THE FREEMAS⊕N'S DAUGHTER

SHETLAND
ISLAND

ORKNEY ISLAND

HEBRIDES

SCOTLAND

ABERDEEN

DUNDEE

EDINBURGH

GLASGOW

NORTH SEA

NEWCASTLE

MIDDLESBROUGH

NORTHERN
BELFAST
IRELAND

ISLE OF MAN

YORK

LEEDS
MANCHESTER

SHEFFIELD
NOTTINGHAM

IRELAND

ISLE OF ANGLESEY

LIVERPOOL

ENGLAND

WALES

NORWICH

BIRMINGHAM

CAMBRIDGE

IPSWICH

SWANSEA

NEWPORT

CARDIFF

OXFORD

LONDON

ST. GEORGE'S CHANNEL

BRISTOL

PORTSMOUTH

SOUTHAMPTON

BRIGHTON

DOVER

N

W

E

S

ENGLISH CHANNEL

FRANCE

THE FREEMAS⊛N'S DAUGHTER

SHELLEY SACKIER

HARPER TEEN
An Imprint of HarperCollinsPublishers

HarperTeen is an imprint of HarperCollins Publishers.

The Freemason's Daughter
Copyright © 2017 by Shelley Sackier

www.epicreads.com

Library of Congress Control Number: 2016949900
ISBN 978-0-06-245344-0

Typography by Torborg Davern
17 18 19 20 21 PC/LSCH 10 9 8 7 6 5 4 3 2 1

❖

First Edition

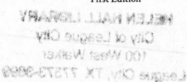

Unlike a drop of water which loses its identity when it joins the ocean, man does not lose his being in the society in which he lives. Man's life is independent. He is born not for the development of the society alone, but for the development of his self.

—B. R. Ambedkar

THE UNITED KINGDOM
OF GREAT BRITAIN
AND NORTHERN IRELAND

SHETLAND
ISLAND

HEBRIDES

SCOTLAND

ABERDEEN

DUNDEE

EDINBURGH

GLASGOW

NORTH SEA

NORTHERN
BELFAST
IRELAND

NEWCASTLE

MIDDLESBROUGH

IRELAND

ISLE OF MAN

YORK

LIVERPOOL

LEEDS

MANCHESTER

SHEFFIELD

NOTTINGHAM

NORWICH

ST. GEORGE'S CHANNEL

WALES

BIRMINGHAM

CAMBRIDGE

IPSWICH

SWANSEA

NEWPORT

CARDIFF

OXFORD

LONDON

BRISTOL

SOUTHAMPTON

PORTSMOUTH

BRIGHTON

ENGLISH CHANNEL

FRANCE

ONE

Scottish Lowlands, September 1714

JENNA WOKE TO THE SOUND OF TOPPLING CHAIRS AND a dish clattering to the jagged flagstones. It was late. She pushed aside the frayed linen hanging over the rime-laden window. The fiery crimson star she used to mark time hung on the edge of the western horizon. And there was no smell of choking peat in the air, which meant dawn was still a fair way off. She was about to roll over, close her eyes, and succumb to sleep again, but a fist hammering the table in the next room jerked her from a leaden stupor.

She padded to the door with the crack in the knothole and knelt to peer through the fissure. Six men stood at the table. Six cups rose high above their heads, their features fixed with purpose and pride.

"*Scientia, Sapientia, Sanctitas.*"

Jenna knew the words. Knowledge, wisdom, holiness.

She sunk back against the door. This toast, this salute between the men, meant they'd been assigned a new post. It was time to leave again.

A crack of gunfire exploded outside, accompanied by the sound of thudding hooves. She bolted from the floor and scrambled for the woolen cloak that was tossed last night onto the end of her flea-ridden cot. And her book, *The Principia* by Isaac Newton. She would never leave it behind.

Her door burst open. She saw the frantic labor of five men snatching leather satchels and weapons before leaping through the cottage's back window and making for the shed where the horses were kept.

Her father's voice hissed rough Gaelic through the darkness. "Jenna, *greas ort*! Make haste!"

She reached for his hand and was pulled toward the window. One last glance over her shoulder revealed the things she would never see again.

Solid hands around her waist raised and tossed her expertly through the open casement. Her feet caught the pitted ground beneath her, but she still skinned her knee. Sixteen years of scars. She was certain she was the only girl who had to wear boots to bed.

TWO

Withinghall House, Cumbria, England

"HE WILL NEVER SEE MY SIDE OF THE STORY. HE WILL blame me entirely, as he always does." The words tumbled out of Alex's mouth, the curt observations of his father breaking through his tightly practiced air of respect.

He looked at his mother, a duchess married twenty-three years to a tyrannical man, and still she held her tongue. Would she not say *anything* about his being dismissed from school?

"Would you mind fetching my brush? I left it on the window-sill."

Alex sighed, crossed the chamber, and reached for the ivory handle. A flash of movement outside caught his eye. Two men in the distance walked with measured footsteps along the outline for a building foundation. Another cleared branches from trees newly felled.

"Alex, my brush, please." His mother peered at him through her dressing table mirror.

He turned and caught his reflection in the looking glass, the image of the University of Cambridge's latest "troublemaker." He turned away. He knew what he looked like and didn't need reminding, but what did his mother see? A tall young man, long legs in calfskin breeches and leather riding boots? Someone who had the same narrow, straight nose as hers?

Or did she see a disappointment the way his father did?

Dust from the road had settled on his white linen shirt, and his fair hair was disheveled and windblown. He'd wanted to get home quickly. Get it over with. So he'd chosen to ride on horseback rather than in a carriage. Delaying the wrath of his father was something he'd made a practice of for the last twenty years. He had made a vow to himself to break the habit.

The duchess cleared her throat and drummed her fingers on the wooden table.

"Forgive me." He returned with the hairbrush and pointed. "What is happening outside?"

The duchess stopped midstroke. "What do you mean? Is there a disturbance?" She rose from her velvet stool, almost upsetting it, and hurried across the room, the fabric of her skirts slapping against the furniture.

"No." Alex raised a reassuring hand. "I see men working, and I'm only wondering on what."

She pushed aside the heavy brocade and peered out the window. "Ah yes. The garrison."

"Garrison? Are we to have soldiers living here?"

"Not to worry. Your father is merely taking precautions."

"Precautions against what?"

She pressed her pale lips together and patted his arm. "That is an excellent question for your father. All he has told me is that there has been talk. I would assume it's related to the rebellions."

"Rebellions? Do you mean the Jacobites?" Alex felt a shiver run through his mother's arm where her hand rested on him.

"Yes. There have been riots—and hangings because of them. I'm not sure the deaths have been . . . an effective deterrent." Her eyes locked on Alex's. "Some people are determined to bring home James Stuart."

THREE

IT WAS SLIPPING THROUGH HER FINGERS. THE permanence of things. This time Jenna studied everything twice, made a point to memorize details. There was the usual bitterness, the sharp tang of vitriol in her mouth, but now dread sprouted as well, an unwanted blossom.

She hated leaving, but her father promised they'd return. He swore on it, and the clan stood behind him.

Except they had never left Scotland before.

She batted the muddle of long russet-red hair from her eyes, but singled out two strands. It was always only two. She pulled until they gave. That tiny tug, the prick on her scalp—it felt . . . good. What she really wanted to do was grab two fistfuls and yank them out, to transfer the ache to a place she could rub away.

But it wasn't her father's fault or the other men's. They were only doing what they must. If it was time to leave then she would go. She ground her teeth and felt her jaw ache. The pain from withholding her words.

But the words of others, the whispering, the snippets of huddled discussion wormed into her head. They sat in the pit of her stomach: *approaching, flee, hide*. They festered, foretold this attempt at escape.

She looked ahead at the men, her makeshift family. Their shoulders slumped from the weight of bedraggled plaids. Filthy and weary from weeks of travel, their clothes had not borne the journey well. Their plaids especially, for when the long pleated cloth was not wrapped and buckled around their waists and shoulders, it was used to cocoon them for sleeping. The ground could be coldhearted.

Standing beside her horse, she heard nothing apart from the rush of air moving in and out of his lungs, tidal and rhythmic. She closed her eyes, swayed, and etched the view of the hardened landscape onto the inside of her eyelids. The morning wind gusted and flapped her skirts, a determined tug forward. She looked up through a tangle of hair, but the scenery became blurry, her eyes stinging. She blinked and swallowed the solid lump in her throat.

One of the men looked back. She fought the urge to shout, to protest his prying attention. Instead, she managed a halfhearted wave and felt a nudge against her shoulder. The horse probed her pockets.

"You'll have to wait, Henry. I have nothing." The truth of the words fueled her frustration.

"It's as expected, Jenna," her father had often reminded her. "Living in the midst of rebellion and finding financial support for the Crown comes wi' a price. Namely one's head on a stake if ye aren't lucky. We need to stay two steps ahead of the English dragoons."

Those two steps between Jenna and government soldiers on the lookout for traitorous activity provided little comfort, and more often, little sleep for them all.

It had been months of running. Months of regrouping, of secret meetings informing the men where they would collect money for James—the Jacobite leader.

James Edward Francis Stuart was a name that beat a constant rhythm in her head. He was Great Britain's rightful king, whose claim to the throne was "given by God." Except . . . she'd heard another name whispered on those late nights when the men thought she was asleep. *The Old Pretender.* He was considered an impostor by some and a political liability by others.

Now that Queen Anne had died, the throne lay empty. Her likely successor was George, a Hannover, and a German. Last night, as Jenna's clan passed through another village, they heard a group of Englishmen outside a ramshackle tavern bellyaching that Great Britain was close to passing into German hands.

"Imagine being governed by a king who not only isn't English— but doesn't speak a word of it!" they had said.

Still, a great many found the Dutch monarch preferable to the Catholic claimant, James.

She had listened to the same grumbles throughout their travels. But now the grousing was growing volatile. Part of her father's responsibility, agreed upon by an intricate network of James's secret supporters, was to keep the impassioned devotees under control.

"Why should they distress at his faith?" Jenna had asked her father.

"Well, many folks think that if their sovereign were Roman Catholic, the king would answer first and foremost to papal authority. They say it'd be like handing the country back to the Roman Empire. Folks would be afraid that James wouldna allow them to practice their own faith. But it isna so. James would fight for religious liberty. As we do now."

Jenna closed her eyes, remembering her father's words, and thought, *Can't we continue to do it from Scotland?* Her father's whistle pierced the air, told her to catch up. She grabbed the folds of her rough woolen skirt and swung up into the saddle. She held the horse back, his eagerness to join the others stressing the reins. The pungent scent of heather filled her lungs. She wondered if she would be capable of breathing English air, or if her Scottish body would reject it.

Beyond the men snaked the dim line of Hadrian's Wall, the old Roman stone barrier dividing Scotland and England. She wished the wall were too high, too impenetrable. Nothing existed on the other side except the people who were making life unbearable for the Scots. Even so, it was the next stop of their miserable journey, where, thankfully, no one knew who they were.

"Ha!" she shouted at the horse, spurring him with her heels.

Henry reared a little and jolted forward. Jenna bent against his straining neck and urged him to race to a speed she knew would earn a scolding, but for a moment she would be feral, wild, uncontrolled.

The horse thundered over the field. She shut her eyes, her fingers threaded through his mane. Every rise and dip demanded she melt into the muscles as they stretched over the bones beneath her. She swept headlong past the men, ignored their garbled warnings. If she continued apace, the horse would have to jump the ancient wall.

But could he do it? It wasn't tall, but it was thick. A deeper spread than he'd ever jumped before.

She sensed a sudden hesitation beneath her, a swift change in direction, mad momentum. Her eyes flew open. Henry's mane slipped from her hands and her weight vanished as the horse veered from the wall. From her. *A body in motion* were the words that leapt to her mind from the pages of Newton she'd read yesterday. Her shoulder slammed into the ground, her body lurched awkwardly over her head like a dropped doll.

She could not breathe. Her lungs compressed, a vise constricting her chest. Black pooling ink spots bloomed before her eyes. She gripped the grass beneath her hands and wrenched a ragged breath from the air. It left her coughing . . . gulping. She rolled onto her back to still her heaving chest. When she opened her eyes she saw the pallid face of her father and those of the five other men. There were many shaking heads and a few clucking tongues, so she gathered she must still be somewhat intact. She sat up and was at once reminded of the painful jolt to her shoulder. The joint was sore to her touch, but she slowly found her feet.

"Serves ye right," her father said, brushing the grass off her skirt with a heavy hand. "Now go get your horse and walk him a ways, aye? You're lucky you didna break your neck, ye wee fiend."

"Lucky?" Jenna mumbled. "Lucky would have been to die in Scotland."

FOUR

ALEX SURVEYED HIS MOTHER'S LAVISH SITTING ROOM, the plush, enveloping chairs, the tapestry-covered walls in jeweled hues. It was a chamber that sheltered and sheathed her. Perhaps it was designed to soften the sharp edges of living with his father. "Your maid said you'd taken to your bed last week." He studied her. He'd never been capable of reading his mother. She hid beneath her perfected smooth countenance: a feigned smile, a shrouded gaze, and always censored words. He wanted the truth and not the polished routine of circumspect behavior.

"Alex, I do wish you'd stop worrying." His mother picked up her brush, taking care with each lengthy stroke.

To Alex, her hair seemed different, dull and brittle brown.

She twisted to look at him. Her wide-set hazel eyes, although tired, still held their warmth. "It was nothing more than a chill." She rose and walked back toward him, her fingers kneading her temples. "Perhaps your concern should be your explanation about school. Your father will want an account, and I'm not sure how warmly it will be received." Her feathery brows knitted with unease. "How I wish I could alter things for you . . . make it easier." She moved a strand of hair from his forehead and let her hand fall to his shoulder to brush the dust from it. "But you are as you are, and in many regards, I am grateful for it."

"You're speaking in riddles, Mother."

"Perhaps I am, but cling to your fortitude with him. I cringe to think of that conversation. He will doubtlessly remind you that being sent down from Cambridge is a disgrace." She shook her head and met his gaze. "Lady Lucia will be arriving from Sicily tomorrow, and I cannot think of how we will explain your early homecoming. Perhaps we'll confess an eagerness for the engagement party and push the date forward?"

Lady Lucia and her flimsy relations to the Holy Roman Emperor. Alex felt his jaw stiffen. "It doesn't matter to me."

"Rumor has it your fiancée is quite a stunning young lady."

"As if that would make a difference." *This engagement is a loathsome sham.*

"It has for some." She raised her teacup from a nearby table.

"Matrimonial matchmaking. Why encourage me to take part in the very thing that has made you so miserable?"

"Alex!" She paused and drew in a slow breath. "I have never admitted to feeling unhappy. Besides, happiness is not the intent here. People find it elsewhere."

"Like my father has."

The icy words made her wince. "I'm sorry if you disagree, but this is the way it's done." She returned to her table and sank onto the stool. "Perhaps we should speak of this later."

His statement was cruel, and she'd suffered because of his careless tongue. "Forgive me. I didn't intend it to come out the way it did. And you're right—let's discuss it another time. I truly wanted to spend a nice afternoon with you before everyone else discovered my return."

"Are they already here?" She closed the lid of her jewelry box with a snap.

Alex prickled. "Why? Do you disapprove of them? Those three are my friends—and they've more than proven that now. We were expelled together. Don't forget they're in this predicament because of me."

"You're mistaken. No one forced them to act as they did. Charles and Hugh behaving as imbeciles is one thing. They've never shown an aptitude for demonstrating sound judgment. But Julian? . . . That I don't understand."

"He was acting in my defense."

"Julian never does anything unless he benefits from it. That apple did not fall far from its tree." She tapped her fingers on the table.

"Well, perhaps people change, Mother."

"Yes . . . and perhaps water will begin flowing upstream."

He smiled tensely and moved to kiss her cheek. "Indeed. I'm off to find my unruly friends. I'll see you at supper."

"Alex, one more thing," she said, her voice lowered. "Stay away from the garrison. The whole idea of it makes me nervous."

FIVE

IT WAS COLD AND DANK. THAT WAS JENNA'S FIRST thought when she stepped into the old crofter's cottage, her new home on the estate of Withinghall. The smell of rat droppings and moldering wood pinched at her nose. She stared at the sparsely furnished room and shivered. *Why must every place be so dismal? With an inch of dust as welcome?*

"Get a move on, lass," she heard Angus McGregor say behind her. "Your da will nay like it if we keep his things out in the rain." He moved past her to set packs from the horses onto the dirty flagstone. "What's got ye so grim? This?" He nodded at the inside of the cottage. "We'll have this place fixed up in no time. Dinna worry."

She watched him unload. Angus was a cheerful, burly man, his bulk compounded by his mass of unruly brown hair. He winked at her beneath a hedge of an eyebrow and left to help the others.

She dropped her own pack on the long wooden table in the middle of the room. A cobwebbed stone fireplace sagged on the back wall, sad with neglect. She moved closer and found a pewter bowl on the mantel, a few stubs of candle ends left inside. "Positively dreary," she sighed, digging a fingernail into the waxy remains.

"What's that, then?" Her father stooped through the warped doorframe. "Angus says you're still sulking. I thought seein' such an estate would put ye in a more appreciative mood."

The soft burr of her father's accent tickled her ears. She turned to look up at him and tried to hide her gloom. Malcolm MacDuff ran a hand through his rough black hair and stretched. His dirty linen shirt pulled across his chest, straining the threads of fabric. He showed no languor, and despite the silver along his temples, he was a force that once started, would not pause for breath.

"It is a lovely manor, Da, and I'm trying to be appreciative.... It's just that I appreciated Scotland more."

He made a sound deep in his throat. "We go where the work is, lass. Ye ken that."

"It's not only the *work*, Da," she said, chancing to meet his gaze.

His black eyes flashed a warning. "It's all part of the work in the end."

Duncan McPhee popped through the door, his hallowed box of medicines under his arm. "We'll need to find a ready place for this. No doubt wi' all the rain, folks'll be coming down with one thing after t'other." Duncan had spent a few years with a healer in his youth, and lucky for the clan, retained much of his knowledge. The other men ribbed him about his remedy box and the fact it contained everything to treat one's ills apart from a cure for his own wildly crooked nose. "Nothing to fix McPhee's McMuzzle," they chided.

The others came in, their shoulders burdened with packs. A few tilts of the head informed Jenna she had best be at her work. She picked up her bag and trudged toward the dark staircase in the corner, and everyone's actions became a familiar reprise.

It was always the same when settling someplace new: the six men split up into the customary two or three chambers and Jenna got the loft, if one was available. Space was a luxury reserved for the rich.

Sometimes, Angus would fix a corner of a room by hanging old blankets for walls. It was cramped during those bitter winter nights when she shared the same room. And though she was grateful for the feeble heat of their fire, it took getting used to the racket that regularly accompanied hardworking, tired men. The snores, grunts, and shuffling on squeaky trundle beds or floorboards was an orchestra unlike any other.

This cottage was shelter in its most basic form. At the top of the stairs she opened the door to the loft, which boasted a twisted bed frame, a battered wooden chest, and three grimy windows. One narrow casement perched on the front wall, while a larger one, deeply set with a roughly hewn window seat, revealed the manor. It was imposing, a formidable retreat. On the other side of the cottage, rolling hills bubbled around a silver loch.

"Not a loch," she muttered to herself, scowling. "It's a lake. This isn't Scotland."

Regardless of its name, the sight was striking, with a grove of colorful trees beckoning one into the woods beyond. Even so, Jenna was used to steeling her heart against attachments, whether they be to places and sights, or people and things.

Once, when she was eight, she'd developed a fierce fondness for a sweet and shaggy highland cow, living in the pasture next to their quarters. She'd begged her father to buy the animal and bring it with them, but as she learned, they would only travel with necessities, and *two sharp horns covered in fur* was not one of them.

She gazed out the window toward the manor and saw a woman, plump as a busty quail, draped in brown homespun, bustling her way down to their lodgings. No doubt someone from the house had noted their arrival. Her own unpacking must wait. She should help downstairs.

At the bottom of the steps, she held back, hearing the men chatting with the hefty woman.

"Mrs. Wigginton. Your servant, madam. We're the stonemasons for the garrison." Jenna watched Colin Brodie bow deeply to the woman. He often said living with five other men tended to make them forget the social graces needed when in polite company. In particular, female company. Therefore, he encouraged them to practice whenever the occasion presented itself. The clan ribbed him after each episode, but he shrugged it off gaily and told them he would soon have a fine, fat wife to look after him in his old age.

Colin schooled Jenna in the rudiments of etiquette. He'd said, "My father spent his days as a schoolmaster and a tutor to a wealthy family. He passed the lessons down to me, not that I had much chance to employ them. Use them or no, it pays to learn them."

Colin had also pressed upon Malcolm the importance of teaching Jenna to speak the King's English. They found folks of this country would soften the grip around their grubby coins when asked in the dulcet tone of their own dialect, versus the harsh brogue of a foreigner.

Her face warmed seeing the lanky-boned Colin twisting his bonnet between nervous hands. He stooped over the woman, his thin brown hair matted and flat. She tittered and patted the white-capped bun into tidy order atop her head.

The bosomy figure turned and made for the entrance to the cottage, saying, "Ye wouldna believe how delighted I am to have fellow kinsmen here. What a fine sight finding men in proper dress again. It's right difficult tending to *their* elegant costuming. The fabrics are too frail." She eyed the men before they followed her in with more packs off the horses.

"My heavens, what a state this is in!" The woman took in the room, her lips pinched with distaste. She turned to the group, revealing an apologetic gaze. "I do wish milady had given me notice ye were coming. We would've had this prepared for your arrival." She poked through the long-ignored chambers in the back of the cottage, muttering in broken Gaelic. Jenna slipped farther into the shadows and pulled a blooming sliver of melancholy with her upon hearing her native tongue.

Mrs. Wigginton marched back to the front room, full of purpose. "Well, I'll see to it that a few of the girls come down to spruce it up." She took a bowl from the table and blew on it, then waved at the swirling dust mites she'd sent flying, reaching for the table to steady herself. Her hand knocked a stack of Jenna's books to the floor. "Oh, pardon me," she said, bending to retrieve them. "It appears that not only have we left the place littered wi' dust, but old books as well. Ye'll not be needin' these round here."

Jenna jumped into the light and reached for the books. "Those are my—"

"Those are for milord's library," Gavin Munro interrupted, his expressive face catching the housekeeper's attention. "A gift of gratitude."

Jenna felt the sudden flush of fire scorch her cheeks and watched as the woman muscled the books under her arm. "How kind of ye," she said with a quick bob. "And I see ye brought a maid wi' ye." The woman turned to Jenna. "Tell me if there's anything ye might be wanting, lass. I'm Mrs. Wigginton, the housekeeper of Withinghall. You're welcome anytime up at the house wi' the other girls. Just use the back kitchen door."

"I'm not a—"

The men's eyes flashed to Jenna and Gavin stepped forward again. "Ah yes, that's Master MacDuff's daughter, Jenna. She's a real help indoors." He put a guiding hand onto her shoulder and directed her outside. "Thanks so much for whatever ye feel obliged to send down. Good day to ye, madam." He mumbled awkward thanks and closed the door.

Jenna felt the heated glare of everyone present.

Gavin leaned his back on the frame and sighed, his rubbery mouth frowning. "The woman had every right to assume you're a wee maid. And as for the books . . . just remember to think before ye talk, lass. This job is bigger than the ones we've done before. It's more than just picking up a few coins for the crown. If anyone on the estate finds out what we're doing . . ." He pressed his lips together. "Now let's get this place sorted."

Jenna dropped her eyes. Gavin was right: she shouldn't have

been so quick to speak, nor upset at the swift assessment. It was likely because of her age. At sixteen, most girls were sent off to work in houses with wealthier families, emptying chamber pots, hauling water, and cleaning fireplaces. At night, they were easy prey for the master of the house, his sons, or whatever guests he wanted to please. Few other options were available. The girls were simply another mouth to feed at home. Another burden to unload.

The men got to work emptying bags, and Jenna withdrew to the table to unpack the leather sack containing pots and pans.

Angus leaned over and whispered, "Dinna fash yourself over it, Jenna. It takes us all a while to adjust."

She studied him as he emptied his sack; soggy and dripping from the relentless trickle of rain, his face still held a smile. Even his cheeks were pink with color, although much of it was hidden by his great bushy beard.

"If ye keep up wi' that kind of chatter, you're doing her no favors—just filling her head wi' nonsense." Jenna looked up at Ian Ross, who'd come to the table and stood in front of them. The scowl on his face was deeper than usual, the lines on his forehead etched with permanence. She thought it improbable that his eyebrows could move any closer together. Pretty soon, she figured, they'd fuse to each other.

"She doesna need any mothering from you, Angus. It's time she pulled her share."

Angus stood from the table. "Now here, Jenna, is a fine example of where the good Lord has given a man more brain than most, but taken the surplus from his heart." He tousled her hair, pulling a few bits of grass from it. "No minding Ian, now, then—he's just a bit of an old woman."

Angus walked away, having filled his arms full of kitchen goods, and retaining a face full of cheer. Ian caught Jenna by the arm and turned her to face his cold, black eyes, "Aye, start using less of your mind and more of your hands like a woman should. Put away the books and find your apron. Stop bringin' trouble to the door."

She bit down on her tongue.

Ian grabbed another armload and left the table, unaware of the hateful glare at his back. She returned to unearthing the kitchen goods and pulled out Angus's frying pan. She inhaled the smoky perfume from its etched surface. Bacon. Yesterday, one of the men had bagged a few rabbits, and their reward at last night's campfire was a rich game stew with the remaining roots and onions they'd foraged along their journey.

"Jenna." Her father's head poked through the doorframe.

She snapped out of her daydream and looked up.

"Your horse is waiting for its bed. Take Henry down to the stables and give him to one of the lads there. Tell them you're wi' me and they'll ken where to put him." His face grew solemn. "And, Jenna, ye must be on your guard here. Speak of James to no one, understand?"

She nodded and pushed herself from the table, putting the pan beside the others.

"A little bit of air will do ye good, I think," he said, and grasped her arm as she passed him in the doorway. "But be on guard. There could be trouble round every bend."

She moved out into the drizzle and graying light and snatched her horse's reins, pulling his head down closer to hers. "Then I suggest we avoid every bend. And make a beeline straight for home."

SIX

ALEX FOLLOWED THE WET FOOTPATHS THROUGH the gardens of the inner courtyard to the long stone building that housed the horses. He couldn't understand why his father had bought the thoroughbred without first seeing it. If they employed a decent horse handler, they might not make such costly mistakes. They'd have a stable full of elegant, well-bred horses, rather than ill-tempered animals the duke passed off as champions. There was nothing gained in arguing with his father on this point, for whatever the duke wanted, the duke received.

The stable hands were lighting the lamps around the stalls, and a dim glow slipped through the windowed slits beneath the eaves of the roofline. He smiled at the sounds the horses made, feathery-soft gratitude for their evening meal. He stopped to glance back toward the house, wishing it too could be filled with horses rather than people.

His father, Edward Abney Clifton, was the Duke of Keswick and the Marquess of Pembroke. As the duke's only son, Alex held the title of Lord Pembroke. Withinghall, their home, was an estate held by the family for the last century. The great stone house with its fortified towers, walled courtyard, and gardens was situated above the banks of Esthwaite Water in the Cumbrian region of northern England. It stood solidly, a mass of bricks and stone.

The house was an oppression. When Alex returned here he yearned only to be among the woodlands and shores of the lake, which held breathtaking beauty. What a shame his perfect world was soured by many of the people inhabiting it.

Trees and water asked nothing of you. People demanded everything you had.

He reached for the stable door when the hefty gate opened toward him. An elderly stable hand hobbled through with two horses he didn't recognize.

"Jeb," Alex said, brightening, "a face I've longed to see. Have you been keeping well?"

The snowy-haired man bowed stiffly to Alex. "I have at that, milord. It's kind of you to ask of my health. And might I add the house is in dire need of your honorable presence." His eyes twinkled.

"Honorable presence?" Alex grimaced. "You slather me with nonsense, Jeb."

"Ah, well, I had to be safe, didn't I?" he said with a smirk. "One never knows what that swag-bellied school has stuffed into your mind. Soon you'll come back all saucy and fatheaded, filled with your own self-importance. I'll be forced to give you a reminder of who you are, milord." Jeb cuffed the side of Alex's arm and shuffled ahead with the drowsy beasts. "I'm sure you're here to size up the newest prize, but have a care, she's got a real temper. Snapped at three of us already."

Alex followed Jeb with his eyes, wondering how much longer he might be able to work. His footslogged gait was the result of one of his father's half-crazed beasts backing him into a stall and throwing him against the rear of the box with a Herculean kick. His leg was fractured in three places, the injuries never healing properly.

Jeb kept his post as one of the handlers, but it was understood he was no longer capable of working with any of the belligerent horses. Alex knew it would be a difficult day when Jeb was forced to rely solely on the mercurial generosity of the duke.

But this matter would have to wait. Frankly, a temperamental horse was the last thing he wanted to tackle. Cook's meat pies and a glass of ale were better options, although a quick peek at his long-time companions was a draw he could not resist.

Alex came in from the drizzle and was enveloped in a murky fog, courtesy of the barn's heavy-breathing occupants and the smoky lanterns glowing around the stalls. He inhaled the tang of hay and wet animals. The scent gave rise to childhood memories of hiding beneath the straw in the loft and spying on the barn's visitors, whether dignitaries taking a tour, or stable lads taking a chambermaid.

He walked with thresh-muffled footsteps and greeted a few of the animals with a soft stroke. The stables were L-shaped, which allowed Garrick Wicken, the latest in a series of overly eager head horse handlers, to keep the edgier, newly purchased animals in an area removed from the serenity of the others.

Alex rounded the corner and heard nervous whinnying coming from one of the last stalls. The newest mare. His jaw went rigid. Damn his father! The man created problems, but never dealt with them. He grabbed a few apples from the barrel by the tack room and approached the horse, offering the fruit. He crooned sweetly, "I'm sorry. You should be treated better. My father is nothing more than an arrant slug who would never sully his noble hands. *Aquila non capit muscas.*"

"An eagle would catch flies if he were hungry enough." A pale-faced girl with wild hair peeked out from behind the horse, a brush in her hand.

Alex leapt back, his eyes widened with alarm. "Who are you there?" he sputtered, mortified she'd heard him speaking to the horse. "Where is your good sense? Can't you see this animal is dangerous? She's not been broken yet! And she's already bitten three handlers." He glared at the girl.

She laughed, patting the horse's rump. "Well, you might want to inform old *Henry* here that he's a girl."

"Wha? I . . ." A rush of heat filled Alex's chest and he tugged at the cravat around his neck, his shirt collar suddenly too tight.

The girl put up a hand, still smirking. "Simple mistake. Don't worry, I won't tell anyone."

"Housemaids are not allowed in the stables, and I intend to take this up with the housekeeper in order to have you dismissed." He jabbed a finger toward the stable door, fumbling desperately to regain a shred of his dignity.

"On this estate, are the stable lads granted boundless authority?" the girl spat.

Alex narrowed his gaze. "They are when they are given the title of Lord Pembroke."

The girl's face flushed with bright pink spots upon her cheeks. She slipped through the stall door and closed it behind her with a perfunctory click, then turned to face Alex. He took in her shabby woolen riding clothes, wet from the day's rainfall.

"I beg your pardon, *my lord*. I seem to have forgotten my place." She made an obedient bow and darted down the corridor and out the stable door.

Alex stood in the center of the barn, looking around to see if anyone had overheard their conversation, or was an eyewitness to the exchange. It was empty. The girl was the only one who had heard him malign his father—for now.

He abandoned his purpose for the visit, now determined to find the housekeeper.

The brisk ten-minute walk from the stables propelled Alex on through the massive house, his step matching his heated pulse. *An ignorant scullery maid all too eager to make a fool of me!* He rounded a corner and smacked into the bountiful form of the housekeeper.

"Mrs. Wigginton, are you all right?" He grabbed her elbows to steady her.

"Oh aye, I dinna keep the extra padding on for naught." She tugged and preened his coat, the brown velvet wrinkles resistant to reform. "Does her ladyship ken you've come home yet? Ye canna go in to greet her all rumpled like."

"Please, Mrs. Wigginton, I'm fine, and yes, I saw her earlier this afternoon." Alex backed up to avoid further patting.

"Well, then, you'd best be getting to the library. Mr. Finch and the two others are here."

"Are they?" He glanced down the hall.

"Will you be needin' anything? I can send in some of the girls if they've not had enough to eat or drink."

The image that appeared in his mind, of his friends and the entitled attitude that accompanied them, made him cringe, and he shook his head in answer. He made to go and then turned back. "Oh, Mrs. Wigginton?"

"Aye, milord?" She looked up, her eyebrows at crooked angles.

"Speaking of girls"—he wondered how to put it, for Mrs. Wigginton took pride and pains to ensure all her staff were suitably behaved—"I've had a bit of a run-in with one of your maids."

"Oh? Which one?" Her eyes narrowed under their graying brows.

"I'm not sure. In fact, I think she must be a recent addition, for I've not seen her before."

"Describe her to me. I'll ken who it is and it willna happen again." Her eyes grew determined. Someone would be receiving a most unpleasant scolding.

Good.

"Well . . ." Alex faltered. He tried recalling the girl's features, which wasn't difficult, for the face that bedeviled him was etched into his memory. An outspoken servant was a small matter, but appearing foolish in front of her left him feeling exposed.

Her skin was light, almost translucent in some places, and her hair was coppery, a circle of heat around her face. How was he to describe her eyes to Mrs. Wigginton? It would sound absurd for him to say that her eyes were shockingly green. Green would have to suffice.

"Well, then?" Mrs. Wigginton said, waiting.

"Green. She was green."

"I beg your pardon?"

"No. I mean . . . her eyes were green. Red face, pale hair—you know the sort of thing." He waved at her.

"Red face?"

"Hair! I meant red hair. Or orange and brown—whatever." Alex shook his head.

"I'm afraid we dinna have any girls wi' red hair in the house. Not sure I ken anyone of that description—save the young lad who washes pots for me." She crinkled her face, thinking.

"Well," Alex continued, heat prickling his neck, "maybe she's his sister—but she most definitely was *not* a boy."

The housekeeper scratched her head. "Well, boy or no, there are three gentlemen in the library making a fuss while waiting for you. Do ye think ye might calm them a bit?"

Alex clenched his fists. He'd been sent to handle an ornery horse, an inappropriate servant, and now his unruly friends. He couldn't wait to sort out things with his cantankerous father. *Yield to all, and you will soon have nothing to yield.* One day he would decide whether Aesop, teller of fables, was advising or warning him.

SEVEN

JENNA SCRAMBLED BACK TO THE CROFTER'S COTTAGE, nerves twisting her stomach into a ball of knots. The cold drizzle added to the frozen sense of dread creeping beneath her skin. The young man in the barn had made an error, and she'd laughed, trying to be witty. It wasn't until he announced his intention of throwing her off the estate that she overstepped and spoke brazenly.

She'd had no inkling he was important. And that he had absolutely no sense of humor.

He'd thought her a servant girl. Was it her clothing—worn and frayed as it was from weeks of rough travel?

"Lord Arrogant," she would call him. A wicked smile crept to her lips when she recalled the tidal flush of red on his face after he discovered he'd been overheard. His livid blue eyes had stared accusingly at her. She wondered if they were still enraged, only now making demands that she be found and dealt with.

Remorse filled in where her pride had leaked out, for if her father, or any of the other men, heard of her talk in the stable, they'd strip her of what was most valuable: the rest of her books. And if Lord Arrogant was true to his word, she'd have to endure six livid faces perched on their horses, on their way out of the estate.

Upon reaching the cottage door, she hesitated. Should she prepare them? Admit to her mistake? She glanced back toward the stables, but steeled herself and swung through the door.

"It's about time, Jenna. I was beginning to think you'd taken the horse and run wi' him," her father said, looking up from the table, a hint of humor around his eyes.

She stepped into the snug, smoky cottage, seeing the men sitting together, engaged in gladsome conversation. These were people who truly loved one another, and with them, she felt safe. It was clear they'd worked quickly to clean and settle the shabby house with their collective furnishings. They never carried much with them, but familiar things eased the transition.

The patchwork quilts, gifted by women friends they'd made along the way, were stacked neatly on a chair, ready for beds. The table was set with their old crockery. Chipped as they were, they had seen this family through years of festive meals and serious discussions. Duncan, when not busy with the clan's ailments or carpentry work with the masons, was adept at bartering. Conveying a resourceful and sweet-tempered nature, he found the salt-glazed earthenware in a town market, and negotiated the set out of their owner in exchange for two hours' worth of labor. Although each of them possessed skills to barter with, Duncan was more than canny.

Angus often said Duncan could sway a bird to part with his song.

A blazing fire in the hearth heated a beefy broth, probably sent down by the housekeeper. She must have included bread and cheese, for those also appeared on the table. Bonnets and cloaks hung on pegs by the door. The copper pots were placed around the hutch on the side wall, and the men sat at the hearth, a jug of ale at their feet.

She watched Angus lean over the pot, stirring with his spurtle—the magic spoon he'd first shown her when she was a child. The spoon that kept them from hunger. Angus once told wide-eyed Jenna that this very spoon could extend a meal made for seven into enough to feed twelve, should they need it. And oftentimes they did. There were many nights when outsiders joined their family suppers.

Many of those evenings had music, stories, and food. Mirthful events. But lately, their dinners were serious-natured, the tone subdued. She was usually allowed to eat with everyone, but then dismissed to an early bed, where she would sit, straining her ears from behind a distant doorway, interpreting muddled words. The conversations began in English, but would switch to Gaelic, and although she understood and spoke the language well, the sound of all those deep voices mingling together had a soporific effect. Sleep would overcome her.

"Well, don't just stand there, lassie. Come and grab a seat by the fire. Tell us what you've seen." Angus pushed a crooked wooden stool closer to the fire and gestured to her.

"Nothing more than the stables." Jenna sat and straightened out the folds of her bracken-colored skirt. Perhaps it was just her grubbiness that had made the young man jump to the conclusion that she was a servant.

"That's it, then? That's the best ye can give us? Ye didna peek in all the corners of the castle to see where the wee fairy folk live, then?" Angus looked around at the other men. "Surely ye remember when it was all we could do to keep Jenna from finding them first thing and deciding to run off wi' em? She'd tell us that they'd much better food than we and the schooling would be less as well."

The men chuckled and nodded.

Jenna reached up for a lock of hair, twirling it between her fingers. "No, Angus, I never did find any fairies, and it's been a long time since I have looked." She singled out two strands and felt the tiny snap of hair parting from her scalp. "I did find a most unpleasant young man, however."

"A young man?" Colin piped up, grinning ear to ear. "Ah, I can see it now, Jenna, you've left the fairies for the fellows." The men erupted with laughter.

Her father glanced up from the kitchen table where he was writing and shushed the others. "What man is this, then?"

"A rude one," Jenna answered.

The men choked back their amusement and Malcolm raised one eyebrow with interest. He put down his quill. "Could ye be more specific than that?"

"Not really." Jenna rose from the stool and walked toward the front window. "Except he wasn't as tall as you, Da, and he had blond hair . . . that flipped around his ears." *I bet he has someone comb it for him in the mornings.*

She reached the casement and lost herself in the dim reflection. "His clothes were tailored. And he wore new leather boots. I doubt they'd ever stepped into a stable before." Jenna breathed onto the glass to make it fog and traced a pale finger through the vapor. "And his hands looked like they'd never seen a hard day's work." She turned to face the men. Each was grinning.

"Sounds like ye weren't paying attention at all." Her father chortled and picked up his quill. "Still, I'm curious to know who it was and ye can only tell so much by someone's clothing or the flip of his hair."

"His name is Lord Arrogant," she said without thinking.

The room exploded with riotous laughter.

"But apparently he is known to others as Lord *Pembroke*."

Her father raised both brows this time. "Jenna . . . I'd think it best ye keep that first name to yourself, aye?"

"Sorry, Da," she said, biting her lip. "It's just that he assumed I was hired help."

"Ye *are* hired help, Jenna."

"Yes, but not in the way he was presuming."

"It doesna matter what people think, lass. It's your actions you'll be judged upon, and I'll not have ye making harsh assumptions of others based on what they wear as well. Do ye understand me now?" He gave her a sharp glance. It felt like a slap.

She blinked hard several times, her eyes stinging from the reproach. "I do."

"Now go get washed for dinner. Angus here has cooked up one of Mrs. Wigginton's meat broths, and I'm sure it'll be ready soon." He nodded toward the door.

She trudged outside to locate the rain barrel the men had used to clean the cottage and found it butted against one of the side walls. Her hand brushed the wall's rugged surface. It seemed to radiate stability, and she wondered how long this building had been standing.

Her entire life was filled with the memories of building sites. She followed their rise from the earth as if day by day the formations grew on their own. She watched as the men fed them stone and mortar, sweat and strength. And at completion, there was nothing more satisfying than to stand back and see how man had altered earth, had improved its beauty and left his mark. How long these structures could stand to face the elements and exist through time's cunning whims was a testament to the builder's skill.

Her father was a master stonemason, gifted with a deft competence bestowed upon few. Many sought his talents, and he was fortunate enough to choose his work. The men who accompanied him had been with him for years, at least as long as Jenna had been alive. Except for Ian. He joined their family two years ago, and Jenna still had a difficult time regarding him as part of their circle.

Each man had unique skills, and when combined with one another, the architectural results were inspiring. Apart from being highly accomplished in stonemasonry, they were also Freemasons, members of a small and secret guild of men who regulated not only their craft, but their philosophies. They clung to virtue and truth as fundamental values, solid as the foundations they built. Charity and morality were held as high in importance as the beams of each vaulted ceiling. These men were brothers, not of blood, but of mindset. And their minds were set on righting a wrong done to James Stuart—believer in the Divine Right of Kings. They must help reclaim his throne.

It was within this world and these walls that Jenna was raised.

And it was by these men and their ideas she was educated. The life she lived and the knowledge she was given were not of the usual sort for women. In fact, Jenna's education was kept secret. What had begun as food to satiate a child's simple curiosity had bloomed into a monstrous appetite. And although her father insisted upon slaking that thirst, Jenna knew, and grieved to admit, that nothing would come of it in the end.

She was female. The options before her were few.

She washed her hands in the rain barrel and took a deep breath. Her lungs filled with the smell of damp leaves and black earth. Autumn was here, changing the land.

One could not control nature, her father would tell her, but controlling the nature of others was altogether a different matter. The fates of many were often altered by the voice of just one.

EIGHT

ALEX HEARD SHOUTING FROM THE FAR END OF THE dark corridor. He approached the library's open doorway and stood back in the recessed shadows.

Hugh Fowler spit onto the carpet. "You call this wine? It puts me in mind of what the maids throw out of the chamber pots." He thumped a glass onto the table, some of its contents sloshing out the sides. A young maid started and scurried forward with a cloth to catch the spill. "Mind it doesn't get on my breeches, you witless dolt," he snapped.

"I'm s-sorry, sir. Might I g-get you another?" The girl clutched the rag and stared hard at the floor.

"Not of that ilk. If I wanted to drink swill, I'd dine at Charles's manor," he said, flashing a grin at his friend. Two dimples pierced the flesh of his cheeks. "As we're already here, find something more suitable. I doubt your employer would be pleased to see we're drinking the dregs of his cellar."

With a quick curtsy in Hugh's general direction, the pale-faced girl fumbled for one of the bottles on the table. Hugh shot out a hand and clamped down on the girl's wrist. "And bring food. It breeds ill will that we should be expected to wait with an empty stomach."

The trembling maid dashed for the door. She flew past Alex without seeing him in the dim passageway. He was about to speak, but pulled back again at the sound of a scraping knife. A flash of brassy firelight caught the blade as Julian Finch sliced mud from his Moroccan leather boots. He flicked the muck into the fire. "You're a first-rate leech, Hugh. We'll be thrown out before we've been welcomed."

Alex emerged from the gloom. "If such a thing were possible, I'd have done it already. Stop harassing the help, Hugh."

Hugh looked up and broke out in his winning grin. "You know I just like a good game, and that little tart looked like an excellent pawn to play with." He leaned back, stretching, his chair tilting on two rear legs.

Charles, who had slyly moved around the table behind his goading friend, darted in and tipped Hugh's chair back, catching him off guard. "We've barely arrived and already you've begun with the servants."

Hugh righted himself and narrowed his eyes at Charles, a sardonic grin curling his lips. "Let the games begin, I say. We're out of school and I feel in the mood for a little mischief."

Charles scowled at him, his pitted skin dull and pale. "It's because of our mischief that we've been cast out in the first place, you clodpoll."

Hugh feigned a look of affront. "Well, it was about bloody time. I'd been behaving myself for far too long, wouldn't you agree, Alex?"

"No," Alex said, fixated with the wine stain on his mother's Spanish silk carpet.

"Neither do I," Julian said, continuing to remove slivers of mud caked to the outside of his expensive boots.

"Julian," Hugh sighed, "you must learn to relax a little. Get dirty. *Be* dirty. You're much too perfect with the press of your clothes and the shave of your chin. . . . Even your hair tonic outperforms. Your locks are so shiny black they're almost blue."

Charles grunted in amusement. "*Disheveled* is not a word Julian Finch will have saddled to his description."

"Shrewd, cunning, and ambitious, but never soiled," Hugh agreed.

Charles picked a strand of hair off Julian's velvet coat and patted him on the back. "Perhaps you should take a page out of Hugh's book, Julian. After the mind-numbing journey from Cambridge, he expects nothing less from the house than a week's worth of free entertainment."

Alex held up an empty wine bottle. "It seems you've begun already. How long have you been here?"

Hugh sniffed. "Well, when one is kept waiting by one's host, one must find some distraction." He reached over for Charles's wine goblet. "I've rather lost track of time, and I had a fair mind to dismiss the maid who sullied our arrival." He took a deep swig and drained the glass of its ruby liquid.

Julian sighed and moved to the adjoining bookshelves, fingering the spines of the gold-leafed titles. "Hugh, you are nothing less than sponging baggage." He opened a leathered tome and handled its delicate pages.

"Me?" Hugh said, feigning shock. "Not at all, Julian, I was simply raised with standards that refuse to be ignored. The impudent maid said our rooms were not ready and sent us to wait here. Then the sniveling one came in with the liquid sludge."

Alex stiffened. "What did the first one look like, Hugh?"

"Like all of them"—he waved a hand—"afraid, meek, lowly. Uninteresting to the extreme, but very easy to frighten." He cast a wicked smile at Charles.

"Well, that couldn't be her, then," Alex mumbled, thinking it impossible it could be the same maid, and turning toward the fireplace. A fire in the blackened hearth warmed the Spanish marble surround, and the mantel of carved wood trapped the light beneath it. A gilded mirror above the fireplace reflected bookshelves filled with poetry, law books, and literature.

"Couldn't be who, Alex?" Charles said.

Alex glanced over. "Oh, it's nothing really. I had a skirmish with a maid myself, and was wondering if it was the same girl. From Hugh's description it doesn't seem so." He rubbed his neck, recalling the embarrassment, the way she'd heard him coo in Latin and—

Wait.

She heard me speak Latin to the horse. And answered back in English. She understood me.

Hugh put a finger in the air. "You cannot let the house staff claim dominance. Who do these onion-eyed vermin think they are, anyway?

Personally, I think the service here is in dire need of redirection. Fire them. Better yet, flog anyone who causes you the slightest vexation!"

Julian delivered a look to Hugh that silenced him. "I think it fair Alex handles his family's troublesome staff in his own way."

Hugh scoffed. "I was only coming to the aid of a friend. He doesn't get much of *your* support apart from licking the boots of anyone important who comes to stay. Tell me . . . is fawning a profession, Julian?"

Charles swatted him and skirted round the reading table an arm's length away. "Try to understand, Hugh. Julian comes from quality and he's used to mixing with an elevated class of people. Being seen with you hampers his ability to move upward socially and professionally."

Alex turned to Julian. "I thought the three of you were going off to your own homes first. Why did you come early?"

"I received a last-minute post from Father. It said they'd be holding one of those dreadful open houses for the peasants this week. The last thing I want is to watch feculent people walk through the estate and put their grubby hands on our things. It takes the servants weeks afterward to clean the piggish mess they've left behind."

"That would explain the law book in your hands," Alex said, a wry smile creeping across his lips.

"Well, I'm desperate to find some precedent—some alternative way of helping my father buy off votes in our borough without having the mass of unmuzzled poor come pickpocketing their way through our public reception rooms." Julian scanned the pages. "It's an archaic way of running the business of Parliament and high time for change."

Hugh leered at Julian. "Next time around just make sure you're born into peerage like old Alex here. It's much easier to know you've got a seat in Parliament—whether you want it or not—than to have to rely on favors or bribery." He collapsed onto an overstuffed chair and threw his feet on an old wooden games table.

Julian snapped the book closed and kicked Hugh's feet from the table, glowering. "Next time you have the audacity to compare family heritage, I suggest you keep your mouth shut, Fowler. I doubt the serving wenches will find a lowly baron nearly as attractive without his front teeth."

"All right, chaps, enough," Charles said. "On to more pressing matters. Alex, have you spoken with your father?"

"No," Alex said, still eyeing Julian. His friend and classmate was notorious for keeping his cool under stress, but this was his weakness. Julian's father, although a member of Parliament, was not in the House of Lords, but rather the House of Commons, where he filled an elected position. Therefore, his future was not guaranteed, as was Alex's, and all he could do was hope for an eventual appointment from the monarchy.

How much easier it would be if Julian were my father's son, Alex often thought. *He wants this life while I want only to escape it.*

"Well, I don't envy you that conversation," Charles went on, grim-faced.

"I assume you'll be part of it," Alex said. "We'll dine with my parents this evening, and I'm certain my father will have plenty to say to all of us."

"Or nothing to say to any of us," Julian countered.

Alex rubbed above his brows. It was difficult to say how they'd be received, but Julian's words left a prickling twinge on his forehead.

Julian admired the Duke of Keswick, respected his shrewd mind. *Yes, his mind is sharp, and will come at you like a battle-ax, ready to shred ribbons of your theories.*

Hugh snorted as Julian pulled another book from the shelf. "Good God, Julian. You're not actually going to read whilst on break from school."

"May I remind you that being sent down can hardly be referred to as a break? And mad as it may seem to your idle head, Hugh, I take pleasure in expanding my knowledge—perhaps as much as Charles enjoys slapping the very source of where yours should be coming from."

Charles leapt at his inattentive friend, and wrapped his arms in a victorious headlock while Hugh struggled for escape.

Julian sighed. "My point precisely."

The maid returned with a heavy tray and the rigid posture of a rabbit about to flee. An older girl, with long hair of corn silk, followed her in. She held a bottle of wine and three glasses in her arms. Charles and Hugh released each other and casually smoothed their disheveled fabrics of shirts and breeches, both watching the girls lay the table.

The young pale-faced servant glanced nervously at them as she laid a plate with cold meats and cheeses, along with steaming rolls and salted butter. The older maid caught Hugh's eye and sidled around the table. She poured red wine into each glass and wiped the mouth of the bottle with a cloth after each tip. When the last goblet was filled, she caught the drip of wine from the glass with her finger and, meeting Hugh's fixed gaze, licked it from her hand. His slow half smile revealed one dimple, and he watched the girls leave. The older one flicked her hair over her shoulder before closing the door.

"This is much better, I must say," Hugh said, casting an eye at Charles.

"You haven't even tasted the wine yet, you pumpion." Charles swiped at him.

Hugh settled into a chair, his face cool and complaisant. He swirled the liquid in the glass. "No need. I'm satisfied with whatever they've brought and perhaps with what's to come."

Alex shook his head, unable to stomach any more. "I propose we settle into our chambers and meet in the drawing room later for drinks. Hugh, Charles . . . Julian, I'll see you anon." He nodded at them and left the library. There would be no room for anything in his stomach this evening. All the space had filled with dread.

An hour later, Alex rushed headlong through the somber halls toward his parents' private dining salon. His mother had filled the room with French and Flemish tapestries, hanging on wine-colored walls, trimmed in gilded leather. She'd had the ivory seat cushions overstuffed for the twelve-foot mahogany table. And each setting displayed gilded porcelain and gleaming English rock crystal. But no amount of eye-catching artistry could compete with his father's disagreeable presence. The room would always be stubbornly bleak and uninviting so long as he occupied it.

Alex cursed his rapid pulse and opened the dining room door. The dinner party was in progress and the polite conversation gener-ated a quiet hum. He surveyed his father for a moment; the velvet waistcoat attempting to gather in the man's girth was the finest to be found, but failed its purpose.

"Kind of you to join us this evening, Alex. I wondered if you'd simply hide your head in shame during your visit," his father said. "Although we shan't call it a visit, since your school doesn't want you back. Please, do sit down." The duke gestured with a ruffled sleeve at an empty spot across the table from him. Hugh made a quiet snort and tried to cover it with a cough. He received a sharp elbow from Charles and a dour glare from Julian.

Alex gritted his teeth and willed himself not to respond to his father's barb, but instead sat in the chair the duke's private butler had pulled out. "I'm sorry I've come late, but I was sorting out a few housekeeping matters with Mrs. Wigginton. I thought rather than passing the burden on to Mother, I would handle them myself."

"You? Whatever for?" the duke said, spearing a piece of meat. "I believe you do your mother an injustice. Running this household is precisely what gives her pleasure. Am I not speaking the truth, my dear?" He opened his mouth to envelop the great hunk of pork.

"No. You are not," she said, her face serene and smiling at the men.

The duke grunted in reply and waved his knife through the air. "Perhaps you did not hear the compliment in my statement. I endeavored to say that you enjoy taking charge of such things as the domestic matters." He stared at his wife, glistening gravy dribbling down his chin.

"Indeed I did. Your assumption that my daily pleasure springs from choosing which rooms will be aired out and making sure the staff are not thieving from us is incorrect."

The duke grew a deep shade of scarlet.

"*Pride* in my work is a given, but that which brings me pleasure is elsewhere."

Alex watched Julian's eyes jump from the duke to the duchess. He knew Julian would seize this as an opportunity to score flattery points, and scowled as his friend leaned forward to say, "Enlighten us, Your Grace. Do tell, what captures your interest these days?"

"That's very kind of you to ask, Mr. Finch, but I doubt it would be of much interest to anyone here," she said, her eyes moving to her husband.

"Quite right, I'm sure, my dear." The duke waved at his butler. "Please bring the next course. I'm certain our guests are still famished from their travels."

Alex closed his eyes and reminded himself to unclench his jaw, then looked to his mother, who seemed to say with a quiet smile there was no need to further irritate the situation.

"I decided this year would be best for fowl," the duke raised a finger. "I informed several of my more superfluous tenants that this season there was to be no harvesting of corn on their lands unless obtained with a sickle." He smiled at the look of confusion around him. "Sadly, many of these ill-bred creatures found it impossible to reap enough of their grain in time to procure the rent. Therefore, I was left with the unfortunate task of throwing them off the estate."

Julian's eyebrows knitted together. "I am perplexed, Your Grace."

Sighing, the duke went on, "Mr. Finch, think of the buffet these birds have been left with—a feast for fattening, and our ultimate benefit in a few weeks."

Julian's face lit with understanding. "Ingenious. I admire your forethought."

Alex cleared his throat. "Have any of these tenants been tardy with rents in the past?"

The duke turned, his receding chin stiffening. "You feel it your place to question my judgment, Alex? I think you rather inexperienced to render an opinion on the matter, particularly when it has not been sought."

Alex wondered where he could possibly take the conversation from here. His father had been raised in the comfortable cloak of an elitist attitude. He sported it as if it were a badge of honor. "I suppose I was simply wondering about the families of the unfortunate farmers and what they will do without means of support."

"It's business, Alex. Surely you can appreciate your father's cunning?" Julian said.

Alex shook his head. "It occurs to me that if you have proposed a business partnership with an individual, changing the terms after the accord has been accepted is dishonest and deceitful."

His father scowled, his glare sharp as the knife in his hand. "There is nothing corrupt in procuring the best possible outcome for one's economic endeavors, Alex. One takes a gamble with ventures and if you are not up for the challenge, you shall fall behind and perish. It is the law of the land. If you are to create any kind of a livelihood, it would behoove you to learn the benefits of shrewdness. As Mr. Finch gathered, if you show signs of weakness, others will gobble you up as soon as look at you. Given the opportunity, you'll not find a man who wouldn't use you as a stepping stool should they see you on the ground and a better place above you."

Alex sunk back into his chair, deflated. He shook his head in amazement. Julian was the son the duke had wished for. He was so willing to play the game.

The rest of the dinner was nothing but polite conversation regarding the travels of the duke and the reopening of Parliament in November. Until then, the duke was planning several hunting trips, and spoke of next month's visitation from a local magistrate.

"A knowledgeable man, I must say," he nodded to Alex. "An individual I think pertinent to your future. That is, if you still have a future."

Alex gripped the sides of his chair and molded a vapid expression.

"He will also advise me on how thick a rope I'll need to hang the blasted rebels running our country amuck." The duke pierced the air with his knife. "Once my garrison is built, this area will be clean of Jacobites and they'll be rotting in a hole surrounded by my soldiers. Loathsome villains, the lot of them, and the filthy Stuarts they support. James will never be king. Stay in France where somebody actually gives a damn!"

The duke mopped the sheen from his face, motioned to the butler, and pushed his bulk back from the table to rise. "We'll take our port in the library. See it gets there immediately." He made a lackadaisical bow in the direction of his wife. "Thank you for dining with us this evening, my dear. The pleasure of your company always adds to the enjoyment."

She gave him a thin smile and turned to Alex. "I do hope you'll find a moment to spend with me tomorrow. There is much to discuss."

"Why don't you join us in the library for port?"

"Not tonight, Alex. I have letters to write and I'm rather weary as it is. I believe I will retire with a cup of tea and the quiet of my room."

Alex sighed with unexpected relief. His parents' forced politeness was something he could tolerate only in small doses. He kissed her on the cheek as she stifled a yawn, and noted again the pallor of her skin and jaundiced eyes. As far as the end to his evening, it was likely a long way off. His father was still wide-eyed and clear-witted.

NINE

THE EDGE OF THE QUILL WAS SHARP. ALTHOUGH NOT as sharp as she needed it to be. Gavin would be sailing through the front door any moment; his assigned Latin verses were to be translated in her finest penmanship. Verb conjugation swam before Jenna's eyes.

She pressed the quill into the wooden table and tried to dislodge a tiny dried pea that had wedged itself into a crack. It was exactly how she felt at the moment: ignored, insignificant, and stuck in an odd place. If she could just get outside and breathe for a few minutes, she might be able to clear her head. But Angus demanded she stay indoors for the week—after the visit from Mrs. Wigginton. She'd been searching for the troublemaker who'd had a clash in the stables with Lord Pembroke, the duke's son. He wanted her found and dealt with. *"Clash?"* Angus had repeated and looked questioningly at Jenna. But he covered for her, saying that she had been bedridden with an irritating cough since they'd arrived. It couldn't be she who had vexed Lord Pembroke.

But it had been her. And now she was paying for her insolence. Her chin sunk to rest on the table and she viewed the parchment with her conjugation exercises at an odd angle.

Amo, amas, amat, amamus, amatis, amant. Conjugation in the present tense. Other tenses floated through her head, adding to the confusion. *Amo, amare, amavi, amatus.* To love.

Jenna sighed. She found if she closed her eyes, some of the words started to disappear. It felt better with her eyes closed. She resolved to do the next conjugation in her head. To read. *Lego, legere, legi, lectum . . .*

"Iaceant canes dormientes," said a soft voice near Jenna's ear.

She sprang from the table and knocked over the inkwell. "Oh, Gavin, you scared me! Don't sneak up on me when I'm studying. My heart is pounding like a hammer." She held her hand to her throat.

"I only said 'let sleeping dogs lie,' and I quite meant it, lass," he said, and laughed. "I'd no intention of waking ye from your vigorous pursuit of knowledge. I ken what it's like to be so immersed in work that your eyes give up and close while a wee bit of drool slips from your mouth." He put the back of a sinewy hand to his head, his tongue lolling out the side of his mouth.

She swatted him with the dishcloth that lay on the table. "I cannot be blamed. I didn't get enough sleep last night." She stretched and yawned like a cat, limbs unfurling.

"It might help if ye didna stay up half the night wi' your ear pressed against the door." Gavin winked a playful brown eye and she flushed red with the second chiding of the day.

"I wouldna have woken you," he said, "except your da sent me down. Ian's almost finished wi' his day's drawings and wants to get your mathematics done before Angus comes to cook the supper. Ian thinks ye dinna pay near enough attention when Angus comes bustling about." Gavin swung a leg over the bench, and arranged the folds of fabric from his plaid. He pulled the parchment in front of him.

She watched him bending over her work, his long, oval face focused. She sighed and nibbled on a fingernail. It's not just Angus. A loaf of bread would be more captivating that Ian's dismal company. If he had walked in to find her lying facedown on her Latin, he would have inked the phrase onto her forehead.

She hoped her catnap had been sufficient, for working with Ian required staunch concentration. She much preferred study with any of the other men. At least they had humor. Ian's expectations often exceeded her capabilities, which only served to exasperate him further.

Although she enjoyed learning geometry with all of its lines, points, and angles, it would be easier if she could see it used practically. Ian refused to take her to the building site to show her how he figured the measurements. He was nervous someone outside the family might see him teaching Jenna something women had no need to understand, nor right to perform. Instead, they worked dryly with a simple straight edge, her problems figured on parchment.

"Well, I think there isna anything left to do wi' this at the moment," Gavin said, holding her exercises in his hand. "I think it's best we continue tomorrow, and maybe we'll throw in a wee bit of Homer, if you're lucky." He grinned, an absent tooth revealing a pink space of gum.

She sprang up, her face lit with enthusiasm. "*The Iliad*? *The Frog Mouse War*?"

Gavin smiled devilishly and shook his head. She would have to wait until tomorrow to find out.

Jenna loved Gavin's storytelling. Sometimes, when they sat around the campsite fire after a day's travel, he would recite in Latin or Greek, and anyone sitting there would swear they understood the tale, whether they knew the language or not.

His audience would lean closer, lured like moths to his firelight. Gavin pounded on his breast with punctuated enthusiasm, and his face molded to the features of his characters, portraying their feelings. The saga unraveled in the flickering glow and Jenna sunk into the story. She wanted to know what their narrator was truly saying. She needed to know. And thus, her Latin lessons began.

Ian came through the door carrying the same heavy scowl on his face Jenna had seen for the last two years, only varying in degrees. She tried not to mirror his image, fearing she'd make the situation worse. She often wondered what brought Ian to the business of stonemasonry. With his lithe, spare-framed body and finely boned fingers, he looked better suited to paperwork and ledger keeping, but according to her father he never shirked a hard day's labor.

Gavin rose and clapped Ian on the shoulder. "*Bene vale vobis.*" He gave her an encouraging smile and headed out.

Ian sighed with annoyance as he pulled the straight edge from his sporran, the fur-covered pouch he kept his tools in. He set himself on the bench next to Jenna, his plaid swinging off his shoulders.

"All right, then, let's get down to it."

He worked out a set of points for her to label with angles and measurements. While she calculated, he paced the room, his impatience heard with every footfall. His grumbling, which made her self-conscious, added minutes to her computations. After the better part of an hour, Angus showed up with two parcels that clearly held the contents of dinner.

"Who's up for venison stew, then?" His face beamed with exuberance. "One of the stable lads had a good bag today and gave us more than we'd need ourselves. Aye, that's a nice group of lads down there." He turned to look at Jenna with widened eyes and pointed with a pudgy finger. "Save for that plumped-up one ye met, I'm sure. Although," he added with a stern look beneath his brows, "ye must remember to keep that opinion to yourself, aye?"

Ian stood to gather his materials and huffed. "I'd say that's enough for today, Jenna. Your entertainment has arrived and your attention has departed."

She beamed at Angus behind Ian's back, but he gave her a stern shake of his head.

"Well, then, if you're sure you're finished wi' her, I wouldna mind a hand in the kitchen. Mrs. Wigginton was kind enough to send down vegetables from the late summer garden, and they need chopping." Angus held out a clean knife, handle end first, toward her.

She looked at Ian, who waved a hand in dismissal and left mumbling as when he first came in, something about Jenna finally doing what she should be in the first place.

They settled into their tasks for the stew and Angus told her news of the building site. He also spoke of meeting the man

Wicken—the duke's new Welsh horse handler, who appeared to be spending more time nosing about the site of the garrison than handling horses. Their knives stilled as there was a knock at the door.

Angus wiped his hands on the old linen apron covering the front of his plaid and heaved himself from the table. When he opened the door, his figure filled the space and Jenna could only make out the high-pitched squeak of a little boy.

"What is it?" she said when he returned and tossed a sealed envelope onto the table.

"One of Mrs. Wigginton's lads wi' a note addressed to your da, so we'll not ken till supper I s'pose. Come on, then. Let's get this all into the pot. I'm famished."

She stood on a chair to reach for one of Angus's bundles of hanging herbs. She thought about the letter, about how unopened correspondence always set the family on edge. Often, the next day found them packing their bags and heading elsewhere. Given that the note came from Mrs. Wigginton, it was an unlikely scenario. Nonetheless, her level of patience was abysmal, and the thought of leaving for Scottish soil left her eager with anticipation.

She spent the next three-quarters of an hour physically preparing the evening meal, but mentally envisioning what lurked behind that sealed wax. It was all but torture waiting for the men to file in. They took their time to wash and tidy before sitting, the sharp scent of Angus's pine needle soap filling the room. Her father was the last to come in, and after cleaning the day's dirt off his hands and face, he sat at the table with no notice of the letter beside his bowl and cup.

"Ah, Angus, another fine meal you've prepared for us. Your skills have gone wasted, I think." The men laughed, but he went on.

"Aye, but it's true. You're a canny fine cook and a good friend." He raised his cup. "To Angus and the way he fills our hearts and bellies!" Everyone lifted their glass in a toast to the dark and hairy man, who suddenly looked as coy as a young maiden.

Jenna couldn't wait any longer. "Da . . . you've got a letter."

"Ah, so I have."

Angus went round filling each of the bowls with the rich, meaty stew while her father sat back from the table to break the wax seal and read the note.

"His Grace has invited us to attend the engagement of his son— day after next," he said at last. There was a lot of looking around, and a dozen eyes settled on Jenna.

"Lord Pembroke?" she asked, her eyes meeting with Angus's.

"Aye, 'tis likely the off-putting young man ye met in the stables a few days back," Angus said, and then mumbled to Jenna, "the one Mrs. Wigginton came about."

She felt her pulse quicken and color rise in her cheeks. She shrugged and added under her breath, "I pity the unfortunate woman who must put up with him permanently." Angus heard her remark and she could tell he wasn't pleased. She glanced at her father. "Must we attend?"

"I think it would be rude not to," he said. "The duke seems to be extending his hand in friendship. To deny it might cause suspicion, Jenna."

She would not look him in the eye, for if she did, he would see the flash of panic, the sickness that spread. She caught Angus biting his lip. He was anxious.

She was in trouble.

TEN

"MAI. È BRUTTO!"

"Lucia, please settle yourself. And use your English."

"I won't wear it. It's dis-gus-ting." Lady Lucia pushed the lavender silk dress away, its embroidered hem swinging buoyantly.

"But darling, *bella*, you thought it exquisite when we had it made for you just last month. I don't understand."

"You never do, Mamma, for you are so—what is the word for *vecchio stile*?—old-fashioned. I said away." Lady Lucia swatted at the outfit, making it slip from the maid's fingers.

The chambermaid dove for the gown before it hit the ground, bowed, and returned the dress to one of several massive trunks containing Lady Lucia's clothing.

The young woman ran her hand down the upholstery of the settee where she reclined. "Their things are drenched with luxury. I must surpass the splendor of this house, or they shall judge me as not befitting, Mamma." She strolled to where the other dresses hung, waiting for her evaluation. She regarded each with a tight-lipped expression indicating an uncompromising resolve. The young servant beside them shuddered at the girl's mood, which was as dark as her pitch-black hair.

The countess glanced at her daughter and the cowering maid. A resigned sigh escaped her lips. "Well, soon these handsome things may truly be yours. And if you are desirous, you shall have money enough for a dress made every day if it suits you." Her mother stroked a discarded dress lying on the sumptuous featherbed, smoothing its shiny fabric.

"It will," Lady Lucia said, her black eyes challenging her mother's. "Soon I will be the lady of this house, and I shall run it as I see fit." She walked to the fireplace in the bedroom and inspected herself in the beveled mirror above it.

"*Tesoro mio,*" her mother said, pleading. "I beg you to be patient . . . and reasonable."

Lady Lucia's thin lips pulled back into a terse curve. "Of course, your words are full of the wisdom that comes with old age, but I see my future here and I must act with strength to secure it." She pointed to the dresses. "Now, please, Mamma, pick out a dress that is appropriate for the occasion or I will refuse to come down to be seen."

The countess pressed a hand to her mouth and nodded to the maid, who began pulling out a series of dazzling gowns.

Lady Lucia snapped her fingers at the girl. "The red one. I shall wear the red one with the slippers matching. This color shows off my skin. *Molto bene!* And something will need to be done with my hair.

I will not wear a wig tonight, for I want everyone to see its true color. Something so stunning should not be disguised, don't you agree, Mamma?" She played with the strands of ink that lay silkily about her shoulders. "You must find my hair jewels," she said to the maid. "And why have we not yet been served tea?" Lady Lucia turned to the girl with a sharp eye.

The maid scrambled up from the side of the trunk, and apologizing, left for the kitchen. Lady Lucia returned to the mirror, and posed from different angles. "I think it appalling the duchess stays away not seeing us. We've been here for a wearisome hour."

"I'm sure she is laboring over our dinner party this evening, not to mention the engagement reception next week," the countess said, looking through her own wardrobe. "There is much one must do in a household of this size to prepare for such elaborate events."

"That is what servants are for. Given fit direction, a household should run uninterrupted by such occasions. She has a most displeasing staff. This will not be so when I am here."

"First things first, *amore mio*. I think you will need to work on your English so that the staff will understand you—don't you agree?"

"*Sì.*" Lady Lucia rolled her eyes and held the red dress against her body, gazing into the mirror. "Perhaps I shall make everyone speak *my* language so I can understand *them*."

"Yes, Lucia," her mother murmured. "Perhaps it will turn out this time."

Alex waited in the library with a glass of sherry and fiddled with his sleeves. He watched the steward return books to their shelves and fluff pillows to invite visitors to recline on them. He would need something stiffer than a pillow to support him now.

The thought of meeting the young lady to whom he was betrothed made his stomach churn. He'd received a miniature portrait of Lady Lucia, painted on an enamel snuffbox. Nevertheless, he had no taste for tobacco and gave the box to his wardrobe groom. Although he had a general idea of her physical appearance from the neck upward, a miniature was incapable of describing a person's intellect, or personality, or even humor. Would they find each other entertaining?

His father assured him months ago, when the arrangements were made, that this was strictly a political union, created for the benefit of both families, as had been done for centuries. This would in no way curtail his quest for other pursuits, as was "natural for every man," and simply advised discretion. His mother was more judicious in her counsel, and encouraged Alex to wait and see if something might develop over time. This, she warned him, wouldn't occur unless he put sincere effort into the relationship.

The door opened and the house butler peered at him. "Sir, the ladies are in the drawing room. Shall I escort you there?" His bushy eyebrows rose in expectation.

"No, thank you. I shall see myself."

"Very well, milord." The butler backed out silently and closed the door behind him.

A shiver ran through Alex as he stared, unmoving, at the door. He hoped his mother would arrive before him. She was much better than he at making idle conversation with strangers. He took a deep breath and swallowed the last of the amber liquid. The warmth it provided gave him a shallow sense of courage, but not enough to affect enthusiasm.

He traveled the long hall and glanced at the wall displaying family portraits. The gallery was filled with fashionable wigs and stern, scholarly faces. He stopped in front of the drawing room doors. The butler stood, one hand on the latch, his face giving no hint as to what lay beyond the threshold. "May I see you in, milord?"

A deep breath and a slight nod was Alex's answer.

The butler opened both doors just enough to be seen and said, "Good ladies, I present Lord Pembroke." He eased the doors open and stood aside, gesturing Alex into the room.

He moved past the butler and looked at the two women, then took a step back.

"Alex, please, join us." His mother rose from her seat. She walked toward him, arms outstretched, and kissed both his cheeks. She turned to face the other woman, who wore an apricot gown of delicate Chinese-woven silk, her black hair piled atop her head.

The woman looked as old as his mother!

"Alex, may I present the Countess of Provenza?"

"Lady Lucia?" His voice was a whisper.

"Lady Lucia's mother."

His heart made a palpable thump and then slowly regained its normal rhythm. He took the outstretched hand in front of him. "Your servant, madam."

"A pleasure to make your acquaintance. I've heard admirable things from Her Grace."

Alex scanned the uneasy face and tried to pinpoint the resemblance from Lady Lucia's miniature. "Please, dismiss half of what she reveals, as she has a rather distorted view of my strengths and achievements."

"As any mother who loves her son would!" The duchess laughed, mischief in her eyes.

The butler appeared at his elbow. He leaned in and whispered, "Would now be a good time, milord?"

Alex tilted back to look at the butler's face. "For what?"

"For the young lady to make her entrance."

"Her entrance?"

"Lady Lucia left earlier after discovering you were not present. She insists she does not wait on anyone; rather people anticipate her."

Alex's eyes narrowed. Could he be serious?

The butler went on. "She asked I come for her once you'd arrived."

"Ah . . . I see. I guess you'd best fulfill her wish, then. Better we don't start things off on the wrong foot." He sighed and turned back to the women.

The countess leaned forward. "Your mother says you are home from Cambridge."

"Yes," Alex said, glancing toward the duchess. "I'm unsure when I'll be returning, as my father would like me to begin my Tour, but I would prefer continuing my studies. We haven't had an opportunity to . . . discuss it yet."

"The Grand Tour, such a wonderful name for travel," the countess said, smiling. "I remember my son journeyed after schooling too. He was away two years and returned filled to the brim with experience, eager to begin work with my husband."

Eager? Alex could barely hope for a transformation dramatic enough to make him *eager* to spend time in the company of his father.

At that moment, the butler appeared within his customary crack in the door and announced, "Ladies and gentleman, I present to you, Lady Lucia."

Alex got to his feet. His pulse quickened.

The butler pushed the doors forward and stepped aside as a slim girl wearing a plush red gown sailed into the room. She was enveloped by the dress, and occupied the middle of it with some difficulty. Alex judged that she needed four feet of clearance to successfully maneuver the costume, and the sleeves that encompassed her slender arms could have housed several others. She held a broad, white-laced fan over the bottom half of her face, which allowed her intense black eyes to peek over its edges. It fluttered back and forth and created a breeze, making the fringe of dark curls above her forehead rise and fall unexpectedly.

Alex bit the inside of his cheek to stop from laughing and covered his amusement with a deep bow. As he rose, Lady Lucia thrust out her hand to be kissed. When she leaned beyond the perimeter of her dress she swayed forward and wobbled. Alex grasped her hand to steady and save her from an unrecoverable embarrassment. Even so, her eyes widened with displeasure as they both noticed he stepped on the trim of her frock. He quickly removed his foot and decided the young lady bore a strong resemblance to an aggravated peacock.

Her demeanor recovered, she curtsied and said in a thick Sicilian accent, "How very pleasant to meet you, Lord Pembroke."

He forced a thin smile and said, "Welcome to our home, Lady

Lucia. Please, do sit." He gestured toward the chairs where both their mothers were seated, and then realized there was no place to accommodate both the young woman and her dress. A brief panic widened her eyes, but he pretended not to see it, and again clamped down on the flesh in his mouth.

The duchess spotted the problem and rose from her spacious settee. She offered it to the young woman and insisted she would be more comfortable in one of the simple, straight-backed chairs. With stiff-necked pride, Lady Lucia lowered herself to the settee and finally removed the fan from her face in order to parade the dress's fine silk and conceal the hoops supporting it.

Alex studied the rest of her features. Her highly rouged cheeks and red-stained lips seemed most comfortable in a pursed position. *Attractive, but unwelcoming.* For his mother's sake, he chided himself for allowing any negativity to color his first impressions. When Lady Lucia finished her preening, Alex said, "Our butler has taken special pains to ensure the house is stocked with grappa. Shall I pour you a glass?"

"No. And your butler is a fool, for no Sicilian of high class ever drinks grappa. It's reserved for the unintelligent and the poor." She cast a scowl in the servant's direction.

"Lucia!" her mother gasped.

"Duly noted," said Alex, barely audible. "I'm sure no offense was intended, milady."

The girl fussed with her billowing sleeves. "I do believe a proper butler would know that."

"Lucia," her mother growled.

The air erupted with the heated exchange between Lady

Lucia and the countess, their bristling Sicilian phrases ricocheting between each other. Alex and the duchess's gazes met. He raised his eyebrows and received a cool, reassuring look in return. Apparently, his mother wasn't the slightest bit fazed by the unusual outburst. For Alex, this would take some getting used to.

ELEVEN

AFTER THE INITIAL MEETING WITH LADY LUCIA AND her mother, Alex tried to disappear. Everyone else spent the next several days preparing for the gathering set to announce the engagement. Rooms were aired and readied for guests traveling from afar, the finest French linens placed on the beds. Furniture was arranged to invite intimate circles of conversation. Long tables were brought in to accommodate diners for the evening, and the house seemed to hemorrhage money in the acquisition of food and drink. Even a modest orchestra would play in the courtyard, encouraging guests to venture outside to the serpentine stroll through mazes and gardens.

The guest list had been hastily finalized, and the duke insisted anyone with influence regarding Alex's future should be invited. The party would balance the subtle dance of calling in favors and marking one's territory.

"Make sure your teeth are clean, Alex. Chances are your father will want to display them for pedigree purposes," Hugh had said.

Between his attempts to avoid his mother, and her requests to become more acquainted with Lady Lucia, Alex also managed to steer clear of his father. The necessary conversation remained lodged in his throat like an annoying small bone from a fish.

Unfortunately, he was found in the horse barn, and given a message to join Lady Lucia in the garden for an amble about the roses. The event was tedious, as far as conversations went, and paralyzed his mind after an hour of unreciprocated efforts at making small talk.

He offered his arm to steady her irregular gait, the result of her insistence to show off fashionable footwear, however erratically shaped and dangerously elevated. Soon, he found she had no interest in books, art, music, and certainly not nature. Bees were a nuisance. Grass and mud stained expensive shoes. The sun wreaked havoc with her complexion. And the only time she wanted to see a horse was when it would be standing ready in front of her carriage.

On the afternoon of the party, as Alex dressed in his chambers, a young steward brought a note from his mother.

Dearest Alex,

I am fully aware of your hesitation at this point, but your uncertainty is somewhat premature, in my opinion. I do hope you will endeavor to further educate yourself in the matters of Lady Lucia's charms and give the young woman an opportunity to become familiar with yours as well. Rest assured they both exist in ample quantity.

Your loving mother,
Charlotte Clifton

He put aside the scripted advice and continued dressing, wondering if his mother was growing delusional in her attempts to see this union come to fruition. Certainly, she'd noticed Lady Lucia's eccentricities. Would she wish them upon her son and any offspring that might result from the marriage? Was the tenuous lineage of Sicilian royalty crucial to the family, or might there be other, more suitable matches with someone else? Anyone else.

This is a farce!

He could not focus and mismatched the buttons on his waistcoat. His valet held open his topcoat and Alex blindly slipped his arms through, plagued by his thoughts.

"Your wig, sir?" the valet offered, holding out one of several available choices.

"No. I have no desire to fashion myself as a dandy tonight," Alex said, fastening his dress sword to breeches. "But hand me my pocket watch. I have the distinct feeling that this evening I will look at it with frequency."

Jenna tugged at the stays that stiffened her midsection, the result of fraying material that allowed its boning to become unsheathed. She had no formal dress to wear to the party, but luckily Mrs. Wigginton had obtained one for her. Alas, the gown, a jeweled green that cast a shimmer of blue in the light, contained more layers of flouncing material, and beaded strings and ties with which to keep them all in place, than most of her clothes combined.

The kindly woman had also procured a corset—the first Jenna had ever worn. Being raised by men since her mother had died meant some of the ordinary ways of women were either unheard of by the bachelors, or forgotten about by her father. For years, her wardrobe had contained nothing more than jumps—serviceable, boneless corsets made of whatever material the family had left from making saddles and linens. The leather jumps were especially comfortable and incredibly adept at keeping her bosom from paining her whilst riding through unforgiving territory at treacherous speeds.

"What in heaven's name are women thinking wearing these ghastly devices?" She poked at the whalebones and walked stiffly up the hill to the manor house, one arm linked with her father's.

"I'm told some women have such pressure for breath wearing them they find it difficult to talk."

"Yes! It's true. I can barely . . . ," she began, and then caught the faint smile on her father's lips. "You jest at my expense. If you'd prefer I remain silent for the evening, you need only ask. In fact, if you'd rather I didn't accompany you at all, I'd be happy to stay back in the cottage and eat Angus's meat pies with the rest of the men."

"I meant no such thing, Jenna, but was only repeating that which I'd heard before. If ye feel the need to pass out, give me a nod just before. I'll make sure ye willna knock over anything expensive on your way down."

She laughed, but regretted it; the whalebones would not allow the muscle movement needed.

They crested the hill and the house came into view. Candles glowed in windows opened to the warm mid-September evening. A string orchestra's music fluttered across the courtyard to them. She wanted to linger there, to enjoy the enticing designs it created in her head. *And avoid the potential retribution for a loose tongue.*

"It willna be a long evening," her father began. "Strange that His Grace invited us to his celebration, but I've nay doubt we've been asked only as a courtesy. A shake of a few hands and we'll be off. Ye may have your meat pies yet, Jenna," he chuckled.

They joined the receiving line in the entry hall and waited to be introduced. Jenna continued to quarrel with the more uncomfortable parts of her dress, the slow-moving queue providing ample opportunity. She noticed all the women had extravagant hairdos. Some were speckled with jeweled pins and pressed into complicated buns. Others hid beneath wigs that provided something equally intricate. She was the only one with hair unfastened and falling.

It was easy to identify the faces of the Duke and Duchess of Keswick. They looked as Angus had described them: he, with a long wig, luxurious velvet coat, and breeches—unable to restrain a bloated waistline—and she, pale and elegant, with a sumptuous turquoise gown that balanced her tall frame and upswept hair. It was no great discovery to identify the person to the right of the couple, and the eyes that locked onto hers. That intrusive blue gaze . . . It pulled at her reserves of courage.

She felt the stays of her gown tighten with each step closer to both the head of the line, and to the interrogating eyes that she knew hadn't moved since the moment they'd recognized her. She couldn't help but wonder, *Is it too late to run?*

The usher announced their names as they stepped in front of the duke. "Master Stonemason Malcolm MacDuff and his daughter, Miss Jenna MacDuff, Your Grace."

Her father made a courtly bow and Jenna tried to remember the men's instructions in the cottage on the proper way to curtsy without falling over, or looking obsequious.

"Your Grace, thank you for your kind invitation, and congratulations to you and your family on the upcoming nuptials," her father said.

The duke nodded and rolled his milky, vein-streaked eyes toward Jenna. "Thank you, Master MacDuff, and I would imagine the same will be said to you in short time. We feel privileged to have a man of your caliber and skill working among us. Perhaps you'll indulge me in a peek now and again at your efforts. I'm eager to rid our region of its devilment."

"As ye wish, Your Grace," Malcolm said steadily.

"Miss MacDuff." The duke blinked like a pawky-faced owl and turned as the usher introduced the next guests in line.

Jenna curtsied to the duchess, but did not hear what her father said to the lady. She knew it was only moments before she would face the young man who probably still wanted her punished for her insolence in the stables.

"Jenna?" her father said.

"I beg your pardon?" Her eyes snapped to his.

"Her Grace asked if you've had a chance to meet her son yet?" he said lowly.

"I, uh . . ." She swallowed and met his eyes. The young lord's head cocked to one side and his brows rose with anticipation. She closed her eyes. "We—"

"No," the young man said, interrupting. "We've not been introduced."

"Lord Pembroke," the duchess said warmly and turned away.

He laid out his hand.

"Yes," Jenna said. "Right." Her eyes darted in panic.

"And you are . . . ?" He raised his brows.

Jenna felt as leaden and stiff as her buckram-lined dress. She couldn't remember her name, but she could count, with great accuracy, the number of whalebones trying to fuse to her rib cage.

"Miss Jenna MacDuff," her father answered without ceremony. He took his daughter's hand, albeit somewhat gruffly, and put it in the young man's still outstretched and waiting one. He leaned in. "First time with a corset. It's taken the wind out of her."

The young man bent to kiss Jenna's hand as her father said these words. She felt the rush of his breath against her skin and knew he had not been able to stifle a laugh. She flamed crimson and snatched her hand back, rubbing the spot he kissed, and now wishing Mrs. Wigginton had found gloves as well.

Once again, those blue eyes challenged hers.

"I—I'm—" Her tongue was leaden. Unwilling. He was enjoying her humiliation. She swallowed her choler and felt her father tug at her elbow, leading her away. She only hoped before the evening was through, she might have a chance to see Lord Pembroke choke on his pheasant.

Alex's jaw nearly dropped when he beheld the red-haired girl standing in the queue. Who was she? He stared at her, trying to imagine how his parents knew her, when twice, his mother had to repeat an introduction of someone standing in front of him. He recalled their nerve-jangling meeting in the stables a week or so ago, and having found no one who knew her, had put her out of his mind. Nonetheless, seeing that distinctive head of hair and the line of determination across her forehead brought about an insatiable curiosity.

As she and the tall, dark man she stood with came nearer, he began to question the nature of their relationship. Were they married? She looked young, although it wasn't unheard-of for a girl to be married off at an early age. And she didn't look like she was enjoying herself. Her dress was becoming, and framed her figure, but she appeared wholly uncomfortable with how it managed to do so.

Alex studied her, and while he had every right to be upset with the girl for her saucy behavior, he gathered she was becoming more nervous with each step nearer. He was still unsure how to address the situation when at last they approached.

He heard their names announced by the usher and noted with interest that the tall man was her father. So this was the master stonemason who'd come to build the garrison. A special invitation, his mother mentioned. He scrutinized the girl while his mother asked if they'd met, but she seemed to be having difficulty breathing.

He held out his hand and took delight that her discomfort was possibly brought on by a case of remorse. He'd started feeling a bit sorry for her when the Scotsman made a crude remark. Alex could not suppress his amusement. The girl jerked back her hand, unnerved. He watched her fumble a reply and leave, cheeks flushed as red as her hair. He heard his mother's voice.

"Lord Pembroke," his mother repeated.

He turned to her, biting back his mirth.

"This is Bishop Drummond."

Jenna and Malcolm moved through the crowd of people, whose lavish costumes echoed the feel of the opulent hall and its contents. "My goodness," she said. "Whatever could this man do to earn money enough for all of these possessions?"

"It is an eyeful," her father said, admiring the handiwork of a French table, "but lest ye forget, this is family money, and these things were passed down by many of their ancestors."

"But still, he must do *something* to sustain his family in this manner."

Malcolm ran his hand across the table and felt the joints. "Aye, he does at that. Politics."

"Yes, but what exactly does he *do*?"

"Wavers on principles when necessary." He walked to the wall to look closer at a painting.

"He was talking about us, wasn't he? When he said he was keen to root out 'the wickedness'?"

Her father raised his chin in answer.

"Does it make you nervous he might find out he *hired* the wickedness?"

Malcolm looked at her sharply. "He'll nay find out, Jenna. Do ye understand?"

She nodded and stared at the lush artwork. After a moment, she turned to her father. "Where is the girl he's supposed to marry? Shouldn't she have been in the receiving line?"

"I couldna say, but aye, one would expect so. Stay put, Jenna. I'll fetch ye something to drink."

She leaned closer to the canvas and tried to see the brushstrokes of the artist. It was an oil painting of a stone vase holding a cluster of white roses, each petal detailed by curve and pitch. She raised her hand to touch the ridged surface of its frame.

"Do you like it?" asked a voice behind her.

She leapt back and pulled her hand away as if she touched a spark. She collided with Lord Pembroke's chest.

"Pardon me," he said, giving her room to turn around. "Apparently we're pretty adept at catching each other off guard. I passed by and saw you looking. I thought I'd ask."

"I *was* only looking," she said, clasping her hand to her chest.

"It's fine if you want to touch it—I won't tell anyone. I promise," the young man said, his mouth quirked in a half smile.

Jenna wondered if he was trying to trick her. "I wasn't going to touch it. Colin says the oil from your fingers can destroy the paint. I was simply trying to see the brushstrokes."

"Well, you needn't be careful with this piece of artwork—there's plenty more where it came from."

"Benefits of the wealthy?" she asked.

His eyebrows shot up. "No, I meant it's one of twenty or thirty of the same thing. My mother painted it, and she's a perfectionist. This is the one she thought best."

"Oh." Jenna pressed her lips together. "Forgive me. I've been told I'm terribly outspoken."

"Only when we're alone. I've noticed you're sparing of words otherwise." Again, there was a slight smirk.

A bell rang from across the room.

"Excuse me, please," he said, making a quick bow and leaving.

She turned to see what had caught his attention and noticed the chatter in the hall quieting. The usher appeared at the top of the grand staircase and boomed, "Your Graces, ladies and gentlemen, may I present Lady Lucia of Provenza."

The young woman stood on the staircase, poised to receive

admiring glances. She wore a royal-blue velvet Mantua, its open robe and lengthy train trailing behind. Her raven-colored hair was scraped back tightly and showed off the tiny features of chin and ears. Her engaging black eyes expressed meticulous patience as she allowed the people below to admire her entrance.

Jenna watched the duke's son swiftly mount the steps to escort the young lady down. She listened to the subdued voices gushing admiration for the girl whom he would be marrying. "A grand entrance for a grand girl, I'm sure," Jenna huffed. A whalebone poked her in the ribs, a reminder not to breathe and speak simultaneously.

She watched the couple greet guests, make introductions, and move nearer to where she stood. She made a path between bulky furniture and excited guests, who swarmed in toward the handsome couple, and scanned the crowd for her father. She spotted him, head bent in conversation. He turned to her when she put a hand on his arm.

"Jenna, would ye wait outside for me? I'll nay be more than a few minutes."

She left and took great care traversing the myriad candles scattered about the hall. A set of grand double doors were opened to the glasshouse conservatory, where the musicians pulled sapphire-sweet tones from the wood of their instruments and spilled them onto the garden's courtyard. She surveyed the area and spied an empty table and chair beside a trellis smothered in ivy. Serving girls made their way through the crowd offering food and drinks. A striking maid with long, fair hair came to Jenna with a tray.

"A drink, milady?"

Jenna looked behind her—*milady?*—before she realized the

maid was addressing her. "Oh no. No thank you," she mumbled.

"Go on. His Grace has put out his finest for the occasion. Might not ever see it again, if you know what I mean." She put a glass in front of Jenna and then raised one herself. "He's a tight-fisted gorbelly—who's forced me on my back more than once, eh?" The liquid disappeared in one swig. "Ah, you'll be pleased you did. It helps to erase the memories." She wiped her mouth with the back of her hand and returned the glass to the tray. It teetered, but she managed to keep it balanced as she walked away. Aghast at the girl's confession, Jenna guessed this was not the first drink the disgruntled servant had rewarded herself with tonight.

A noisy group of young men ambled out another doorway from the house and seated themselves on the other side of the ivy screen.

"An unsociable man," one of them stated.

"It doesn't matter one whit to me which club he coffees at," another voice began. "He's a damn fine shot." The voice slurred a little. "We need another drink."

"That's hardly the way to judge an individual, Hugh," the first voice went on, "and I think you've had enough."

"Ha! That's what you think, Julian—and don't spoil my fun. Where's the girl? Wine! We need wine over here!"

Jenna flinched with the sound of an iron chair toppling onto the flagstones.

"Charles, do something with him, will you?" The crisp voice sounded galled.

The maidservant sidled around the ivy lattice. Jenna heard her say, "Still up for more, lads? Haven't had your fill yet?"

"I think he has, actually," someone told the girl coolly.

"I know I could give you your fill," the other garbled.

Jenna heard the girl squeal in false protest.

"Charles, don't take her away. You're both ruining my fun."

"You leave me no choice. Someone has to look out for you, and you're far too much a dolt to look after yourself."

Jenna picked up her glass and walked to the edge of the conservatory doors leading to the garden, to where the breeze blew against her face and the light from the house was dim. She looked into the darkness and listened for familiar sounds. Autumn spoke with the quieting of summer insects and a cool foretelling wind.

How long would they be here? The gathering of coins was not a long process, but Gavin had said this was different. She knew they were to build the garrison, but what else? And what if this duke found them out? They would be prisoners of their own making. She looked back at the grand house, tried counting the number of palatial windows, and then spotted her father approaching.

"Looking for wee bitty ghosties, or cracks in the foundation?"

She smiled. "None spotted thus far. Of either." Her gaze fell to her father's clothing. His brown unlined waistcoat and best dress plaid may not have matched the quality of the other guests, but the men had found a pale yellow shirt to compliment his woolen stockings, and buckles for his shoes. He was a striking figure.

"Well, you'll have a tad more time on your hands to survey them if ye dinna take great offense to it. Have ye got your dirk?"

Her mind flashed to the *sgian dubh*, the sharp knife she kept strapped to her leg at all times. "It's where I always keep it, Da, but this is a party."

His eyes brimmed with gravity. "Party or not, you're on your own. I'll need a bit more time than I thought. An important conversation was interrupted, as there was quite a commotion in the house a moment ago. The foreign girl fell to the ground having come over wi' a spell. Most folk think it was just the excitement of it all, ye ken. I'm sure she'll be fine. Are ye all right for a while longer?"

She nodded. "I'll be right here appreciating angles and apparitions."

He winked and left her wondering if it was not the excitement of it all that caused the girl to faint, but rather another corset drawn too tightly. Not a flattering way to see the bride-to-be, sprawled on the floor in a heap, but that's the result of stuffing a dress to its limits. Most of these women would be much more comfortable by simply adding a yard of material to the upper parts of their gowns. Many of them looked as if they were on the verge of spilling out of them.

She walked off the stone pavers of the courtyard to the English boxwood gardens beyond, and admired the few late blooms, not yet giving in. She closed her eyes. "And summer's lease hath all too short a date," she quoted Shakespeare. Still holding the glass of wine in her hand, she took a tentative sip and continued on her tour.

She rounded the corner of one of the flower beds and felt her foot catch. She pitched forward with a cry of alarm and landed facedown, a splintering crack muffled beneath her.

I'm no better than the bride.

"Ow," the girl said as Alex lifted her from the ground. She looked up through a haze of feverish red hair.

"Good God—Miss MacDuff? I didn't see you coming. Are you all right?" he asked, alarm surging through him.

She pushed the hair from her face and looked at the remains of the goblet, a thick piece of glass wedged between thumb and forefinger.

"Damn!" he said, glancing back to the bench. "You have all of my apologies. Come quickly—sit down."

"There's no need," she said, peering closer at the wound.

"Please, sit," Alex protested. "The shard must come out, and I wouldn't want you to injure yourself at the sight of blood."

"Injure myself at the sight of it?" She pulled back as he tugged her toward the bench.

"I am *not* going to have *two* women faint on me in one evening!"

"I assure you, milord, I will not lose consciousness before I purposely put my head on my pillow tonight."

He refused to let go. "All the same, I'd prefer if you didn't look until I have it bandaged." He pulled a linen handkerchief from his breast pocket.

"Is it clean?" She jerked her hand back. "Duncan says if you bind a wound with a dirty linen, it will fester."

"Yes, of course it is," he said, looking at her curiously. "Now hold still." He bent his head over her hand. She had a clean, sweet scent . . . marigolds?

After a moment he asked, "Who is Duncan? Your husband?"

"No."

He felt her fidget, aiming to see her hidden hand. "Well, then, is Colin your husband?" He pressed her fingers down, opening her palm.

"No. They're just the men I live with." She hissed with an indrawn breath as the glass was pulled free.

"The men you live with?" He held the linen to the cut. "You live with two men?"

"Oh no," she said through clenched teeth. "I live with six."

He peered up at her. "Six?"

"Yes. Six. Well, one of them is my father."

"Are the rest your brothers?"

"Not a one." Her lips curled.

Clearly, she was enjoying a tease. He wrapped the handkerchief around her hand and pressed on the wound. She stiffened and Alex looked up to see Julian, Charles, and Hugh heading toward them.

"It's not what you think," she filled in quickly. "They all work for my father, building the garrison. We've lived and traveled together for as long as I can remember. They're sort of my family."

A simulated family, Alex reflected. *Just like the motley trio that masquerade as mine.* The young men reached the bench, one raising an eyebrow and another coughing politely at the interruption.

Hugh stumbled to a stop in front of them. "What have we here? Sowing the last of the wild oats before it's forbidden, old son?"

"I most certainly am not. Miss MacDuff, may I introduce you to my friends from school. And in some cases I use the term *friends* loosely. This is Mr. Finch, Mr. Gainsford, and the insulting one is Mr. Fowler. Miss MacDuff's father is the master stonemason who's come to build the garrison. I've . . . eh . . . injured her hand."

"I think it'll be all right now," she mumbled, pulling her hand out of Alex's grasp. "If you'll excuse me, it's growing late. I should find the master mason. Good night, milord, and to you, gentlemen." She rose, made an awkward curtsy, and began walking toward the house.

"Miss MacDuff! You'll have to change the dressing soon. Don't forget!" Alex called.

She held up the bandaged hand, giving a small wave.

Julian turned to Alex, his eyes calculating. "So, who is she?"

"What do you mean?" He stooped to retrieve the remaining pieces of glass.

"I mean, you're out here in the garden with a girl other than your intended. Who is she?"

Alex released a harsh sigh. "First of all, dismiss your suspicions of my whereabouts. I simply needed fresh air. This was a result of my *intended* creating yet another scene to garner attention. I wanted to clear my head as she was resting hers. I came to the garden and this young lady happened across me—specifically, across my foot, and fell upon her wineglass. I did what any gentleman would have done by giving her aid. Now, I'd appreciate it if you didn't spread some scandalous rumor." He stood, the broken goblet cradled in his hand. "Have I made myself clear, Hugh?"

"As glass." Hugh leered. "Your secret is safe with us, old chap. And it's a wise choice to pick someone like a migrant worker's daughter. She won't be around long enough to present you with a bundle of trouble," he whispered, winking.

"Oh, shut up, Hugh," Julian said, glaring at him. "No offense was meant, Alex, and we didn't need the lengthy explanation. We only came looking for you after your mother inquired as to your whereabouts. Apparently, Lady Lucia is feeling well enough to rejoin the festivities and requires your escorting services." He raised his eyebrows and added, "It appears the leash is tightening as we speak."

TWELVE

DUNCAN HOVERED OVER JENNA'S DEEP GASH WITH equal parts worry and fascination. His concerns were infection and disability. His curiosity filled the pages of his medical notebooks. He changed the dressing every day until the wound could be covered with a simple bandage. Angus created a daily poultice, which Jenna applied after soaking her hand. Fortunately, Duncan told her, it was healing, and soon he would give her a series of exercises to do each day to strengthen her thumb.

Everyone had been anxious, for a deep gouge like Jenna's could spell disaster for the recipient, but that worry had been replaced with another: Lord Pembroke. Uninvited attention was a great risk. They hoped he'd forgotten the entire incident.

A week later, after the evening meal, Malcolm announced, "Jenna, you're looking a wee bit tired, so ye may leave your clearing chores to the rest of us. Take your books and turn in. Get a good night's sleep and rest your hand. Duncan says the bandage may come off in the morning."

"But, Da, I'm not tired and my hand isn't hurting in the least bit. I don't mind helping."

"Jenna. Good night to ye."

His message was implied and familiar. When something interesting needed discussing, she was sent to bed, or put on an errand. *They treat me as a blithering child. As if there's someone I could gossip to!*

She rose from her seat wanting to pout, but said a polite good night to each of the men. As she dragged her feet on the stairs, she heard Ian grumble, "Dinna see why she can't at least clean up. All she does is study round here."

She paused at the top of the stairs and shrank back into the shadows, eager for her father's response.

"And that's how we'll have it." In a louder voice he announced, "Good night, Jenna. Now, in your room and close the door."

She scooted inside and made a point of letting them hear the latch close. Then she slid to the floor and peered through a low crack in the door. She was determined to ferret out information however she could.

Although muffled, she recognized her father's voice.

"Duncan, I think I've left a chisel out back. Would ye mind much putting it away?"

It was their code. Either someone left tools outside, another needed fresh air, or a trip to the privy was in order. It all meant the same thing. Patrol. One of the men stood guard when Stuart matters were discussed.

Her father continued. "I've gotten word the Hanoverian prince has arrived in London. His coronation will be in one month's time. Opportunities have been wasted for us since the death of Queen Anne, but there's nay to be done about it now."

Jenna wondered what opportunities he was referring to and strained to hear more.

"We must continue wi' the building until otherwise told. When I hear further, I'll report it."

Ian sat forward. "Surely now that the prince has arrived, it changes everything. I canna imagine why we would stay. I say we pack up and move on."

Jenna saw the others murmur with surprise, but Malcolm cut them short. "It's nay for you to decide. We'll carry on."

"Informers snatched two in our chain just last week. They're headed for Newgate—as will we be if we're caught," Ian continued. "I say it's too dangerous."

"Fighting for what ye believe in has always been dangerous, Ian. We all ken that. If ye want to pull out yourself, then ye have my blessing, but if ye still stand for James, then find some courage. Dinna pull the rest of us down." Malcolm looked him straight on, heavy brows lifted.

Jenna pressed her eye to the crack with such force, she felt a splinter of wood pierce her cheek. She held her breath in anticipation.

"Ye ken I've no choice in the matter. I'm forced to stay. But I still say things should change round here. That girl of yours is a liability, Malcolm, and she sticks out like a sore thumb wi' all she kens and the little she does. She shouldna be tutored so. Pretty soon she'll be putting her nose in *this* business."

Gavin slapped the table in front of him. "Then at least she'll be doing it wi' an educated head." The rest of the men agreed, apart from Malcolm, whose dark features were fixed on Ian.

"Ye've all spent countless hours teaching her things she'll have absolutely no use for," Ian growled.

Gavin leaned over the table with a blissful grin on his face and said, "And all for the sheer pleasure of seein' her learn."

"You leave Jenna to me, Ian. If ye dinna want to teach her the mathematics, I'll find someone else to do it."

Ian glared at him, steely-eyed. "Ye do that. I want nay part of it. Women should cook, clean, and keep quiet, in my opinion."

"No one asked ye for it," Malcolm whispered. He turned to the rest of the men. "The meeting's over. Good night to ye all." He pushed his chair back and headed for the front door, but stopped and turned back. "And, Ian, I'll nay have ye giving her any trouble, understood?" He opened the door and walked out into the cool night.

Jenna pulled her head from the door and sunk back against the wall. She breathed a heavy sigh and looked across her room through the window at the moonless night. Newgate? That was where they kept criminals condemned of high treason awaiting hanging at Tyburn. She shuddered. There'd be no further study with Ian. Still, it left her with the feeling that life around him would become, if possible, even more unpleasant.

The following day baited Jenna with sunshine. She craved a short walk and a break from her studies, desperate to absorb the rays of warmth. She left the cottage and followed the path through the fields of thick grass to the creek below. Garrick Wicken, the fussy horse handler she'd seen when first bringing Henry to the stables, wrestled with a sleek chestnut mare beside the stream.

He straddled the horse, which bucked to rid herself of her passenger. The water was shallow but swift, and the horse splashed, snorting and whinnying. The sandy-haired man's clutched arms about her neck lost their grip with one fierce twist from the animal. Catapulted, he flew, arms and feet splayed, panic in his wide eyes. He landed in the rushing water, sodden and furious.

Jenna ran to him. "Mr. Wicken! Are you all right?" She offered a hand as he slogged out of the stream. He refused her help and stomped to the horse. He raised a boot and kicked a mound of dirt close to where she stood. Again, she reared, and took off toward the open fields.

"Bloody stupid beasts!" He threw a rock into the stream and turned to glare at Jenna. "What are you doing out here? These are the duke's lands, and one needs permission to enter."

She stepped back and looked toward the cottage. "My father is building the garrison. We've been given license, sir."

"Have you, then? And have you been apprised of the danger in this area? The purpose for the garrison? The evil that lurks?"

Her legs stiffened, ready to run. "No, I've not heard of any such thing."

He stood watching her, water dripping from the tip of his nose. "Consider yourselves warned then. These are dangerous times, miss." He wagged a finger at her, turned on his heel toward the grazing mare, and strutted off.

She sank to the edge of the water with a shivering chill and watched the man make his way toward the barn. She would need to tell the others of his watchfulness and warnings.

For a moment she trailed a finger in the icy stream, following the trout that lived in the shadows. The sound of the trickling water saturated her ears, but her eye caught the high-spirited approach of her father moving toward her.

"Da! What are you doing down here?"

"I came to find ye, to look at your wee hand now that the bandage is off." He held out his own and offered her a warm smile.

She rose to her feet and brushed her skirts free of moss and dirt. "Duncan says I should be ready in a day or two to start his exercises. I'm still clumsy-mannered." She stretched her long, pale fingers wide. "But I suppose that's from lack of use, yes?"

His thick, level brows lowered. "My understanding of medicine falls woefully short of a healer, Jenna. That's why we have Duncan. So I'll leave it for him to say. In the meantime, there's something I s'pose we ought speak of."

"Is it Ian?" She noticed his jaw twitch.

"It isna just Ian, although I guessed you've heard enough through that door of yours to put two and two together. It's the least he's taught you." He smiled a little at this. "It's just what we're attempting to do here . . . it isna easy. There's great risk for everyone involved. Including you." He paused to rub his dark, stubbled chin. "Although the conversation with Ian last night wasna a pleasant one, and I didna take kindly to the things he said, he did have a valid point."

"Which was?"

"Well, you're my daughter and I dinna want to see ye getting hurt. Funneling money and gathering support for James Stuart is *treason*. While my decision to fight for the rightful king is a choice I make, it's nay one I can make for anyone else." His gaze was so solemn she felt the hair prickle on the back of her neck.

He took her injured hand and held it between his, rough and warm. "Jenna . . . this life isna safe for you anymore. The one I lead could spell disaster for me and the men helping. I've been thinking maybe we need to reconsider where it is ye live and with whom."

"What?" Jenna's eyes widened in shock. "We don't know anyone else I could live with, and besides, I want to be with you."

"'Tis an easy thing speaking those words now, while no one's pounding down our door."

She thought about Mr. Wicken. His declaration of sinister threats.

Malcolm took a deep breath. "I'm thinking of approaching Mrs. Wigginton, to see about getting you a place in the house to work. Ye'd be safe there—"

"No," Jenna begged. "Please, Da, don't send me away!"

He grabbed her shoulders. "It isna safe wi' us. Ye could get killed!" His grasp loosened and he held her in front of him, his eyes wide and determined.

"He's my king too," she whispered.

Malcolm looked away and pulled her to him, his grip fierce. "Lass, I promised your mother before she died nothing would hurt you. How can ye ask me to let her down? I couldna bear it if anything happened to you. I'd go straight to my *own* grave."

"Then we must die together," she said into the muffling folds of his shirt, a determined curve in her lips.

"Good God in heaven, if she could see ye now," he murmured. "She'd not ken what to make of ye, all fierce and stubborn like."

"You mean just like you?" Jenna turned away from him and found a place to sit on the bank. The water gurgled as it passed in eddying swirls. Malcolm sighed and eased himself next to her, spreading his plaid beneath him.

"Da, what does it mean to become a Freemason? I've heard your ceremonies," Jenna said, watching him carefully. "But what is it really?"

He held an edge of his kilt, fingering a hole in the wool. "Well ... that's a good question. I've spent the better part of my life finding that out, and still, I feel like I'm at the beginning of my search.

"I've found a lot of people have their own ideas as to how the whole thing began. Some I believe and some I don't. Some folk are certain it started back when the Tower of Babel was being built. And then mathematics and geometry were passed down by the Egyptians to help build Solomon's Temple in Jerusalem. Likely it's a myth as everyone has a part of them wanting to be caught up in something worthy and important—to be an extension of the past that's surrounded by some such mystery.

"Even though the history may be confusing, its ideals are the same wherever ye go. A Freemason has an obligation to his craft, to mankind, and to God. It's a pledge one makes when joining, to improve the world in which ye live—to leave it better than when ye first came to be in it. We're men who preach and practice tolerance wi' one another." Malcolm's eyes strayed across the stream, into the yellowing fields beyond.

"I first joined because I ken I had the skill to work with stone, make it answer me. I learned the craft from others before me and I'll teach it to those who follow. But now, my skill has a . . . a higher calling, I guess, and I must allow for my hands to be the conduit." He shook his head and turned to her. "I doubt I've made it much easier for you to understand me. I've always been honest with ye, Jenna, and I willna start lying now. There's too much at stake."

"Gavin said this time was different. How come?"

"Well, we've collected a bit more than coins this time." He pressed his lips together while his eyes swept the area around them. At last he said, "Deliveries of that which will aid us winning the rebellion—should there be one. I ken it's a bit confusing for ye to understand an all, but it's a bloody bold move right beneath their noses."

She shivered, recalling the determined gleam in the duke's eyes as he told her father how eager he was to "rid our region of its devilment." She tilted her head. "Why are we here in England if the English are happy with the German as king? It doesn't make sense. We should be back in Scotland to help the Scots."

"Nay, lass. There are plenty of English who would tell ye James has the right to the throne, especially here in the north—not to mention a good handful in Parliament. Ye see, it's no just politics, but also religion that forces some to choose allegiance."

He paused, and the stream babbled at their feet, filling the silence.

"I want ye to think about what I've said. You're young, and you could have a good life. Babies and all." He eyed her intensely. "Please say no more until you've had a chance to mull it over."

He stood and straightened his plaid. "I'm sure I've been missed, and there are aye things for you to do as well." He started back toward the garrison, but stopped. "Jenna." He stood still a moment, gazing at her over his shoulder. "Think carefully."

She watched him walk up the trail away from the stream, his broad shoulders straight and strong. Although her father's path wasn't well traveled, it was obvious he was sure-footed. Clearly, he was concerned for *her* next stumble.

THIRTEEN

THE LAST DAYS OF SEPTEMBER HURRIED PAST, AND October crept in on stealthy paws, carpeting the woods with frost and crisp leaves. Jenna woke on the cool mornings and scraped a fingernail across the hoary-rimed windows, peeking at the anxious, snatching squirrels and birds, busy with their autumnal gatherings.

Her life took on a rhythm as well. Rising early, she helped Angus fix breakfast and tidy the cottage, settled into lessons with her tutors, and took an afternoon walk by the garrison to view the progress.

As the village of Hawkshead was a quiet hour by foot through the woods, Jenna was often given the task to fetch something one of the men needed. And since she was also skilled with a bow, she was granted the liberty to hunt on her way to and from the hamlet. Veiling her hair beneath a brown hood, she camouflaged her body under russet leaves and waited. Usually, she'd bring back a prized catch for the stew pot. But she came to realize this was her father's way of giving her time to think, to wrestle with their recent conversation, and to ponder the merit of his argument.

The choices were plain. *If I stay with them and fight for James, I'll be hunted. If caught I'll be tried for treason, killed along with my family.*

It was how they lived right now. Just beneath the surface. Always on guard.

If I leave them, to live safely, I will never see them again. The results would be the same as if they were dead. *The price of my security will be the loss of those I love.*

Which to choose: sanctuary and loneliness, or kinsmen and persecution?

She stopped short. "Who's to say victory would be impossible for the Jacobites? It could happen with enough support." A twig snapped and she whirled around, her senses returning to full alert. If anyone had heard her speaking aloud, her reckless behavior could cost them dearly, but after scouting the woods and spotting only a frenzied squirrel, she felt safe to carry on with caution.

She brooded over her choices. The declaration to her father at the stream, the need to stay with him, fight with him, came from exactly the place her father had guessed: one of worry, of being without them. She wanted to see herself as she saw the clan. Because they had a purpose, a desire so strong they'd risk anything to succeed. But did she share it?

The thought needled her further as she approached the cottage on her latest errand from Hawkshead, a brace of rabbit hooked to her belt. She spotted Angus speaking to someone on horseback.

Angus waved and peered hopefully at her. "Ah, Jenna, you're back. Did ye get Duncan's book? I hope they had it because he's been a right gudgeon having lost his own copy in the move."

The mounted figure turned in his saddle. It was Lord Pembroke.

"Yes—yes, I have it," she said, raising the book and coming to him.

She widened her eyes in question, but Angus just nodded upward. "You've got a visitor as well." He backed into the cottage and peered at her from under his bushy eyebrows. "I'll just be inside, but it's such a nice day, I'll leave the door wide-open."

She turned to see the young man alight from what appeared to be the tallest horse she'd ever seen.

"Good afternoon, Miss MacDuff," he said with a swift bow of his head. "I hope it's not inconvenient, but I came to view your hand and see how it's healed, or rather, *if* it's healed." He brushed the sleeves of his spotless coat.

Jenna smiled and held her hand up. She wiggled her fingers in demonstration. "More than sound." She stuffed it into the pocket of her woolen skirt. "And it's Jenna."

He tilted his head. "You don't hold much with convention, do you?"

She burned at her blunder. "I have not been schooled in unwarranted etiquette."

"Nor in holding your tongue."

She pressed her lips together and shrugged.

He took a tentative step forward. "Might I take a closer look? I have an interest in medicine."

"I think you'll not find anything to further it in my palm."

He smiled. "Please, I insist." She reluctantly presented it. He turned it over and uncurled her fingers to reveal the laceration. With his head bent low over her palm he said, "Medicine *is* a curiosity of mine, but in your case, I was curious about the healing."

She stood still, the pale gold crown of his head visible, and felt him probe the flesh of her thumb and forefinger.

"Can you feel this?"

"Mm-hm," she mumbled, biting on the urge to pull away.

He traced the line of the scar and looked up. "Well, it doesn't appear you've lost any sensitivity, does it?" He let go of her hand.

"No, it does not." She curled her fingers into a fist. *In fact, I've gained some.* Her mind raced in search of a distraction. "Your hand-kerchief," she blurted out.

"Did you need one?" He searched the inside of his coat.

She raced into the cottage. "No," she called from inside. "I just remembered Angus spent two days trying to return yours to its original color." She came back with the folded square cloth, white and crisply clean.

"It needn't have been laundered. I wasn't expecting it back." He threw her a questioning glance. "Did you say Angus cleaned it?"

Jenna was about to fumble a reply when Angus called her name. He popped his vast, hairy head out an open window, wide-eyed. "Do ye remember how much ye had to pay for the book, Jenna? Your da will want to ken for the record-keeping." He held up the leather-bound object in question.

"The shopkeeper wouldn't take any money. She said she'd settle with him later."

"Send your gentle blood to the merchant, and see what it will buy, that's what I always says." Angus nodded and disappeared inside.

"What did he mean by that?" Lord Pembroke said.

"It means I probably looked like I couldn't spare the cost and she was doing us a favor."

He turned to scratch the stallion's head after getting nudged in the back for attention. "So Duncan is a healer *and* he reads as well?"

"A little," she mumbled, picking burrs off her skirt. She avoided looking at Lord Pembroke, whose eyes she felt heavily upon her.

"And you?"

She kept working at the burrs and shook her head.

"What is the book you brought back for him?"

"Something medical, I think," she said, head bent low.

"A medical book? Do you recall its name?"

"No." She moved over to a sad-looking apple tree whose low branches were stripped bare of its best fruit.

"Then how do you know you were given the right one? The shopkeeper could have slipped you anything."

"I trusted her."

"You've done business with her before?"

Jenna shook her head as she reached for an apple just beyond the stretch of her arm.

"There are many shopkeepers who wouldn't hesitate to take advantage of the innocent and ignorant," he said, coming to the tree.

She jumped and took a swipe at the apple, but missed. "Duncan will check to make sure."

"Ab uno disce omnes?"

Her mind immediately translated the Latin, *From one learn all.* "Precisely," she said, swatting at the fruit again. But then her mind caught up with her ears and she glanced over to find Lord Pembroke's narrowed gaze focused on her.

He grabbed her arm to stay it and closed his other hand around the apple, then plucked it effortlessly from its perch. He let go of her arm and held the apple out to her. "Precisely."

Her spine stiffened and she took possession of the fruit. "I was hoping to give your horse that apple."

Lord Pembroke paid no heed to her reply. "You can read quite well, can't you?"

"I can read the signs of a hungry horse and was trying to do something about it." She knew his eyes followed her as she approached his horse with the treat. It disappeared behind his velvet-lipped muzzle.

"You're welcome." She stroked the beast's shoulder. Then, turning to Lord Pembroke, she said, "Thank you for your courtesy, milord." She bobbed her head, stepped into the cottage, and closed the door.

Angus opened his mouth to speak, but she put her fingers to her lips and ducked beneath the open window.

She heard Lord Pembroke speak to his horse. "I cannot begin to understand how the female mind works, and if you could talk, I'd be grateful for a second opinion." She heard the creak of leather as he swung into the saddle. "Now, there's a book that needs to be written." He clicked to the horse and they trotted away.

Jenna sagged against the wall and looked to Angus, her heart hammering in her chest. "He knows we can read."

FOURTEEN

IN EARLY OCTOBER, MUCH OF THE DUKE OF KESWICK'S house was emptied of visitors and its regular occupants. The Cliftons left for their London residence two weeks prior to the coronation of their new king. They brought with them all the necessary staff for the house and a few guests to entertain or be entertained by. Alex, who dreaded the journey, found himself accompanying his parents, Lady Lucia, and her mother on the excursion.

"Use the traveling time," his mother advised, "to gain an appreciation for who Lady Lucia is."

Halfway through the journey, Alex had a word with his mother. "What I have gained is an earful as to the substandard conditions of our coach's interior. And apparently, she is suffering through the driver's incompetence in maneuvering the coach around the poorly maintained roads. She says it will soon negatively affect her cheerful disposition."

Lady Lucia did surprise him, however, by commenting on the beauty of his pocket watch. When considering the frequency with which he brought it out to check the length of time left in the journey, it created ample opportunities to view it.

On October twentieth, the Prince Elector of the Holy Roman Empire, the first Hanoverian monarch of Great Britain, was crowned king of England and Scotland. George of Hanover spoke his native German, which made it somewhat challenging to reign over a country wherein he had little knowledge or interest. Alex raised a brow when Lady Lucia expressed a kinship with the king.

She put a hand to her heart and said, "My mother and I are experiencing the same agonizing tests of strength and composure. No one can know our struggles."

The new king's coronation was extravagant. Every purchase for the new monarch was a colossal expense, and only utilized for the momentous occasion, most everything being immediately disposed of following the affair.

"You can't be serious," Alex balked after Lady Lucia announced her desire to model their May wedding after the coronation.

While in the city, Alex thought Lady Lucia might enjoy learning a bit more about the country in which she would soon become a citizen. He took her to view the Houses of Parliament, where his father worked during the months of November through April. *An address that will soon be mine if my father has his way.* St. Paul's Cathedral, recently completed, was another outing. And last, he attempted a stroll through some of the city's more exquisite gardens.

None of these expeditions produced the intended enthusiasm he hoped for. Instead, they evoked the young woman's crisp politeness. She nodded absentmindedly at whatever Alex called attention to.

Soured by her indifference, he grew rash. "Milady, I must point out that every year a slew of London's Sicilian visitors are hung upside down by their feet for sport from the tree branches of the very park we're strolling through. Coincidentally, the event for this marvelous festival is today. Would you care to participate?"

She gave an inattentive nod. "And then we can go shopping?"

While the duke and his entourage were away, Jenna watched her father and the men work solidly through the quiet days of mid-October. Progress at the building site was hurried due to the new political state. Riots broke out across the country in small pockets of protest against the new king's coronation. Efforts to gather support increased, for the longer it took raising funds to allow James Stuart to challenge the competitor for his birthright, the less likely it would be that it would take place at all. Ian attempted to raise doubts in the men's minds, but remained mostly distant and quiet.

Angus crooked a finger at her one morning. "I suggest ye keep a wide berth from Ian at the moment. The man's in a curmudgeonly state that's itching for argument."

With fewer watchful eyes, she was allowed greater freedom to the duke's lands, but the reminders of vigilance were unrelenting. She'd roam through the wooded areas in the cool mornings and search for mushrooms to add to Angus's meals. Often after her studies, she'd escape to the open fields with her horse, and bow and arrow, scaring up pheasant and grouse as she hunted the hedges.

On one crisp afternoon, the air thick with the smell of molding leaves, she brought Henry into a pasture for a nibble on whatever last green shoots the horse could find. She thought about dismounting and sitting on the ground to wait while the horse took his rest, but the field's surface looked rutted and bristly. She simply swung both legs to the side of the horse and lay on her stomach across Henry's wide unsaddled back. She found that hanging limply over each side stretched the kinks out of her spine, and was the perfect way to end a vigorous ride.

She moved with Henry's breathing as he bit off tufts of sour grass, his jaws munching loudly. His massive rib cage expanded and contracted with the movement of air. "I bet a saddle is like wearing a corset, isn't it? It's a horrible feeling, and I speak from experience." She played with the long strands of hair that fell past her head.

"Imagine trying to hunt whilst bound up in one, or grappling in a spar." She thought of the practice duals she had with the men. She'd been gifted a smallsword, its weight almost nothing, and given lessons on usage from the age of seven. Crossing blades while wearing a poking corset would leave her constantly wondering if she'd been skewered.

"It has taken more than a month to heal my aching ribs. Rather a long time to suffer for such a daft evening, don't you think?"

He moved his head in the direction of her voice, and she took that as an agreeable response.

"Such a lavish affair for two people who I'd wager have barely exchanged half a dozen words with each other. I would never marry for family connections. I would rather stay at the mucky bottom of the social heap than wed my way into better living conditions. Sleeping in a straw-tick bed on my own is much more enticing if the alternative was marrying some dimwitted ignoramus just for the feathered mattress. Truthfully, I'd rather sleep on rocks."

"Well, you could always sleep on your horse, it seems."

Snapping up with surprise, Jenna slipped off the horse and fell to the ground in a mound of scratchy woolen riding clothes. She scrambled up to confront the intruding visitor. Standing before her was the sun-wrinkled face of Jeb, the elderly horse handler from the barn.

Putting her hand to her heart, she said, "Oh, you gave me such a start. Have you been listening?"

"Listening to what?" His voice had the rasp of old age and disuse.

"To me talk—babbling about . . . It was private."

He patted the rump of Henry, who Jenna thought betrayed her by not notifying her of approaching company. The horse paid no heed to the gnarled, warm hands resting on his backside.

"I've found over the years that you needn't hear so much of what a person says to figure out their story. Just paying attention to their behavior tells you who they are." The corners of his mouth curved, but he showed no teeth, which Jenna figured must not fully occupy the spaces provided for them.

She mentally scanned back through the one-sided conversation with Henry. *Well, I doubt you discovered anything about me by watching my backside hang off my horse.* "Did I reveal anything shocking?"

"Miss MacDuff, is it?"

She nodded.

"Shocking? No. But it seems you don't have many friends at the moment, and a horse makes a poor substitute. If you're like the rest of them, I'd say your interest is sparked with the duke's son, despite that he's spoken for, and . . ." He paused, seeing her eyes pop outward.

"I'd suggest you find one of the scullery maids to chatter with, to keep out of trouble."

Jenna's face flamed like a bright spark. "I—"

"Don't pretend to be shaken with what I've said." Jeb wagged a crooked finger at her. "I've been around the barnyard long enough to know when one animal is sniffing another out."

She winced. *I think all the manure has left you addled!* "I've taken no notice of . . ."

"The marquess."

"Yes, the . . . ," Jenna said, dismissing the florid title with her hand and wishing the whole conversation could just stop.

He gave her the crooked smile again, but revealed a hint of amusement. "Well, I would never call him that either, so you've made a good mark with me. And if it's naught but a figment of my mind, I beg your pardon. But I'd hate to see either of you get mixed up in the middle of something that could lead to trouble."

"I assure you I have no intention of getting into the sort of business that could create problems for anybody." She raised her chin and nearly choked on the fact she'd just told a barefaced lie. "I'm simply out for a quiet ride."

"And talking to Henry about marriage, don't forget." Jeb looked at her from under his bushy white brows.

"Well, Henry isn't particular with the content of our conversations. He merely likes the sound of my voice."

"I know a great many people who like the sound of their voice, but because it never spoke of common sense, it did them little good." He scratched the thin white hair under his cap, gave the horse one last pat on the rump, and turned to go.

Jenna watched him limp back toward the barns, brushing off the absurd conversation. She had no designs on anyone. Her mind was focused on her family's problems.

Looking down, she noticed she'd mindlessly been tracing a finger back and forth over her scar. She itched with the uncomfortable realization that once you've told the first lie, the second one comes easier.

FIFTEEN

HER NOSE WAS COLD. JENNA REFUSED TO PUT IT UNDER the woolen blankets with the rest of her body because she felt, almost absurdly, that she would suffocate with the lack of air beneath the heavy covers. She knew this untrue, but the panicky anxiety that started without fail after the first few inhalations was difficult to suppress.

She raised one reluctant eyelid. Objects were fuzzy in the muted gray light with only half her sight, so she opened the other and confirmed her suspicion. Snow. Delicate flakes pirouetted among one another in a deceitful dance. Harmlessly intoxicating until one had to face it without the protection of four walls, a fire, and a bowlful of Angus's parritch.

It also helped to have the long brown serge stockings Mrs. Wigginton instructed her how to make. Colin, despite his gangly-limbed appearance, had skilled, nimble fingers as well. He'd shown Jenna how to sew and knit from the time she was old enough to sit still, but he continued to do most of the family's repair work. Sadly, he possessed few patterns to draw from, and Mrs. Wigginton took pity on Jenna. She believed Jenna should be capable of creating more feminine designs and took it upon herself to tutor Jenna in snatches of spare time. Thankfully, they finished one pair of stockings before the weather made them a necessity. To Jenna's disappointment, no one would ever admire her newfound skills, since every inch of her handiwork was covered with the heavy fabric of her skirts and quilted petticoats.

She poked one toe out from underneath the bed linens and decided no other body parts would be brutally punished by following suit. She curled her body into a ball, wishing she could ignore the persistent calls coming from below.

The men, who she heard at the kitchen table, were taking turns calling her to breakfast. She burrowed deeper. Their next effort was to serenade her out of bed. She covered her ears, but knew further lingering would bring on severe reproach. Finally, she heaved herself out from her cocoon and, wrapping her body in as many quilts as she could muster, trudged down the stairs.

The room fell silent as she settled in a bulky heap at the table, and Angus popped up from the wooden bench in pursuit of his long-handled spurtle. He stirred the contents of the kettle above the glowing coals and scooped a bowlful of his much-loved brose. He placed it before Jenna, whose eyes were determined to remain shut. The steam rose from the dish and carried with it a scent that slithered to her nose. Her sleepy gaze and smile turned to Angus.

"You've added whisky," Jenna said, inhaling its aroma.

"Aye, I have. It's cold out there, and I'll nay have anyone complaining I didna do what I could to protect them from the wee bits of snow flying round." He moved his head an inch in the direction of Colin. "Especially Mr. Brodie over there, who canna keep enough fat on his bones to attract a proper wife."

"And until I do, you're making me a fine one—I'll nay complain!" Colin quipped.

Jenna glanced down to Ian at the end of the table, his head over his bowl, not participating in the men's rallying banter.

"Aye, ye spoil the child with all your antics," he grumbled. "She'll be good for no man with a tongue that loose and a head that tutored."

"Ye afraid of a woman wi' a mind, then, Ian?" Duncan goaded him.

"Do ye see how she has the lot of ye dancing about, trying to please her?" Ian pointed his spoon at each of them. "You've done her no favors by making her think she'll find a husband who'll do the same."

"Perhaps I'll be the kind of woman who'll choose not to marry," Jenna said.

"Given as ye are, Jenna, I doubt you'll be presented an offer to refuse."

The words stung.

"That's enough, Ian." Her father's normally hypnotic voice sounded narrow and checked. Ian's agitated reproach created an icy atmosphere and dulled whatever warmth the whisky-infused porridge had fashioned. Malcolm pushed himself from the table. He leaned on his hands and stood looking at the men.

"I've gotten news," he said, his eyes dark and serious. "The site plans have been approved, as has the location of the . . ." He paused and then murmured, "chambers. We'll soon get directions for what'll happen next. When I've received word, I'll tell. We're also being sent a lad. He'll be joining as an apprentice and arriving in Hawkshead late in the day."

Jenna stopped eating to stare at her father. "Someone's coming to live with us?"

"Aye. It's a terrible time for us to be takin' in someone new, but we've really no choice, and he's nowhere else to go. He'll be learning the trade and then life as a Freemason, should he want it. He's very young, though." He leaned in toward her, his tone softening. "Treat him kindly, Jenna. He lost his family to fever just six months past. Ye ken what he's going through."

She nodded. It was how her mother had died, or so she'd been told. At four, Jenna's memory of her mother was that one moment she was there, and the next not. Although she found it difficult to mourn someone she could not remember, there remained a void, the loss of the individual's promise with their presence.

Malcolm continued. "Right now I'll need Colin, Duncan, and Ian on the site to begin with." He turned to Jenna. "Duncan has brought ye a present from town. After you've had a peek at it, ye need to do your studies with Angus and Gavin. Then head to the barn and clean all the gear in the tack box before goin' to town. I want ye to pick up the lad later." Finally, he looked to the two men. "When you've both finished, make your way down, aye?"

The men left and Duncan returned from his room with a brown

parcel, tied and tucked under his arm. He offered it to Jenna, who took it with widened eyes. She unwrapped the package and stared.

"*Newton's Cambridge Lectures*?" she read.

"Aye, it took some doing, but I got them sent from a friend in London. We've all agreed it'd be worthwhile to instruct you of his latest theories. Much has changed because of the man. I think you'll enjoy his teachings." Duncan nodded toward the papers.

"Lectures from a real school." A smile curled her lips, and she looked up at Duncan. "I don't know what to say."

"Say you'll be quick to ready yourself for your lessons, lass." He winked at the others.

Jenna laughed and climbed the stairs to the loft, but her thoughts returned to Ian's caustic remarks. He considered her unmarriageable. Perhaps these men and her father had done a disservice by teaching her things useless to her life, or the future of a happy union. Was it time she concentrated on attracting a prospective suitor so she'd no longer be a burden to her father? The thought both disturbed and intrigued her. But first she wanted to find out what had moved the members of her family to decide Newton's lectures should be added to her daily curriculum. Clutching the lectures to her chest, she beamed with giddiness and said to herself, "Although my academy walls are invisible, I nearly feel like a true scholar."

Finished at last with the studies Angus and Gavin had given her, Jenna rushed to the barn to begin the arduous task of cleaning the bits and bridles, saddles and reins within the tack box Mr. Wicken had assigned to her when first arriving. They were ample chores keeping her from examining the pages of Sir Isaac Newton's works that would clarify many of the clan's lessons in mathematics and astronomy.

She recalled Ian's less than enthusiastic teachings on the laws of motion and the law of universal gravitation. Hands-on experiments, contrived by many of the men, helped her grasp the general concepts, whetting her appetite for more.

The hunger to devour Newton's words spurred her labors onward, but as she cleaned and polished, she could not help repeatedly staring at the tack box, the treasure chest where she'd placed the papers. She sighed with gratitude when Jeb and Mr. Wicken came around the corner, deep in conversation while picking up their barn tasks on her side of the stables. At last, something to keep her mind off those alluring writings.

"I've no doubt the duke will see your efforts here, Master Wicken, as long as those efforts prove successful to that which interests him now. If you wanted his immediate notice, 'twould be better if you'd been hired to serve as the estate steward rather than head groom." Jeb bent to adjust the ironworks on one of the stall doors across from where Jenna sat polishing. "Truthfully, His Grace is too taken up with his new garrison to notice much else, but the young Lord Pembroke has a keen eye on much of the same things and visits the stables frequently. He'd be the individual I'd advise you to set your sights on impressing. If you're hoping to work your way up through the ranks of Withinghall, he'll soon hold the key to most doors."

Mr. Wicken glanced thoughtfully around, taking in the expanse of the stables. "Is that it then? Be ever present and hands-on?"

Jenna heard a piece of hardware click into place, and Jeb stood to test the swing of the door. "That and perhaps hinting at a long-term pledge to the estate. You might consider taking a wife to show you're dependable and serious." Jeb glanced over to Jenna. "There are plenty of young kitchen maids eager to do the same."

A shiver of apprehension rippled across her arms as Mr. Wicken's gaze followed Jeb's and landed on her. He quickly turned toward the stable's main door. "I think I see Lord Pembroke now. He'll need know of the state of things as last I've checked. Excuse me." Mr. Wicken made a quick nod of his head to Jeb and bolted down the corridor.

Jeb gathered his tools and raised a bushy white brow at Jenna as he hobbled off in the other direction. Jenna gave him a withering glare as her parting gift and then glanced back down the hall to see Mr. Wicken trailing a very determined, if somewhat dismissive, Lord Pembroke.

"When is she due?"

"Well, far as I can see, should be around cross-quarter day of Beltane, sir."

"And the rest of the foals, what about them?" Lord Pembroke's eyes caught Jenna's and he made the tiniest note of acknowledgment as they moved closer to where she worked.

"All are due anywhere between Lady Day and St. John's Day, milord," he said, attempting an authoritative voice.

"Mr. Wicken," Lord Pembroke said, abruptly stopping and causing the other man to bump into him. He sighed with irritation and went on. "I prefer you state the dates from the calendar we share and not report everything to me in terms of Catholic feast days. New Year's and Midsummer, then, correct?"

"Yes, milord."

Jenna made a mental note of Lord Pembroke's aggravation, curious as to what lay behind it, while Mr. Wicken spoke again.

"Milord, I don't know if anyone's informed you, but there's been rumor as to some unrest in the area."

"With the horses?" Lord Pembroke pulled back, his face perplexed.

"No, milord. What I meant was there's been talk of difficulty . . . in pledging fealty."

"To whom?"

"Well, to the new king, of course, milord." Mr. Wicken seemed surprised his cryptic message wasn't decipherable. "Might be some are disappointed with the fact he's German."

Lord Pembroke looked toward Jenna and rolled his eyes. "He could be God himself and people would still grumble. It's the fact he's not inherently English is what's likely bothering them. I wouldn't let it worry you."

Mr. Wicken straightened himself and persisted, "It's not just that, sir, but there's other whisperings as well." He looked around and lowered his head. "Talk that there might be one . . . better suited for the job."

Jenna's heart suddenly strained to beat.

"Mr. Wicken"—Lord Pembroke sighed—"if I had a coin for every time I heard a drunken man utter the words, *If I were king . . .*" He let his words trail off, shaking his head.

Mr. Wicken's face grew dull with confusion and Lord Pembroke exhaled again. "Everyone thinks they have a better way, a superior idea. In any case, I'm not disposed to speak of politics—in fact, I'd give a day's wages to anyone who would avoid the topic altogether in my presence."

Jenna's brows shot up with surprise. Disinterested in both religion *and* politics? Did he think there was any way of escaping it, coming from his lineage? She lowered her head and industriously went back to polishing.

"That's enough for now, Mr. Wicken. You may take your leave. Just tell me where you've put the new double bridles you wanted me to see."

Mr. Wicken made a deep bow. "The tack box at the end of the row, milord. Good day." He spun on his heel and left. Jenna snuck a peek to see Lord Pembroke staring off at Mr. Wicken as he departed, a slight shake to his head. He then turned and made for the bridles, but moved toward the wrong tack box. Jenna panicked and leapt from her seat, the silver bit in her lap clanking in a heap as it fell to the floor.

"That's the wrong box, milord!" she blathered, rushing toward him. But it was too late. He'd lifted the lid and was peering inside.

Jenna felt the blood drain from her face. She clutched the front of her skirt, squeezing the fabric into a ball beneath her fists.

"What are these?" he asked, holding up the cluster of pages. Jenna's heart thumped madly, her mind whirling to fabricate an explanation.

"You are searching the wrong box for your bridles, milord," she stated.

"Clearly." He shuffled through the papers.

Her mouth went dry.

"*These* are Newton's lectures." He held up the sheaf.

She raised her brows innocently. "Are they?"

"Shall we dispense with the tired pretense that you've the educational level of a doorpost, Miss MacDuff?" he said sardonically. "And perhaps you can tell me why you, a young lady, possess them." He thrust forward the text of Latin that was part of her day's lesson.

Half of her was desperate to upset his perfunctory thoughts about women. But the more reasonable half, or maybe the more fearful, was telling her to invent a logical fiction for why these things were in her custody. She watched him for signs of danger. Most people, her father had told her, would find it surprising she could read, being of nomadic background. But almost everyone would find it *alarming* that she could read and understand Latin. That she studied French and German and spoke fluent Gaelic would only compound her problems. The men warned her to err on the side of caution.

"You'll be strung up by your wee toesies should anyone find out," Gavin had told her.

To study, to be educated, you had to be a man. To the ignorant country folk—the class they mixed with—the only reasonable explanation for her skills would be that she was a witch. But Lord Pembroke? He appeared to be more . . . enlightened.

She took a calculated breath and cleared her throat. "I possess them . . . because I want to read them."

Lord Pembroke took his time studying her, his eyes narrowing suspiciously, and she had the distressing notion he was reading her mind.

"Who are you?" he asked, his eyes fixed on hers.

She twisted the fabric in her hands, terrified of revealing too much. "Just someone who is determined to learn, milord."

"And so you carry around the works of one of the greatest professorial minds of our day?"

Her jaw went rigid. Why must it come as such a surprise? Was her brain any less capable than his? "My father, and the men of my clan realized I had an interest and have endeavored to support it with those lectures. They were a gift."

"Really?" He made a sad grunt of amusement. "What I wouldn't give to have *my* father support my interests. But not for one moment would I fool myself into believing that His Grace would give me permission to pursue my fascination for medicine, or the sciences."

"At least you are allowed to pursue *something* properly. But why are you here? Aren't you supposed to be wandering about the halls of your university?"

His face darkened, and there was a moment of silence before he looked up to answer. "I've been sent down." He said it flatly. "And so have the other three lads you met at the party. The school will review my papers in the spring. We'll see what happens after that."

Dismissed from school? On what grounds? Jenna wondered desperately how anyone could forfeit such an opportunity, but she was determined to remain on Lord Pembroke's good side, and held her tongue. "Perhaps once you return you'll be granted the opportunity to study the art of healing."

She saw his mouth twitch, his skepticism growing. "Never," he murmured, lowering to sit upon the tack box. "My path has been chosen for me. It is one paved strictly with the text of law and politics. I am to serve in Parliament."

Jenna leaned back against one of the stalls. "It is a prickly path.

Especially now, when so many people have their dander up over the line of succession."

Lord Pembroke looked up at her. "Just to be clear, are we talking about the dander of those in your clan, everyone in Scotland, or the all-purpose gripes of the British in general?"

She smiled. "I doubt I could speak on behalf of all the king's subjects. Suffice it to say, most complaints I've been privy to, have been uttered with a broad Scots dialect."

"Fair enough." He chuckled. "What have *you* been hearing?"

She heard Ian's words echo in her head. *Informers snatched two in our chain just last week. They're headed for Newgate—as will we be if we're caught.*

She straightened. She needed to act with more caution. It would be easy for her to slip and say the wrong thing, pitching her family toward not only arrest, but also the verdict of treason.

But at the same time, it struck Jenna that here was an opportunity to express the concerns of a considerable group of people to someone who would eventually have the ability to do something about it.

She searched his face for the signs of chicanery and, finding nothing, took a leap.

"Well, from what I gather, the Union idea, the merging of Scotland and England into one kingdom, is a fairly sore point for most people north of here. And then you dismissed our country's Parliament."

"You make it sound as if there was no benefit to Scotland at all regarding the Union," he interjected. "Don't forget the worth of free trade with England and all of her colonies."

"That wasn't an advantage to joining the Union; it was used as a threat of loss to us if the country voted against it," Jenna said. "And you never let us participate in determining Queen Anne's successor!"

Lord Pembroke kept his voice calm. "You do understand if England allowed Scotland to choose its own successor, it could prove fatal."

"How so?" she demanded.

"Well, the line of succession Scotland wanted, and apparently still desires, is quite cozy with two countries we have recently been at war with. Both France and Spain would love nothing more than to divide and conquer Great Britain, to stake claim on a country weakened by civil war and unable to defend itself."

"And so," Jenna countered, "England will likely conclude we should fight off these horrid foreigners by banding together in a war against them—a war that would put our Highlanders on the front line."

"The clansmen are fierce warriors, and we would need to put our best defense first," Lord Pembroke offered.

"Perhaps the English don't want to get their red coats muddy," she snapped.

"Putting James on the throne of Scotland would make your country a back door for kings Louis and Philip, and put England in a compromising position. Tell me, would you rather be speaking French or Spanish than the queen's English?"

"To be frank, I'd rather be speaking Gaelic," Jenna said bitingly, forgetting herself.

"Then why are you here?" he said, rising from the tack box,

bewilderment shadowing his features.

Jenna flushed, suddenly aware of having lost herself within the heated debate. "I beg your pardon, milord. I have spoken . . . so out of hand."

"You only spoke passionately. I see no reason for condemnation."

Air rushed out of Jenna's lungs. "I am accustomed to reproof, sir. And if anyone in my clan gains knowledge that I have spoken to you in this manner—or released the fact that I am granted access to scholarship—limited as it is—I shall be soundly punished for it." She paused. "They worry. For my safety."

Lord Pembroke puffed with a small chuckle. "Few, I'd think, should worry about you." And then paused, sizing her up. "And what exactly *is* your access to scholarship—apart from these?" He held up the lectures.

"We have a few books. Only a couple of stories."

"You're welcome to come up to the house. We have a full library. All the publications you could possibly desire." His head tilted to one side. "Can you do numbers as well?"

She gave a slight nod, watching for his reaction.

Lord Pembroke tugged at the lobe of one ear. "How novel. To be encouraged to stray from one's cast in life."

"Angus always says that the road before and behind you matters little if you can push to follow the path that calls from within."

He looked at her sadly. "Sage words for a mason. If only it were true."

SIXTEEN

JENNA'S STOMACH GRUMBLED. THE IDEA OF ANGUS'S dinner waiting for her return from town meant casting a blind eye to cunning distractions—such as the whiff of spicy gingerbread.

Like a bloodhound, once she caught a scent, there was little else she could focus on, and the pungent aroma drew her toward the stall of an elderly woman, bowed as a twisted tree.

Her cart stood at the entrance of the local tavern and lured people to the fragrant treat. The mellifluous sounds of a fiddler's tale trickled through the cracked window behind the stall, coaxing passersby. It worked as well as the pied piper's flute, inviting men to drown themselves in ale rather than in the river. The woman perched like an old bird on the side of an upturned wooden crate. She watched Jenna through tiny black eyes, following her as she passed.

Jenna felt the gaze of the sharp-eyed women and turned. "It smells wonderful." She nodded toward the gingerbread.

The old woman bobbed her head and, taking a hand from its warm hiding spot beneath her woolen cloak, pointed a shaky finger toward the cakes. "The baking is such labor, but the reward is worth the effort."

Jenna's heart was heavy with pity. The woman's survival was probably dependent upon her sales. She smiled at the figure wrapped in the worn-out brown wool and was rewarded with a fairly toothless grin. She led Henry, who would have been more than happy to help eat the woman's entire day's labor, away from the stall and farther down the cobbled street.

The path bustled with animals pulling carts and people running errands, their breath crystallizing in an ethereal fog around them. With the December days short on light, those working outside scurried from one task to the next and attempted to keep warm in the process. Jenna was no exception. Her father sent her here to meet the boy, Tavish Buchanan. She tried not to think of the bitter ride back to the cottage, the challenge of having to make idle talk with a stranger—especially someone morose over the recent loss of his parents. But she supposed anything new to challenge her mind would be a welcome change. For more than the last few hours, her thoughts had been solely focused on her conversation with Lord Pembroke in the barn. She'd trusted him with information she'd been warned never to reveal. Her instincts told her it was safe to do so. Or was it the flutter in her stomach that encouraged her to share? To impress upon him the fact that she wasn't as common as he might have once thought.

Still, his last statement left her unsettled, after she'd offered Angus's quote as encouragement.

Sage words . . . for a mason.

Was he questioning the truth of the quote as it applied to him or the validity of Angus's stated profession?

If it was the former, then she felt sorry for him, but if it was the latter, then it might be an ominous clue that he held suspicions about her clan. She pinched her eyes shut to rid herself of the worrisome images flooding her thoughts.

Concentrate on other things. Like finding the boy.

She spotted him, as her father had said, waiting in between the ironmonger and the cooper's workshop. Perhaps no more than nine, he sat hunched on a wooden cask, his strawberry blond head resting on his hands, elbows wedged between dirty knees. Chickens pecked and scratched the ground beneath him. At the sight of her and Henry, he leapt from his roost, a little fist grabbing the ragged satchel at the side of the barrel, and strode right to them.

"Your hair is truly red. They said it would be red, but I've never seen hair as red as yours." He smiled a freckled face at her, revealing a few missing teeth. Jenna wasn't sure if it was because they were about to be replaced with new ones or if the gaps were the result of the typical roughhousing of boys.

"Ye must be Jenna, and I bet that's your horse. They said to look for a girl wi' red hair and a horse, and here ye are, so I guess it's you, aye?"

Good heavens. And I was worried about having to do all the talking.

She raised an eyebrow at Tavish. "Yes, you're correct. It's the girl with red hair and a horse."

"*Really* red," he added with emphasis.

"It's my mother's fault."

"What do ye mean?" He looked as if perhaps she were suggesting her mother might have dropped her on her head and caused the insult of hair color by accident.

"I mean she has red hair too—or rather . . . *had* red hair."

"Has it gone gray, then?" he asked, eyebrows knitted with curiosity.

Jenna smiled. "No, I mean my mother passed away."

Tavish's eyes went soft and clouded.

"A long time ago," she added.

"I'm sorry for your loss," he said, echoing a phrase he'd probably heard a thousand times.

"And I'm sorry for yours too. Have you been waiting long?"

"Maybe a time—I hadna really noticed. There's so much going on round here, people passing wi' their baskets, and the smells . . ." He paused, closing his eyes. "The smells are enough to drive a man wild."

"Drive *a man* wild?" she repeated, grinning.

"Aye, it's taking all the strength I have to control myself. I feel like running up and down the market street, robbing the stalls of what I fancy."

She tried to keep a solemn face. "It must have been torture for you."

"Well, it would be for any savage, aye?"

"Savage?"

"Och aye, all Scots are savages, but mainly the men."

Jenna bit her cheeks. "Ah yes, I think I've heard that somewhere."

She tried not to come across as humoring him. He seemed too sensitive for that. "Who told you that you were a savage?"

"My grandmother. She was English. My mother said she was none too pleased having her daughter marrying into a clan o' wild men who eat their own kin. Wild blood—that's what I have in my veins, and because of it, I have a terrible time controlling myself."

She wanted to laugh until tears came to her eyes, but she pressed her lips together until she could speak again. "I think you've done a fair job thus far. You should be rewarded." She looped Tavish's satchel onto Henry's saddle and turned to him. "Do you like gingerbread?"

"I've been doing nothing but thinking 'bout it since I first passed it. Hoping it might somehow make its way into my hands through magic and such like. But my mother always said, *A man who lives on hope has a slim diet*, and in this case it couldna be truer, aye?" He smiled so excitedly at the mention of the cakes Jenna thought perhaps his face would split in two.

"Your mother sounds like she was a wise woman," Jenna said, leading Tavish and Henry back toward the tavern. Lanterns were lighting in the houses above the shops and on the streets.

"Aye, that she was. Had a saying for all occasions, so I spent a good deal listening."

"And your da? Was he as wise?"

"According to my mother, no one else would have him. She said she din him a favor—and the way he'd look at her all the time, ye ken he believed it." He stopped to look at the ground and kicked a stone in his path. "They died holding hands. I guess it was a good match after all." Tavish made a meager smile.

They walked down the street in silence and approached the smoky tavern where the old woman still sat, wrapped as tight as a caterpillar in its cocoon. Jenna watched Tavish's face grow with anticipation once the smell of the cakes made its way to his nose. She'd reached out to request two when she heard shouting from inside the tavern.

She peered through the grimy window and saw several men make their way to the door, hollering farewells. Three of them came through the door, two stumbling out onto the street. She identified them at once as Lord Pembroke's less-than-well-mannered friends Mr. Fowler, Mr. Gainsford, and Mr. Finch from the engagement party, the first two now well lubricated with liquor. One of them, she thought it might be Mr. Fowler, made a wobbling beeline for the old woman's stand.

"What have we got over here?" he slurred, trying to remain upright.

Jenna was glad for the dim lighting, not wanting to be recognized, but seeing the state he was in, his cognitive skills were of little use to him now. She pulled Tavish back so he wouldn't be stepped upon.

Mr. Fowler leaned over and put his nose onto one of the cakes. "Ah," he said, slipping backward and grabbing on to the cart, "jussst what I need at the moment." He turned to his friend, who seemed a little steadier, and garbled, "Venison pasties."

Mr. Gainsford moved closer. "You're an idiot, Hugh. Not venison pasties . . . They're likely fish chuits, and they look disgusting."

Jenna stared at them in disbelief. It wasn't so dark one couldn't make out what they were looking at, and even if their eyes were swimming in brandy, surely their noses still worked.

"Fish chuits they are, then, thank you very much," Mr. Fowler gurgled. "I need sssomething to keep the liquor down." He leaned in, telling the old woman, "And fish love to swim, do they not?" His toxic breath made her lean back. "Pay the man, Charles. I'll have three—no, four!" He grabbed at the cakes and began loading them into his arms.

"I'm not paying for that filth," Mr. Gainsford spat, and tottered away down the street.

"You're ssso right," shouted Mr. Fowler after him. "I'm not paying for it either." With his arms full of at least ten gingerbreads, he smiled drunkenly at the old woman, who now looked panicked, and sauntered off toward his friend.

Jenna gasped and watched with disbelief as the two men walked away with stolen goods, no one attempting to stop them.

"They're not worth the money she asks for them anyway," an acidic voice said from beside her. She turned to see Mr. Finch. "They're probably as old as the hills. They'll break their teeth on them for sure."

"Deservedly so," Jenna mumbled. She looked down to see Tavish watching her, fear in his eyes.

"She's been selling stale goods all month and taking advantage of those who have temporarily lost their wits from drink." He nodded his head toward the tavern door.

"Some never had them to begin with," she said coolly.

Mr. Finch peered at her in the faint light and then pulled back. "Oh, well, surprise. It's you . . . the injured garden waif."

Jenna smelled the strong reek of alcohol on his breath too. "Perhaps this woman is doing the best under her circumstances. Can you not conjure up a sliver of pity for someone who has clearly traveled a path in life full of hardship, Mr. Finch?"

He shrugged. "It is her destiny. Not a shred of pity will change that."

"I cannot agree. I would encourage anyone unhappy to wrestle with their fate until they find a more agreeable circumstance."

He shook his head once, decidedly. "I wouldn't know the first thing about it. My fate is as agreeable as I could have it. And as a word of warning, the old woman is the town's ancient fortune-teller. If anyone should be aware of her predetermined course and the futility in fighting it, it should be her. Good day, miss." He made a quick nod of his head and walked toward his friends.

The elderly woman began to whimper. Jenna bristled with anger and searched for her leather purse with its shilling and pennies. She tried shushing the woman. "Here," she said, holding out a few farthings. "It may not cover all, but it should help."

The old woman's grizzled hand shot out, snaking cold, tuberous fingers around Jenna's wrist as she took the coins.

"There will be trouble," she croaked. "It cannot be avoided, but the Great Soul will guide you."

Jenna yanked her hand from the grasp of the woman. She stared at her and felt the young boy, Tavish, slide back, away from the stall. "What did you say?"

Her withered lips pursed and whispered. "These are wicked times."

"Indeed they are," Jenna said, backing up and leading Tavish to the horse. "Worrisome too."

Alex stood in the courtyard and stared up at the glassed windows of the house. He had spent yet another evening avoiding. Avoiding people, avoiding responsibility, avoiding action. The girl was right. Somewhere there was a path within him that begged for his determined footfalls. One that would quiet everything—that spoke to him of duty and obedience—that encouraged him to ignore the track that had been selected for him.

He wondered if he'd ever have the strength to follow it.

Miss MacDuff. He'd never had a conversation like that with a woman before. And that had him wondering if she would ever exercise the invitation to wander the shelves of the family's library. It stood to reason that she could find the threshold of the main house an obstacle too high to surmount.

He gazed at the one window which hampered his own success. Unlike those that surrounded it, with their faint candlelight and flickering shadows suggesting drowsy movement, this one released a vivid glow. His father's study. Determined to remember the sweet release of truth, he decided to speak with the duke regarding his future.

He pondered his father's state of mind, and noted with each step closer to the room, he left a sizable amount of courage behind. By the time he reached the study's doorway, he had all but decided against having a discussion on the subject of anything with the man. His palm rested on the wooden door. His fingers refused to curl. They would not make a fist to knock, to ask permission for entrance.

The door swung open and Alex leapt back. A wild-eyed young maid dashed from the room, clutching the top of her open garment to her chest, and disappeared down the hall. The Duke of Keswick was also at the door, housed in a plush indigo dressing gown, and holding an empty decanter. He too appeared disconcerted at seeing someone unexpectedly.

"Alex? What is it?"

"I only came—well, I was about to knock. . . . I wondered if we might speak?" He tried slowing his breath to stay his pulse.

"Fine," his father said. "I'd intended to refill my port decanter, but I shall wait as long as you are brief. Take this from me, Alex. I need the chamber pot. And fill my glass with sherry." The duke caught the heavy door with the back of his foot and kicked it closed. Candled sconces flickered with the wind and a few pictures hiccuped on the walls.

Alex took the vessel from his father and searched for a place to set it down. He attempted to find an audible distraction—anything to prevent the disturbing sounds of his father relieving himself behind the Chinese screen from reaching his ears. With nothing else to do, he eased the stopper out of the sherry decanter and poured the wine. The duke came from behind the screen just as Alex replaced the crystal cap. He offered the glass to his father, who nodded curtly and settled into a chair.

"What is it, then? What have you come to see me about?"

The duke's tone was a familiar sound to Alex's ears: one of brevity and aloofness. If he were asked to pinpoint the exact time in which he and his father had lost any vestige of warmth in their relationship, it wouldn't be difficult. He'd seen his father court many a mistress as he was growing up. In some ways, he'd grown immune to its shock. It wasn't until the duke cast aside all consideration for his wife, sometimes dismissing her presence all together by flaunting his affairs, that he began to feel hostile in his presence. He'd never been certain as to the cause of his father's callousness, but he'd assumed it was the result of the duchess's increasing apathy toward the man she married, the slow unraveling of the marriage knot.

"I wanted to speak to you regarding my schooling."

The duke sighed and took a deep swallow from his glass. "It does not amuse me to discover that my son believes he has a choice in the matter of education."

Alex shifted in his chair and cleared his throat. "It's not an issue of declining education, but rather the line of instruction, if you will."

"Whatever line you have set your sights on, if it differs from mine, it will not be entertained. Although at present, your school may not even extend an invitation for your return.

"Your future was laid out with great care. To secure the continuance and prosperity of this family name. But as I recall, you have little respect for those in search of success."

Having prepared for this type of discourse, the words stung less than Alex figured they had intended to. Thus, he ventured further. "I assure you, sir, I have the greatest respect for those seeking triumph in their endeavors. I understand your concern for lineage and its survival, but I feel I have a capacity for subject matter other than politics. In particular, medicine."

"No," was the curt reply. "I shall not support anything other than the schooling route prepared for you—even with this disastrous delay. You have no idea the amount of work you've cast in my direction. The things I will have to do—or, more to the point, the people I will have to pay—to get you *re*admitted makes my blood boil, a malady no medicine has been able to cure."

Alex pressed on. "What if I were to school in both subject matters?"

His father leaned over the table and set his glass down with a jolt. "If I have failed to make it clear, let me take advantage of this most important moment. You are being groomed for a life of public service in the House of Lords. A prestigious position where you will legislate law—not work in a hospital where you will leech blood and lance boils! When I step down, you shall take my place. You shall carry on fulfilling your duty to your country and king. And you shall do it in the same vein of mind-set as your father and my father before me. You will not be a snag in the tapestry of this family's carefully woven dynasty. Its members have built their accomplishments with solid allegiances to meticulously selected allies." The duke sat back, the veins of his forehead protruding and purple. He took a few restorative breaths, poured another glass of sherry, spilling half the contents onto the table, and guzzled the remainder.

Alex eyed his father and felt the tendons in his arms tighten. He envisioned his hands clutching the man around his neck and constricting the flow of air, imagined a plea for mercy. He felt his heart pounding in his rib cage, but then he slowly gained control of his rage. Although he had anticipated this reaction from his father, he hadn't realized how much it would affect him physically. He thought he would at least have the opportunity to *discuss* his interests. He had not expected complete dismissal.

Myriad thoughts flew through his mind, conversations with countless endings—all of them finishing poorly. *As usual, I have no control over my life.* He stood and made a quick nod to the duke. "Thank you, sir."

The duke made no acknowledgment, but rose and faced the picture above the fireplace mantel. He gazed at it in quiet reflection. Alex turned and walked the length of the room. When he reached the door and pulled it open, his father spoke. "Your life has little to offer you with regard to preference, Alex, but remember this: choice comes with power. You will not be graced with one until you are triumphant with the other. And at this point, you have neither."

Alex left without further delay. His father's words stung like little daggers. Obviously, there were still chinks in his armor.

The fire crackled in the hearth when Jenna and Tavish arrived at the cottage. The men were clearing the table while Malcolm and Ian spoke, details of the building site strewn before them. Angus was the first to greet them and gave Jenna a smothering bear hug, then warmed her icicled fingers. When he discovered his enormous frame was intimidating Tavish, he bent down on his knees to make his introduction.

"How do ye do, lad? I'm Angus," he said with a tenderness Jenna hadn't remembered he possessed.

Tavish pulled himself up to his full height and thrust his hand forward. "I'm well. The name's Tavish. My father was Buchanan. I'll work hard and be no trouble. My mother always said, *Stay nay longer in a friend's house than you're welcome*. And I intend to be welcome for a while."

The men and Jenna broke out in rollicking laughter, and Tavish's face beamed back at them.

After the introductions, Jenna showed Tavish around the cottage and upstairs to the loft, where she and Colin had prepared a little cot in her room. They'd hung an old quilt so the boy could have a space to call his own, just as the men had for her years ago. He gushed over the cozy nook and thanked Jenna repeatedly until she put a hand on his shoulder to quiet him. "You're welcome. Now, I'll not hear another word of your good fortune until we've had a proper supper. Are you hungry?"

His eyes widened at the suggestion of food.

"I'm sure Angus kept something warm for us, so let's . . ." Tavish was out the door and down the stairs before she could finish.

"The lady Jenna mentioned something about food perhaps still round from suppertime? Is it so, Mr. Angus? For if it is, I'd be willing to do a bit of work for it—whatever it may be—no complaints." Tavish skidded to a halt before Angus, who was stacking the last of the bowls into the rough wooden cupboard.

Angus turned around with a look of pure bewilderment. "You'll do no such thing, lad." He paused as Tavish's face crumpled. "You'll not work a second for this meal. It comes wi'out need for payment."

Jenna saw the look of confusion surface in his eyes. "Tavish. If you're hungry, you'll be fed."

He grinned, again showing his missing teeth.

"If there's one thing Angus can't stand, it's a growling tummy somewhere within earshot. He's determined to cure the countryside of hunger—belly by belly."

Angus whipped the edge of his dish towel at Jenna, snapping the air at her shoulder. He turned to Tavish, his face grave. "You know, lad, everything ye feel shows on your face, and ye should never let everyone ken how ye feel all the time. It looks as if we men have a lot to teach you."

Tavish nodded with enthusiasm.

"Perhaps we'll have to start wi' a few games of cards."

"You'll do no such thing, Angus McGregor," Jenna chastised him. "I think it's adorable Tavish hasn't yet learned to hide what he feels." Her stomach twisted with sorrow. But she enjoyed the idea of having someone younger than herself around.

"Did ye hear that, son? Jenna thinks you're adorable."

Tavish turned from peeking inside the massive cast-iron pot and responded earnestly, "I *am* adorable—my mother told me of it all the time."

"And what mother wouldn't?" Angus winked at Jenna. "Sit ye down, lad, and let's see if we can fill your wee belly. Ye need plumping."

After Tavish devoured his supper, Jenna and Angus watched the boy's head grow heavy with sleep as he gazed into the glowing fire, a hand wrapped around his cup of watered-down ale. Even weakened, it proved too strong for Tavish to stay awake. Malcolm, having come in from his frosty late-night chores, scooped up the languid child and took him upstairs.

One by one, the men bid their good nights. Jenna and Angus sat in front of the fire drying wooden bowls and spoons, preparing the table for tomorrow's breakfast. The fire was quieting, its embers hot and glowing. It still warmed the room and released the odd pop and spitting crack.

She listened to Angus hum a mindless tune, and found herself weaving through the memories of the day. "Angus?"

"Umph?" His dirk lay between his teeth, and he bent under the sideboard. She watched him settle back with his chunk of whittling wood.

"Who is the Great Soul?"

He chuckled. "Why do ye ask?"

Jenna shivered. "I ran into a spaewife today."

"A fortune-teller?" He looked up at her.

She nodded. "She said I'd see great trouble and that—"

He held up a hand. "Rubbish. They all say that. Pay her no mind."

"She said the Great Soul would guide me."

Angus laughed again. "Well, maybe this one wasn't such a charlatan, as we do know someone of that name. But, lass, ye need only follow your heart as a guide and your head as counsel. Together they'll not steer ye wrong."

She was quiet again, remembering the men from outside the tavern. They seemed to make a habit of ignoring all sound wisdom. She smiled at Tavish's stories of his parents, how happy they'd been. Perhaps they had been meant to find each other, their marriage destined from the start.

"Did you ever want to get married?"

He smiled without looking up and answered, "Not a lass in the world would want a burly old fool like me, Jenna."

"You know that's not true."

"'Tis true; I'm set in my ways, dinna like to stay in one place for too long—and I snore like a great bear!"

She stared into the fire. "But don't you wonder what it would be like to love someone so much you'd want to spend the rest of your life with them? Maybe even die for them?"

"I do have that." He stopped his knife. "I've surrounded myself wi' people—whether related by blood or not—whom I consider my family. People I love wi' my whole heart, and I would do anything for each of them." He began carving again. "I consider myself a lucky man."

She was quiet again, her thoughts wrestling for attention.

"Are ye thinking 'bout yourself, then, lass?" Angus eyed her briefly.

"Not so much. . . . Well, maybe sometimes." She would never have said this to anyone else. Nothing she said to him ever raised an eyebrow. "Do you think that odd?"

"Odd? Nay. In fact, 'tis the most natural thing in the world. Although we love you like ye belong to each one of us, we ken ye deserve a life of your own—a place to call home and likely a husband to go wi' it." He set his dirk down and looked hard at Jenna. "You're a young woman now. Your da's made it so ye can have a say in your future. Not many have that option, lass, so use it wisely."

She paused. "What if what I want isn't available to me? What if my future was determined by . . . fate?"

Angus set his carving aside and turned to her. He picked up her hands with his own deeply calloused ones. "Jenna, look at all the things that would normally have been denied to you because of who ye are—a woman, I mean. No schooling, no chance to develop the sharp brain . . . and the tongue to match. The travel—even though ye dragged your feet through much of it. It let ye see how others lived . . . gave ye something to compare your own life with. Are ye telling me we havena set a good enough example of what can be done if ye put your mind to it?" He looked at her from under his great brows, a challenge in his gaze.

"Your life is what ye make of it, and sometimes that means you'll sacrifice in other places. Whether you're giving up a dream because of promises made to your kin, or you're giving up your life because of pledges made to your king. 'Tis much the same in the end. Ye have a choice, though. Ye have a choice, always. Dinna be foolish wi' it."

"Did you give up your dreams for this life, Angus?"

He took a deep breath and rose. "I'm telling ye that I gave up everything else to make *this* dream my *life*." He bent to kiss her head. "Good night, sweet lass."

She listened to his heavy feet make their way down the hall. She sat for a long while afterward and heard Angus's words repeat themselves in the empty room. It was the one greatest gift her family had given to her, beyond that of education, or a keen mind. It was that of choice.

SEVENTEEN

"LORD PEMBROKE, I DO NOT THINK YOU PAY ME ENOUGH attentions," Lady Lucia said.

"Whatever do you mean?" Alex scanned the library's bookshelves.

"I mean, the other suitors I have had. They gave me things to keep me interesting."

He smiled. "Surely, you mean interes*ted*, milady."

"Regardless. *You* haven't given me anything," she said through pouting lips.

He pulled a book from the shelf and turned to look at her sitting on the settee, a puffy cloud of blue silk ballooning around her. He had made the effort, at his mother's request, to spend time with the young lady each day. He noticed how she preened herself wherever they were. Most of the time, she was busy arranging her dress, presenting it in the most flattering way, or glass-gazing to fix her hair—whichever one was out of place.

"I've given you what I consider most valuable to myself. My time." He meant it sincerely, but she wasn't moved.

"Time doesn't sparkle. You cannot put it on your wrist or around your neck. You cannot show it to your friends over tea and have them admire it. That is what I want, milord," she said, giving him a doe-eyed look.

"And that would make you happy? Trinkets?"

"It would be a good start."

Alex turned back to the bookshelves. "What if I gave you a book?"

"No. I have no use for the books. I find it a chore to read, and all those letters on the page make my head hurt looking at them. I learned to read because I had to, and that was enough."

I could say the same for a thousand things in my life. "I'm sorry to hear that," he responded. "I'm hoping we can find something in common. It helps with conversation."

"I would be happy to talk about the things I want. That could be my conversation."

"Perhaps you're right." He moved to the settee to sit beside her, and she pulled a sliver of her dress out from where he'd sat on it, smoothing it. He pressed his lips inward, but continued, "Why don't you tell me? What *things* would make you happy?"

She took a long breath in and closed her eyes. "Where do I begin? Well, there are the things every young woman wants. A fine home to show one's wealth, filled with servants to do one's bidding. Of course, many jewels and clothing for the entertaining—my head is happy with the thoughts of them." She stopped, a secretive smile curving her thin lips. "There are many others. Little things, like a grand carriage with the horses beautiful and a place in the city."

Alex tried to keep his eyes from bulging at the list she presented. Nevertheless, he had been a fool to ask. Plus, what she wanted wasn't unreasonable. Not in her world. It was what she'd been promised and what had lured her into this particular arrangement. He sighed and scratched his head, then jokingly said, "Perhaps I should capture the moon?"

She clicked her tongue and rolled her dark eyes skyward. "I grow tired of this talking when you don't tell me the things I want to hear." She rose from the settee and swished toward the door. "I must go and change my gown for supper."

Alex stood as well. "Why? Your dress is fine."

"*Fine* will not do." She sighed harshly. "If I come into a room and everyone is not immediately captured by my appearing, it was not the correct choice."

He studied her for a moment. She was a stunning girl, and once or twice he'd allowed himself to wonder what it might be like married to her. Would she demonstrate any affection? Would she want to be touched? It was hard to envision, seeing how she reacted any time he came in contact with her clothing.

He couldn't remember the last time he'd seen his father or mother show any warmth toward each other, and in his mind, a marriage like that would be torture. But it was moments like this, when Lady Lucia showed such vanity, that he found it impossible to imagine spending a lifetime in any marriage. Inviting the possibility of love into the equation was ludicrous. Confident women he found alluring, but Lady Lucia's lack of humility had the opposite effect.

"I see. Well, then, by all means don't let me keep you." He bowed. "I look forward to seeing you at the evening meal, and I'm sure you will, as always, be thoroughly captivating."

Charles's head popped around the library door. "I heard the word *captivating*, so I assume the two of you must be speaking of me."

Lady Lucia jumped at his voice. She scowled at him and hissed something too quietly for Alex to make out, but regained her composure and moved past Charles.

"I don't mean to frighten you away, milady; I only came to pass on juicy gossip to old Alex here. Please don't leave on my account."

"I assure you, I do nothing on your account." She brushed past him on her way out.

"And lest you forget," Charles continued, his voice louder, "those who leave the room are the next in line to be gossiped about."

"Charles, don't tease her," Alex warned, returning to the bookshelves.

"But, Alex, she's like a cat and I hold the yarn. You can't expect me to pass up a little entertainment, now, can you? I'm sure she's enjoying it just as much."

"You'll enjoy it a little less when her claws come out," Alex said, his head tilted to read a title in the stacks.

"So what's keeping you locked in this stuffy old room? It's glorious outside. We should be hunting, or riding, or wreaking havoc with the locals. What do you say?" Charles flopped down on a stuffed chair and threw his boots on the table in front of him.

"Maybe in a little while, Charles. I'm trying to find a book."

"Again with the books," he grumbled. "Take a break—enjoy the day."

"I am. And the book is not for me, so quiet your criticisms."

"Who for, then?" Charles ran a hand along his cheek and jaw, fingering his blemishes.

"A friend." Alex bent to pull out a leather-bound volume.

"A friend? Julian? Certainly not Hugh," Charles said. "What friends have you here apart from the three of us?"

"It's no one really," Alex said, leafing through the pages. "Just the young girl down in the stonemason's cottage."

Charles leapt from his seat. "You mean the one from your engagement party? The one whose hand you were holding?" His eyes glistened with mischief. "And to think, I was the one *delivering* gossip today, not hearing it."

Alex quickly shut the book. "I wasn't holding her—"

Lady Lucia burst into the room, red and furious. "How dare you! No wonder you're not interesting in me!" Her face was a storm erupting in front of them, her eyes glittering and black.

Charles broke out in a sly smile. "Listening at the door, milady? That hardly seems befitting of your station. Could you not get a scullery maid to do your dirty work?"

"Be quiet, Charles." Alex turned to Lady Lucia. "I wasn't holding anyone's hand—well, not in the way he thinks," he said, motioning toward Charles. "There's nothing to get upset over, milady, and you shouldn't have been listening in on our conversation."

"I heard what I needed to hear. You have been giving gifts and courting another woman."

Julian and Hugh appeared at the door behind Lady Lucia.

"Who's giving gifts to another woman?" Hugh asked, his eyes hungry.

"Alex wants to give a book to that stonemason's daughter," Charles said, smirking.

Alex turned and gave Charles a daggered look to quiet him.

"Miss MacDuff?" Julian said coolly. Alex moved his gaze to meet Julian's and felt a flush of heat.

"She has a *name*," Lady Lucia hissed, *"and you all know it."* Her jaw grew square and tight.

Alex felt a rigid knot developing in his stomach, and he tried taking a moment to think before talking, but Lady Lucia turned on his friends in a flash.

"You all knew about this," she accused them. She moved closer and jabbed a finger at them. "You have been keeping this a secret and allowing him to make foolish of me." She whirled on Hugh. "You, I can understand. You play all day with the women like they are toys. And you"—she pointed a long finger at Charles—"think it all great fun the way your friend acts." She turned to face Julian. "But I thought you might have been better than the rest of them. You seem to have . . . What is the word? *Intelligenza* . . . a brain." She scowled at him, dared him to deny the accusation.

"Lady Lucia," Alex began, his voice calm, "you are gravely mistaken. There has been no infidelity. My friends have kept no betrayal hidden from you. I give you my word."

She scanned each of them, bitter vitriol displaying itself in her eyes. An exaggerated "Humph!" accompanied the whirl of her gown as she stormed out of the library.

They were silent as they listened to the swishing skirts of an angry woman making her way down the hall. When at last it was quiet, they looked at Alex. His own jaw set firm, he raised his eyebrows and said, "Well, thank you very much for that." Running a hand through his hair, he heaved a sigh. He felt Julian's eyes press into his skull.

Julian surveyed him skeptically. "Are you telling me there is no truth to this, then?"

"Of course not. Apart from having the desire to help someone, I've done nothing. One can hardly be accused of something sordid there," Alex snapped.

"Are you sure your desire is truly to help and not *have*?" Julian's gaze was unconvinced.

Alex felt the color rising in his cheeks and fought to keep the flush from showing. "This conversation is over, Julian." He walked out the door and leaned against the cool wooded wainscoting just outside.

"Oh, I don't think it is," he heard Charles sing gaily.

"Why would you say that?" Julian said.

"He's taken the book." His voice was smug. "And perhaps it's only me, but I wouldn't give just anybody Shakespeare's sonnets, wouldst thou?"

EIGHTEEN

"IT DID *NOT* GO WELL. I DOUBT HE HEARD A WORD I said," Alex murmured, leading his mother to a chair in the conservatory. A short walk in the garden was nearly more than she had stamina for, so they would speak here, surrounded by the late fall greenery, the ivy vines and philodendron weaving in and out of the lattice screens around them.

"Well," she said, lowering herself onto the broad limestone garden bench, "if you mumbled then as ineloquently as you did just now, I can sympathize, and wouldn't blame the man for refusing you. Chances are he *didn't* hear a word you said."

Alex sighed and sat next to her. "I requested he give some regard to who I am. That was all. I was not unreasonable. I did not refuse. I simply . . . asked."

"What did you ask for, Alex?"

"Consideration."

The duchess looked at her son with weary eyes. "What is it you want, Alex?"

He turned to her and said, "I'm not entirely sure, but I know that which I *do not* want. I do not want to sit in Parliament. I do not want this marriage. I do not want . . ." He waved his hand about. "This. This life," he finished lamely.

His mother raised a hand and let it rest on his arm. "I suggest you think very carefully. For some choices, once made, cannot be undone." She drew in a long breath and rose from her seat. "I must go in to rest now, Alex. I shall see you this evening. But think on it in great measure. A divergent course is often a lonely one."

He helped to steady her on her feet and made a slight bow as she turned to leave the glasshouse. Slowly, he took a few steps backward, moving toward the exit closest to the stables. His foot clipped something beneath him—a shiny boot of fine Moroccan leather. Alex looked up to see both Julian and Lady Lucia sitting on the opposite side of the screen from where he'd sat with his mother. And the faces of two people who'd heard the entire conversation. Apparently, this time, his words were unmistakably clear.

The look on Lady Lucia's face was thunderous as she swept past him, leaving without a word. Julian's expression was less revealing; he was excellent at keeping his emotions in check. Another feature his father surely admired.

"Is it us?" Julian asked. "Are we so dull that we cannot provide you with enough excitement?"

Alex shook his head. "It is not that, Julian. It is not excitement that I seek, but *fulfillment*. They are fruits from two different trees."

Julian cast a hand to sweep the vista in front of him. "Just look,

Alex. You have an entire orchard in front of you. How can you ignore what is ripe and right here for the asking? You are handed the Garden of Eden in a basket at your feet every morning as you wake." Julian looked skyward with frustration. "You absolutely cannot throw it all away—certainly not at this point. Not when your father is depending upon your support. The garrison is rising before our very eyes for a reason. Because we live in dangerous times! The estate *needs* you, Alex. This place is your past, your present, and most important, your future. And it would be churlish of me not to mention how mine is inextricably interwoven with yours."

Alex settled back in his chair and said quietly, "The road before and behind you matters little if you can push to follow the path that calls from within."

"I beg your pardon?" Julian said, his face unreadably stiff.

"It's nothing," Alex brushed off. "I'm simply repeating advice someone wisely offered me recently—about wrestling with my fate. It's given me pause for thought."

Julian's eyes narrowed with his reply. "Funny, the sentiment rings recognizably familiar to me as well." He suddenly leapt from his chair. "May I suggest we go for a hunt? Yes, a tour about the grounds on horseback is always the thing that sets you straight, Alex. What do you say? A bracing breath of fresh air? It will clear our heads and have a tremendous good effect on these ridiculous notions of yours to dismiss the treasures at your disposal. I shall see you in the stables in an hour."

It *would* be an impressive structure when finished, Alex supposed. He brought his horse closer to the garrison's building site, admiring the framework taking shape and envisioning the architecture once complete. But the reason for its existence managed to tarnish any pleasure he might have found in it. He was about to turn his horse around and leave the worrisome thoughts behind when he spotted Miss MacDuff traversing mounds of stone and great beams of wood, a basket in her hand and a contented smile upon her face.

He pulled alongside her and dismounted his horse. "Good afternoon, Miss MacDuff. You appear in good spirits. Could it be you have been gifted further workings from the men of Cambridge?"

She attempted to hold in her smile with meager success. "No, milord. Today is nothing more than a series of riddles."

"Wordplay, you say?"

"Numbers. Mathematical puzzles, actually. I've just brought the men their lunch and have triumphantly beaten them in deciphering a string of puzzles they wagered I'd fail to solve."

"Undoubtedly a grave error on their parts, for I would never place a wager against your skills with the fresh understanding that pure determination stands behind them." He gave her a congratulatory smile. "Perhaps you would indulge me with a peek? I've always enjoyed unraveling enigmas."

Miss MacDuff tossed aside the linen cloth that covered the basket and pulled out a roll of coarse brown paper, ink smears marring the surface. Alex unrolled and studied it, following the quill markings that showed the complicated equation and the ingenious cipher she used to resolve it.

"Ordinary arithmetic leaving you wanting?" he asked, handing back the scroll.

She smiled contentedly, looking over her shoulder to the garrison. "It was their assignment—and there is nothing ordinary about any of these men." She wheeled back to face him, her eyes suddenly wide. "I only meant they are simple men who are stuck with someone who needles them for knowledge."

He considered her curious reaction. "Yes, Miss MacDuff. I would wholly agree. It is *you* who is the extraordinary one." He reached into his saddlebag and pulled out a glove, then looked about on the ground. "I thank you for sharing the puzzle. It's one I'll not forget. But I am late for an appointment, and now fear I will compound my tardiness." Alex looked beneath his horse and finally up to Miss MacDuff's confused face. "I have lost a glove. Ah, well, perhaps this will be *my* puzzle to solve by the end of day. Good afternoon," he said, mounting his horse and giving her a wave.

Jenna chased the afternoon sun, trekking to the lake and pastures beyond Withinghall. She walked alongside Esthwaite waters, to the old stone church, which sat embedded into the side of a grassy hill, moss-covered steps leading to its entrance. Behind the old building was a graveyard, its gardens unkempt. The trees were barren of leaves, and the old winter grass was withered and yellowed. But there was solace here, soberly offered, undisturbed, and it called to her.

The sun gave its watery winter light grudgingly at this time of year, a subtle appearance, a hastened departure. The winter solstice was a difficult day to weather as her mother had died on it thirteen years ago, and because of it, the numbing gray hours left her fragmented. Yet it marked another beginning: the methodical plod toward longer, brighter days, which restored her source of strength. And the men helped her through it.

She thought of the family she had now, their curious observations, their science, their illuminations. She'd begun to appreciate their bond, and fierce love for family, friend, and sovereign. It was an easy path to be led along when one's teachers were so devoted. But a new question formed in her mind, struggled there. These men were exactly where they wanted to be. Where did *she* belong?

A figure in black caught her eye, a dark crow in clothing. Mr. Finch rested against the side of the church, his eyes closed in deep reverie as he took in the scent of something he held to his nose.

Jenna narrowed her eyes and mindlessly leaned forward to see.

It was a glove.

It was Lord Pembroke's glove.

A twig snapped beneath her boot, and she pulled back with a gasp. Mr. Finch's eyes flew open and he whirled to stand at attention. Their eyes met and Jenna watched the young man's expression go from one of panicked surprise to one of disagreeable realization.

"What are you doing here?" he demanded. He quickly shoved the glove into a pocket within the fold of his cloak and glared at her.

Jenna stepped back, resting a hand on the stone wall, aware she'd trespassed on a very intimate, private moment, but there was nothing she could do. "I was only . . ."

"Grave robbing? Or are you merely looking for fresh supplies?" He eyed her hand on the stone wall.

She blanched and snatched it away, wrapping it protectively with the other. "I am not, sir, and I take offense at your suggestion of thievery."

He snorted. "It's hardly a far-fetched charge, as it appears you are attempting to snatch Lord Pembroke's attentions away from where they once were focused."

"I have come here for no other gain than solitude." She pulled her woolen cloak tighter about her shoulders.

"Privacy you seek? Another clandestine encounter?" He smiled scornfully, the finely drawn bones of his face conveying true hostility. "Lord Pembroke is above your station, and it has become evident you are upsetting Lady Lucia."

She swallowed the tight lump forming in her throat and felt a wave of cold panic creep through her body.

Mr. Finch continued, eyebrows forming a high arc. "I could imagine the duke and duchess becoming most displeased if anything—or anyone—could be found damaging the conjugal bond they are trying to create for their son. One that required years of preparation on their part. Wouldn't you agree?"

Her stomach somersaulted mercilessly. She found herself incapable of speech, and moreover, he might take her silence for an admittance of guilt. Why wouldn't words come to her mouth?

He frowned. "I wouldn't be surprised if they'd ask the offending party to leave, and that would be a terrible embarrassment for your family, wouldn't it?"

She felt his eyes scrutinize her face, which she presumed was effortless to read.

"Let me give you a word of advice," he went on. "Leave him alone. Stop putting ideas in his head that are interfering with his well-planned future. That way, your father can finish his work on the garrison and you will remain in his good graces." He swept up the stone staircase and out of sight behind the old kirk.

Jenna slumped against the stone wall, her muscles paralyzed and slack. Mr. Finch, clearly rattled, made it seem like she'd been throwing herself at Lord Pembroke, flaunting an infatuation that was ruinous to his future. How could he accuse her of such a thing?

But then, part of his criticism was true. She *had* encouraged him to see beyond the box he lived within. But these were not revolutionary thoughts—and certainly she had not tried to tempt him inappropriately. The butterflies in her stomach, at the remembered feeling of his finger tracing her palm, carried with them an uncertainty that she stuffed to the back of her mind. She needed time to think, to calm the chaotic thoughts in her head. But no amount of time could erase the wretched conversation with Mr. Finch.

Determined to resurface from her woolgathering stupor, she brushed bits of dried grass from her skirt, as if the physical act could dislodge her anchored, disturbing reflections. She climbed the stone stairs, her boots grazing the lichen with her slow, deliberate steps. A faint whirring sound rushed by her ear as she reached the last one.

She heard a sharp thwack, and then saw the quivering stem of an arrow in one of the broad oak trees, and the flash of white in the woods beside her as a red stag leapt away in an explosion of soundless movement. Stunned, she whirled in the direction of the arrow's path, her heart pounding. With the sun setting, she could just make out the silhouetted figures of a band of hunters farther down by the water's edge. Someone ran toward her out of the gathering, almost as quickly as the arrow had. Jenna assumed it was the arrow's owner. She turned to wrestle it out of its missed target, intending to give the hunter a piece of her mind. She heard his hurried footsteps crushing the fallen oak leaves as she struggled with the shaft.

"Do you know how close that was?" Jenna said through gritted teeth. A strong hand grabbed her shoulder.

"Yes," a voice panted, laboring for breath, "I do."

The arrow suddenly gave way and Jenna turned, squinting into the sun to see the anxiety-ridden face of Lord Pembroke looking down at her.

"Mo chreach!" She took a step backward.

"Good God, did I hurt you?" He grabbed her arms.

"What are you doing here?" Jenna looked around wildly, wondering where Mr. Finch was, and handling the skittering, fractured thought that perhaps he'd set up a trap to snare them together.

"I might ask you the same question." His eyes searched her for signs of injury.

"Did you not check the public grounds before hunting?"

"I did. Or, rather, *Julian* did." His gaze moved back to the group of men.

"I see." She swallowed that familiar lump. "He told you it was clear, did he?" Her voice sounded hollow as she imagined the probable conversation.

His eyes clouded with bewilderment. "He did. Wait here. I shall speak with him," he said, holding up a hand. He turned and hurried toward the men again.

The last thing Jenna wanted was another encounter with Mr. Finch. She looked around, frantic for an escape, and decided on the same path as the frightened red stag. She ran, clutching the arrow in one hand. The other seized the cloak around her neck as it fluttered about like an expanding wing. She tore through the forest, branches snatching at her as if they were the fingers of some ominous spirits, trying to hinder her way.

NINETEEN

THE SNOW RETURNED, AND WITH IT THE PERCEPTION of safety. Perhaps it was because Jenna could make out the sounds of approaching feet as they crunched their way through freshly fallen snow. Or because she could see the tracks of unrecognizable footprints as they patterned around the exterior of the cottage. Yet the urge to hide was constant.

It had been three days since the incident in the woods, and Jenna noticed the men growing suspicious of her behavior. Choosing to stay buried indoors was not her usual manner. Still, after finishing each day's lessons, she attempted to find things to do inside. She couldn't bear to tell anyone what had happened. They might pick apart every moment she'd shared with Lord Pembroke, maybe tell her she was actually at fault.

More than once, Angus tried to persuade her to run an errand up to Mrs. Wigginton at the main house, or to collect something from the stables. Jenna always found an excuse not to go. She maintained the need to study further on her Greek or Latin lessons, argued the necessity of finishing a sewing repair, or feigned exhaustion from a bad night's sleep and put off the request. She was running out of reasons.

"If ye want me to tell him you're not interested, I shall do so, lass, but ye needn't keep to the cottage just to avoid seein' him, aye?" her father had said at one point.

Her eyes had gone wildly round. "What?" she'd whispered.

"Mr. Wicken. I heard from Jeb that he's been actively pursuin' the hunt for a wife, and I thought that perhaps it was the reason we've seen so much of him down at the garrison lately. That maybe he was going to ask about your level of interest, aye?"

"Of course," Jenna breathed out. "Mr. Wicken. Yes. I mean, no. I'm definitely *not* interested. I shall address him eventually, Da. Soon. I promise." But she had kept to the cottage a little longer.

The ruse was over when she came down the stairs and saw the men, who were finishing their predawn breakfasts look up from their bowls and exchange nonverbal messages.

"Good morn to ye, Jenna," her father said. "Have ye slept well?"

"Yes, sir," she said, aware of the many eyes upon her.

"I've never slept better before coming here," Tavish interjected. "I'm beginning to think maybe Angus is putting something in my food at night. For the second my head goes down, I canna keep my mind awake—even to the end of my prayers."

Malcolm leaned in to tousle the boy's hair. "I think perhaps it has more to do wi' your mind and muscles working all day, aye?"

Tavish smiled. "Mama used to say, *Idle hands will make for mischief*, an' I havena gotten cuffed once since coming here."

Ian snorted. "If ye want to keep it that way, I suggest ye get yourself ready. I've found that when your hands are idle, your mouth isn't, and I for one prefer it the other way round." He rose from the table, grabbed his coat by the door, and left.

Tavish, unaffected by Ian's gruff remarks, grinned and said, "Angus, whatever it is ye might be putting in my food at night, I think ye might want to put a double dose into Mr. Ross's. For if ever there was someone in need of a better night's rest, I'd guess it's him." A general agreement was the response around the table as everyone got up to clear.

Jenna sat on the empty bench and her father came to stand behind her. Malcolm settled his muscular hands on her shoulders. "Do ye think ye might feel up to going to town for me today, lass? I've Ian's printed plans all finished and coded, and I need them taken to the smithy. They mark precisely where we'll be hiding. . . ." He stopped, and Jenna looked up at him.

"Hiding what, Da?"

He sat next to her on the bench and looked at her, grim-faced. "Arms. And ammunitions. The blacksmith will ken what to do wi' them, but you're the only one I'd trust to get them there."

"I was planning to help Angus finish the beeswax candles today. We haven't made the wicks, and they really should be done."

"Nay, lass," Angus said, his face turned to the task of washing the breakfast bowls. "I need to visit the brewhouse with Mrs. Wigginton for a spell. We're nearly finished wi' the ale for the winter and it's got to be casked straightaway. The wicks can wait another day, aye?"

She knew this most likely had been rehearsed with her father earlier, and was resigned to accept without creating any more raised eyebrows.

"All right, then," she said. "I'll go."

"Fine. Just after your lessons, then. The papers are on the table by the window. Roll them up nice and tight like, aye? For anyone capable of readin' these plans would find they point in one direction. Understand, lass?" Malcolm put a kiss on her forehead. "Tavish? Are ye ready, ye wee fiend?" He lifted the boy and threw him over his shoulder.

Tavish giggled and waved to Angus and Jenna as they left the cottage and made their way out into the snowy landscape.

After everyone had left the cottage, Jenna sat at the kitchen table eyeing the pages in front of her. She tried to concentrate on the long string of math problems, but her mind wandered as she traced the numbers printed in clean script. The paper smelled faintly of berries and walnuts and something metallic, since Angus was forever concocting new tinctures to be used in place of ink. It was an expense they could not afford to squander away on her calculations.

She scribbled a few halfhearted attempts, numbly processing the figures. A solid knock at the door made her jolt in her seat, and she marred the paper in front of her with a smear of bright color.

Her stomach lurched. She dropped the quill and ran to the side of the door to peek through the window from behind its rough curtain. The glass was covered in a thick layer of frost and hindered her inspection. It might be Mr. Finch coming to finish the job without the drawbacks of a group of witnesses. She searched for a place to hide in the little cottage. A stifled sound of fear escaped her throat as the caller knocked again, more forcefully.

"Miss MacDuff!" a muffled voice called out. "Open the door. I know you're there because I just saw Angus."

Lord Pembroke.

Without thinking, she raced back to the door and flung it open. Biting wind swept across her face. "What are you doing here?" she blurted out, ignoring the sting at her cheeks and looking beyond him for followers. "Come inside, hurry!"

He wiped the dusting of snow upon the shoulders of his coat before moving his tall frame through the doorway. He pushed the door closed and turned.

"Are you ill?" He peered at her. "Angus said you haven't left the house for days."

She shook her head in answer.

He appeared unconvinced. "Listen," he said, scanning her features as if he were searching for symptoms of poor health, "I wanted to talk to you about what happened the other day. I meant to speak with you right away, but when I returned, you'd gone. I was mortified when I discovered I'd almost shot someone . . . and then finding out it was you, I . . ." He stopped.

She watched his eyes leave her face and take in the room, a quick look at its contents.

He rubbed the cold from his arms. "It's been years since I've stepped into this cottage. It hasn't changed a bit. I spent much of my youth here, slaying dragons and fighting great battles. I've always claimed this cottage as a castle in my mind's eye, my own private fortress." He chortled at the memories.

"Slaying dragons? Yes, your imagination is well developed,"

Jenna said, astonished anyone could envision this hut as enchanting. She busied herself, arranging the meager woodpile at the hearth.

"Well"—he hesitated—"actually, it's *your* imagination I'm worried about."

"Mine? Whatever for?"

He rubbed the tendons at the back of his neck. "I know you haven't had the most gratifying encounters with my friends. More than likely they deserve the unflattering opinion you may have developed. I'm not making excuses for them, but I wanted to let you know how awful Mr. Finch felt about the other day."

I'll bet he did.

"He said he'd made a sweep of the area, had found you, and mentioned where it was we were hunting. Mr. Finch said he advised you to reverse your direction. He blames himself for the error. He's plagued me for three days straight, not letting *me* out of his sight, certain I'm still furious with him."

Jenna pulled back. She was convinced her mouth must be hanging open. She stayed her features, determined not to draw undue curiosity from him. How in the world could she explain it all now?

"He's begged me not to mention anything to you, fearing your likely embarrassment for not heeding his warning. I told him you probably had good reason for continuing on, and he needn't feel inappropriate guilt on your behalf." Lord Pembroke looked at her, his eyebrows raised in anticipation.

She shut her eyes and thought carefully before speaking. "No," she said, letting her breath out. "I'm certain Mr. Finch will not suffer long from *my* errors. Please rest assured my feelings toward him have not worsened."

They could not grow any more negative.

Lord Pembroke looked at her sideways and then smiled. "I think I'm pleased to hear that. Although I'd be infinitely more pleased to hear you accept my invitation to a wedding. Not mine," he added quickly, "but Garrick Wicken's, the horse handler. He's marrying one of the kitchen maids, Elizabeth. You might know her?"

Jenna shook her head but felt a sliver of relief.

"Regardless, everyone is invited, and my father has insisted I and all my friends attend. Typically, once a year he feels it necessary to show the servants and staff just how . . . generous a man he is and has decided to show his charity by paying for the wedding and excusing the staff from work."

"You needn't have invited us yourself. Surely you've more important matters to attend to."

"Yes, there is another important matter." He reached into his inner coat pocket and pulled out a slim, leather-bound book and offered it to her. "I meant what I said when inviting you to avail yourself of our library. If you wish, I'll show you how everything is arranged."

"Shakespeare's sonnets," she read aloud. A smile crept at the corners of her mouth. "Gavin used to have a copy, and would read to us after dinner."

"Well, then, don't feel obligated."

"No—thank you. We lost his copy long ago, plus the book was secondhand and missing the last twenty or so poems. I think they were torn out, so I've never read them."

"Really?" he said, amused and watchful. "Well, that would be the poetry supposedly written about his married mistress. It speaks of pain and love. And longing."

Her face bypassed the usual ruddy hue caused by embarrassment, and went straight to scarlet. She swallowed and felt her mouth had gone most uncooperative.

"I hope you'll find them intriguing. I wasn't sure what type of literature you're drawn to, so I chose one of my favorites."

"I'm sure they'll be captivating." She glanced down and went to work busily picking bits of lint off the folds of her skirt, desperate to change the subject. "You mentioned Mr. Finch has been at your side these last few days. How was it you managed to get past him this morning?"

He gave a low, rueful chuckle. "I made sure he was offered our best port last night. Julian cannot refuse unparalleled quality." Lord Pembroke smiled. "In other words, he drank his fill, and I expect he's feeling the effects of it this morning. My whereabouts will be his least concern."

"When is the wedding?" Jenna asked, glancing toward the window.

"Twelfth Night. Will you come?" He followed her gaze and wandered to the casement, leaning on the spindly table beneath the glass to examine the snowy world outside. He bent over the garrison's plans and looked down to the drawings, to the sketches written in the same coded puzzle language Jenna had revealed to him just three days ago.

Jenna's breath came short and fast. "I don't think . . ."

"Ha!" he cried out. "I recognize this little brain-twisting riddle." He turned to look at Jenna, pointing to the plans. "More of the same, is it not?"

She nodded lamely.

He picked up the plans and held them out. "And would this be the final shape of the garrison?"

She reached out to take them from him and swiftly rolled them up. "Oh dear. Someone must have forgotten to bring these with today. I must deliver them straightaway."

"Why don't I do it and save you the journey?"

No! It was one thing to trust him with the knowledge of her education, but she unquestionably could not afford the risk of the duke's son, the heir to a seat in the Parliament in King George's court, studying the plans he'd glanced at. The very composition meant to help unhinge the current king and replace him with another.

Think! What do I do? "Wholly unnecessary, but I do have something for you nevertheless."

She placed the rolled-up plans back at the entrance to the door, scurried to the mantel, and plucked the arrow that had narrowly missed eliminating Mr. Finch's problem. "Your fletchings are damaged. I'd say you have a poor spine, so it's not surprising you missed the stag, but I thought you might want this back anyway." She attempted to show amusement on her face. She held the arrow out and hoped to entice him away from the table, but fate intervened. Someone hammered on the door.

Lord Pembroke peered out the frosted glass, sighed, and said, "Julian's here."

Jenna thought she might explode with fear. She fought the desire to run upstairs and hide beneath the bed. The door burst open. "Is he here?" came the biting voice—a voice, if possible, colder than the piercing air outside.

"Rather a dramatic entrance, Julian," Lord Pembroke said from behind the door.

Jenna couldn't breathe. She felt her chest tighten as Mr. Finch's bloodshot eyes locked into a defiant, accusatory glare with hers. He narrowed his eyes at the arrow in her hand, stepped through the door, and then, remarkably, changed his expression entirely into one displaying care and concern.

"Oh, thank God," he sighed, closing the door to find Lord Pembroke behind it. "Lady Lucia has been beside herself, sick with worry."

"Why?" Lord Pembroke said.

"When I woke, no one could find you in the house or stables. We were certain you'd come to harm in the storm and were in need of rescue."

"And your next thought was that the stonemason's daughter held me hostage here?" Lord Pembroke's face showed a picture of ludicrous amusement.

"Don't be ridiculous," Mr. Finch said, brushing the snow from his cloak. The ice crystals landed on the clean flagstones, a soppish mess mixing with the mud of his boots.

Jenna eyed it hatefully while Mr. Finch continued.

"You have no idea the distress you created at the house. Lady Lucia turned the place upside down in search of you. Your parents have become *most* concerned." He turned to face Jenna when he said this.

"Have they indeed?" Lord Pembroke said, turning from the window. He leaned back against the table and folded his arms in front of his chest. "That would be remarkable, seeing as my father is in London presently. I believe he's sitting with the rest of the members of Parliament, finishing the business of the week. Has he returned unexpectedly, then?" He arched an eyebrow in the direction of his friend.

Mr. Finch flushed but, without faltering, smiled. "Did I say *parents*? Of course, by that I meant your mother. More important, what are you doing *here*?"

"Miss MacDuff has allowed me a peek at the garrison plans. A wonderful privilege to see architecture in its most base form." He reached for the papers by the door and quickly unrolled them in front of Mr. Finch.

Jenna's stomach dropped, and she wanted to snatch the plans out of Lord Pembroke's grasp, but clenched her hands together in front of her.

"Whomever created that plan is truly clever. In fact, this is a group of the most ingenious Scotsmen I've yet to come across."

Mr. Finch glanced at the plans and then at Jenna.

"Well, my errand is complete, but now that I think about it," he said, returning the roll to the table by the door, "I'm glad you're here, Julian."

Both Jenna and Mr. Finch looked at Lord Pembroke, their eyes widening in question.

"I made mention to Miss MacDuff of your remorse over the hunting incident. Told her how you've been a puppy at my heels, full of regret regarding our terrible error."

"Yes, thank you for that," Mr. Finch said tightly. He turned to Jenna and made a slight bow in her direction. "My sincerest apologies, Miss MacDuff. I mistakenly thought you'd taken heed of my warning. Perhaps the winds about us were too strong, and you misheard?"

Something snapped in Jenna. She'd had enough. "I do beg pardon, Mr. Finch," she said. "I believe I was so delighted to see that you had recovered Lord Pembroke's missing glove that your message must have sailed right over my head." She smiled and made a quick glance at Lord Pembroke and then back to Mr. Finch.

Mr. Finch made a slight audible breath inward.

For a fleeting moment Jenna felt ashamed of her action. It was a mean-spirited thing to do. But surely Mr. Finch's maneuver was more atrocious than hers, for she could have easily been killed. The puzzle pieces fit neatly together soon after Jenna had given the situation some thought. Mr. Finch was in love with Lord Pembroke, and Jenna was getting in the way.

Lord Pembroke looked back and forth between the two of them with a somewhat puzzled expression. "Heartwarming news. It was one of my favorites." He walked to the door and held it open for Mr. Finch. "I think we'd best take our leave now, Julian. Lady Lucia should not be kept worried and waiting."

Mr. Finch gave Jenna one last, cold glare and she turned to face the fireplace, hearing Lord Pembroke's final remarks just before pulling the door shut. "Enjoy the book, Miss MacDuff. I'll see you at the wedding."

She focused on her breathing, taking a few moments to restore a steady, calm heartbeat and a clear, thinking head. The book. She would spend a few moments reading a page or two and then journey with the plans to the smithy. Except, upon turning around, she'd discovered that this would be an impossibility. There would be no journey.

For there were no plans.

TWENTY

THE NERVES IN HER STOMACH WERE A KNOTTED BALL of twine, writhing about in too tight a space and unforgiving of breath. The garrison's coded plans had been stolen right beneath her nose! The end for her clan had finally arrived. Her every thought urged her to run to the building site and sound the alarm so that they'd have time to escape before being fitted for a noose.

But just as she donned her cloak, ready to rush out the door, she stopped and gave pause.

Which one of them took the plans?

If it was Mr. Finch, then yes, this could be retribution. She'd just forced him to return a private treasure, and slyly informed him that she knew of his feelings toward Lord Pembroke. If they became publicly known, he would be in ruins . . . or worse. But, she reminded herself, Mr. Finch could not read the codes, so the plans were of little use to him.

If Lord Pembroke had taken them, it was likely because he was insisting on showing gallantry. He was on his way to deliver them to the garrison so she wouldn't have to set foot out in the snowfall. And in that case, whomever he will give them to will shortly realize that Jenna had not only failed at her assigned task to bring them to the smithy, but also that Lord Pembroke had likely viewed them as well. Surely, that clansman will believe Lord Pembroke's next move will be to measure the rope needed to hang them.

She shook her head and finished knotting her cloak. Either way, it didn't matter. They needed to be told. It gave them a few more moments of precious time in case they needed to escape.

She threw open the cottage door and pulled back with surprise to see her father hastily approaching, a bull about to charge, the plans in his hands.

Jenna stepped back in alarm.

"I've just been *congratulated*, lass. For my architectural savviness." Her father held the plans in the air and growled. "Lord Pembroke delivered the compliments as well as the designs. Imagine my surprise, Jenna!"

She could. And stuttered with her explanation. "He—he took them without me knowing, Da, and apparently only to save me the trouble of delivering them."

"Clearly, he's seen them."

"Yes . . . but only briefly," she rushed on. "It was a glance of admiration—nothing more." She could not form any other words. Somehow the slight relief at discovering it was Lord Pembroke rather than Mr. Finch who took the plans was enough to convince her the clan was safe—that there was no need to reveal that Lord Pembroke could decipher the code. Was there?

Her father stared at her in silent calculation, and then spun on his heel toward the door. "I'm off to the smithy, Jenna. To put them in their *rightful hands*."

Three days later, apart from having to survive the prickling discomfort of the agitated clan, nothing out of the ordinary had transpired. Jenna had convinced herself it was safe to breathe again and had finally begun to move about the estate accomplishing her normal daily errands when she came upon a picture that filled her with unease.

A well-muscled horse grazed upon a tuft of winter grass at the entrance to the cottage. It was one Jenna didn't recognize. It wasn't unusual for her family to have guests, but much of the time they came on foot, not having adequate finances to support a beast as fine as this one.

She'd been at the garrison to peek at the week's progress and was enjoying the brisk evening hike down the hill to the cottage when she spied the animal. She approached it quietly and put a hand close to the velvety nose, offering her scent as a means of introduction.

The cottage door opened wide and spilled light into the chilly darkness. She turned to see the outlined figure of Angus heading to the woodpile. He spotted her by the horse and crunched through the snow toward them. His hand came to rest on the horse's flank and his face broke out into a massive grin. "Daniel's here."

Daniel. Her heart skipped a beat. As it had for as many years back as she could remember whenever anyone would say his name.

"Daniel?" Jenna said. "Why?"

"News for your da, I'spect," he answered, sliding his hand across the horse's back. "He'll be pleased to see you too, ye ken."

She thought for a moment and asked, "How long has it been?"

"Three years? Nay . . . four. Aye, four years since we've seen him. Whatever it is, it's been too long. He's kept well, I think, but you'll have the chance to see for yourself in a minute." He gave the horse a solid pat. "Would ye mind putting her in the stable before ye come in? It's been a long time of travel. I bet this old girl could use some warmth and company. And she's finding none so much to eat by this fence post."

"Of course," she answered, now noticing the small thrill of exhilaration thrumming through her veins. Daniel Delafuente—the most intoxicating person she'd ever met. And the one that caused her the greatest embarrassment.

Angus went into the house with another armload of firewood as Jenna untied the horse from the stud and led the weary animal to the barn for a long deserved rest. She crossed the distance between the cottage and the stable and listened to their footsteps as they broke through the thin crust of snow. A cloud shifted and the moonlight came strong and bright, the white floor around them illuminated. Their breath came in steamy clouds and rose above their heads to disappear into the brittle night air.

They entered the stable, where the smell of sweet hay saturated her senses, and the warmth of all those bulky animals enveloped her—like a womb. She smiled demurely at Jeb and Mr. Wicken as they assisted the animals for the night. She avoided making eye contact with Jeb, as his well-developed sixth sense might recognize that, even unintentionally, she had not heeded his advice to stay away from Lord Pembroke. The two men worked to feed the horses, brush them, and supply fresh bedding. Without a word, Jeb nodded in the direction of Henry, to an open stall for the visiting animal. She tethered Daniel's horse to one of the rails alongside and found a clean brush to work over her neck and mane.

She stroked the animal and tried recalling the last time she'd seen their family friend and her childhood white knight.

Daniel used to visit with much more regularity—certainly more than every three or four years. And he used to come with his father, but her memories of the elder man were few. Recollections of Daniel were indelible, for as a young girl she told anyone who would listen that she intended to run away with him. She wanted to lead his life of adventure after he'd filled her ears with his stories of people and places. These weren't the ordinary towns and villages she'd grown used to living in, but were wild and exotic places she hungered to travel toward. The hot, dusty sands of Egypt, the spicy wealth and splendor of India, Spain and France and Poland—all places Daniel brought to life.

For a man now of around twenty-four, he'd had his share of exploration. At the time of his last visit, her only concern was leaving with him. She'd packed her bag, hugged her father good-bye, and waited by Daniel's horse, waited for him to come and put her on it. To her shock, she'd been given a kiss on the forehead and a book of ancient Indian poetry in place of a seat behind him. She was told she must wait her turn for adventure, but that in good time, it too would come.

She'd done her best to bury those tender, fragile feelings. She had only been twelve, after all. Her plan, she could see now, was quite absurd. And so pining for Daniel had been replaced with more practical matters of learning and living. She turned at the creaking sound of the stable door.

Daniel. After all those years, he was exactly as she'd remembered, and her heart leapt, boiling over with emotions like an unwatched pot.

He was silent as he advanced, his warm smile growing as he reached the stall, his deep golden eyes gleaming.

"Jenna, is that you? I can't believe it. *Tu eres hermosa*," he said in a low voice, his accent thick and velvety to her ears. Daniel shook his head and walked around the mare to where she stood. He looked her up and down and then swallowed her in his arms. He smelled of horses and leather and damp earth. He kissed the top of her head and moved her out at arm's length to search her face.

"It cannot be you—*No lo puedo creer*. You were a scrappy little girl when I last left. Bright red hair, round red face, and a very red temper to match, if I remember correctly. This cannot be the same girl, no?" He smiled broadly, showing well-kept teeth, even and white.

"You had the chance, and you let it slip through your fingers, Daniel," Jenna said, feigning disinterest. "I would have run away with you, but you wouldn't have me, remember?" She gave him a cursory once-over. "You don't look as I recall. Your hair is too long and you need a bath." She bit the inside of her cheek to keep from smiling and picked up the brush to continue working over the mare.

"Oh, *mi querida*, you have not forgiven me for leaving without you?" He attempted to look contrite, but failed, unable to get past the humor of the situation.

"Well, you might have at least made the effort to write," she said, giving him a frosty sideways glance.

"I did write! I just never trusted letters to arrive here, so I waited until I could deliver them myself. It is my present to you, Jenna, a journal of all my travels."

She scrutinized him and calculated his unexpected appearance. His family was from southern Spain, that much she remembered. With his inky black hair and olive complexion, it would be easy for anyone to place his background, but his accented speech created confusion for the best of ancestral scholars. He could be Spanish, Portuguese or Greek, or even Egyptian. It was a talent he'd developed, in order to fit in wherever he went.

But Jenna was sure it was impossible for Daniel not to draw attention to himself, at least from the females he'd come across. Even after weeks of weary travel, the smudge of smoky bristles upon his face could not hide the true depth of striking attractiveness in the man.

"The book, where is it?" she asked, putting a hand out toward Daniel. "I want to find out what I missed, and what was so important it kept you away from us."

"Well, first let me finish what you've started here. I do not expect anyone to look after me or my horse. These things I can do myself—and if I do not mind Pazya here"—Daniel tapped the rump of the animal—"she will anger with me and treat me badly the next time I ask of her." His eyes were playful as Jenna handed him the brush, bristles first.

"I think that's a fine idea," she said. "I'm going back to the cottage, where I shall pilfer through your belongings until I locate the book you seem nearly as determined to keep from me as the travel itself." She turned and left Daniel with a grin of sheer amusement on his face.

Back at the cottage, everyone was busy making room and dinner for Daniel's visit. Angus was at the hearth, preparing a stew of rabbits— a timely snare from the morning—and the smell of gingerbread slid through the house, a come-hither invitation. Appetite whetted, Jenna felt that waiting for the celebratory meal would be unbearable if she wasn't allowed to participate somehow and keep her mind occupied.

She surveyed the rest of the family. Colin was helping Angus with the kitchen work by chopping winter vegetables and setting the table. Duncan and Gavin were fixing a pallet in the far corner of the room, a place for Daniel to sleep. Her father was traipsing in and out of the house, gathering firewood and arranging it in a tidy stack hearthside. Even little Tavish swept the cottage floor, useful in all the commotion.

Ian, she noted, was absent.

"Angus," Jenna said, coming to him by the fire, "give me a task to do—Daniel wouldn't let me finish rubbing down the horse. And anyway, I'm starving, so I must keep busy."

"Aye, there's plenty to do," Angus said, nodding his great hairy head. "Go on up to Mrs. Wigginton's kitchen and tell her you've come for some of the new ale in the brewhouse. And bring Tavish wi' ye; he'll help carry the load back." He gave her a wink and whistled for the boy.

Outside, the frost-fettered air slapped against her woolen skirts, determined to discover any bare patches of skin. She and Tavish skidded through icy patches to the house and Jenna explained to the newest member of their clan who this old family friend was.

"I can't remember when he first visited, but he always came with his father. They traveled endlessly, one voyage after another. And they always brought us books. Plus spices for Angus. Their visits were too short, and after they'd gone, just when I'd finally stop asking about them, they'd come back."

"Why did they come?" Tavish said.

"To pass along important news and take any with them thereafter." She glanced at Tavish and wondered how much he'd been told about why they themselves were here.

"Daniel is Spanish, but I imagine you could tell just by looking at him that he was foreign. He talks a lot about religion and philosophy, but when I was a little girl, what he said didn't matter. Just the sound of his silvery voice would have me curled up on the floor by the fire and drifting off to sleep. Don't say I didn't warn you." She mussed his hair.

"Philosophy?"

"It's like worldly points of view."

"Well, then I'll have to share a bit of mine wi' him. I've got more opinions of this world than I've had hot dinners."

"Truer words have never been spoken!" Jenna laughed.

They reached the house kitchens, where Mrs. Wigginton sent them down to the brewhouse with instructions. Together, they rolled a miniature cask down the hill, back to the cottage.

They met Ian heading home from his day's work, his typical

sour disposition present in his greeting. "What's this—a party, then?"

"It is. Our friend Daniel's come." Jenna looked at him warily.

"He has, has he? I expect you've brought out the fatted calf as well, then."

His nettlesome statements no longer fazed her.

"Do you know him?" She recalled Daniel's last visit; Ian hadn't joined them yet.

"Aye, I ken him. Met him before wi' your da. And I've heard all the stories as well—the ones where ye followed him round like a pup at his heels." His eyes regarded her with scorn. "So why aren't ye in there brushing your hair a thousand strokes? Gone off him, have ye?"

She bit her tongue and knew that responding with any off-handed quip would only vex Ian. But even his wretched mood wasn't going to alter her excitement for the evening. They walked inside the cottage and were greeted by everyone, happy to see they'd brought the ale.

"Who's hungry, then?" Angus bellowed as he began filling bowls, putting the first one in front of Daniel.

Malcolm MacDuff stood at the head of the table with a jug of wine in his hands. He gave a faint nod to Colin, who stretched and said, "I think I'll make a quick trip to the privy, but go on and get started." Jenna knew it was his turn to patrol and felt a pang of sadness he couldn't be here for the start of this special meal.

Her eyes returned to her father, who poured some of the ruby liquid into a tall, stout glass. She'd seen the goblet before. It had its place, a part of meetings, hushed and clandestine. It was carved with delicate roses and thistles, and three sections displayed Latin writings in italics. Each segment showed one word. The first was *fiat*, meaning "let it be." The second carving was *revirescat*, which meant "let it grow again," and the last etching read *redeat*. "May he return."

She felt a familiar shiver run up her spine as she watched the ceremony of the Loyal Toast. It was such a simple thing, but she knew the consequences of anyone seeing them do it.

Her father passed the hefty glass over a water-filled wooden bowl and said, "To the king over the water. *Redeat!*" Then he took a liberal sip and passed the glass to the rest of the men, who each drank deeply from it.

She glanced at Tavish and smiled at the confusion on his expectant face. He was too young to understand what the ritual meant. Turning back, she found Daniel watching her. He raised an eyebrow in question. *Yes,* she thought, *I do understand.*

Another toast was raised in welcoming Daniel back into their clan, but hearing the salute, "At last—the return of the Great Soul!" gave her pause, and she looked at Angus for an explanation. He simply shrugged the coincidence away with humor and encouraged everyone to eat.

Warm brown bread was passed around the table, along with a generous crock of butter sent down from Mrs. Wigginton. Tavish did his best, in between mouthfuls of rabbit stew and watered-down ale, to explain to Daniel how it was he came to reside with the clan.

"I dinna ken how it is God works, but He must have a sense of humor. First He gives me my mum 'n' da—two people I never complained about. Then snatched them right out from under me like old socks I didna want anymore. Now He throws me into this lot. It's like having a houseful of fathers. One da for every day of the week!"

He was giggling so hard, Jenna thought he might choke on his bread.

The evening meal went on for hours, everyone taking turns asking Daniel for news from the places he'd traveled through. Foreign politics were foremost on the men's minds, and as was expected, Tavish soon slumped over the side of his plate, sleep catching him unaware as the discussions slipped into drowsy tones.

The mesmerizing pull of the hearth beckoned the men to clear the table, set up chairs fireside, and uncork flasks of whisky. Jenna began to yawn as the candles shortened, and she rose for the privy outside. She shuffled out the cottage door and fumbled with latching the bolt. Bleary-eyed, she turned to see a shadowy figure round the side of the cottage. The sharp slap of the fiendish cold and the surprise of the unexpected silhouette brought Jenna's senses up at once.

"Who's there?" The words rushed out to form a spinning white cloud of alarm. Her wisps of breath dispersed, and through it stepped Mr. Wicken, an apologetic expression lit by the thin, flickering firelight through the cottage's front window.

"'Tis Master Wicken, maid. I only come to return a riding crop of your guest. 'Twas on the floor near his stall."

The image of Daniel, his precision, everything just so in his tack box, flashed through her mind. She didn't believe it. Especially as he would never use a crop on his prized horse. "Allow me to fetch him for you." She rushed for the door latch, but Mr. Wicken put a hand across the door.

"No need, lass, see? You'll give over." He dropped his hand and searched the pockets of his outer coat, finding nothing. A chagrined expression flashed across his face. "Must have dropped it on my way down. I'm off, then. Stables need locking. Horse thieves abound, do they not?" He skirted across the frosty ground, back toward the stables, the horses, and in Jenna's mind, nothing out of place within Daniel's tack box by Pazya's stall. There was no crop. He was simply on the prowl, determined to find *something* to raise his current status from that of newly hired hand to invaluable attendant of the estate.

She skipped the privy and rushed back inside. Her abrupt entrance made the men corkscrew in their chairs. Her breath short, she hastily explained the odd visit.

Her father put a hand up to stop her. "Clearly, whatever message of disinterest ye may have *tried* to communicate to Mr. Wicken was unsuccessful, Jenna." He winked at her. "Ye can't blame the man for goin' after something he's set his heart on, now, can ye?"

The men murmured bits of agreement, and she noticed Daniel raise an eyebrow at her.

"No," she persisted. "I overheard a conversation he had with Lord Pembroke in the barn a month ago. I really thought nothing of it at the time, but perhaps I should have brought it to your attention."

"With Lord Pembroke, ye say?" her father asked.

Jenna nodded but decided not to reveal the contents of her own dialogue with the duke's son. It would only bring further suspicion to a person she wanted to keep out of the bright light of inquest. "And also," she added, "Mr. Wicken *is* to be married—to a kitchen maid he barely knows. We've received an invitation to attend the celebration in three days' time."

All eyes turned to Malcolm, apart from Daniel's, who kept his gaze fixed on Jenna, quietly making small calculations behind an expression of mild disapproval—or perhaps it was concern, she guessed.

A small nod of Malcolm's head had Gavin out of his seat and through the door, the others moving themselves ever tighter toward the hearth. Another glance from her father was enough to have Jenna bid her good nights and stumble up the stairs to her bed, regretfully giving up precious time with Daniel and the other adults.

Once in bed, she placed her hand in a patch of moonlight that washed her quilt with silver, softening the edges of her fractious mind. For an hour she listened to the faint vibration of deep voices, but hovering on the verge of sinking to that somnolent place, the tones began to rise.

Or rather, one voice began to rise. She raised her head from the pillow and cocked an ear toward the door. It wasn't her father or Angus. Their voices were much too low to confuse with this tone. Likely, it was Ian.

"I swore an oath to be here, Malcolm—to your family and to mine. And as much as I see wrong wi' the situation, I wilna go back on my word."

Her head was heavy with weariness, frayed nerves, and Ian's constant aversion with their current plans. Somewhere in the back of her sleep-woolly mind, Jenna wondered if Ian wouldn't have been better off just finding a stonemason's guild where they simply worked on the raising of buildings and not the uprising of a country.

In the morning, the men prepared to leave for the garrison, having found no great alarm from Mr. Wicken's appearance. "Most say he's naught but short of friendship and too arrogant to be offered any," Gavin remarked to Jenna. "But he must be watched, as his interest is too close to ours."

Angus folded the last of his linen dishcloths and turned to add, "Jeb says he's desperate for praise, that Mr. Wicken drives him to distraction wi' all of his queries."

"Perhaps he assumed I knew no one here and searched me out to offer friendship," Daniel said, donning his coat before joining the men. "I find it common on my travels."

Jenna's ears pricked with interest. "Angus is right. In fact, Mr. Wicken is following every bit of advice he's been given by Jeb. Even to the point of following through with a wedding to establish his commitment to the estate and its occupants."

Daniel's dark brows rose. "Then we shall attend, the two of us. It will give us a chance to speak of my travels and, most important, observe this man."

"How long will you stay this time?" Jenna asked.

"Only a couple of weeks, I think. There is much to be done, and I will be expected in France to give an update to the court in exile."

James Stuart's court. Her eyes clouded with disappointment, but she understood he was as committed as the rest of her clan.

Daniel raised a finger and pointed at her. "Fret over tomorrow steals the joy of today. I am here now, and here is my journal from the last four years. It will tell you many things—some you may not want to know." His mouth quirked in a sly smile. "But mostly, it should be very interesting. Not the same as being there, but as close as I could get you."

She took the book and looked at it with longing. "I will savor every page."

Daniel made a gallant bow. *"Hasta más tarde."*

Jenna glowed. *Yes, later.* Up until this moment, she hadn't planned on attending the wedding, fearing the great possibility of seeing Mr. Finch. Likely he was still upset with her over the glove, but his acrimony would be a small price to pay if it meant she'd receive an earful of rousing adventures delivered in a mellifluous Spanish accent.

TWENTY-ONE

TWO DAYS LATER, JENNA PEEKED IN THE CARRIAGE house where the wedding reception would be held in the evening— the twelfth night of Christmastide. For the better part of a week, it had been bustling with preparations. Decorated by the womenfolk in their precious spare time, they had transformed the great house into a handsome hall for the evening's celebration.

The walls were adorned with pine boughs and holly, and the air inside, spicy from its greenery, made her nose twitch. Candles were placed about the hall on makeshift wall sconces, and tables, lining the sides of the room, had been pushed back until needed for dinner. The rough wooden floor had been cleaned of mud from the carriage wheels, readied for the hours of dancing that would take place after the banquet.

She came across Mrs. Wigginton, who said she was near to pulling out her own hair. "I've not seen my bed for near a week now." She yawned and rubbed her eyes. "The kitchen staff is cooking in their sleep, trying to keep ahead of it all. The cold cellars are plum filled wi' salmon, venison, and pigs.

"Aye, and I've yet to make my syllabub. Folk come from miles for that dish. Canna disappoint this year." She mopped her brow and headed back to the kitchens.

Jenna couldn't wait to see Mrs. Wigginton's efforts, but later that day, her enthusiasm waned. She sat staring at the few pieces of clothing she owned, the same things she'd been wearing repeatedly for the last year and a half. She possessed nothing appropriate to wear to a wedding, and decided against going altogether, when someone knocked at the thin wooden door to the loft.

In her father's arms was the dress she'd worn to Lord Pembroke's engagement party. "I thought I'd never see that dress again after I returned it to Mrs. Wigginton. One can hardly hope for two great acts of generosity for the same problem from the same person, can they?" She smiled.

"It appears that good woman has offered not only charity, but mercy as well." He handed the dress to Jenna. "She's taken out the wee stiff bits ye so detested the first time ye wore it. Said ye didna need to be uncomfortable on behalf of this couple getting wed." Her father chuckled and walked toward the door. He stopped with his hand on the door frame and turned around, smiling. "That first one had you trussed up wi' nearly as many ribs and joists as those on the garrison's plans."

He closed the door and left Jenna chewing on her lip. Sharp pangs of guilt needled her, refusing to be driven away. She hadn't told anyone about unknowingly providing Lord Pembroke the ability to interpret the plans. If she kept herself wholly occupied with her studies, it was easier not to fret. A little. She switched to nibble on a fingernail. *Of course there's nothing to worry over . . . right?*

She plopped down on her bed and fingered the green satin fabric of the dress, revisiting the tempting thought of not attending the wedding. But Daniel felt the need to scrutinize Mr. Wicken, and it would be a shame to miss out on Mrs. Wigginton's efforts. Plus . . . if she was being honest, she wanted to be admired.

The warmhearted housekeeper had done more to the dress than remove the whalebone stays. She had sewn in another layer of soft, cream-colored petticoat. It created a sumptuous contrast to the outer coat's deep emerald green. Frilly strips of lace had been added to the sleeves in the same luscious ivory, and there were matching long gloves and a delicate lace cap to complete the ensemble. After many tiresome minutes of trying to pin her mass of hair beneath it, she gave up and tossed the cap onto the bed. Her hairstyle would remain outdated in that department. A small sacrifice when considering the rest of the costume.

Satisfied she'd done her best in dressing without a looking glass, she descended the stairs, careful not to trip on the many layers of fabric determined to get underfoot. When she reached the bottom step, she glanced up to see everyone sitting around the table, silent and admiring.

"What?" she asked, disconcerted.

Daniel rose from his chair and crossed the few steps to where she stood. He took her hand and bowed low. "Your servant, Miss MacDuff."

She pulled her hand back and laughed at them. "Stop staring, all of you. I wore this very thing not three months back."

"Aye, but you've finally washed behind your ears, I think." Colin grinned stupidly.

She flushed the color of beetroot, and was relieved when Angus shushed the other teasing remarks and said, "The dress suits ye fine, lass."

"I'd agree," her father said. "You've grown into it well—and there's a lot less fidgeting."

"Are *you* the one getting married, then, Miss Jenna?" Tavish asked with widened eyes.

"No!" she said, shaking her head definitively. "Indeed I am not." But looking at Daniel would change most anyone's mind, she thought. A surge of admiration flooded her thoughts as her eyes feasted on his handsome clothes. He wore a gold waistcoat to match his eyes, and an outer coat of black velvet with a lily-white jabot. He adjusted the layered ruffles upon his linen shirt and caught her eye. "Perhaps it's time we leave." He offered Jenna his arm.

"Just a minute." Malcolm leapt from his chair and came toward them. "I've got one more thing for ye, Jenna. Something I think might be appropriate for the evening." Her father opened his sporran and pulled out a fragile gold chain. He crossed behind her and lowered the necklace to settle in the hollow of her throat, fastening it beneath her hair.

She looked down at the finely cut ruby beneath her chin and smiled. "Is it my mother's?"

"It's yours now, lass. I wish ye health to wear it." His face warmed and he turned to grasp her woolen cloak by the doorway. "I think ye best wear this the whole night through. There's a chill out there."

"Then I might as well change back into my old skirt and shift for all anyone will see of the gown." She grabbed a thin shawl and turned to smile at her father. "If I'm cold, I shall dance."

Jenna and Daniel walked through the side entrance of the carriage house. She hoped they might slip in without being noticed, to give her a moment to take in the crowd. Unfortunately, she neglected to consider the fact she'd be on the arm of an individual who'd never had the term *inconspicuous* applied to his description. Therefore, as they walked past the rows of wedding attendees, heads turned and gloved hands covered many whispering mouths. Most people had never seen Daniel before, and he and the clan gave little thought to the need for explaining his presence since he'd soon depart.

She knew the faces of the people they passed, but few of their names, as the men were insistent she stay clear of the house and keep to herself.

The less they ken of us the better, Jenna, her father had said. *Be ever mindful of that notion.*

But she could not help but embrace the kindness of Mrs. Wigginton, or the softening shy nod of Jeb. And even seeing the shabby, desperate efforts of Mr. Wicken brought a piteous form of humor to her day. But there were so many others here as well: the kitchen staff, housekeepers, stable lads, groundskeepers, and footmen employed by the estate. Seeing them dressed in their holiday finery was gladdening, despite the fact that many, like Jenna, wore clothes borrowed from friends and relatives. Most were ill-fitting or sported outdated fashions, the result of gifts from past employers, or secondhand purchases.

The room was thick with an unmistakable air of anticipation, most everyone having just walked from the local parish, where the family's pastor had given the service and married the couple. The Duke of Keswick was to appear shortly to congratulate the pair and begin the celebration in earnest. Jenna and Daniel found a seat toward the back and fell into an easy, quiet conversation about life on the estate.

"I am not allowed friends, but even if I were, I'd find it pointless to make the effort," Jenna commented, aware that people were still turning to stare at them.

"*De veras?* Really? But why?"

"I am stuck between two worlds, Daniel. In one, I have the tongue of the learned, but the look of the lower class, and in the other I have the look of the lower class, but the tongue of a witch. I am viewed with suspicion in both."

"I find that hard to believe, Jenna. You used to make friends with anything that breathed."

"I think there's a considerable gap of time between the ages of twelve and sixteen, from when you last remember me. People change and it is oftentimes a miserable existence."

Daniel nodded. "I agree. On the outside you have altered greatly, and it is a shock to see. But I cannot believe inside you could have changed so much, especially since you were so happy to begin with." He paused, the corners of his mouth rising. "You're no longer a child, Jenna. And although the world is unfolding in front of you in surprising ways, I assure you they will not all be disappointing." Daniel raised his eyebrows and waited for her response, but one of the immense carriage house doors swung open. A rush of cold air created a stir, and everyone turned, craning their necks to watch one of the duke's carriages grandly roll to a stop at the entrance. The duke and duchess stepped out, followed by Lady Lucia and her mother.

The Cliftons were seated at the front of the hall. They smiled and nodded at everyone. Jenna noticed Lord Pembroke wasn't around his parents or Lady Lucia, but the latter was dressed in a gown that made many of the girls seated on the benches groan with envy. The ruby-red velvet fabric was luxuriously thick, and Jenna guessed if Mrs. Wigginton could get hold of the material, she could redecorate the entire house with new curtains, upholstery, and cushions.

Envious as Jenna was over Lady Lucia's holiday apparel, she could not stop her eyes from scanning the room in search of Lord Pembroke. Where was he?

Casually glancing about, she pinpointed Mr. Finch and his faithful companions, Mr. Fowler and Mr. Gainsford. She watched the latter two, in constant playful battle, and it seemed an unremitting source of bother to Mr. Finch. It struck her as odd that Lord Pembroke would maintain a friendship with young men who were so immature in comparison, but she added it to the list of his growing mysteries.

Alex sighed wearily as he stood alongside Mr. Wicken in the back of the hall and watched his friends carrying on with their horseplay. He had agreed to stand as a witness out of consideration for

Mr. Wicken, who was still new on the estate and had yet to find luck making friends. It was providence, then, that the yearly Twelfth Night celebration was to be combined with the wedding party; otherwise, it may have been poorly attended. Alex wondered if it was his mother or Mrs. Wigginton who had whispered into the duke's ear with the sympathetic suggestion. Regardless, he wished for the event to start so it might end quickly. Today had been a monumentally wretched day, and he craved an escape—a chance to be alone and not hounded by those who took note of his every move.

He glanced around, looking for Lady Lucia's mother, the countess—the one most responsible for his current state of distress. She had been a hawk following him these last few days, watching his whereabouts, obviously informed of the conversation her daughter had overheard where Alex had confessed his wishes to be anywhere but there.

The countess had cornered him alone earlier today, her face nervous but resolute. Clutched in her bejeweled fingers was a piece of his mother's fine stationery. She thrust it toward him with a shaky hand.

> *Dearest D,*
>
> *I desire the same of you as always. Rest assured, my friendship is as strong as ever, and I am still of the same opinion.*
>
> *I am ever mindful and grateful for the many essential services you have rendered. You are a tender gardener to my white rose. I am aware of the thrills the white cockade receives at the honor of such favor. Do me the justice to*

believe me at all times, my dear doctor. Pray keep our
tending to this rosebud a secret.

I am heartily glad of our great health and pray God
may keep it so. Remember me with all your affection and
esteem possible. I am with great truth,

Yours,
Charlotte

Alex had lowered the letter. "What is this?"

The countess swallowed and raised her chin. "My security."

"Against what?"

"It is an insurance. If you care for the welfare of your mother—a woman whose scandalous behavior can easily strip her of both title and security—then I suggest you put aside any further interest in altering our future plans."

Alex felt his face drain of color. "You have pried into my mother's personal effects?"

The countess glanced about the empty room. "I have traveled a vast distance and with great cost to see this union come to fruition. If you should be tempted to change your mind and dishonor my family, I will be forced to ruin yours." She snatched the letter from his hands and left with a whirl of skirts and petticoats.

Alex had put a hand to his chest, the bands of matrimonial ties, nothing more than iron clamps, squeezing the breath from him. His mother was . . . having an affair? This was not wholly a surprise, nor was it of such scandalous nature that it would raise more than the odd eyebrow—under normal circumstances. But Alex knew his father, and if he was proven a cuckold, the duke would see that his wife paid an abhorrent price. And whomever "D" was would fare far worse.

The interaction was a blood-chilling memory that now forced him to be ever vigilant of the countess's whereabouts. It also added another worry to the list of growing concerns regarding his mother: the treatment she received from his father, her health, and the revelation of a brewing threat. The countess dangled extortion from her fingertips as easily as colorful beads dangled from her necklaces.

He passed the time scanning the crowd but grew roiled that last-minute guests were still being seated. It was a simple affair. He only needed to walk the couple to the front of the hall, present them to the duke and duchess for a formal congratulations, and then he could be off. But his gaze came to rest upon an unadorned head, one whose color he could recognize at fifty paces. The deep red of Miss MacDuff's hair was unmistakable, long and shiny . . . and now with a man's hand resting on the back of the bench just beneath it.

"Who the devil is that?" Alex said out loud, peering around hats that refused to stand still.

"Oh, that's my aunt Henrietta. She's come all the way from Leeds." Mr. Wicken pointed to a woman standing in the aisle, near the front of the hall.

Alex pulled at the collar of his shirt, damning his tailor for mistaking his measurements. What was the point of explaining who he really meant? Most of them were strangers to Mr. Wicken. He tried getting a better look at the man without encouraging further conversation from the groom. The buzz of voices in the hall made it difficult to hear what anyone was saying, including the person next to him, who was obviously trying to get his attention.

"I beg your pardon?" Alex said.

Mr. Wicken put his hand on Alex's arm and leaned in. "I asked if you were aware there's still the smell of dissension in the air round these parts?"

Good God. Not again.

"No, Mr. Wicken. Since our initial conversation, I am not aware of any discord to speak of." Alex knew full well his father was building the garrison to be prepared for that precise situation. He was also aware of the dangers involved by sharing too much with someone he knew so little. "What sort of talk are you hearing?"

"I've not been privy to any firsthand, milord, but I am aware of a new visitor on the estate, and expect you'd want notice of him."

"A new visitor? Who is this man?"

Mr. Wicken pointed into the crowd, and Alex followed his finger. He caught sight of Miss MacDuff again, her head pitched toward intimacy with the owner of the hand. The dark-haired man spoke into her ear, evidently trying to make conversation easier, but Alex found the man's proximity to her far too close for polite dialogue. When the man raised his head, it was clear this was not one of her clansmen. He appeared a wholly charismatic individual, for Miss MacDuff was intensely drawn to what he was saying, her eyes drinking him in.

The skin on the back of Alex's neck prickled uncomfortably and he turned to feel the heated gaze that came from a pair of eyes solely focused on him. They moved to rest on Miss MacDuff, and then returned to meet his again. The countess was a harbinger of warning.

Again Mr. Wicken tapped him on the shoulder, this time

motioning to the front of the hall, where the parson had just requested their presence. He *needed* to identify Mr. Wicken's stranger, in case there was cause for concern, but in doing so, he would increase the ire of the countess who would only see him studying some female other than Lady Lucia. Damned if he did. Damned if he didn't. Either way, his choices could burn him.

Daniel had much to share with Jenna regarding the four-year absence. His stories held her spellbound. They had barely shared more than a few minutes' conversation, difficult as it was amid the noisy gathering, when Daniel nodded toward the beginning ceremony. She turned just as Mr. Wicken and Lord Pembroke walked past their bench. Lord Pembroke stared with such sharp intensity she felt the swift and unforgiving blush of embarrassment wash over her. Her sudden intake of breath alerted Daniel something was amiss.

"What is it?" He leaned over, concerned, then looked up at the passing groomsman and received an unfriendly glare. "Who's that?"

Jenna didn't answer, but instead kept watch of Lord Pembroke's confident stride as he led the newly married, and clearly nervous, couple toward the duke and duchess. Appraising Mr. Wicken and his young bride, it looked as if they were about to meet their king, and their earnest gravity infected the crowd, which hungered for a taste of pomp and circumstance.

The vicar bestowed a quick blessing on the bride and groom and to the gathered crowd on the eve of Epiphany. A perfunctory kiss passed between the young pair, who then glanced sheepishly at the duke, awaiting his acknowledgment and felicitations.

The duke stood and faced the murmuring crowd. He motioned for silence. "I'd like to express my congratulations to both Master

Wicken and his now good lady wife, Mistress Elizabeth, on their successful nuptials. I'm sure I speak for all present when I say we wish them good fortune for the future." He turned and motioned for his wife to join him.

The duchess rose slowly, her face blank as she greeted the crowd before her. Her eyes swept over the guests and paused for a moment where Daniel and Jenna sat, and then carried on through the rest of the room. Jenna smiled. *Even the duchess has an eye for the handsome.* The woman was wrapped in a fur-trimmed cloak that all but hid the festive dress she wore beneath it, and Jenna wondered if the duchess felt the cold more than others. She looked bone-weary and eager for the whole affair to end.

The duke continued, "This evening we will also celebrate Twelfth Night, and shortly the tables and chairs will be arranged so Mrs. Wigginton's yearly feast may be presented. We wish you each a prosperous New Year. All hail the king!"

An abundance of cheers rose around Jenna. She saw many of the faces, not yet red with drink, clear-eyed and enthusiastic, heartily echoing the duke and his sentiments. Daniel raised a furtive eyebrow and leaned over to murmur, "*Sí*, all hail the king."

She shifted uncomfortably in her seat, and seeing movement just past Daniel's shoulder, noticed Mr. Gainsford and Mr. Fowler poking at each other in an attempt at swordplay without actual accoutrements. She rolled her eyes and turned her attentions back toward the duke, who still addressed the crowd.

"This being Twelfth Night, one is obliged to follow proper procedure. The Lord of Misrule must be named, and then I will find myself and my wife a quick departure, for before long, the pursuit of merriment will surpass good sense."

He surveyed the room and spotted Mr. Fowler and Mr. Gainsford, still engaged in foolish trifling. He thrust a finger at the former and bellowed, "There is your man! Hugh Fowler shall reign as your Lord of Misrule. I can think of no finer person suited for the position."

Mr. Fowler looked up and let a broad smile spread across his features. His eyes filled with mischief while scanning those around him. They alighted upon a fleshy-faced woman with a tall, feathered cap. He bounded to her in two princely leaps and, to the crowd's delight, plucked the adornment from her head and placed it on his own. He then sprung himself upon the nearest table and caught an oak walking stick Mr. Gainsford tossed to him. His scepter in hand, he bowed low to his audience and declared, "I humbly accept the honor cast upon me and promise a night of delicious debauchery."

The crowd hooted with pleasure.

"The chairs and tables, my friends!" Mr. Fowler shouted.

Men sprang from their seats and pushed creaking benches to the far sides of the room. The tables began filling with Mrs. Wigginton's procession of enticing dishes, all paraded in by the young maids from the kitchens. Jenna was about to tell Daniel she felt it best they head back to the cottage, when Mr. Fowler clapped for attention.

"As usual, the Lord of Misrule is in charge of the evening's festivities, and in the traditional manner of Twelfth Night, everything one might expect is turned upside down and reversed. So to launch the celebrations, the choice of the first dance is given to the women."

There was a great stir among the audience—sounds of delight from the female half of the group as they hastily scanned the men. The musicians took up their instruments, brightly colored streamers hanging from their scrolls. The party officially began by way of Mr. Fowler shouting from atop his perch and encouraging anyone he saw peering tentatively around to sift through the riffraff and find a suitable dance partner.

"Do not fall for the first pair of pleading eyes you come upon. Be choosy. Be specific. Demand a dowry up front!" The men responded with spirited laughter, and the women set about with serious intent.

Jenna noticed several women making their way toward them with purposeful strides, their ardent eyes fixed on Daniel, prey to be speared. She turned to face him and was again about to suggest they leave—or at the very least, that *she* leave—when Daniel spoke.

"*Pídeme que baile.* Ask me to dance." He ignored the look of surprise on her face and grabbed her hand to lead her to the dance floor. Jenna noted they'd left behind a gathering of girls, crestfallen at what appeared as an inequitable stroke of good fortune in her favor. Jenna bit her lip, suppressing a smile, and let Daniel lead her into the crowd.

Alex stood in the front of the hall with the newlyweds. He'd observed the entire interaction between Miss MacDuff and the mystery man from his position, and watched a dozen brazen women push others out of their way to get there first. Even his mother's eyes strayed to the dark-haired man during his father's speech.

Lady Lucia's intent was clear and meant to attract attention as she cut a wide swath through the crowd to where Alex stood. When she reached him, he bowed and extended his hand. "You look lovely," he said, forcing a smile of welcome.

"Much too lovely for an occasion such as this, I think." She eyed the hall with distaste. "There is dirt on the floor, and my dress is sure to be the recipient of it."

"Mrs. Wigginton will be most willing to put forth whatever efforts necessary to restore your dress. Do not fret, milady." Alex attempted a cheerful facade. He gently whirled her through the throngs of other dancers, and scanned the crowd for Miss MacDuff and her partner.

Lady Lucia stiffened in response. "I most certainly do fret. I worry that perhaps this is what one would think was an appropriate place to hold *our* wedding." She narrowed her eyes. "Although, after hearing recent revelations, I am to understand that there may *be* no wedding. That you are simply taking time to make a thorough fool out of me." She refocused her features and stared off in the distance.

He politely acknowledged the heated gaze of the countess and took a slow breath in before continuing. "I apologize profusely for how my simple confession of momentary frustration upset you, milady. And I assure you"—he swallowed—"my intentions are dependable."

They must be, Alex thought glumly, *as I have no other choice.*

He stole a glance at Miss MacDuff and the stylish man, bitterly resigned to his future. The two danced gracefully, their eyes locked as they spoke. And clearly she was not aware of the many eyes focused on them, which might have been a blessing, for most of the women looked as if they would happily claw their way through her to be next in line to dance with the stranger.

Daniel spoke in furtive tones and leaned in close so no one would overhear. He asked Jenna about the duke and his family, who everyone was, and what she knew of them.

She answered him honestly. "I don't know any of them well, but first impressions speak a lot in my book." She glanced around. "Most of the people here work on the estate. You saw the duke and duchess. They play their parts well.

"They have a son"—her eyes briefly settled on Lord Pembroke and his betrothed—"who's soon to be married. I heard his bride-to-be is utterly controlling. He doesn't deserve that."

Daniel proved most perceptive. "And what does he deserve?"

She blushed. "I don't know. Something else. Some*one* else. Could be anyone but her." She steeled her features. "Observe the girl for five minutes and you'll know what I'm speaking about."

"I see," he said, and raised an eyebrow. "Any others you've developed an aversion to?"

"Well, there are Lord Pembroke's friends from school—two of which are tippling buffoons. I can't imagine why he keeps them around. And another"—she bit her lip—"who keeps a spot close to the hearth, which he guards with bared teeth."

"Jenna," Daniel said, leaning in, "did you ever consider that these were people the son *must* mingle with? That he has little say in those who surround him because he is being groomed for a political position?"

"But he has a *choice*. His family has money. It shouldn't be that hard."

"Not necessarily. There are those in this world who feel that choice is out of their hands, and you must admire the strength it takes on their part to fulfill the destiny chosen for them."

She shook her head with skepticism.

"There is the chance that what this young man wants is worth the unhappy marriage and the pestering friends. Do you know what he is after?"

Jenna felt her heart skip a beat. *What is he after?*

The choice to study what moved him? A life unshackled from duty? Meaningful friendship? And as much as he denounced his attraction to politics, he spoke with a voice that demonstrated a passionate position.

Perhaps he was a loyal supporter of the House of Hanover. She thought about the garrison plans. "I . . . I don't know," she answered, feeling a bloom of doubt seep through her veins. "I don't know enough about him."

Daniel smiled. "*Chiquita*, you are yet understandably naïve about the world. As much as it goes against your ideals for integrity, people will do things not initiated by love or friendship if it means they'll get what they want in the end. If it is as you say, it may be possible this young man is highly motivated by political gain. Power and money may not make good bedfellows for you, but for some . . . there is little else that will entertain them."

"He's not like that," Jenna said brusquely.

He raised a brow, his eyes widening. "I thought you were unacquainted with him."

"Overall," she said, stopping mid-dance, desperate to hide the measure of their friendship. "It's just . . . he doesn't come across that way."

The music stopped, and people, still well mannered, politely clapped and looked up to where Mr. Fowler whirled about for attention.

"Now, simply to be fair before the women become wanton, the men will have their chance to choose. Ladies, put on your best faces, and do be gracious if old Mr. Gainsford here comes and asks for a twirl." Mr. Fowler ducked as his friend had thrown an orange.

Lady Lucia parted the other dancers around her and ignored the new instructions. She sailed toward Daniel. "*Scusi*," she said thickly to Jenna and pointed at Daniel, "but I will dance with *you* now."

Jenna threw Daniel a look of *I told you so* and backed up graciously. He gave the impression of being thoroughly amused, but bowed to the forthright young woman. Turning her head, Jenna met the even, fixed stare of Mr. Finch from across the room. She hastily searched for the nearest exit from the hall, hoping for a break from the jostling crowd and penetrating eyes. She found a side entrance behind the fiddlers, wrapped her shawl about her shoulders, and opened the door to the crisp bite of night air.

Mere moments passed before she heard the door behind her click and Lord Pembroke's voice. "Too warm inside?"

She turned to face him, his eyes washed silvery pale in the dim light of the moon, like those of a ghost. His voice was flat but resolute. "Who is he?"

She raised a brow in question, scrambling for an answer she hadn't prepared.

"Your guest."

"An old family friend."

"Another member of your clan?"

"Far from it." She smirked without meaning to. She watched him stiffen, and his eyes grew dark, pupils widening.

"How long have you known him?" He took a step closer in.

"I have always known him," Jenna answered truthfully, trying to remain calm.

"From where does he come? Is he here to help with the garrison?"

She felt her face tighten, and the butterflies in her stomach began their familiar flutter. "What does it matter?"

"It does matter—a great deal. Withinghall is my *home*. It's very important that I know everyone who visits or takes residence here, for the safety of all concerned."

"Really?"

"You find my interest unfounded?"

Jenna opened her mouth to respond, but he continued.

"You of all people should realize the seriousness of the situation. You and your family . . . building the garrison?"

Jenna was positive her face betrayed the angst that sat like a stone in her stomach. Did he know what was going on? She took a deep breath. "Of course, the garrison," she began innocently. "Terrible times." She had to move the conversation away from this dangerous topic. "His name is Daniel Delafuente. He's Spanish by birth, but makes a point of not staking claim to any particular soil long enough to become a resident in it. He's probably the most fascinating person I am acquainted with. And when I was twelve, I decided to leave all I knew and loved behind to become his wife and journey with him."

"At twelve." Lord Pembroke's response was a simple statement of clarification rather than a question, but his face showed something unreadable. "Are you betrothed to him, then?"

"Promised? No! I was twelve."

"I meant perhaps by your family."

She grimaced. "My father would never arrange *my* marriage." No sooner were the words out of her mouth than she realized her blunder. She cast her glance downward and took in a slow breath. "What I meant was . . ." She pressed her lips inward to keep from saying anything further.

"I see," Lord Pembroke began. "Well, now that you're . . . what— sixteen?"

"Almost seventeen."

"Almost seventeen—and are far more experienced in such matters—are you still planning to run away with him?" It was as penetrating a gaze as Jenna had ever felt.

She understood the men in her family by their guttural sounds, unfathomable to anyone who wasn't Scottish. And Daniel controlled everything about himself. You knew only what he decided to reveal. But this person who stood before her, a hair too close for courtesy, baffled her, as she'd never had anyone pay her such curious attention that she could not define.

"Well, he wouldn't have me at twelve, and I haven't restated the offer . . . ," she joked. Had she not been paying close attention, the slight twitch of his jaw would have passed unseen. She wished she had simply answered yes or no, but it was too late to reel her flip reply back in.

Lord Pembroke was silent, his gaze fixed upon the tiny ruby at her neck she nervously fingered. She let it rest at her throat and pulled her shawl tighter about her shoulders as the cold wind blew around her face. She shivered. He looked up and said, "Something has come to my attention—something awful and grave. I am saddened immeasurably to say this, but it forces me to end our friendship."

Jenna's lungs crushed together within her rib cage, and her heart stopped dead in her chest. The plans. Had he decoded them? Was her family in danger? She panicked. Bursting into a flurry of movement, she turned to run, but he caught her by the elbow and wheeled her back to face him. Bewilderment spread across his face, his eyes searching for an explanation.

"I have to go," she tried to say solidly, but it came out as a whisper. She put her hand over his and tried to remove it, but his grip was firm. She wanted to run and she wanted to stay. The details around her were so precise: the moon haloing the back of his head, the music seeping through the cracks of the wooden carriage house, the people laughing inside it. She smelled pungent smoke from the nearby kitchens where the food had been prepared, and saw his breath meet the cold air, then turn misty and white. Growing close enough to mix with hers.

"Yes, I think it's time we leave."

At Daniel's words, Lord Pembroke dropped his hand as if he'd touched fire and looked up. Daniel's face was grave and tight-lipped. He walked the few remaining steps to where Jenna stood and took her by the elbow. Turning to Lord Pembroke, he made a curt bow and said, "Good evening, sir, and I was led to believe congratulations on your upcoming *marriage* are in order."

Jenna's cheeks flushed with unwelcome heat, and she fought to steady her panicked breath as Daniel led her away.

What have I done? Her thoughts screamed in her head. *Or, more important, what have I un done?*

TWENTY-TWO

JENNA'S FATHER PACED THE FLOOR IN FRONT OF THE fire. The other men sat in their usual spots, apart from Ian, who stared out the window by the door. He rubbed a shoulder that stretched the fabric of his shirt across his back.

"I ken she'd get us in trouble one day—and dinna say I havena warned ye." Ian spoke out of the side of his mouth, his voice a low growl, but Jenna could hear from upstairs, the door to her room opened a crack. She rested her head on the frame and closed her eyes, mindlessly allowing the sharp edge of her *sgian dubh* to trace the pink-ridged scar along her palm.

"Said she needed a tighter rein, and all I got was grief, aye?"

"Be quiet, Ian," Malcolm snapped. "We've precious little information as to what the duke's son knows—if anything. And I willna have ye passing judgment on anyone unfairly."

Jenna's stomach pretzeled and writhed from where she sat listening.

Most of her discomfort stemmed from her secret—that she'd mistakenly revealed the method to decipher the garrison's codes.

How was I to know that my daily math assignment was not simply some pleasurable number riddle?!

She peered down, watching her father walk to the table and take a swig from his glass. "Daniel only heard the words *our friendship* before steppin' in to interrupt."

"Doesn't it seem likely he was trying to canvass information from her?" Ian asked. "Perhaps he was tryin' to sway her to see the plans again!"

"Even if he did," Angus spoke up, "what could he make of them? They're nothing but a bunch of lines to anyone save us. They're coded!"

Angus rose from his chair, grabbed an iron poker, and jabbed at a few bits in the fire. Sparks exploded upward in bright bursts of orange. "Jenna said he wanted to ken who Daniel was, that's all."

But that wasn't all, she thought, curling tightly around her knees. What would the men do if they discovered Lord Pembroke *could* break the code? Would they immediately pack up and haul out—or would they head out to hunt him down? She couldn't imagine the men doing anything drastic to silence the young man.

And was Lord Pembroke telling her that he'd uncovered their schemes? His words hung in the air:

Something has come to my attention—something awful and grave.

Awful enough to end their friendship, but was it awful enough to end their lives?

Malcolm sighed heavily from below. "I say we wait to see what

Daniel comes up with. It's about this time most of the free liquor's been drunk and the men who've taken advantage of it will be more than keen to waggle their tongues wi' a man who'll spend his coin for their drink. He's most canny, that Daniel. If there's news out there that's shining a light on our cottage—he'll find it."

Jenna felt relief, however slight it was. She remembered how Daniel had grabbed her by the elbow and pulled her away, a bull barely controlling the urge to charge. She was certain Lord Pembroke had been watching.

"What were you thinking?" Daniel had growled as he hauled her toward the cottage. "I mean, Jenna, of all the people . . . why him? You do realize who he is, don't you?"

She skittered on an icy patch, but Daniel held her arm firmly so she wouldn't fall.

"Of course I know who he is, but I also know I haven't done anything."

"He was trying to elicit information from you!" Daniel hissed.

She tried to remain calm, for she'd never seen Daniel angry, and certainly not with her, but she was resolute in her defense. "The only information he was trying to extract was whether I was betrothed to *you*. And I think the behavior you just displayed suggested exactly that."

"Good."

Jenna's head snapped around to look at him. "Good?"

"Let him think that's the reason I interrupted your intimate conversation. I'm only grateful to the man Mr. Finch for coming to inform me my escort might be in need of assistance. Any number of things could have taken place had I not come when I did." Daniel kept his eyes forward and didn't meet her look of incredulity.

"I wasn't about to tell him anything," she insisted.

Daniel had stopped at the threshold to the cottage, his hand on the door. "There were many things you told him . . . without uttering a word." It was the last thing Daniel said before they entered the house and her interrogation began.

After telling and retelling the events, she was brusquely dismissed to her bedroom, where Tavish was already asleep. She undid the maddening hooks and fastenings that bound her into the borrowed dress, slipped into her cotton shift and wrapped a heavy shawl around herself for warmth. And she sat watching through the loft door crack ever since.

Daniel had been sent out to gather information about any suspicions that might be forming regarding the men or the garrison, but had she ruined everything? Would they now conclude she was a liability they could no longer afford, and that discussions would— nay, *must* lead them to where she'd be sent? She recalled the talk she and her father had on the bank of the river. He was serious in her consideration of leaving them. At the time, she'd interpreted his offer as being with her comfort and safety in mind. She hadn't given a thought to theirs.

She heard the front door open and close, and the scuffling of chairs. Then Daniel's voice. She held her breath and waited to hear if it was time to pack and depart. It wouldn't be the first time, but it would be the first time because one of their own had made an error.

"Nothing," she heard Daniel tell the others. "Most think there are a few local rebels closer into town. They're pretty closemouthed. Not so foolish to spread their opinions to just anyone, soused or not."

A collective sigh permeated the room. "I blame myself for the scare," she heard her father say. "I should've taken the plans myself, and I didna talk to her about explaining Daniel's presence."

"None of us did, Malcolm. Dinna fash yourself over it," Colin said. She saw his long-limbed figure sit back down and stretch. "What's done is done, and now we best get on wi' how to prepare her come next time—should there be one."

Jenna's breath caught, filled with the flicker of hope.

"She needs to be sent away." There was no doubt in her mind who said that. "Ye promised her mother ye'd protect her, Malcolm. She's either going to get herself killed or all of us—but nonetheless, you're ignoring the woman's final plea!" She saw Ian stand. His jaw was set firm, his eyes hard as he challenged the leader of their group.

Malcolm moved slowly toward Ian. His voice was as low as the growl from a dog. "I said . . . not a word more from you about it." Malcolm's eyes blazed hot and black, his bulk filling more space than seemed possible. There was a flash of rebellion in Ian's glare, but it was quickly covered.

Malcolm turned to face the rest of the men. "It's time we all find our beds. In the morning we'll speak to Jenna and set things straight, aye?"

Everyone agreed and Jenna silently closed the door to the murmurs of good nights. She crawled her way back to bed and slid beneath the cold quilts. But her mind would not quiet. It wrestled with the uneasy realization that once again, Mr. Finch had her in his sights.

She woke in the night, shivering, and all attempts to welcome sleep back proved impossible. She wrapped her warmest shawl around her and grabbed the quilt from the floor. She would stoke the fire downstairs and warm herself in front of it for a while. But the flames had already been revived. Daniel sat at the table, his head bent low. He read by the light of a candle and the quivering glow from the hearth. Upon spotting him, she thought better of interrupting his privacy and turned to reenter her room.

"Jenna, don't leave," he said.

She looked back at him, but his head was still over his papers.

He spoke again. "Don't turn away on my behalf. I'm inviting you to come down, if you wish."

The breath she hadn't realized she was holding escaped. She tiptoed down the stairs, careful not to trip on the quilt as it dragged along the floor. "I wouldn't want to disturb you," she said stiffly, and walked to the water jug. She glanced to the table where he sat. "Would you like tea? I'm making some."

He nodded and kept reading. Jenna busied herself for the next few minutes heating the water over the fire and preparing the cups. She placed a mug beside his papers and sat on the bench a few spaces away. "What are you reading?" she asked, sipping her tea.

"The Mishnah," Daniel said, without looking up.

"Is it a novel?"

"*En absoluto*. By no means."

"Well, what, then? It doesn't sound Latin or Greek," she said, peering over to see the writings.

He raised his head. "It is the Oral Law. Discussions and decisions made to interpret what God said in the Torah."

"You mean the Hebrew Bible?"

"Some would call it that. 'Torah' means teachings, or laws, and in this case, the Law of Moses. It is what the Jewish people must do, must follow, and sometimes without question."

Daniel took a sip from his cup and eyed Jenna speculatively. After a moment, he said, "Your father and Angus said you have studied well these last few years. They said your curiosity has propelled your education."

"I suppose it has," she answered with a halfhearted shrug.

"For many, knowledge is a great risk."

"I don't understand."

"Well, to find a servant girl who can read is not unheard-of. One who can read in several languages—if only passably—figure mathematics, and discuss philosophy and logic—is a rare find. It marks you as unusual."

"So I've been told," she said dryly.

"The thing is," he went on, "you may not understand that all of the knowledge you've been given carries responsibility with it. But to be truly responsible with it you must obtain something that no one can give you. It is an instinct one gains through experience. *La confianza*. Figuring out who to trust." He swung his leg over the bench to face her. "I read the Mishnah away from other eyes because there are many who would do me harm upon seeing it. You cannot help the family you are born into, but I think you can help direct your fate thereafter, if you are wise.

"Many people have secrets," he continued, "and are capable of working with others, never revealing what must be hidden. We all keep information back. I'm sure even you do, although you never could play cards." He raised his eyebrows at this, but Jenna noted his face displayed a matter-of-fact expression, rather than the mirth she wished to see.

"The time has come. Your father and these men are risking their lives to do what they feel necessary. You are peripherally involved, and put an element of chance into their situation. They question whether it is safe for you to be here, and whether having you here is safe for *them*. They need to know you will follow what it is they ask of you . . . unquestionably. I do not know that you can." He returned his gaze to the pages on the table.

Jenna held her jaws together and willed her pulse to slow. "Have you quite finished?" she asked tightly. She received no response from Daniel and ventured further. "You come back after four years of absence and treat me as if I were an ill-behaved child?"

He looked up to meet her seething gaze, his own eyes simmering. He crossed his arms. "That criticism is unfounded, and your exaggeration rather illustrates the fact that you are currently *speaking* as an ill-behaved child."

She spluttered in astonishment.

"Do you realize that had you been a man, and circumstances unfolded as they have, where your irresponsibility may have put this entire process in jeopardy and everyone's lives at stake, the first thing the clan would have done is flogged you?"

Yes, she thought with a flutter of alarm, *they might have.* But her clan was *different.* They would *never* elect that option.

"I've said it before, Jenna: you are no longer a child, but you are new at being a woman, and as such, your family has exercised a great deal of control. You would not have gotten off so easily in any other household."

She stood and balled the quilt in her arms. There was no doubt she had little use for it now. She was livid. Heat rushed through her veins, making her fingertips tingle. Yes, she knew these things, and she'd been carrying around the guilt and the fear from that reality for the last several days. But she didn't want *Daniel* to be the one bringing it bubbling up to the surface. And so she cast her dagger of anger at him.

She backed away from the table toward the stairs and hissed, "I may be new at being a woman, Daniel, but I believe your own maturity has slipped back to a level of barbarianism." She marched upstairs, bristling with anger. When she reached the top of the landing, she glanced quickly at Daniel, who had chosen no response other than to return to his reading, a small smile on his face as he shook his head.

TWENTY-THREE

TWO WEEKS WENT BY WITH NARY AN ADVENTURE OR escape from the cottage. Jenna knew she was being watched, and everyone went to great pains to remind her how to avoid suspicion and detect oncoming trouble.

She spent a good deal of time trying to convince her father that allowing her to stay was in the best interest for both of them. He wavered. In fact, he presented her with a proposal. The men had been called to an overnight meeting a few hours north. It was a "Stuart supporters" conclave, and a dangerous one. Last week, Mrs. Wigginton had asked if Jenna would be available to help with inventory of the storage cellars, a two-day job. Malcolm thought it was a fine solution all around.

"Ye needn't go to the clan gathering, ye'll be safe wi' Mrs. Wigginton, *and* ye'll get a taste of working in a fine house—something to keep in the back of your mind as an option for employment."

Jenna felt certain that disagreeing with her father would be perceived as ingratitude, so she would stay at the house with the rest of the girls . . . for one night.

That morning, she and Angus were making bread for the week while the others were on the site of the garrison. Shortly, the men would be leaving for the north, and Jenna would head up to the kitchens, but they had a little time together before departure.

The flour lay in a vast wooden bowl between them, and they scooped a handful of it whenever the dough became sticky and unmanageable.

"Have I been forgiven, do you think?" Jenna said suddenly, as she wrestled with her mound of dough.

"Well, now, that depends upon who we're talking about."

"I would imagine most everyone apart from Ian?"

"Aye, maybe." His dismissive manner did little to calm her anxiety.

"Why does he stay, Angus? He argues with Da about every decision, seemingly on principle—and he clearly despises *me*; why doesn't he simply leave?"

Angus gave her a sharp look. "Ian supports this cause wholeheartedly—he's just . . . meticulous of nature and guards all our blindness. But as far as *you*? *Despise* ye?" He shook his head and looked heavenward. "Good God, no—not even close. He'd lay his life down for ye, Jenna. You're his *family*."

Jenna snorted, but decided not to waste any more time debating that opinion. "What about Daniel? Is he still grumbling?"

"Pay it no mind, lass. He's just not used to seeing you all

grown-up like, ye ken?"

"Is it that I'm taller? Or more conversational? Or opinionated? What exactly is it about me that vexes him so?" Jenna scowled.

"More like the fact you were about to be kissed," Angus said, not looking up from his work.

"I wasn't. It's not true. It—it never happened," she said, her face flushing.

"Aye, but I believe what really bothers him is that he thinks ye *wanted* it to."

She sat down and put her head onto the table, her floury hands still resting on the dough. "Maybe it's true, Angus, and I'm too ashamed to admit it." There. She said it. Relief came in fragmented bits, like the quenching of thirst to a parched throat.

With his hands covered in flour, there was little physical comforting he could offer, but he put aside his dough and sat down across from her. He patted her powdery hands, trying to ease her embarrassment. "Do ye think you're such an abhorrent individual you should be unlike everyone else? That ye shouldna crave love? Do ye believe none of us have ever gone through the same as you? When I recall the number of times I've gotten my hide tanned for doing things I shouldna have—and most of them dealing wi' girls an such like—I'm surprised I still have a backside agreeable enough to sit upon." He sighed loudly and, as a result, blew a tiny cloud of flour onto her head. He squeezed her hands until she looked up, flour on her nose and forehead. Angus smiled at the sight.

"If it's not such a horrible thing to want, then what's created Daniel's disdain?" She looked sadly at him.

"Perhaps your taking him off his pedestal. He left us last wi' ye clinging to his shirttail, talking of nothing but adventure and how you'd perish wi'out him. 'Tis a hard slap in the face when ye come back to see people have moved on, and ye werena there to see it happen and ye werena there to make it so." Angus patted her hands. "He wants nothing more than to protect ye, as he's always done."

"That's ridiculous," Jenna said quietly. "I'm not twelve anymore."

Angus got up and gathered his dough. He bit his lower lip, which made his beard sprout hedgehog-like, and then overcame his hesitation. "That's what he said."

Jenna counted the minutes until it was time to leave, relishing the idea of tallying supplies to clear her head. At this point she would agree to anything that would free her from a house full of overbearing and overprotective men. The opportunity came a little earlier than expected, when one of Mrs. Wigginton's kitchen boys arrived requesting that Jenna collect some bottles from her at the ale house.

Angus nodded to her, "She probably wants to get a head start on the work. Ye best take your things and head up. We'll see you tomorrow on our return."

She wrapped herself in the warmest woolen cloak she owned and waited as Angus cased the freshly baked bread loaves in cloth.

"Here. Take this to Mrs. Wigginton. Tell her I'm willing to put my rye against her wheat any day. If she wants the recipe, she'll have to part wi' hers for the syllabub." Angus winked and gave her a rough hug and the bundle, its warmth still radiating from within.

She stepped out into a January day grim enough to depress the stoutest of constitutions. The ale house was located behind the kitchens, its path muddy from the cold rains of the last two weeks. The rain had also left the air smelling of damp earth and leaf mold, scents Jenna felt glad were the same in both England and Scotland. Upon reaching the rough oak door of the ale house, she turned the handle and peered inside.

"Mrs. Wigginton?" She poked her head in and was greeted by the pungent smell of hops. A chair scraped against the floor. She slipped in and closed the door. "Mrs. Wigginton?" Jenna called again, allowing her eyes a moment to adjust to the room's murky light.

"Not exactly," said a voice that most assuredly did not belong to the housekeeper.

Jenna gasped as Mr. Finch's face came into focus. He sat at the round table in the middle of the room and moved a candle in front of him.

"What are you doing here?" she demanded, a slight coppery note springing to the back of her throat. "Mrs. Wigginton asked me to collect some bottles. Where is she?"

"Hmm . . . an obedient girl for some, but you'll ignore the sage advice of others," Mr. Finch said, his jaw firm, and his eyes narrow. "How is it you decide whose bidding you'll do, because you certainly have taken no notice of mine? I saw you leave the carriage house, and you somehow compelled my friend to follow you. Your campaign to divert his habits of mind is about to bring him ruin."

She heard the scuffle of feet and recognized Mr. Fowler and Mr. Gainsford as they came out from behind the barrels by the door. She turned to reach for the door handle, but Mr. Fowler made his way to it first.

"Oh, don't leave—you'll spoil the party. Julian says Alex finds you most entertaining, so perhaps you'll amuse us for a spell while you're waiting on Mrs. Wigginton."

"Yes, don't be in a hurry to go on our account. Come here—we've much to discuss," Mr. Finch drawled.

"You wouldn't dare—" Jenna began.

"Dare what? Dare to be as bold as you? Dare to do as we wish, despite the consequences?"

A wave of cold dread washed over her as she realized what they intended to do. "I will scream," she said, her eyes darting between Mr. Finch and Mr. Gainsford.

"That you might," Mr. Finch countered. "Thank you for the warning."

A surge of terror ran up her spine and she swallowed hard to rid herself of the rising fear.

Mr. Finch pushed himself away from the table and edged toward her.

"You really don't want to do this," Jenna said, trying to stay her hands.

"Oh, but I must," Mr. Finch retorted.

"I won't tell them what I know about you," she promised, cutting her gaze toward Gainsford. "It's not their business, in any case."

Fowler snorted. "What in the hell is she talking about, Julian?"

Mr. Finch rushed at her, grabbing her by the throat with one hand and pinning her against the cold stone wall. "I'll tell you what's *my* business. Meddling wenches who forget their place."

He wrenched her neck forward and, before she could react, snapped it back again toward the wall.

"Now wait a second, Julian," Jenna heard Mr. Gainsford call out. She felt a sharp pain at the back of her head where it hit the wall, and blinked her eyes against the tiny starbursts floating in front of them. It was hard to breathe with his hand encircling her neck. His breath smelled of licorice.

She dropped the bread and brought her knee up sharp and fast. When her foot came up, she grasped the small dirk she kept strapped to her calf. Mr. Finch hunched over, sputtered, and tried to upright himself. Jenna fumbled to toss off her cloak and untangle the *sgian dubh* from her skirts.

She heard Mr. Finch choke out the words, "Grab her," to Mr. Gainsford.

"What?" Mr. Gainsford cried. "Julian, you said we were simply going to give her a fright."

Jenna finally managed to pull the knife out. She held it in front of her and scrambled to the other side of the table and chairs. Her breath was shallow with fear, and she could not calm her beating heart.

Mr. Gainsford stood dumbly in place, peering at his friend. "I suggest we simply leave, as I'm not very fond of knives—"

"Just help me!" Finch hissed.

He circled in front. Mr. Gainsford lunged and grabbed Jenna awkwardly from behind. It was clear he was not much of a fighter. He gave Jenna the split second she needed to jam her elbow into his stomach. But she also struck a bone on what must have been a very solid buckle, and gasped as a burst of pain shot down her arm. Her fingers went numb and the dirk dropped.

"A good blow to the stomach is never enough to stay one's

attacker," the men had instructed her. "You must also render them incapable of walking for a few moments to aid your escape." Jenna brought the back of her heel down with a bone-cracking force and hoped to hit the target. Mr. Gainsford doubled over in pain, and for the briefest moment, she was given the necessary time to concentrate on Mr. Finch.

The dirk had skittered across the floor a few feet in front of her, and both she and Mr. Finch lunged for it. He managed to reach for the knife with one hand and shoved her away with the other, the side of her head crashing into the heavy wooden table next to them. She fell to her knees and found her vision become a tunnel, her focus of the floor fading. She wrenched air back into her lungs and looked up to see Mr. Finch on all fours, watching her.

She grasped the table for support, the pain in her head making her crazed with anger. "They don't know, do they, Mr. Finch? And so to keep your secret—" But before she could finish her words he launched himself and pulled her to her feet. He wrapped a hand over her mouth and then set the cold blade of her *sgian dubh* against the hollow of her throat.

"I might have guessed correctly at your poor parentage and upbringing," he panted, "but I must admit . . . I underestimated the amount of gumption you have." The words rushed out of his mouth in bursts, and Jenna could feel each rise of his chest in search of air. "Well . . . no one can accuse you of just lying down . . . and playing dead, can they? It seems you're willing to hurt anyone who gets in your way."

Jenna felt the sharp prick of the knife pierce her skin.

"But what to do with you now? What will leave a permanent

reminder . . . that you may not claw your way . . . out of the filthy class you were born in?" His breath was hot in her ear. His anger squeezing the air from her lungs. "Nor can you drag Alex down into it."

The sound of frantic voices outside made them both stiffen.

"You must *do* something! I can't stop him!"

The ale house door burst open and Lord Pembroke charged in, panicked. She saw Mr. Fowler behind him. Both of their faces were wide with alarm.

"Let go of her, Julian!"

The words sounded far away. Pinpricks of light dotted her vision again as the vise around her chest increased. The last thing she saw before slumping to the floor was Lord Pembroke's fist driving into Mr. Finch's face.

TWENTY-FOUR

JENNA WOKE IN SOMEONE ELSE'S BED. SHE OPENED her eyes and took in the low ceiling and whitewashed walls, all bathed in flickering amber light. Shadows fluttered on the wall, a fair imitation of children's puppetry. She closed her eyes again and tried to escape the blurry vision and throbbing pains in her head. *Am I ill?*

She brought her hand to her forehead in search of fever, came to rest on a bandage just above her temple, and recognized the source of one of her pains. The other tender area was on the back of her head—a modest lump, but impressive enough to jar her memory.

Carefully, she sat up on her elbows and tried to focus on the rest of the room. There was the strong but not unpleasant smell of food permeating the air. A door to her right was closed to whatever lay beyond it. On the other side, a slender shelf attached to the wall held a few books and a polished wooden cross, which sat atop a lace doily. Tavish leaned his head against the shelf. His eyes were shut, but his mouth was open. At his feet lay a sack of almonds. His lap cradled a bowl, divided into two segments: shelled and unshelled nuts.

Her eyes edged to the left, for moving them quickly brought on a searing pain, and objects swirled haphazardly if she wasn't cautious. The dithering light, a beeswax candle, rested in a thick pewter base and burned on a sturdy wooden cupboard along the far wall, opposite the bed. Its flame quivered from a feathery breeze, the source flowing from the breath of a slumbering figure in the wooden chair next to the hutch.

She squinted. A pair of long legs splayed in front of the chair. One hand grasped a strip of gauze and the other propped a head from falling to a chest. Lord Pembroke's face was turned toward the candlelight, a deep crease between his fair brows.

The light attached itself to his features, and she stared for a moment, watching him doze, but felt it almost voyeuristic to satisfy her curiosity when he was clearly unaware. It was then she realized her own vulnerable state and saw that apart from the warm quilts covering her on the little cot, she wore nothing but her shift. Where were her things and who had removed them? She panicked at the thought of Lord Pembroke having seen her in this state of undress, snatched the quilt to her chin, and lunged to get out of bed.

Her head reeled and she grasped it, falling back against the cot. She moaned in response to the hammering throb.

Lord Pembroke woke to the sound and leapt to his feet. He scrambled to the side of the bed. Blinking back sleep and fumbling for wakefulness, he gushed, "Miss MacDuff, you're awake. Thank

God." He snatched her hand and pulled it to his chest just above his heart, searching her face and squeezing her fingers. Her eyes shot fully open and he pulled back, alarmed at his own actions. He quickly replaced her hand on the cot and stood, stuttering. "I . . . I'm so sorry. My apologies." He rolled his eyes skyward and let out a deep breath. "I'm just . . . so relieved you're okay."

"Okay?" Jenna groaned. "Of course. This is how I feel every day. How could I have forgotten?"

His shoulders relaxed a little and he rubbed his eyes. "What I meant was, I don't think you've been done any permanent harm. And you're safe here."

She peeked from behind the hands cradling her head and squinted at him. "Am I? I am in nothing but my shift, lying in someone else's bed, in front of a person I barely know. Apparently, this is a sense I have not yet associated with the term *safe*."

He chuckled. "Well, at least we know you still have your wits."

She sighed and pulled the quilt closer to her chin. "Somehow, I don't think that was what those abominable men were after." She paused and glanced at the sleeping young Tavish with his almonds. "Where is Mrs. Wigginton?"

"In the kitchens, I'd assume. I see you've noted our *chaperone*." Lord Pembroke nodded toward the lad and pulled a chair closer to the bed. "The stubborn woman insisted on complete decorum when I informed her I would be staying. She said your father would have her drawn and quartered if we were left unaccompanied. I argued that I would attend to you, but apparently she felt your family's young lad would do a much better job."

Jenna looked at him, raising her eyebrows ever so slightly so as not to set off a new ripple of pain. "Whose room is this?"

"We're at the back of the kitchens. The room belongs to our parish priest. He's off visiting the infirm for a few days and won't need it tonight."

She bit her lip and tried to think clearly. "How long have I been asleep?"

"A few hours. You may not recall, but we came straight to the kitchens. When Mrs. Wigginton saw you, and started asking questions, your speech was so muddled she decided that sleep was of the first order. It was the only way she could tend to your wounds. You were quite uncooperative," he added.

"And how did I come to be . . . in my shift?" She was unwilling to make eye contact.

"Don't worry. Mrs. Wigginton had me wait in the hall," he said, looking skyward. He paused for a moment and then took a breath. "Do you make a practice of carrying a weapon?"

"Yes, and I make a practice of using it."

"Did your . . . family teach you how?"

The word *family* made her jolt. "My family," she said, and regretted the sudden movement. "Did you send anyone in search of them?"

"No," he said with a tilt to his head. "You were quite insistent about that. And Mrs. Wigginton said that since your wounds were not life-threatening, the men could come back tomorrow and fret then, but at least they'd have their supplies."

Thank goodness. Jenna again rested her head gently on her pillow. "She's a practical Scot." A quiet moment passed between them. "So you needn't stay," Jenna told him. "I have Mrs. Wigginton and"—she paused to stare at the immobile Tavish—"my vigilant attendant."

"Yes," Lord Pembroke said, looking at her and then lamentably at the door. "I really must go. There are things—"

Mrs. Wigginton bustled through the door with a tray. "How are ye feeling, lass? Head hurting like someone's taken a chisel to it? Oh aye," she went on, ignoring Jenna's pained expression. "The tea wi' the cherry bark will help ease the pain a bit. And I've brought ye some broth. It'll restore some of your strength, although I dare say you're a tough nut to crack. From what I've heard, ye defended yourself like a cornered wolf."

There was no time to answer, for Jenna realized the housekeeper was content to keep a running conversation by herself. Mrs. Wigginton handed her the steaming mug of tea. She put it under her nose and separated the scents: chamomile, peppermint, comfrey, and a trace of almond too. Mrs. Wigginton put the tray on the cupboard with the candle and turned to Tavish. "Wha—?" She pinched his arm and he yelped awake. "Och, ye silly clout. What use have ye been to me? Neither watchful nor shelling!" She huffed and then, looking at his fearful face, reached into her apron pocket and handed him a biscuit.

"It's high time you leave now, milord. This is entirely improper, you being here." She stood, roughened red hands on her ample hips.

"I agree, Mrs. Wigginton. But I need just a moment more. I won't be long." Seeing the concern growing in the housekeeper's face, he added, "I promise not to tax her unnecessarily if I find her temperament suffering."

Mrs. Wigginton tutted twice. "Fine, then, milord. I'll give ye a few minutes more, but when I return, I expect to see the tea all but finished and a hearty start to the broth." She bent to smooth Jenna's mussed hair. "Ye poor dear. What I think of when your family finds out . . ."

Jenna smiled weakly at her. "I know they'll be ever so grateful for your endeavors, Mrs. Wigginton. Thank you."

The housekeeper turned to Tavish. "And you"—she poked at him—"had better be awake when I return." She scuttled out the door but left it open.

Afraid to look at Lord Pembroke, Jenna ducked her head and went to work, sipping the hot tea. She was dreading the probable moment when he would announce his discovery of her family's traitorous behavior. Would he have them all arrested? Was that what he was waiting here to say? Jenna clambered about in her brain for a way to change his mind. "I imagine I owe you a debt of gratitude," she offered.

A humble smile curled his lips. "You owe me nothing of the kind. Truth be told, I must offer my sincerest apologies."

Her brow crinkled with confusion.

He went on. "I feel that upon arriving here, you have suffered an endless amount of injury. And much of the responsibility lies at my feet. I hope you might find it possible to set aside your grievances and forgive my inhospitable actions, and those of my guests. And," he said quietly, "the ones that are to come."

She stared dumbly at him, her heart in her mouth.

He nodded and stood. "Now drink your tea, or Mrs. Wigginton will have my head."

She took a nervous sip, and bowled forward with the need to keep talking. "How was it you came upon us at the ale house?"

"For that, we have your young Tavish to thank. He was in the stable as I was leaving it. I saw your clansmen saddling up to head out somewhere, and overheard your father ask Tavish to help you bring some ale back to the cottage. Assessing the size of the boy, and knowing the amount of ale men can drink, I followed him. Little did I realize how fortuitous this run-in was."

"Speaking of family and relations, why are you friends with . . ." Jenna hesitated, swallowing. "With them?" she finished. She kept her face unreadably stiff.

His eyes shadowed. "Well, Miss MacDuff, I cannot consider them friends now, regardless of the years of history between us. Both my father and Mr. Finch's serve in Parliament together—and we are expected to fill their shoes when they no longer occupy them."

"Are you not tied to them—or at least Mr. Finch?" Jenna ventured.

"Perhaps . . . perhaps not." He sighed. "Mr. Finch is not guaranteed a spot in Parliament as my family's title grants me, but . . ." He shrugged. "The truth of the matter is, lately, I have found myself defending their behavior. More so Mr. Gainsford and Mr. Fowler than Mr. Finch, as I've come to believe that Mr. Finch is motivated by the unsettling thought that I am unhappy and wish for things he cannot comprehend. He believes I am blind to the treasures before me."

She knew then that Lord Pembroke had no knowledge of Mr. Finch's feelings toward him. She weighed the option of telling him, and dismissed it.

"Miss MacDuff, you must know . . . how exceedingly happy I am for your health despite the ordeal you have just suffered." An expression that spoke simultaneously of grief and relief came across Lord

Pembroke's face. In a blink, he once again held her hand in his and just as quickly pressed it to his lips.

Jenna heard footsteps in the hallway. She watched Lord Pembroke deftly place her hand on the cot, turn, and nudge Tavish, whose eyes had grown heavy with sleep once again.

Mrs. Wigginton frowned at the door. "That's it? That's all you've had?" She turned her heavy gaze toward Lord Pembroke. "All right, then, off wi' ye. I ken better than to leave you in here, chattering away." She tugged at his sleeve as he rose to his feet. "Mind ye—if I'm questioned at all about it, I willna come to your defense," she said reproachfully, and went to pick up the bowl of broth on the table.

Lord Pembroke put a quick hand to her arm. "Mrs. Wigginton, I beg you not breathe a word that I was here." He turned to face Jenna, his expression bleak and regretful. "And I am left hollow with misgivings over what I am compelled to do, but my actions are for the greater good and those who count on my service and strength. Good-bye, Miss MacDuff. I wish you well, and again, I'm sorry." Without waiting for a reply, he left.

Mrs. Wigginton—a well-trained servant—pretended not to have heard Lord Pembroke's veiled words of departure and simply reached for Jenna's tea mug and replaced it with the broth. "Drink up, lass, then go to sleep. I'm here if ye want to talk about it." She gave Jenna a gentle pat, sized up Tavish's efforts while pointing to the sack of almonds, and bustled out the door again.

As much as she appreciated Mrs. Wigginton's offer, Jenna didn't want to talk about what had just happened. She wanted someone to tell her what was *about* to happen.

TWENTY-FIVE

ALEX LEFT HIS FATHER'S STUDY, DISGUSTED WITH HIS botched attempt at suggesting Julian's departure. He endeavored to point out that his friend was perhaps *missed in his own home* and too polite to beg his leave. Could they encourage his parting for his parents' sake?

The brittle reply from Alex's father was that Julian remained the only sensible companion Alex had, and although doubtful, his influence might dissuade further pointless conversations, such as this one.

Fuming and humiliated, Alex charged down the hallway and was stunned to find Julian walking toward him. Here was the man half responsible for the state of madness he currently suffered.

Alex kept his face calm, but couldn't help his fists from clenching, his sorely bruised knuckles a reminder from their last encounter.

Julian's face showed eager expectation, but Alex could no longer hold back. He lunged. He grabbed Julian by the throat and watched the face above his hands drain of blood and fill with fear. He wanted to squeeze out his anger that stemmed from too many sources: his father, Julian, Lady Lucia, the countess . . . everyone tugging and pulling at him, and all for their own benefit.

"What are you doing here?" Alex said through gritted teeth. He released the pressure on Julian's neck and seized him by the shoulders, shoving him against the wood paneling.

Julian swallowed hard and rubbed beneath his thick cravat. He looked at Alex with desperation. "Please . . . I—I must speak to you." His voice came out in a wretched croak. They were both heaving with breath, and Julian put his hand upon Alex's chest to distance him. "I know you may never forgive me, but give me a moment to explain." Julian searched Alex's eyes wildly.

Alex pushed himself away, his teeth clenched. "There is nothing you can say that would make it pardonable. No defense you could muster that would explain your despicable behavior."

"Please—I beg you."

Alex tried to check his anger by slowing his breath and studying Julian's battered face. His voice was cold. "You have but one minute of my attention. Speak."

"Alex, there is much you are right to despise me for, to loathe my actions and manner." His black eyes glinted with sincerity. "But everything I have done is because of the depth of my feeling for you. I feel it urgent to save you from yourself as of late. Undeniably, I have dishonored myself in trying to honor you. But understand I would cast away all principles and self-respect if it meant I was able to prevent your ruin."

"What ruin?"

"The list of people who are concerned for you has grown substantially. They beseech me to exert whatever influence I may possess to sway you from this disastrous path. Many people are frightened over losing their place in your future. The future you're casting aside in favor of something other than your true calling." Julian put his hand on Alex's arm, which remained firmly crossed with the other in front of his chest. "Your mind is clouded and confused, no doubt, but I am here for you . . . as I have always been . . . and want to be."

Alex moved back from Julian's reach. "Were you intending to kill her?"

"No," he said, eyes fastened to Alex's. "My aim was to frighten. Only to the extent that she would leave you be. Even spurn any misguided attentions you may be directing her way."

Julian took a lungful of air before continuing on. "Did it ever occur to you that she may be using you for political advantage?" He paused. "King George did an impressive job of cleaning out his cabinet. Those individuals who have been so abruptly replaced will use any ill-gotten means to gain access back."

"You're accusing the girl of *political impropriety*? That she intends to influence—nay, brainwash me into developing sympathies for . . . for what?" Alex asked, exasperated.

Julian raised his eyebrows. "She is . . . Scots, is she not?"

Alex's face grew keenly edged. "This is utter nonsense and you know it."

But Julian leaned in. "What need have plain masons to devise plans in coded language?" he asked in patient tones.

Alex was silent and then glanced up to look at Julian. He tried to push away the ridiculous note of disquietude, but what Julian said struck a nerve.

The young man looked at Alex imploringly. "Do not dismiss this as a mere attempt to lure you away from my abhorrent conduct. What I say has merit, and I believe if you give but a moment's thought to the concerns I have raised, you will concur my alarm is not unfounded."

Alex stood tall and looked away from him. *This is who should be my father's son. A man who sees ulterior motive and wrongdoing in everyone within a stone's throw of him. And Julian wishes it were as well.* He turned back and glared at him. "I will think on your words, but that is the extent of my promise to you. Now leave me, for I swear, Julian, yours is the last face I wish to see, and one I may ban from my future." He left Julian, his anger still unmitigated, but it was now tinged with a hint of apprehension.

When she had woken from several more hours of a drug-induced sleep, Jenna, despite being tired and still pressed with pain in her head, felt the flush of dread wash over her body as her mind began to clear.

She found her clothes and, with the aid of the protesting housekeeper, pulled herself together. "Ye shouldna be out of bed, lass. It's cold and damp on the floor, and it'll do your head no good moving it about such like." But as grateful as Jenna was for the hospitality, she felt she should not chance the angry questioning of her family. More, she needed to be with them should whatever Lord Pembroke intended to do come to light.

Mrs. Wigginton made Jenna wait until she returned with a tray of tea and spiced bread, along with fresh bandages for her head. She brought the cup to Jenna and tended to her wounds one last time.

"Ye poor child, has it happened much to you?"

"Has what happened much?"

The housekeeper sighed. "The men. The rough play and all, ye ken."

Jenna shook her head. "No. Never."

"I've seen it a good deal." She sighed. "I always tell the new ones in my care to stay away when the lads are about wi' drink in them. And there are definitely some they watch wi' more care than others. A few of those boys think the world's theirs for the taking and there's little negotiating about it. I've told milord about his friends time and again, but this one's gone too far."

Her face grew serious. "I didna call ye down to the ale house, ye ken."

Jenna nodded. "That would explain much."

"How timely it was that milord came. He's a good lad." She scratched her head, as if just thinking created a bit of an itch. "Such trouble he was as a wee bairn. Always taking things from the kitchen to tinker with. I've lost a great deal from the scullery because of his curiosities." She smiled, then the expression faded. "Something's come over him, though, recently, and I canna put my finger on it. It's almost as if he's shifted directions—like a weather vane." She shrugged. "But there's a lot going on that's changing for him, I s'pose—the wedding and all."

Jenna bit her lip, deciding now was the right time to ask. "Mrs. Wigginton, do you know why they were all sent away from Cambridge?" She thought it better to include all, rather than single out

Lord Pembroke, whom the housekeeper might staunchly defend.

Mrs. Wigginton's chin thrust upward. "Aye, I ken the gist of it. He defended the studies of a crippled man who was visitin' the university. Some blind professor, I think." She shrugged. "Milord's friends came to his *aid* by usin' their fists. Then all hell broke loose and milord was caught in the midst of it."

Elizabeth, the newly married kitchen maid, skittered to a stop at the door to the priest's room. "Excuse me, Mum, but it seems the fish has all come spoiled for the dinner tonight."

Mrs. Wigginton's eyes went wide and she lunged for the door. She called to Jenna over her shoulder, "I'm here should ye need anything else, lass. Get some rest!"

Jenna sank to the edge of the cot and placed a hand gingerly to her head. Mrs. Wigginton had fashioned a kerchief to hide the new bandage. The swelling had lessened on both knots, and she wondered if, after the bandage on her temple came off, her hair would sufficiently cover the injury.

She left the priest's room and traversed the muddy slope toward the building site of the garrison, mindful not to slip and drop the basket filled with freshly baked bannocks for the men. Colin Brodie's long-limbed frame unfolded from where he stooped over a vat of mortar. His clothes were covered with a dusting of lime. The broad split grin emerging beneath his white powdered features made Jenna think of silly pantomimes and traveling theater troupes. She lifted the basket in greeting and then caught sight of her father coming toward them.

Malcolm dusted off his hands and wiped his face with a handkerchief. "Jenna!" he bellowed with gruff gaiety. "You're back early. I thought we'd nay see hide nor hair of ye till Mrs. Wigginton had the whole of the pantry spotless. Was she none so short-handed after all?" He hugged her roughly.

"No, we've just finished. I've been sent down with warm bannocks and butter as . . . thanks for my help." She felt a niggling pang of guilt writhe in her stomach. Although she'd begun to make a practice of withholding information about her interactions with Lord Pembroke, this was the first time she'd purposefully lied to her father. It made it impossible to look him in the eye.

"I smell food!" Tavish shouted, running to them.

"Ye do not, ye wee fiend. But your eyes ken it normally comes in the form of one of Mrs. Wigginton's bonny baskets, aye?" Malcolm grabbed the child and tucked him under one arm as he tried to run past, and held back the laughing, squirming figure as he reached for the container.

"Wash your hands of the dust, Tavish." Jenna laughed at him. "I promise there'll be plenty, but only if you're clean." She'd also promised him that if he did not breathe a word of last night's activities, she would reward him with a small bag of sweets next time she went to the village. She impressed upon him that it was nothing more than a minor tumble that would unnecessarily alarm the men, who had no time for extra worry.

"Thanks for bringing it down, Jenna," her father said, releasing the boy. "Are ye heading back to the cottage, then?"

She handed him the basket with a nod.

"Tell Angus we'll be a bit late tonight, but this'll help to keep the bellies from rumbling."

She wanted to ask him about the meeting last night, but knew he'd not answer here. When she neared the cottage, she felt for the kerchief, making sure it was still in place.

Angus was seated at the long table in front of the fireplace, which popped and crackled with fresh wood. Next to him, head bent low over something, was Daniel. Both men looked up in surprise as she came in.

"Jenna, love, what brings ye back so soon? I thought Mrs. Wigginton would have ye counting dried apples and piles of onions for days. Have ye finished, then?"

"I'm finished for now," she answered, coming in and removing her mud-caked boots. "It's cold out there," she added, moving closer to the fire and keeping her cloak on.

The initial look she'd received from Daniel was briefly unguarded, but had been replaced by a faint acknowledgment of her presence. Jenna thought how different things were with him now. Four years ago, life was much easier, as she loved him simply: a child's hungering fascination with someone enticingly unusual to the everyday.

But now she was forced to read faces and judge body language whilst coming to the discomforting realization that others did the very same with her. Growing up, it felt like one was thrust onto a stage and under a bright light. Every curve of brow, curl of lip, or narrowing of eye could be picked apart and refashioned together in some keen new interpretation.

It was exhausting.

"Come and sit down by the fire. It'll warm your wee bones." Angus patted the bench.

Jenna sank down and peered across the table at the writings spread before them on scraps of parchment. "What are you looking at?"

"Daniel here's showing me the workings of a new machine for pumping water out of mines. What's it called again, then?" Angus scratched his beard in question.

Daniel moved his quill across the paper to sketch the diagram. "An atmospheric engine."

"Oh, do you mean the one Thomas Newcomen configured?" Jenna said.

Daniel looked up at her. "How do you know of it?"

"Ian explained it to me during a math lesson. Apparently, he met Newcomen's partner before joining us and was able to see it operate. And if you've spent any amount of time with Ian, you'll know he found fault with it," Jenna said dismissively. She watched Angus sneak away to stir the pot over the fire.

Daniel's interest seemed piqued. "What was his criticism?"

Jenna tried recalling the details of the conversation. "Something about wasting too much coal. Ian told me about it purely to figure out a mathematical computation. But it was difficult to calculate without the aid of an image." She peered down at the illustration. "Have you drawn a scale of it here?"

Daniel put a hand over the drawing. "Before you look, pull the image into your mind."

Her mouth tightened briefly, about to refuse, but then she saw Angus put a finger to his smiling lips behind Daniel and shuffle toward the bedrooms. She knew he wanted them to talk and rolled her eyes at him before he disappeared. Jenna closed her eyes and tried to conjure an imaginary form.

She heard Daniel rubbing his bristled chin with the knuckles of his hand. "The practice of recall is a skill one should put to use every day, as it can serve you in matters of both academic need . . . and of a lonely heart. Envision the details here first . . . *en tu imaginacion*. . . . See it in your mind's eye.

"I used to make a picture of what all of you looked like after each one of my visits, and at night, before sleep, I would remember the fine points. It was never difficult to recall your hair—always on fire. Don't wear a kerchief to hide it all." Jenna felt the cotton scarf slip from her head.

Her eyes flashed open, wide with panic. She wasn't quick enough to grab the scarf before Daniel had it in his hands, concern flashing across his face. *"Qué pasó?"*

Her hand flew to the bandage still secured to her head. She reached out toward the scarf. "It's nothing, just a trifling mishap. May I have it back, please?"

His eyes narrowed into miniature black pearls, rimmed with gold. "Jenna, you forget I've known you all your life. I could see through your colorful stories when you were little, and plainly, you have not yet learned the skill of deception."

She remained silent and attempted to keep an indecipherable face.

"Fine. Shall I go to your father? Do you think he would be so dismissive?" Daniel made to rise from the bench.

"Don't," she said, casting a hand out to stay him. "All right. I'll tell you, but"—she lowered her voice—"you must agree not to go running to him afterward."

"Why would I make a foolish promise if it meant keeping you in danger? Tell me now, or you give me no other choice than to take you to the garrison, where your *father* will force an explanation from you." He glared at her.

"Why must you always be so pigheaded?" she hissed.

"I would prefer to define my actions as choosing right over wrong."

"You may think—" she began.

"Don't tell me what I think," he interrupted, "tell me what *happened*."

She pulled back, surprised by the authority in his voice. "I was confronted and attacked."

His eyes widened.

"Assaulted, with the intent to do harm."

"By whom?"

"By another pigheaded individual."

Daniel took a long time inhaling, and Jenna counted the seconds it took for him to release it. He shook his head. "Who? Who did this to you?"

"The telltale—Mr. Finch. The one who came to your side a few weeks ago, impressing upon you my apparent need for assistance."

"If I recall correctly, you *were* in need of assistance." His voice regained its silken cadence, but his lilting accent still held the intonation of warning.

"I beg to differ," she mumbled.

Daniel's eyes simmered darkly as he studied Jenna's face and stared at the bandage. "*Por qué?* For what reason?"

"He didn't provide one," she said sourly. She held back. Determined not to give away too much information. There was no way of gauging his reaction if he found out who'd come to assist in her struggle with Mr. Finch. Nor did she want to reveal that Lord

Pembroke had stayed at her bedside for the hours thereafter.

Daniel leaned in closer, and she heard the snap of the quill in his hand. "I don't believe you. Now tell me why."

"Mr. Finch doesn't like me," she began with difficulty. "Apparently, he believes"—she paused—"that I put myself above my appropriate station."

"He's right."

Jenna's eyes flashed with surprise. "It's only that he's afraid of a woman with knowledge. I'm beginning to think men simply want women stupid. Senseless enough that they can exert their brute will on us as they please."

"And when you find yourself with one of these *barbaric* individuals"—he emphasized the one word—"it seems you cannot hold your tongue, but must speak on behalf of all wronged women; is that so?"

Jenna rose to the bait. "I don't know why I'm surprised at your judgment of the situation. You're no different from him."

"I would not assault a woman."

"Maybe not, but you are agreeable to suppressing one." She stood from the bench, her face glowing.

Daniel shook his head. "Can you not see the scope of contrast between the two? They are wholly different methods for . . ." He paused.

"For what?" Jenna interrupted. "Go ahead. Say it. Compelling *obedience*. Isn't that it?" She backed up.

Daniel rose and came toward her, his eyes glittering. "I was going to say *maintaining order*. But is the first word so distasteful to you, Jenna? Is there no one you would abide by?"

She glared at him, an unfamiliar energy crackling through her body. "I have done nothing but obey people my entire life. You will live *here*—and therefore I do, we will now *move*—and consequently I pack. Study these verbs, compute this equation, review these lectures. Show me, Daniel, where it is I have been rebellious?"

She breathed heavily and tried swallowing the heat that burned brightly within her. "I live with a band of traitors to the crown who follow their hearts without the least bit of hesitation in acknowledgment of *their own* defiance, and yet I am to remain meek in the face of this constant demonstration?"

"You are wrong to think they act blindly," Daniel said, in level tones. "These men are wholly aware of the risk that accompanies their mutiny. If they are caught, they are killed." He came to stand before her and took her hand in his. "And you, *mi amor*," he said, "cannot change the injustices of the world with a sweep of your hand. History has many examples of those who were ill-content, but the ones who succeeded in their endeavor for change were perhaps less headstrong than you."

He stood back, holding Jenna's gaze. Her eyes, moments ago blazing, were now searching his, taking in his words. He went on. "I think if you insist upon traveling such a difficult path, then you should prepare for many more encounters such as this one." Then the corners of his mouth turned up slightly. "And perhaps I should brace myself for future conversations with you—a young woman whose internal flame of candor grows brighter each day." He paused.

"Suppress you?" He chuckled and kissed the top of her head above the bandage. "I pity the man who tries."

TWENTY-SIX

"HIGH TREASON!" THE DUKE SHOUTED TO THE gathered crowd in front of the garrison. "The worst of felonies!" His voice bellowed justified anger across the heads of those assembled. "Two men levied war against our monarch, and for those actions they were punished to the highest extent of the law."

Jenna's extremities went numb with fright as she listened to the duke address the people. She stood behind Jeb and another stable lad, who kept leaping up to see above the heads in front of him. The press of people consisted of not only those who worked upon the estate, but also those who lived within it.

"Those two Englishmen were hanged for their crimes of rebellion in the hamlet of Hawkshead—in the middle of the square—as a deterrent to others who may be entertaining similar ideas, but mostly as a reminder to the rest of us, illustrating the cold fact that we are in the midst of trying times. We must stand strong against the surge of baseless rebellion."

Jenna looked about the crowd, scanning it hungrily, and she threaded her way quietly through the crush. Her eyes remained fixed on the tall head of Mr. Finch and on Lady Lucia, who stood next to him. They were insiders. Perhaps words about this situation were passing between them, words Jenna could use to her clan's advantage. She pulled the hood of her cloak tighter around her face and came to stand silently behind them.

". . . he was granted special dispensation . . . ," she heard Mr. Finch say. "To administer discipline as he saw fit."

The words filled Jenna with a cold dread.

The duke clamored on. "Lest anyone need a sign of our strength, glance to your right to see the rising fortress of our preparation. This garrison is a symbol of the times to come, and represents our backbone of protection against the rebellion."

Jenna watched the duchess, who stood beside her husband, close her eyes and press her lips inward. A terrible pang of guilt sliced through Jenna's stomach. Nearly everyone here believed the garrison would be a pillar of preservation, but her clan had other plans.

Mr. Finch turned again to Lady Lucia. "And you and I must work in tandem to ensure Alex's personal rebellion is quashed. We must strive to erase any wayward notions he still possesses about leaving this life. He is *needed* here, milady. By you. And me." Julian fanned his hand across the crowd in front of him. "And everyone here who is dependent upon his future."

Jenna turned her head so as not to be seen, and Lady Lucia

replied, "I am worried still. I believe he will cast us all aside, and we shall have nothing."

"Rest assured, milady, I have had words with him of recent, and now, more than ever, I feel confident that he sees the threat upon his home is real, and that he is obligated to remain here to confront it."

Jenna stifled a gasp and fell back into the crowd behind her. She needed to understand more about what was to unfold when the garrison was complete. Raising her head, she found Mr. Wicken watching the men of her clan. They stood close to the building, listening to the duke finish his address to his estate's constituents. Their faces were unreadable, but their stances strong.

A ripple of fear bloomed within her as she stared at her family. Regardless of the strength of one's stance, once the floor was pulled from beneath you, it was impossible to get a foothold on air.

"I'm begging you, Daniel. Please."

He looked at her, his eyes busy with quiet assessment.

Jenna put a hand on his arm and felt the hard-strung tension beneath the white of his fine linen shirt. "The barest of details— that's all I'm asking for," she pleaded. They sat in front of the slumbering fire, a late-night book on Daniel's lap, Shakespeare's sonnets on hers.

Following the duke's announcement, Jenna had found a moment to question her father, hoping for further details on how *exactly* their family was building support for James Stuart. His answer had left her less than satisfied.

We, the garrison, and soldiers are part of a lengthy chain of folk collecting money and such like.

It was like asking about the details of a book only to be told there is a beginning, a middle, and an end. She repeated her father's answer to Daniel and asked for clarification.

"When will the garrison be complete? Where will the smuggled arms come from? Who are the soldiers? And what did he mean by *such like*?" She puffed a little with discontent. "Answer any of these queries, as I'm tired of being in the dark."

"You've been kept uninformed for a good reason, Jenna. No one wants to give you enough information to put a noose around your neck."

Jenna looked at him, incredulous. "It's a little late for that, don't you think? I've read the laws, and as I am related to a man who could easily be found guilty of high treason, the smallest punishment I would find cast upon myself is the forfeiture of all property and the right to any livelihood. I would surely perish, but it would be a long and painful death of slow starvation. Better the courts would find me guilty as well so that at least I would find a quicker end."

Daniel looked away and stared into the fire.

"So the garrison has a hidden chamber?"

He took a slow breath and then raised two fingers.

"And it's here that money will be stored?"

"Among other things," he pointed out. "Weapons and ammunition, which have been shipped from France."

"And the soldiers?"

"Some hold positions in the king's army, but actually support James Stuart."

"But how? When they've pledged fealty to the king?"

He chewed on his lip, thinking. "When you ask about these soldiers and how they could deceive in their position, you must think first about their prior pledges. To serve one monarch and provide unwavering loyalty is a great thing. But when that individual is replaced with another, not of your choosing—whose ideas contradict all you stood for previously, how could you switch allegiance? Especially if you believe in the Divine Right of Kings. If God gave these individuals their monarchy, and you believed in this God, how could you cast aside your faith to support a ruler who took another's place by force?"

Jenna nodded with understanding. "And those soldiers will be here—in the garrison?"

"The duke is preparing himself for the possibility of rebellion, but he will not know that most of those he'll soon employ to protect him will in fact be there to take up arms *against* King George."

Jenna leaned back in her chair. She thought about Lord Pembroke. About Mrs. Wigginton and Jeb, and all the innocent people here who have no forewarning as to the danger they are in. But mostly, her mind filled with the painful thoughts that her family was responsible for what could be tantamount to their devastation.

Her face must have revealed her guilt, for Daniel added, "I know it may be impossible for you to make allowance for the deception involved. But understand, in a situation such as this, each side believes they are right. And many will fight to the death to prove it."

She felt sick. "I can't help but think of the innocent people who'll be harmed."

He leaned forward, his gaze serious. "Jenna, you must not

struggle with the hopelessness of how it seems. There will always be tragedy in our lives. People get hurt, and unfairly so. There is little we can do to stop it."

That might be true, Jenna thought forlornly, *but in this case it appears we are doing everything in our power to* start *it.*

TWENTY-SEVEN

WHEN THE CHANCE TO GET AWAY FROM THE COTTAGE presented itself it seemed like an opportunity for a welcome adventure. The men needed supplies, and Malcolm couldn't spare the loss of anyone's labor. Since Daniel needed to depart for France in a few days to bring news of support to the waiting monarch, Jenna was given the opportunity to accompany him to Preston—a much larger town than Hawkshead, with a market superior to their own. There, she and Daniel would gather the crucial provisions for the men at the garrison, and for his journey. Furthermore, they would meet someone who would present them with a list of names to bring back to her father. The list contained the credentials of soldiers who were to man the garrison. It also identified which of those men were Jacobites—infiltrators working on behalf of James Stuart. Daniel would return with her halfway and leave for the coast at midday. One half day's travel was more than her usual distance away on her own, but she hungered to be anywhere, far from the estate, if even just for a day.

They left well before the sun rose, with both horses packed to their limits. Daniel always traveled with very little, but the men had sent them to Preston with the intent they trade for the goods needed at home. She would either come back with new tools and equipment, or return with a fair amount of money, hidden in various places. Jenna listened to everyone's warnings and had been served more sage advice than breakfast that morning.

Angus had reminded her, "Ye must be constantly aware of your surroundings—never turn your back on anyone for a moment."

Colin had pressed upon her the importance of appearing well mannered and knowledgeable. "So people won't assume you're a naïve adolescent who could easily be taken advantage of."

Of course, Duncan had spent a few minutes with her, assessing the worth of all their goods for trade. "Anything less than my appraisal and ye should walk away from the deal."

Her father simply checked to see she was armed. A finely tuned bow and arrow and a razor-edged *sgian dubh* were her tools of choice, should it come down to that. Daniel disagreed, saying her tongue was the sharpest weapon she possessed.

She had no fear of her assignments for the Preston market. Daniel would be close at hand, even though she insisted she could do the bartering on her own. Ian thought her foolish. "'Tis rightly a man's job, and I say it's downright reckless to have her traveling wi' the list of Jacobite soldiers on her person."

Duncan shook his head. "No one would suspect a young maid of having such a thing in the first place, but beyond that, Jenna is the most capable female I've ever known."

Gavin said, "Dinna worry, Jenna. Even if the record falls into hands other than those intended, it'll make sense to none other than us, because it'll be printed in the code *I* created." Jenna grimaced and thought, *The one I've shared with the enemy.*

They traveled through the dark February morning in silence as it was still too early for birdsong to accompany them. Even the horses plodded along dazed and sleepy, their hooves reluctantly liberated from the suctioning mud beneath them.

After those first quiet hours, streaks of pink and peach began to mingle with the horizon's hazy clouds, as if a painter had strewn a few bright colors from his palette about the sky without concern for where they landed. The dawn roused Jenna's spirits, and she found herself smiling as she rode, watching the sun creep past the edge of land.

"You are happy today?" Daniel said.

Jenna glanced at him. "I'm always happy." She turned back to the sunrise then heard him make a faint grunt. "You disagree?"

"I would not dare," he said with a smirk. "But it pleases me you are content."

"I am not content in order to please *you*."

"That is not what I meant," he said in his heavy accent, meeting her gaze.

"But it's what you said."

"Then I phrased it poorly. I only commented because I saw you smiling now, and most mornings it is difficult to gauge your mood until well after sunup."

"Yes," she began crisply. "You did phrase it poorly. And I can make it clear that each and every morning I wake as happy as a new-born lamb. I would remain that way *as long as no one would have the gall to think I was doing it to please him.*" Jenna bit her lip, determined not to let Daniel see she was enjoying the act of goading him.

He rolled his eyes skyward, paused for a moment, and then said, "Jenna, *mi querida*, perhaps it would be best if I spoke my thoughts in Spanish so they would not be misinterpreted."

"You know I don't speak Spanish."

"Exactly."

Jenna looked at him from beneath her brows. "In whichever language you choose, in your way of thinking, women should still try to please men with their placid attitudes. I'm not like that."

"That is for certain."

He'd taken up his verbal sword, but Jenna quickly returned. "So you agree—your thinking is old-fashioned."

He lowered his head and sighed. "I only asked if you were happy."

Jenna turned her head to face the opposite of his and pressed her lips inward to stifle a smile. She would miss their games when Daniel left again.

"Daniel?" Jenna ventured, when the sun had gone as high as it would for the day. "Where are you going? Where do you always go?" She asked the question that until now, everyone had answered with responses she found vague and insufficient.

"To check on things."

"What things?"

"My business. I go to mind my affairs." He stared at the horizon in front of them.

"What is your business?" She watched his face.

He rubbed roughly at his chin, nodded at a mass of rocks, and said, "We will stop now. There's food in the pack."

She was confused at his reluctance to answer, but dismounted and led Henry to a cluster of leafless trees where Daniel hobbled his horse. She reached into one of the saddlebags and pulled out a cloth sack Angus had prepared for them. Daniel hunted for something in his own leather bags. He brought out a gleaming silver flagon, and came to sit where Jenna was arranging bread and cheese. He offered her the container.

"How marvelous," she said, taking it from him. The flask sparkled with Spanish engravings, and was partially enclosed in a leather covering. "What is it?"

He only raised his eyebrows in response, so she unscrewed the bayonet-fit lid and put her nose to its spout. Taking a deep inhalation, she closed her eyes with approval.

"What do you smell?"

"I smell raisins and oranges." She breathed in again. "And almonds." She opened her eyes and smiled. "What is it?"

"Drink."

She brought the flask to her lips. The liquid was round and perfumed, its taste blossoming in her mouth. She swallowed and mentally followed the warm path of the fluid. "Is it wine?" She licked her lips. She'd had wine before, but nothing as decadent as this.

"It is sherry," he said, chuckling at the delighted expression on her face.

She studied the engravings and traced them with her finger. *"Amor no es voluntad, sino destino,"* she read. "Something about love. What does it mean?"

"It means that love is not a will—not a choice—but a destiny. It suggests that love is a divine mistake. The flask is from my grandfather. He made it."

Jenna was silent, still fingering the soft curve of the urn. "What about the sherry? Where did you find it?"

"It's mine," he said, tearing off a chunk of bread. "I made it."

"Where did you make this?" She looked at him with disbelief. "Here?"

Daniel took a sip from the flask. He chortled and shook his head. "No, Jenna. You cannot make sherry here. The grapes would not grow."

"I don't really know anything about grapes." She shrugged. "Does it take many to make this?"

He laughed again. "*Sí*. A whole field full." He swept an arm in front of him.

She reeled back and pointed to the slim container. "For that?"

"For many of these, *mi amor*."

After their meal he got up and stretched. He walked to his mare and returned the elixir to the saddlebag.

She stared after him. "Do you make a lot of this?"

"Many, many barrels full. It is my business." He unhobbled his horse and led her to the road. Jenna scurried to catch up.

"So you're a winemaker?"

Daniel swung himself into the saddle and turned to face Jenna, still packing her horse. "*Sí*," he nodded. "A winemaker . . . and a thief." He clicked his tongue and trotted down the road.

"A thief?" Jenna called after him. "Wait—as a profession? I don't understand."

Daniel raised a brow. "Here you call it smuggling."

"For James Stuart?"

He nodded.

"Why? You're not even English."

His face softened. "For many reasons, not least of all, I owe your father a great debt."

"Whatever for?"

"My life," he said bluntly. "He saved it long ago, and I've yet to repay him in full." Daniel shook his head. "It's a long story I will tell another time."

Jenna gaped at him. She'd never been told. No one had ever given her so much as a clue as to how the two families knew one another. "Do you smuggle the wine into England? I would assume it comes over in barrels on a ship, yes?"

He nodded.

"But I thought ships had to go through ports with custom houses—and that you're taxed on the number of barrels you bring into the country."

"True, but there are numerous coastal towns that do not have custom houses or proper ports. They're set up to allow smugglers to operate their business through them as long as they receive a share of the profits. It's a risk to participate, but plenty of the locals feel they're willing to wager a little security for the end result."

Jenna felt her forehead creasing.

"When a boat lands with the contraband in the middle of the night, the goods must immediately be stored until they are picked up by the next in line for distribution. That means you need horses and wagons to carry the load to a hideaway—usually somebody's barn or empty grain house. For these things you must receive the consent of willing allies."

She eyed him. "What if you come to a village where the people refuse to help you?"

"Well, there are ways to make those who oppose become at least *unwilling* supporters, but I refuse to participate in such a fashion."

"Oh, so there's a line you've drawn for yourself to distinguish your fraudulent behavior from the other man, who's obviously an immoral miscreant." Jenna looked at him smugly.

Daniel's eyes grew dark. "Yes, if you put it that way. I will not burn someone's barn if they refuse to conceal my goods. I will not steal their sheep as retribution. I will not kill to send a message to others that they must participate or suffer . . . but others will." His eyes remained unblinking and Jenna had to turn away, abashed at her criticism.

"So are you saying your barrels never go through any of the ports or custom houses?"

"I did not say that." Daniel raised a finger and a tiny smirk appeared on his face.

"Why do I feel there's more you're *not* saying?"

He shrugged. "My cooper has created a special barrel in which I am taxed on that which the inspector believes to *be* in the barrel."

"Sherry?"

He nodded.

"Are you saying sherry is *not* in the barrel, Daniel?"

"No. It is, but there is also gunpowder." He quirked an eyebrow. "In a separate compartment."

"A trick barrel?"

"Yes. The inspector inserts a pole through the middle of the barrel to test the contents. My new barrels have three angled compartments: two on either end for the gunpowder and one in the middle filled with sherry—allowing movement for a prodding stick."

Jenna shook her head. "That is a most impressive ruse you have going on."

"Jenna." Daniel looked sternly at her. "Before you cast judgment, remember we are all fighting in some war or another, and I would rather give everything to a cause I support, even if it might cost me my business or my life, than contribute nothing because no one is after *me*. For if I do not stand up for those who need me now, there will be no one left to stand up for me when I need them later. They will come for us all in the end."

How was it that each time she demonstrated a sliver of disdain at some shocking statement of Daniel's, it took him merely seconds to point out she was seeing it from only one side?

The wrong one.

TWENTY-EIGHT

EVENING FELL AND THE COLD SET IN. JENNA SCRUBBED at her arms to warm herself. At intervals, Daniel would take out his flask of sherry and have her drink—more for warmth than enjoyment. And when they had finished its contents, he brought out another, but in a plain leather flagon. Jenna did not refuse the gracious offers, for it made the journey's cold tolerable, if not pleasant. It was like having a miniature campfire in her belly, kindling a feeling of quiet contentment.

They came through the edge of town where humble farms grew closer together and the crofter's cottages were found nearer to the road. Soon there were people crisscrossing in front of them, going home to their dinners as shops closed for the night. The streets were lit with oil lamps that cast black wisps into the frigid air, and the aroma of smoking peat fires crept from the hearths of each home.

The cold snap had come on suddenly with the dark, and the tips of Jenna's fingers grew numb and lifeless.

Daniel stopped the horses in front of an inn. A green sign hung out into the street showing a great barrel outlined in gold. He dismounted, handed the reins to Jenna, and told her to stay put. She watched him enter through the arched brick doorway with a sign above it displaying the tavern's name in curling black letters. *The Hogshead.*

As she waited, she squinted through the hazy glass window, trying to follow Daniel's movements. He spoke to another, shorter figure behind a long wooden bar with a mess of shelved bottles at the back. The windowpane was leaded and mottled the figures behind it, but she saw the man come around the bar and clap Daniel on the back a few times, his other hand pumping Daniel's arm. Whatever caused the enthusiasm, Jenna was glad of the warm reception, as she was chilled to the bone and ravenous.

Daniel came out and headed straight for the packs on the horses. "We're all set, we shall sleep here, and they've got food too. Plus they'll put the horses in their stable out back."

Jenna slid off Henry and began unpacking a few things from her saddle. "Apparently, you know someone here. That must have come in handy," she said over her shoulder.

"Yes, he's the owner, and a man I've done a little business with over the years."

"He appeared awfully glad to see you."

"No, it wasn't that. I told him there'd be two of us staying and he was actually apologetic at first because he had only one room left," he said, his head bent low to his task.

"Then why did he embrace you so?"

"Because I told him it wouldn't be a problem."

Her brow creased. "And why was that?"

Daniel raised his head and looked her in the eye. "Because I told him we'd just been wed."

The pack she held slid to the ground and landed on the paved stone with a dull thud. "You told him what?" she said, raising her voice.

He rushed around the horses to face her and looked about. "Be quiet," he hissed. "I had no choice."

She made a face clearly showing she didn't believe him.

"It is late and cold. This is a man I know who'll not rob us in the middle of the night, and he reminded me that, tomorrow being market day, most of the other inns will be full."

Jenna huffed, but Daniel raised a hand to quell her anger. "Don't worry—you'll have the room to yourself. After everyone has gone to sleep, I shall find my way to the stable."

"Why can't we both sleep in the stable—I'd be much more comfortable there than in the inn with strangers," she countered.

"No," he stated firmly. "It is important we not draw unwanted attention. Sometimes, you must play a part to fit into the game. No one is going to look at us twice if we are newly wedded and just passing through, but a foreigner accompanying a single young woman would raise eyebrows and suspicions. And I want no ripples of doubt to follow us anywhere. Trust me, Jenna. I've done this many times."

"You make a habit of pretending to be newly married?" she asked pointedly. "How scandalous."

He looked at her with disbelief. "When a situation arises, I assess it and make the best calculation I can. You should apologize."

She looked at him indignantly. "For what deed? I'm not the one who has put the other in a compromising position."

"You are not *compromised*, Jenna," he said, a look of warning in his eye. "But you will play along, understood?" He held her by the elbow too firmly for her comfort, but she nodded.

They walked with their things to the door where a lad came out to grab the reins of the horses. Daniel flipped him a coin from his pocket and nodded at Jenna to enter before him.

The first thing she noticed was the smell of roasting meat, and in her mind, all was forgiven. If this meal promised to deliver as much taste as it did scent, then she would gladly accept far worse a situation than pretending to be Daniel's wife. Daniel's traveling cook, or even laundress, would have been palatable enough to suffer through for a decent meal at this point.

The room was strewn with dark wooden tables and chairs, its patrons scattered about. Some were in animated discussion. Others participated in a spirited game of dice in the corner, and it appeared that one or two individuals were already half in their cups.

A dowdy barmaid cleaned the empty tables, and a boy in a food-stained jerkin shuffled in from another room toward the back, his arm stacked from wrist to shoulder with plates of steaming fare. A short man with a generous girth came from behind the wooden bar to greet them, his eyes shining as he neared Jenna.

"Rather captivating eyes and a fair complexion," The chubby man looked Jenna up and down. "A reasonably flattering figure . . . and that hair," he continued, peering closer to her. "I bet she's a wild-cat, eh?"

Jenna turned to Daniel and whispered heatedly, "Am I for sale? Do you think he wants to see my hooves?" She lifted the hem of her skirt an inch or two in demonstration.

The man had heard and bellowed with laughter, his red face wheezing. "Oh, Daniel, lad, are you in for it!"

Daniel leaned in close to Jenna and smiling, said, "Play nice."

She narrowed her eyes but bit her tongue, and turned as ladylike as possible to the innkeeper, a demure smile on her lips.

"You'll have to forgive my young wife, Thomas. It's been a most taxing journey, and we are both weary." Daniel took Jenna's hand and led her to a chair to sit down.

Thomas followed after and said, "I never thought you'd be one to choose the settling-down kind of life. Got tired of all the women, did you? Or are you still hiding them in each port?" His belly rollicked with laughter again, and Jenna had to use every ounce of restraint not to rise up and thump his shiny, balding head.

Daniel nodded toward the kitchen. "It smells as if Margaret has been busy. The scent of her food comes clear into the street."

"And I carry it to bed each night. It clings to every ounce of me." He rolled his eyes.

Jenna gripped the sides of her chair. After silently pointing out that Thomas allowed himself more ounces than necessary and could easily reduce his complaint, she grew determined to find another means of distraction. Daniel walked Thomas to the bar, probably with the aim to get them food, so Jenna turned to watch the game of dice, which grew in fevered pitch.

The men crowded around the table, standing and leaning in above those who had ringside seats. One of the players caught Jenna's eye as he was about to take his turn rolling and pushed his chair back from the table. "You there," he called thickly. "Come here, lass. Kiss my dice before I roll them. For good luck."

His speech was troubled by copious amounts of booze, and the thought of having to kiss anything belonging to the man made a shiver run through Jenna's bones. She turned her head, pretended not to hear.

"Hey, you . . . Red," the dice man called louder, and stood. "Bring yourself round and I'll buy you a drink," he slurred. "I need the favor of a woman to get me fortune back. And I bet you've given a fortune worth of favors away to whoever asks for it." The man slammed a hand down on the table and howled at his own rude behavior, as did his intoxicated cohorts.

Words rose in her throat. Jenna stood from the table and pushed her chair back. She took three steps toward the group of men, prepared to give them an earful, when she felt two hands encircle her waist.

"I am afraid you will have to wait for another. This lady's favor has been given to me, and I am not a generous enough man to share." Daniel made a courteous bow in the direction of the men. Then he spun about and thrust Jenna under a table, turning back just as the man's fist made contact with Daniel's jaw.

Thomas vaulted from behind the bar and bellowed at the troublemaker. He settled the room and Daniel whisked Jenna toward a table close to the kitchen door. He rubbed at his jaw. "Have you never encountered men who have lost their sense to drink before? Do you not have the good judgment to stay away from such a scene?"

Jenna bristled at the criticism, but noted Daniel's split lip with a hint of guilt.

She'd grown up in a house full of men and their occasional rowdy manners. Of course, there had been celebrations where her family had passed around their flasks, the men becoming flush-faced and more than agreeable, but never had they acted in the way of *that* man.

Daniel leaned across the table. "It is like sending a sheep into a pen with a pack of wolves. You must secure yourself from every angle and size up danger quickly. Trust no one."

Thomas interrupted their conversation with two plates of steaming food, held in each hand with the edge of his bar cloth. "Well, it may not be a wedding feast, but it'll take the chill out of your bones." He set the plates in front of them, grabbed two glasses and an emerald-green bottle from the bar's shelf and placed them between the plates. He thumped a hand on Daniel's back. "A wedding present—my finest brandy. Now how long have you been wed? A day? A week? The blush of marriage is ripe on her cheeks yet," he said, waving a hand toward Jenna.

"About a week," Daniel said, wincing as he took a swallow of what Thomas generously poured.

Thomas nodded. "I figured as much. Well, we'll have you fed and upstairs in no time, my friend," he said, pounding Daniel on the back again.

Jenna nearly choked on her food, and brought the edge of her cloak to her mouth to stifle her mortification.

"It must be a good match, Daniel; your lass is trying to hasten the meal as much as you." Thomas looked at her slyly and winked a puffy eyelid in her direction as he left.

Jenna's face must have been like young Tavish's, scrubbed raw and red, clean from the day's work. "Why couldn't I have been your sister or your cousin?"

Daniel gave her an incredulous look.

"All right, then, you could have been my servant," she countered.

"Your clothes are not fine enough and this man is already aware of what I do."

"I'm hardly old enough."

Daniel met her gaze, holding it. "You are more than old enough."

She fumbled for a reply, but found nothing. Instead, she worked to control the flush of warmth that spread up her neck and settled on her face. She was immediately reminded of what it felt like when Daniel's hands had wreathed her waist. The words of *my young wife* echoed in her head, and she hastily picked up her spoon so she'd have something to do.

The food was delicious and hot. Of that, Thomas spoke the truth. His wife had made a mouthwatering lamb casserole, filled with onions, raisins, and prunes, and simmered them together in strong dark ale. The chunks of lamb and fruits were made even more delectable by the abundant herbs she had mixed into the stew. The pungent scents of rosemary, thyme, and clove reached Jenna's sensitive nose. She closed her eyes and took the next bite. She appreciated Margaret's efforts, even if they were wasted on her rude husband.

When she reopened them, she found Daniel staring at her, humor apparent on his face. He leaned forward and said,

"At meat her manners were well taught withal;
No morsel from her lips did she let fall,
Nor dipped her fingers in the sauce too deep;
But she could carry a morsel up and keep
The smallest drop from falling on her breast . . .
And she would wipe her upper lip so clean
That not a trace of grease was to be seen
Upon the cup when she had drunk; to eat,
She reached a hand sedately for the meat."

He fell back against his chair.

"Well, I see your youth was not entirely wasted on learning the ins and outs of criminal conduct, but what I'm to make of your excerpt from Chaucer, I'm not sure. Are you commenting on my fine table manners or the fact that I'm so famished I refuse to waste one scrap of food?" Jenna asked, sipping from the glass of brandy, which sent circles of warmth spiraling through her.

"Perhaps I am only suggesting you are as chaste as a nun," he said playfully, taking up his own drink.

When Jenna had cleaned her plate she lifted her cup. Daniel continued to speak, but his words became lost to her, as she now found herself staring at his lips as he spoke. They were a sculptor's muse, an exquisite shape, and she wished to reach out to touch them. The room had grown heavy with the modulating sound of men reaching the pinnacle of their evening's entertainment. Raucous laughter, the occasional lewd jeer at the poor barmaid as she dodged an overfriendly hand, and calls for another round circled her head.

When at last Jenna stood from her chair, she found her legs had trouble remembering how to walk. She wobbled and clutched the side of the table, then took a faltering step.

Daniel caught her arm to steady her toward the stairs. "Perhaps it is time to retire?"

She looked up at him, his eyes glittering, and felt the rest of the world around her grow spellbound and out of focus. "Do you know that I have never been kissed?" She put a hand on his chest and leaned toward him, but he took hold of her shoulders and spun her to face the stairs.

"No," he said with a quiet chuckle.

Indignant heat flushed her face, and she wrestled her arm free from his grasp. He struggled to maintain his hold on her, but she twisted around to face him and grabbed him with both hands. Forcing his head down to hers, she kissed him soundly amid the garbled noises in the room. He tasted of brandy and faintly of blood, as well.

Her knees, already in a weakened state, defied her as they buckled under the pressure of trying to stand. Daniel grabbed her by the waist to keep her steady, and she clutched at him, trying to right herself. When at last she felt the security of her feet, she pushed him back and straightened her skirt. With shoulders squared, she moved cautiously toward the stairs and refused to look behind her.

"Chaste as a nun," she muttered, ascending the steps. "Not anymore."

TWENTY-NINE

JENNA PUT HER HEAD INTO HER HANDS AND GROANED. Her fingers waded through the clusters of knotted hair. One strand after another snapped free from her scalp as she created a small red nest, like a bird depluming. She peeked at the bed out of the corner of one puffy eye. The events of last night were foggy, but Jenna could easily recall how uncomfortable she'd been, sleeping in a foreign place with none of her family to hand. And she could hardly refer to what she'd done last night as sleeping. Rolling about on the mattress was more like it.

Her mind, dizzy and distorted, had startled with every sound of boots above her, or creak of floorboard outside the room. She'd reprimanded herself for being so jittery and wrestled with the true reason she could not close her eyes.

Daniel. Why had she kissed him? She asked the question a

thousand times. The first kiss she would ever give—or receive—an event she had built in her mind as an occasion that should matter, had been handled as carelessly as the dice the drunken men tossed through their hands. Used to make a point and prove her fortitude, what she had actually demonstrated was how she couldn't hold her liquor, and that Daniel was right. She *did* ask for trouble. But trouble, as it turned out, had been soft and warm—and magnetic.

And now she stared at the door, willing him to be on the other side, to knock and tell her it was time to go. There was nothing but silence. Except for the throbbing echoes in her head. She wondered if he was angry.

He'd been silent coming up the stairs behind her last night, and when they'd reached the second floor he'd simply said, "Left. To the end of the hall."

She'd crept down the corridor, and kept her hand on the dusty wainscoting to aid her balance until she'd come to their room. She slouched against the doorframe, taking in the cramped space with its one curtained window. Two lit candles perched on a spindly-legged table near the window and bathed the room in a muted glow. Daniel retrieved an iron key from the coin purse at his belt and held it out to Jenna. She looked at it stupidly and he grabbed her hand, pressed it into her palm.

"I will not leave until I hear the lock engage. Go to sleep and I will wake you tomorrow."

He nudged her inside and began to close the door. She snapped with alertness, grabbing the handle. "What of the men downstairs? Need I be worried?" She searched Daniel's face.

His eyes narrowed darkly. "I assure you, all who are downstairs assume you are unavailable." He pulled the door closed and sighed audibly as she fumbled with the key. When the lock clicked into place, he tried the door, and presumably satisfied with its resistance, walked away down the hall.

She refused to think back on his words. She had behaved brazenly last night, and deserved everything that followed his leaving.

She had moved to the bed and eased herself on her back. The room was spinning. This was not nearly as fun as it sounded. It reminded her of the days when she would do it for entertainment, to whirl in a circle and flare her skirts only to collapse onto the ground and clutch at tufts of grass so she wouldn't fall off the earth. But the spinning always ceased within a few moments, and she could continue the game, only if she wanted. *This* rotating room, however, was intent to maintain its course, and even closing her eyes would not stop the dizzying effect.

She leapt suddenly from the bed, located the chamber pot, and after a few horrific moments, let her head rest on the cool, plastered wall, plagued with bitter thoughts of a good meal wasted. Apparently, sherry, ale, and brandy did not make for good bedfellows.

Her head rose at the soft tapping on the door. Daniel appeared surprised to find her ready when she opened it. She moved past him without a greeting. "Jenna. Where are you going?"

"To the market, of course." She stopped in the hall but did not turn around.

"The stalls do not open for another half hour. We shall breakfast first," he said quietly.

"I'm not hungry, thank you," she said, ignoring the lurch of her stomach.

"Perhaps you do not like the food here. Did it not sit well with you?"

She turned to face him and saw his eyes, alight with mischief. "Of course I'll have breakfast. I loved Margaret's cooking." She forced a smile and turned to the stairs.

The room where they'd eaten last night was almost empty of customers, but it irrefutably held the scent of those who'd occupied it hours earlier. The smell of ale and wood smoke, unwashed males, and grease filled the air. Jenna tried to breathe as little as possible until her nose could adjust to the unwelcoming assault, but she was not about to admit to Daniel she was suffering with a delicate condition. In that he would, no doubt, take great delight.

He pulled out a chair for her to sit in and made his way to the kitchen. A moment later he came back with a smile on his lips. "Margaret is making us one of my favorite dishes. She always starts it the night before so I can have it for breakfast before I go. *Muy delicioso!*" He rubbed his palms together and sat across from Jenna.

The plump, red-faced woman came out of the kitchen with two steaming bowls in her hands. "Here you are, love. I've made it just as you like. Olios stew." She put the dishes in front of them, beaming.

Jenna looked at the muddy liquid and asked in a wretched voice, "What is it?"

Margaret laughed and put her hands on the broad hips that supported her frame. "Well, what *isn't* it, is more like it. Let's see, there's mutton and fowl, pork and beef and veal, all slathered in a broth made from every leftover vegetable I'd had in back. Then, Daniel always likes for me to top it off with a couple of eggs, not quite cooked through. I guess it thickens it a bit."

This was more than Jenna's stomach could handle. She pushed back from the table and made a mad dash for the door.

Twenty minutes later, Daniel found her sitting by the stable's entrance, pale-faced and eyes closed. He made a clucking sound, emphasizing his disapproval, "I do not understand it. Most people love Margaret's cooking."

She opened her eyes and looked up at him dully. "Isn't all of France waiting for you?"

He laughed and offered his hand to help her up. "Come on. Let us go to the market."

As they drew near the center of town, Jenna heard the bell tower pealing its announcement of the start of trade. The town's crier spread news to the public and the reek of animals began to mingle with the smells of cooking sausages, dried hops, and sour pickles. Unfortunately, they couldn't compete with the squalid stench of unwashed bodies.

Jenna's eyes swarmed with the sights. Preston was a variable feast of animation, and made Hawkshead's market seem pitiful and spare. The minstrels and tumblers, quack doctors and fortune-tellers all laced themselves through the motley arrangement of livestock and booths. The stalls were set up by vendors who were experts at enticing buyers to release their coins. They passed a street seller with earthenware jugs of fresh milk, and another advertising newly baked pies stuffed with meat and dried fruits of apple and pear. She watched a merchant selling newspapers, rags, wool fleeces, and doormats. Whatever odds and ends his customers needed he pulled from a remote corner of his cart.

Servants, sent out by their employers to buy kitchen goods,

loitered about the tinkers selling cookware. Couples ambled, their heads bent over tables with bits of ribbon and jewelry. The sounds of a pennywhistle slithered in between those of cattle bells and children's squeals.

During the next hour and a half, whatever they took off Henry's back to sell was soon replaced by other goods they purchased. It was a fair outcome, and although it wasn't everything they requested, whatever was missing would be bought later with the weighty pouch of coins Jenna would be bringing back. Her father would, undoubtedly, be pleased.

Last, they needed to meet the printer, William Way, and procure the *other* list. Then, finally, she could make her way home. Daniel noted the address and Jenna followed behind as he wound his way through the tangle of back streets. Although it was early, the paths were clogged with people who jostled about on their way to or from the market. They had to be careful with the horses, especially Henry, because he wasn't used to children darting in front and underfoot. It unsettled him, and Jenna did her best to keep him from becoming too skittish to control.

They stopped in front of a cooper's shop. Jenna slid off Henry and almost onto the foot of a passing hawker. As he nimbly stepped out of the way of her oncoming boot, their shoulders collided. She heard the tinkling of trinkets he carried in a box, strapped about his neck and open for everyone to see. He apologized for the run-in and turned, dashing off in the opposite direction, but met up squarely with Daniel's chest.

Daniel grabbed him by the shoulder with one hand and put the other in front of his face, open-palmed. "Give it back," he said evenly, "or I will strip you myself until I've found it."

The scrappy man rolled his eyes skyward and pulled a leather coin bag from the inside of his skirt coat. He politely handed Daniel the purse and slipped, waiflike, back into the thick mass of people. Daniel stood only a few steps away from Jenna, who had watched the entire incident with complete surprise—especially the part where her coin purse emerged. She gaped at him, horrified, aware that because of her lack of market skills, she came across as easy prey.

Daniel threw the bag in the air for her to catch, but it was intercepted by a stout man with wiry ginger hair. He wore no coat, and his sleeves were rolled to his elbows to reveal thickly muscled forearms, covered in the same coat of curls as his head.

"I'll take that," he said, walking up to Daniel and giving him the stiff embrace of a man who's used to keeping a wide berth of personal space.

Daniel smiled warmly but took the bag from the man's beefy, ink-stained hands. "Not all, William. Not this time. Malcolm needs some of it back." He opened the bag and took out a handful of the coins, which William quickly pocketed. "Here, Jenna, now put it out of sight." He tossed the bag into her hands.

William's gaze turned to follow the coin purse and met with Jenna's eyes. "Christ! Ye look jest like your mother," he said, putting a hand over his heart. He looked to Daniel. "It's like seeing a ghost."

Daniel nodded. "She should get used to hearing it, I expect."

"Even her eyes! Green as moss and I thought I'd no' see that color again." William peered at Jenna once more, shaking his head.

"Hello," she said tentatively, "I'm Jenna."

"I ken who ye are. I saw ye as a snot-nosed bairn, years ago." He tilted his head upward and scratched under his neck, where the bristles of his beard ended in pale skin. "Has it been that long since I've been in the company of her kin?" he wondered aloud.

"Perhaps it is time to remedy that," Daniel said.

"Oh aye," William agreed, looking seriously at Daniel under the broad rim of his eyebrows. "It's getting too crowded down here for my liking." He turned to Jenna. "Tell your da I'll see him soon."

Not wanting to appear rude, but wary of the time, Jenna leaned closer to him. "My father. Yes. He sent me for—"

"I ken what you're here for. And ye have it. It's in your purse." He made a quick nod of farewell to Daniel and disappeared behind a fruit cart.

Jenna looked at Daniel, again stunned by the quick interaction, and then fumbled for the coin purse she'd already hidden on the inside of her skirt. Sure enough, a miniature scroll of parchment had been placed in it. She refastened the pouch and looked up to see Daniel nod his head to follow.

They reached the outskirts of town and rode in silence for hours. Jenna wanted to talk to Daniel, to explain last night, but her tongue was thick, and her head too muddled. At noon, they crossed a narrow wooden bridge with the horses in tow and stopped on the other side. Daniel looked up into the heavy, gray sky and said, "You need to hurry. Your father will be worried."

She steeled herself, took a breath and said, "I didn't mean to kiss you last night."

He chortled. "I disagree."

"Well, you also didn't protest. And if I remember correctly, you kissed me back." Flustered, she fought for control.

He shook his head. "First of all, you were so affected by the wine I'm surprised you have any memory of yesterday at all. And second, if I should ever kiss you, you would not forget it." One side of his mouth curled with humor. "I will see you next month, when I return." He swung into his saddle and turned his horse back toward town. "I have put food in your saddlebag for later. Now be off and do not stop for anyone." One amber eye flashed over his shoulder before he took off at a gallop in the opposite direction.

Apart from the occasional stumble from the odd protuberance under foot, Henry instinctively led the way with nary a comment or correction from Jenna.

The sky grew a deeper shade of heavy gray, and she spurred their progress on until at last, she decided the horse needed a few minutes of rest and water. She led Henry to a screen of thin oak saplings off the path, to a little creek where he lapped water thirstily. She pulled one of the bags from the saddle, amazed at Daniel's efficiency in distributing all of the goods.

Inside the leather pouch, she found a few withered apples, obviously intended for the horse, and several tidbits she guessed Margaret had thrown together for their departure. She also found Daniel's luminous silver flask, the one with the etchings from his grandfather. A tiny piece of paper peeked out of the leather case. She unrolled it. *In vino veritas* was penned in black ink. "In wine there is truth," she translated from the Latin phrase. She stood quietly, fed the apples to Henry and listened to him crunch the flesh of the sweet fruit. "In wine there is nausea, is more like it," she said aloud.

She flipped open the cap and inhaled the fragrant scent. Recoiling a little, she capped the sherry and returned it to the leather bag. She would have to be very cold indeed to warm her insides with that particular potion today.

A few chunky snowflakes began to swirl and fall from the lead-colored sky. At least it wouldn't rain. There was nothing worse in her mind than having to spend the day soaked to the bone, wrapped in layers of dripping, smelly wool. She wondered how sheep could stand the smell of themselves when sodden.

She apologized to Henry for the short respite as she clambered back into the saddle and took the reins. He didn't mind and faithfully picked up his pace, likely content to head onward, where he knew he would find rest and recompense for his efforts.

As the light grew dim and the falling snow began in earnest, she calculated the rest of the journey. They'd done well, with only seven or eight miles to cover before reaching the cottage, but it would be well into the night when she'd finally come upon it. The ground was covered with a blanket of white, and the surrounding countryside had grown quiet, any noises now muffled by the snowfall.

In the distance, she recognized a carriage. It stood in the middle of the road, pitched at an awkward angle, one wheel lying broken. There were no horses attached to the yoke, and Jenna guessed the cart had been abandoned.

She came alongside the carriage door and noted the Clifton crest. With a glance inside to make sure it was empty, she jerked back, spotting what looked like a bear. It rolled along the seat from side to side, suddenly caterwauling. Henry shied away from the outburst of sound and whinnied in protest as Jenna tried to rein him in.

The fur-covered figure flung open the coach door and shouted, "It is about time! I nearly froze to death having to wait for you—*idiota*!"

Jenna peered through the gloomy darkness. "Would that be the Lady Lucia?"

A livid face appeared from beneath the fur blanket. "Of course it is. And you'd better be my driver." The face retreated under the covering, clearly expecting the delay to be over.

"I'm sorry to disappoint you, milady, but I am not," Jenna said, again trying to hold a skittish Henry from bolting away from the hairy beast. "Might I be of assistance?"

The face did not reappear but said loudly, "Do you have a wheel?"

"No, I'm afraid not."

"Then you too are an idiot," she snapped, muted by the fur.

"I beg to differ, milady," Jenna said, keeping her tone even. "I seem to be the one with transport."

A dampened "Humph" came from beneath the coat.

"You cannot stay here. Are you aware of the storm?"

Lady Lucia threw back the cover. "Of course I am aware of it. That is why I sent the man out to find a wheel, but apparently if I want something done, I must myself do it."

It was almost like prodding a rabid boar, Jenna decided. "I would suggest you not wait any longer for your man. I doubt he'd be able to find his way back. The snowstorm is growing heavier. You'd best come with me. I'm heading to your home, as it is."

"I will not walk. I would rather stay here and freeze than be eaten by wild animals," she stated emphatically.

"I think most of the wild animals will be tucked away in their own homes by now—at least until after the storm. And you needn't worry about walking; you can ride Henry." Jenna patted the horse on his shoulder, an advance apology.

"I do not ride pack mules," Lady Lucia huffed.

"Well"—Jenna bristled—"it may be a difficult night for you, then, and I wish you luck surviving it." Jenna spurred Henry forward. For one fleeting moment she thought how she'd actually be doing Lord Pembroke a favor by allowing the spoilt woman to remain here, stubbornly on her own, succumbing to a frozen demise.

But then she paused. *This* young woman was the idiot. Was she truly so dense as to believe she could survive the night in a coach during a snowfall? She was turning back when Lady Lucia poked her head out the open window. "Wait!"

Jenna turned the horse and walked him back to the carriage. "Milady, we need to go. The choice is to either walk or ride my *pack mule*. Henry is loaded as it is, and cannot carry both of us."

Lady Lucia stretched a hesitant foot out of the carriage and onto the first step.

"Have you no walking shoes?" Jenna gaped at her ridiculous footwear. A delicate leather sole and a tiny, perilous-looking heel. "Oh, for heaven's sake, you'll have to ride. There's no way you'll get anywhere in those things."

It took a while to get Lady Lucia and her bulky fur blanket into the saddle, as the lady did not care for horses and stated so with great regularity. It took longer for Jenna to make it clear they would not take anything other than her person. Lucia griped at the injustice of leaving her myriad private possessions.

Henry remained wild-eyed and fearful of the other animal he

was now forced to carry, and continued to sidestep in an attempt to see over his shoulder. But Jenna's hold on his rein was firm, and she pulled his attentions forward and down the path through the snow. After three quarters of an hour, Jenna halted the horse.

"We have to stop," she announced, raising her voice above the wind. She was covered in snow and fearful of losing her way. "I think I see the lights of a cotter's farm, and I'm going to ask for shelter for the night. We won't make it home at this point, that's certain."

"Is it a villa?"

"A *villa*?" Jenna repeated.

"*Sì. Grandioso casa?*"

"Is what a villa?"

"The *farm*! Is a farm the same thing as a villa?"

Jenna snorted and bit down on the insides of her cheeks. "Yes. Exactly. There will be servants, featherbeds, and massive amounts of hot food."

"*Benissimo*. I would step inside nothing less. And they must have good wi—" Lady Lucia abruptly stopped speaking and let out a piercing scream. Jenna turned around in time to see Henry's ears flatten, the whites of his eyes flash, and his front legs rear in an attempt to shake off the frightful burden wriggling on his back. He was successful.

The horse took off, spooked, and squealing almost as loudly as Lady Lucia had. She'd landed in a bundle of fur and snow, shrieking Sicilian insults at the second male to abandon her today.

Jenna rushed over. "Milady, are you all right? What happened?"

Lady Lucia spit long locks of her hair out of her mouth and sat up. "Your stupid mule threw me off—that is what happened!"

"I meant what happened to make you scream?"

She flung an accusatory finger to the sky. "The snow—it fell inside . . . onto my skin!"

Jenna stared at her. "What? The snow touched you and you felt the need to scream?"

"It is cold and I don't like it."

Jenna thought she might scream herself, but took in a deep breath of icy air and searched around for Henry. She could hear him snorting and stamping the ground in the woods not far away. She whistled for him and turned to Lady Lucia, shouting above the growing wind. "Get up. You need to get back on Henry. More important, we need to get out of the storm."

Lady Lucia grumbled but found her feet, while Jenna whistled again for Henry. The horse pranced at a distance, eyes wild and white in the dark. He refused to come any closer. Jenna shook her head and shouted, "You'll have to walk. It's not that far."

Lady Lucia balked. "What? Never. How can I walk in this?"

"Let's go!"

"Wait. Give me your shoes."

Jenna was at her wits' end. "You've got to be mad."

"No. It is the only way. My feet are not used to this cold, but yours . . ."

Jenna wanted to choke her. She flipped her skirt up and reached for her dirk.

Lady Lucia backed up, crying, "What are you doing?"

Jenna reached for the large fur blanket Lucia had rewrapped herself in and yanked it off her shoulders. "Step aside," she said icily.

Ignoring the young woman's whimpering protests, Jenna laid the fur on the ground and sliced off two ragged squares. "Put your feet in the center." Lady Lucia did so with mild suspicion. Jenna wrapped the fur around the girl's feet, ripped off a length of leather cord at her waist and the piece holding back her hair, and bound the fur around Lady Lucia's calves. She stood up, brushed the snow from her skirts, and said through clenched teeth, "Now walk."

They did. But the light was impossible to find. One moment it was directly in front of them, then for an agonizing few minutes, obscured by the squalling snow. When it reappeared, it was farther away and on their left—or their right, but never where Jenna thought it should be. The wind whipped from all directions.

After thirty minutes, Lady Lucia threw herself to her knees. "I cannot go on. . . . I must rest. . . . I am too cold. . . . We shall die! We are going to die!"

Jenna whirled to grab the girl by the shoulders, seizing two fistfuls of fur and probably little else. She shook what she held viciously. "Get up!"

"I cannot." She wept.

"Fine. Then know this. *We* will not die. *You* will die."

"When you reach the villa . . . send them out to find me."

Jenna wanted to turn and leave her. Henry whinnied in protest a distance away. She knew she had to get them all to shelter or they truly *would* die. All of them. She looked at Lady Lucia, her pale face, her loss of resolve. Something had to be done. They were so close. Jenna took a bracing breath, raised her hand, and slapped the girl across the face as hard as she could.

Lady Lucia's eyes went wide. Her tiny white teeth revealed

themselves beneath two curling lips. Jenna guessed there would be an outline of her handprint across her cheek.

The young woman growled, "You have just slapped a *lady*!"

Jenna blanched and felt the blood drop to her feet. "I'm sorry, milady! It's just—"

"You will pay for this," Lady Lucia said evenly.

She would, Jenna thought. If they came out of this alive, Jenna would be drawn and quartered by her father before sundown. The icy snow scraped across her skin, raw and biting, and she peered through the blinding snow, desperate to find Henry. She heard his fervent whinnying. "Henry!" she called, "Oh, for God's sake, where are you?"

"Well, I never...." A large hand landed on Jenna's shoulder and she spun to see the rosy, weathered face of an old man staring down at her.

Jenna nearly burst with relief. "Oh, thank God," she cried, her lungs ragged and desperate. "Sir ... we've been searching ... for shelter. We are lost...."

Jenna looked at Lady Lucia, whose hair was covered in white, crystals clinging to her pale, delicate skin. They needed to get inside.

"Please ...," Jenna begged the man.

He pointed to a door six paces from where they stood.

"Take her, please." Jenna gave the man a beseeching look. "I've got to find my horse. Do you have a barn?"

Again the man pointed. "Your horse is standing by it. That's how I come to find you. Heard his bellowing, then yours." The man, covered with snow, picked up a rough length of knotted rope and put it in Jenna's frozen hands. "I've tied it to the doors of both barn and house. Don't lose it, for I'll not be out to seek you."

Jenna followed the rope, and *did* find Henry at the barn door, none too pleased. She unloaded the horse and settled him in a stall next to an aging dappled mare. She rummaged through the saddlebags, looking for something to give the man in exchange for the night's lodging. She'd decided on a bottle of whisky from the several she'd been asked to bring back. Her father would be upset had she not offered something as recompense.

After bringing Henry water and a meager bucket of oats from the rough sack hanging on the wall, she ruffled his ears, apologized, and wished him a good night. He murmured softly at her in between mouthfuls of his supper. Jenna left the stable and found the rope. She braced herself against the snow and wind, and soon arrived at the door to the house on the other end.

She pushed through the cotter's door and found a woman's shriveled face, peeking from beneath several layers of worn knitted shawls. Beyond her was the elderly man, arching a white eyebrow that sprouted more hair than the top of his head.

The woman opened her mouth to speak, revealing toothless gums, and grunted while pointing toward the meager fireplace. Jenna discovered Lady Lucia, stretched out on a straw tick bed, placed in front of the fire. The fur she'd been using as a cloak was beneath her, and her deep saffron-colored silk dress was spread out in golden waves about her legs. The makeshift boots Jenna had fashioned remained strapped to her feet. She looked pale and distressed. The old woman looked up at Jenna, her eyes asking for an explanation of what lay before her.

Jenna came around the side of the cot. She would not show

further bad manners in front of the couple. "Milady, are you well?" She almost choked at the sweetness in her own voice.

Lady Lucia moaned in answer and rolled her eyes. "How could anyone be well in a place like this? I am being tortured for my sins and only the Holy Mother of Christ could know how it is I suffer. I expect I will die from this snowstorm, won't I?"

Jenna smiled at the old woman, embarrassed, and perched on the edge of the cot. She leaned closer to the girl. "I understand this is far from what you are accustomed to, milady, but these people are doing their level best. Could you kindly sit up?" Jenna looked into her coal-black eyes and saw them shift from self-inflicted despair to a dark fury.

"You think I do not feel true anguish?" She sat up on her elbows. "You have *no* idea what a lady must feel like in a situation such as this."

Jenna leaned in and whispered, "Perhaps you're right. I may not know how you feel"—*because I would never allow myself to wallow in such self-pity!*—"but these are only the temporary symptoms of being wet and cold, and probably hungry. It will pass."

The old man approached Jenna and announced, "We've got naught but stew—will it sit right with her?"

Jenna glanced at him, summoned a face of gratitude, and nodded yes. He dragged a low stool from the corner of the room to the rickety table, and tipped a wooden crate onto its side and close to the other chairs. He sat on the crate and motioned for them to join him while the old woman brought bowl after bowl from the fireplace. Finally, she set a glass jar and something round, covered in a linen cloth, in front of the man.

Jenna rose from the bed and waved at Lady Lucia to come. The young woman cast a suspicious eye at the table's contents, moved slowly toward them, and edged into one of the chairs. Her presence in the cottage, with her elegant clothing and jewelry dangling from neck and wrists, conflicted with the rest of her surroundings.

The furnishings were sparse and antiquated, the only luxury being a few tattered quilts on a rickety chest, by the bed. The fireplace sputtered feebly, unable to compete with the freezing temperatures. Jenna noted everything else was likely made by hand, or gathered from outside. Dried herbs and flowers hung from the smoky ceiling beams, a number of hand-carved household tools resided in the corner, and a few bits of scarred pottery stood on a sideboard.

The old man uncovered the mound in front of him and revealed a loaf of bread. He tore off chunks, doling it out, and then slid the glass jar of warm molasses to the center of the table. Jenna's mouth watered at the sight of the steaming bread and smiled in thanks to the old woman.

"The name's Samuel Banks, and that's Celia," the man nodded while pouring ale from a stone jug. "She's not got a tongue, which suits fine, for I've ears that hear poorly anyways."

Lady Lucia looked at the woman, wincing. "She has no tongue?"

"Her father thought her too wordy a lass and fitted her with a scold's bridle when she were young."

Lady Lucia reeled back and looked to Jenna for an explanation.

"A scold's bridle. A torture device made for women who were found outspoken or who liked to gossip." She turned to Celia. "I'm so sorry."

Samuel continued, "After a few days, her tongue swoll up and they needed to cut it off."

Celia shrugged and sipped her stew.

Lady Lucia stippled the sweet molasses onto her bread. "If any person tried to do that to me, I would tear out their heart first."

She probably would, and spread it on toast for breakfast, Jenna thought.

They ate the food in relative silence, pieces of bread sopping up the thin stew. The pot held few vegetables, as it was the end of winter, but the onions and sparse chunks of bacon, mixed with the venison, made for a delicious meal. When they had finished, Jenna cleaned the bowls and spoons with Celia, and placed them back onto the dilapidated sideboard.

Lady Lucia balanced on the edge of the bed, gazing into the fireplace, sighing with boredom. Jenna fetched the whisky and set it before Samuel, who was filling his clay pipe with a few pinches of tobacco. "Thank you," she said, but Samuel shook his head.

"No need, lass." Samuel lit the pipe. "I've got no stomach for it any longer, and Celia never took with drink. Thanks all the same."

The withered old woman picked up the pile of quilts and motioned for Jenna to follow. With a candle for guidance, they scaled a narrow ladder to the cramped, frosty loft. Celia laid the blankets on a tattered straw tick mattress and, turning to Jenna, raised her eyebrows in question.

"Of course it will be all right. Thank you again."

Jenna prodded Lady Lucia up the ladder, ignoring her complaints.

"This is most ridiculous," she said, watching Jenna lay out the quilts. "I should not be expected to sleep in a pigsty." She sighed crossly, her breath a white fog. "Is there no way to make this place warmer? I will freeze before morning comes."

Jenna glared at the girl, who stood with her hands on her tiny hips. *Do you ever stop complaining?* She retrieved the whisky from her bag. "Here," she said, thrusting the bottle at her.

Lady Lucia took a step back and eyed Jenna suspiciously. "What is it?"

"This is the cure to all that ails us at the moment. If you drink enough of it, you will become warm, the room will seem more than sufficient, and I will become appealing company."

Lady Lucia's distrustful gaze never wavered. "What is this magic potion, then?"

"Just whisky, and I can tell you right now you're not going to like it, but . . . ," Jenna said, putting a hand up to defer any objections. "If you can get past the taste, then I promise you, all of this"—she gestured with a wave—"will no longer be an issue."

Lady Lucia shrewdly assessed the truthfulness of the pledge and the element of risk involved. Then, sweeping her eyes around the tiny loft, she grabbed the bottle from Jenna's outstretched hands and uncorked it. She took a long slow breath in, as if she were about to go underwater, and bringing the bottle to her lips, squeezed her eyes shut, and tilted it toward the ceiling.

After the fourth swallow, she brought the bottle down quickly, and her watering eyes popped open, wide and hysterical. She clutched her throat and tried to breathe in, but couldn't manage the effort. She coughed and spluttered, fell to her knees, and crawled to the quilt-covered mattress, where she collapsed. Her breath came raggedly, interspersed with Sicilian curses.

After a few moments of reestablishing her intake of air, she rolled onto an elbow, put a hand to her chest, and murmured, "It's like a tiny fire. I thought it had ripped open my throat, but now something glows from on the inside of me." She lay still for another moment, and turned again to Jenna. "It will not kill me?"

I wish, Jenna thought, but shook her head and knelt beside the mattress.

Lady Lucia lay back onto the quilts. Her gaze focused on the mellow candlelight flickering on the ceiling. "You are right. It tastes horrible, but I am finally warm. I could probably walk home now."

"Feel free to try," Jenna murmured.

Lady Lucia looked glazedly at Jenna. "Aren't you going to have any?"

"No, I'm still full from last night."

Lady Lucia hiccuped quietly. "Where were you last night?"

"In Preston. I went to the market."

"There is no place to shop here. Nothing to do . . ." She paused in quiet contemplation. "I hate this place. It is nothing like the kingdom of Sicily, with everyplace beautiful—every*one* beautiful." Her eyes watched the shadows dancing above the mattress, and she sighed deeply. She turned and peered hard at Jenna. "I have seen you dancing with that dark man . . . at the wedding." Her words were softened with liquor, but Jenna was wary.

"A family friend."

"I knew someone like him once," she said, a shock of glossy black hair falling across her face. She grew quiet, lost in her reverie. "We belonged to each other. I suppose we still do."

Jenna looked at her, confused. "But you're a woman about to be married."

Lady Lucia sniffed. "What difference does marriage make? It is for influence. For money. A title." She shook her head at Jenna. "You do not know how it is. I am property to be bought."

"But what about the duke's son? Don't you have feelings for him?"

"No, but it doesn't matter if I did. He'll not be faithful to me. Already his eyes wander."

Jenna's stomach twisted uneasily. "Then why don't you do something about it?" She couldn't believe she was giving this advice.

"No. All I must do is marry this man, and then I am free to find"—her eyes searched the rafters—"how do you say . . . distractions. Although nothing will ever compare to my . . . *friend*." She sighed heavily. "I am lonely. I miss him so."

Jenna looked at Lady Lucia and saw a fragile, young woman, unhappy and terribly out of place. "It must be difficult. To be told who you'll marry."

Lady Lucia sat up and frowned. "Money is who I marry. The face of it matters little." She lay back down, her hands across her stomach, and closed her eyes. "My mother forces me. My family forces me, as our fortune is depleted, and I am their only hope."

Lady Lucia puffed out a hot breath of air. "For the longest time I was able to foil their plans—to break each engagement by making myself as unimaginable a prospective wife as possible. I wanted to go home, to be with . . ." She sighed. "But Mamma tells me this is my last chance. If I do not marry, we will be destitute." She laughed ruefully. "And now I am faced with someone who does *not want* to marry me."

Jenna's eyes widened with shock. "What?"

Lady Lucia waved a hand in the air and let it fall beside her head, her words beginning to slur with sleep. "He promises he will. But I feel sorry for him."

"Why?" Jenna whispered.

Lady Lucia was silent, and Jenna feared she may have fallen asleep without answering, but she took a big breath in and shook her head as she pulled the quilt up to her chin. "Because I have forgotten how to be kind. And I know I will never love anyone else . . . again."

Spools of pity unfurled in Jenna's heart as she studied the sleeping girl. But as easily as the fragile facade poured out of her, beneath those silk gowns was a core of rock. Lady Lucia, Jenna realized, was more dauntless than half the clan in her cottage.

The next morning, Jenna rose early and had Henry loaded and ready to go before Lady Lucia had risen. Once up, she was cantankerous and petulant, leaving Jenna to wonder where the pitiable and touching young woman from last night had gone. Jenna wished she could just leave and be rid of the returning, unlikeable version of the Sicilian girl. But she couldn't do that to the Bankses. They didn't deserve it.

Jenna managed to assuage Henry's fears long enough to allow Lady Lucia to ride, and although the trek was somewhat rough, Jenna led him carefully.

After an hour, and perhaps no more than four or five miles from Withinghall, Jenna heard the distant sound of men's voices calling. She stopped at one point and tried to make out the words. Suddenly, a man stepped from behind a screen of trees. It was one of the duke's men of arms, who Jenna regularly saw parading around the grounds of the great house.

"I've found one of them!" he shouted, cupping a hand to his mouth. He blew a piercing whistle through his fingers and turned to Jenna. "Have you seen Lady Lucia?"

She pointed at the mound on top of her horse. "Probably sleeping . . . still."

There was a great deal of commotion, with the echoing shouts of men, and the thudding of approaching hooves. Lord Pembroke appeared on horseback, accompanied by several other men following close behind. Each of them looked as if they'd not seen their beds last night.

Lady Lucia, who recognized the precise moment for squeezing the most out of the scene, carefully came to, lifted her head, and moaned in discomfort.

"Where am I?" she whimpered, looking around dizzily. "I . . . I'm so cold," she cried, sliding out of the saddle and into the arms of the brawny guard.

"Bring her to the carriage!" another guard ordered.

Lord Pembroke dismounted and stepped closer to Jenna, aware of the many people around them. "Miss MacDuff, are you all right?" he said quietly, relief apparent in his eyes.

Jenna nodded and smiled, tight-lipped. She looked around at the gathering crowd of men and murmured, "Delightful girl. We've so much in common." Jenna brushed the snow off the front of her cloak and raised her eyes to see Lord Pembroke biting his lower lip, trying desperately not to smile.

"Yes, well . . . thank you," he mumbled roughly, sweeping his hand across his chin. He turned to peer into the woods. "Last night, when the lady's carriage had not returned, we dispatched a group of men. As we were preparing the horses, your father came in to saddle up in search for you. We've been working together all night. It was near impossible with the storm." He hesitated, "Of course, finding the two of you together was the last thing I'd pictured."

"That would make two of us." Jenna frowned. "But I'm sure she'll fill you in on all the captivating details, once she's had a chance to be deloused."

"Jenna!" Angus's voice boomed from across the woods. His husky frame made surprisingly good speed through the thick snow. She had just enough time to see Lady Lucia being carried to the coach, covered in blankets, before Angus grabbed her with both arms and engulfed her in his bearlike hug. He muffled something into her thick hair, growling in Gaelic.

"I thought ye might have finally decided to run away wi' Daniel. Canna say we'd be at all surprised."

She pushed back from the folds of his plaid and glanced at Lord Pembroke, who made a polite bow and excused himself from the circle. He headed toward the carriage and the distressed damsel.

THIRTY

THE NEXT FEW DAYS PROVED BUSY, AS ALL OF THE things Jenna had brought from Preston were put to good use. Small bits to repair the masonry apparatus, new chisels, trowels, hammers, and plumb bobs, and a few household goods, cheaper to buy at the larger markets than local ones, were gratefully accepted as they were unpacked from the saddlebags. There was only so much Henry could carry, but Jenna made sure to bring home a gift for each of the men, as they had done over the years for her whenever they had traveled.

For Angus, Jenna had found a riddleboard and a ridged rolling pin, so he could make oatcakes the way Mrs. Wigginton had shown him in the estate's kitchens, delicate and wafer fine. Duncan was easy to please. Jenna had found a great number of herb packets, picked and pounded for ready use, from a well-known medicine woman who, according to Daniel, regularly held a stall at the market and could be trusted.

Colin was aghast when Jenna gave him a merino wool scarf. "You should have seen Daniel when we came upon the stall," Jenna began. "One of his countrymen was selling woolen goods. They started rattling on in Spanish and then got very quiet. Lucky Daniel was introduced to the *hidden* inventory of goods that came from the peddler's one merino sheep." Jenna's eyes widened. "Here's where it gets interesting. After the quick exchange of money, we zipped away, and Daniel told me that Spain is extraordinarily protective of this breed, and the export of merinos is a crime punishable by death—hence the reason for haste and secrecy." She smiled and pointed to Colin. "Tell no one, and the peddler lives."

She gave her father pipe tobacco but guessed knowing she was back with them, no worse for the wear, was what he cherished most about her return.

Gavin's rough, calloused hands unwrapped a soft leather-bound edition of Giovanni Boccaccio's *On Famous Women*; a collection of one hundred and six biographies, written about either historical or mythological females. It was a book Gavin had been referencing to Jenna for years, trying to recall the details of many stories without success. The gleam of delight in his eyes was unmistakable. "Queens, wives, daughters, and prostitutes shall be your teachers for weeks to come!"

Deciding upon a gift for Tavish was the easiest task. Anything that contained sugar was sure to please his wide grinning mouth. She had filled a cloth sack with comfits of every description: sugarplums, aniseed balls, and candied citrus peel—their sweet perfumes gushing from the open bag. The little boy bounced off the walls with excitement, trying to decide which to taste first.

Finally, Ian. Jenna had no clue if anything would bring even a nominal amount of pleasure to this sour man. She almost bought him a miniature Chinese abacus, hoping its colorful red wooden beads might at least provoke a pleasant reaction, but instead, settled on an intricately hand-carved *sgian dubh*, its pointed tip and razor-sharp edge indicative of their recent exchanges. It was received with a fair amount of indifference.

A week after the excitement of Preston, the clan lingered round the breakfast table, attempting to put off the cold drizzle outside for one last moment of warmth before work.

Jenna's father came in from outside, his eyes bloodshot from a predawn meeting on the outskirts of Hawkshead where a Stuart informant came to deliver him news. He leaned against the door and stared down at everyone around the table. "The first of March. The rooms must be ready by then. The shipments will come in each day thereafter, in the wee hours."

The room crackled with nervous energy as all the men nodded silently.

"And on the night of the seventeenth, the men. Clan leaders will show up somewhere after midnight and the soldiers by dawn." He looked to Jenna. "Your birthday will act as cover. We shall throw a *cèilidh* to celebrate. No one questions extra guests at a party."

A knock on the cottage door brought them to attention and Angus rose to answer it. One of Mrs. Wigginton's stewards handed him a letter. "It's for you, Malcolm," Angus said, setting the soggy correspondence by his hand.

Malcolm opened the letter and skimmed the writing. He raised his eyebrows and looked around the table. "It appears one of us is to be honored." His face formed a half smile and settled on Jenna. "We're invited to take tea with Lord Pembroke and Lady Lucia. They've asked ye be the guest of honor to thank you for the timely rescue of the lady," he read.

Jenna's stomach somersaulted. "No, thank you."

Malcolm's brows lowered and his eyes grew narrow. "I beg your pardon?"

"I would assume you'd think it a terrible idea. Mixing with the family in the estate when at any moment they could discover what it is that we're doing—"

There was a muffled thump at the door. Everyone jumped and Gavin dashed to open it. Beyond it was the scrambling figure of Garrick Wicken, brushing mud from the back of his breeks. Flustered, he put up a filthy hand and pointed toward the house. "Sorry to bother. It's that I saw a young lad messing about your cottage and thought him up to no good. Slipped in the spring mud, now, didn't I?" He looked about at the unwelcoming faces at the table. "Seems he was just dithering. No harm done, see? G'day to you." He bobbed his head in farewell and slogged toward the stables.

The room was silent, but Jenna knew everyone was reviewing the last words she'd said, appraising what might have been overheard.

Malcolm leaned in toward Gavin. "Take him to town. Buy him as many rounds as he'll stomach. And spin a tale like ye've never done before, Gavin. Convince him that his nosin' round this cottage is all for naught and lead him down some other lane. Feed him a whole barrel full of red herring, for we need to get this bloodhound off our scent, understood?"

Gavin dashed for his coat and was out the door in a flash.

Jenna cleared her throat and then began to gather crumbs from the table in front of her. She noticed her father's clasped hands, one thumb making lazy strokes on the other.

The thumb stopped. "Be ready at three."

With timely precision, the rest of men rose and filed out the door. Jenna sat at the table, staring at a small pile of crumbs. She didn't want to go. She couldn't go. Because she knew that beneath Lady Lucia's fine exterior, there lived something primal and hurting. And if provoked she would eat Jenna alive. The way things stood now, she was nothing more than fish bait.

The afternoon continued its gloomy drizzle, all the snow from the past week having melted, leaving rivulets of thick mud in its place. Jenna had spent the last of the family market money on a dress Daniel insisted she buy. It wasn't new, but it showed no signs of heavy wear, and the color, a soft sunny yellow, suggested a hint of spring. It was plain, but she had always been drawn to simple and trouble-free clothing. Bows and ties got in the way, lace was always catching, and excessive folds, in Jenna's mind, were an indulgent waste of material.

The gown, while not the height of fashion, would suit Jenna for many occasions to come, but showing up in Lord Pembroke's parlor to be honored by him and his bride was not one she'd envisioned.

She smoothed the front of the primrose-colored skirt and looked down at her roughened leather boots. Grateful for the height of the dress's previous owner, Jenna noticed it nearly covered her grubby, serviceable shoes. One last brush of her hair left it falling down heavily around her shoulders. Even if it wasn't fashionably upswept, it would provide the extra benefit of warmth on this damp day.

She found her father at the table, going over his new inventory list, and noticed he was outfitted in his finest kilt and snowy-white linen shirt. His rough, wiry hair had been pulled into a neatly plaited queue in the back, and he'd even taken the time to comb his beard. He was resplendent in his formal wear. Little did he know he was dressing for her funeral, for when he'd hear of Jenna's behavior—slapping Lady Lucia—it would be time to find a pine box. At least he would appear handsomely dressed when losing his temper. That seemed to count for a lot with these people.

When shown to the parlor, Jenna looked around uneasily for a place to sit that would neither break from antiquity, nor present a level of discomfort so unendurable she would fidget throughout the entire event. She settled on a modest but well-padded chair with the hope that when their hosts arrived, she would not find she'd chosen somebody else's preferred seat. Her father's tight smile did nothing to buoy her confidence, and she soon discovered the chair had a most precarious wobble. Jenna vowed to sit perfectly still, and the two of them watched, in rigid silence, as one of the maids poured the tea in preparation.

When the door opened, Lord Pembroke entered with his and Lady Lucia's mother on either arm, both immaculately dressed in gowns of colorful blue and green silk. Jenna and her father stood as they came around to the suite of chairs and the tea.

Malcolm made a formal bow to the women as they were introduced and announced grandly, "Your servant, madams." He lowered his head to Lord Pembroke, saying, "Good day, sir, and thank you for the honor."

Jenna made polite curtsies to each, and only raised her eyes when Lord Pembroke spoke. Her heart thumped loudly. She was shocked by the thrill she felt in seeing him again.

"The honor of your company belongs to us, sir. And the tribute of the tea is in admiration of your daughter's, uh . . . courage," he finished with a smirk.

Lady Lucia's mother took Jenna by the shoulders and kissed her on either cheek. "*Non posso ringraziarla abbastanza!* I cannot begin to thank you for what you've done."

Jenna shook her head. "I am only grateful for Mr. Banks and his wife. We were lucky to find the shelter."

The countess nodded. "We have sent a gift of thanks. We've heard much about them."

Jenna's brows rose. *I'll bet.*

"But Lady Lucia would not be here today, if it wasn't for you," she said, eyes bright and glistening.

Jenna looked back and forth. "Where is milady? Is she unwell?" she asked, hopeful. "Perhaps it was the whisky?"

Lord Pembroke choked on a mouthful of tea, his eyes bulging. Lady Lucia's mother looked confused and stood awaiting further explanation. The duchess, whom Jenna thought unusually pale, merely raised her eyebrows, one side of her mouth curling upward, while Jenna's father turned to her in shocked surprise.

"Jenna!" he said, his brows furrowed together.

"She was cold." Jenna shrugged. "And it helped," she murmured to him.

At once the heavy wooden doors of the parlor opened and Lady Lucia waltzed in like a spring breeze, her gown the epitome of dappling sunlight. It was softly quilted with yellow folds of silk falling from gathers and tucks all across her tiny waist, and miniature spray roses of red and gold sprinkled about from head to toe. The bodice was squarely cut across her chest and displayed a delicate choker of striking red stones. Her sleek hair was piled high on her head and pinned in place with jewels that matched her necklace.

For a brief moment, Jenna's nerves disappeared as all she could focus on was how utterly stunning the young woman looked. Everyone turned to watch Lady Lucia and her grand entrance. Everyone, except Lord Pembroke. He had *not* turned around to face the door, but instead stared at Jenna. She raised her eyebrows in question, and he smiled, faintly shaking his head.

"Lord Pembroke, where shall I be sitting?" Lady Lucia inquired in her affected glossy tones. She held out one velvet-covered hand; it needed leading.

"Wherever you please, milady. Pick whatever suits you," he answered.

Malcolm gestured to his chair and to Jenna's. "How about one of these, milady?"

Jenna's eyes flew to her father. "Not my chair," she tried to whisper to him, but he glared back.

"Don't be rude," he hissed.

"Thank you," Lady Lucia said, gliding across the floor toward them. She curtsied delicately at the duchess, made an indiscernible nod in the direction of her mother, and then, dexterously pivoting toward Jenna's father, put her hand out to be kissed. She lowered her gaze and gasped. "You are wearing a skirt!" She pulled her hand back. "Why for are you wearing a skirt?"

Malcolm glanced around uncomfortably before answering. "Well, milady," he faltered. "This isna a skirt. It's a kilt."

"Are you mocking women? Is that your intent?" Her eyes were round and disapproving.

"Nay," he replied, taken aback, "this is the formal dress of my country and clan."

"Lady Lucia." Lord Pembroke and the countess broke in at the same time.

"How preposterous," she said. "Do you know how silly you look in that costume?" She ignored the bulging glare of her mother.

"I wasna aware, but I'll try to appreciate your candor." He turned to Lord Pembroke, who looked aghast, and said, "Perhaps a trip to the north may be helpful in acquainting the lass wi' the habits of my kind."

"Yes," Lord Pembroke said, glowering at Lady Lucia. "A fine idea."

He nodded toward the chair Jenna had vacated to indicate everyone was waiting, and Jenna noticed a small look of regret that clung to the young woman's face. Jenna felt a thread of compassion among the tangled ball of worries in her stomach. The girl truly was stuck in this role of abominable behavior.

When at last her bottom made contact with the cushion and her weight fell upon it, it teetered. A splintering crack filled the air as the chair gave in to its burden. She pitched sideways, nearly falling before Lord Pembroke and Malcolm leapt from their seats and saved her from the spill. They settled her into a new chair and had the butler remove the broken furniture. Lady Lucia's eyes flashed angrily toward Jenna, but there was nothing she could do to defend herself from the accusatory glare.

Jenna tried fixing a sympathetic expression on her face instead. She watched Lord Pembroke pick up his teacup and the line of conversation. "Where is your clan located?" he asked Malcolm.

"Mainly in Fife and throughout up to Aberdeen, but our family home is at the foot of West Lomond—nay far from the village of Falkland," he finished.

Family home. Jenna huffed. *I can't even remember what it looks like.*

"I've never been to Scotland myself," the Duchess of Keswick said. "I understand it's stunning."

"Oh aye." Malcolm turned, a smile brightening his face. "According to Jenna, there isna any other place we should be. She pines for it every day." He patted her hand.

"Well, I'm sorry His Grace isn't here," she continued. Then turning to her son, she said, "You know he's very keen on hunting in Scotland and would have enjoyed discussing the places he's visited. But as it is"—she turned back to Malcolm—"he's away on matters regarding further local unrest. There has been growing talk of the rebellion and rioting. I myself will rest easier once your men have completed the garrison and we can employ several soldiers in it." Curiosity filled her face. "Has it been difficult going? The progress with the garrison, that is?"

Jenna's stomach twisted, thinking of her discussion with Daniel.

What would happen to these people once the soldiers arrived, the ammunition—and now the clan leaders too? Would they be held captive? Would they be injured? She would force her father to answer these questions as soon as they were alone.

"Nay, not a bit." Malcolm stroked his dark beard. "Apart from a few storms, it's been a mild winter, and we havena had to stop work on the masonry."

"How many men do you have?" the countess asked.

"Six—and a half, if ye count the wee apprentice." He chuckled. "We've all got specific jobs. Some masonry—cutting and shaping the stones. Others do carpentry—making shutters, floorboards, doors, and such like."

"What does the half do?" Lady Lucia said haughtily.

"I reckon we'll both find out eventually," he said, amused.

"Well, I'm pleased to hear the work is progressing. I will not sleep well until all the Jacobites are rounded up. I hear they've done a great amount of damage thus far," Lady Lucia's mother said, shaking her head.

The young woman's eyes widened in fear and she leaned back into her chair. "How large are their teeth? Do they have horns?"

"Who?" Lord Pembroke asked, his brows knitting.

"These ferocious biters—we do not have this animal in Sicily."

"They are not animals, Lady Lucia, they are people. Rioters, dissenters, revolutionaries, certainly." Lord Pembroke waved a hand. "Their unpatriotic quest for power will doubtless cause a civil war."

The parlor doors opened again and the butler appeared, crisply apologetic for the interruption. "Master MacDuff, sir, a message for you."

Jenna's father rose and gave Jenna a look of warning as he departed.

Lucia carried on, distressed. "A war? How close are these Jaco-biters and how do they look, so I can recognize them? You must tell me, milord, for I do not want to be taken by one."

"Lucia, *bella*, you do not need to worry. Nobody is after you," her mother cooed.

"She's right, milady." Lord Pembroke sighed. "And I cannot describe what a Jaco*bite* looks like—it could be anyone. It could be Miss MacDuff, for all we know," he said, turning his gaze to her.

Jenna's heart stopped, but she made a feeble shrug, desperate to appear game.

The young woman turned her widened eyes toward Jenna and splashed a bit of her tea, spilling it across her lap.

Lord Pembroke put up a hand. "I wasn't serious, milady. It was only an example."

Lady Lucia rose, dabbing at the tea stains on her gown, tears of frustration brimming at the edges of her eyes. She no longer lis-tened. "I must go change," she said feebly. She left the parlor with the countess following after, a trail of muttered Sicilian in her wake.

Malcolm came in amid all the confusion and, expressing regret, explained he was needed back at the garrison and must beg his leave. He asked Jenna if she could manage her way back to the cottage without him and Lord Pembroke interjected, saying, "I will see her there."

Malcolm, whose face was turned away from Lord Pembroke's, raised his eyebrows in question to Jenna. She answered, "I'm sure I can cope on my own."

"I won't hear of it," Lord Pembroke said firmly. "It's getting dark. Let me get your cloak."

Malcolm put a hasty peck on Jenna's cheek, and a flash of warning in his eyes before departing. Jenna curtsied and thanked the duchess, then left with Lord Pembroke.

They walked down the hill from the house toward the cottage, an uneasy silence between them. Jenna dug her nails into the palms of her hands, steaming over his last comments during tea. She itched with the festering criticism but feared his hunches were becoming finely tuned, so she kept quiet and worked at keeping the hem of her dress above the mud.

"When are you going to announce it?" His eyes searched the horizon and settled on the lake in the distance.

Her heart plummeted to her stomach. "Announce what?"

He turned to her, one graceful brow curved. "Your engagement to . . . what's his name."

Engagement? Jenna's mind scrambled to make use of Lord Pembroke's misinformation. "Do you mean Daniel?" she asked. She thought about denying it but suddenly felt a terrible pang of sympathy for Lady Lucia and didn't want to complicate matters further. "Does it really matter? You have the lovely Lady Lucia."

They walked together, the sounds of muck beneath their feet. After a moment he spoke. "You make her sound as if she were some sort of gift."

Jenna wasn't inclined to have his bride be the subject of their short conversation, but she made another effort to show an element of kindness. "I'm sure she has her redeeming qualities."

They were approaching the cottage and Lord Pembroke slowed.

"Yes, I would imagine she does, but locating them has proven impossible. Strangely enough, I feel obligated to apologize. For her ignorance, at least. She possesses neither skills of diplomacy, nor knowledge of politics." Lord Pembroke turned a questioning blue gaze at her. "But I sense that you do."

Jenna shifted uncomfortably and would not make eye contact with him. "What do you mean?"

"Well, it's just another remarkable characteristic you possess, isn't it?" He eyed her calculatingly, put a hand across the lintel of the doorframe, and barred her way in. "If it were just the fact you could read or write, it would be easy to dismiss the matter. But there are questions about you and your family that keep making the scenario in front of me far more complex than I first thought. You are an enigma, and I've been warned to be suspicious of you." He leaned closer to her, his voice almost a whisper, "So tell me . . . *are* you a Jacobite?"

A gunshot exploded behind the cottage. Jenna saw the ground rushing toward her as she felt Lord Pembroke's weight forcing her down. They lay still for a moment, listening to the wide silence surrounding them. She lifted her chin and scanned the immediate premises while attempting to steady her heartbeat.

Lord Pembroke raised himself to a crouch and whispered, "Go to the rain barrel—stay by the wall."

"Not on your bloody life!" she hissed back. "I'm coming with you."

Apparently, her response did not come as a surprise, for he made no protest. They inched up the cottage wall and pressed against it, then edged to the corner to peer around back. Another blast of gunfire filled the air. Jenna clutched the back of his coat. "Stay back!"

she pleaded. She pushed herself against the wall, nervous of what lay on the other side. The sounds of voices were close approaching.

> *"The auld Stuarts are back again,*
> *The auld Stuarts are back again;*
> *Let howlet Whigs do what they can,*
> *The Stuarts will be back again."*

Two distinctly drunk singers belted out a rowdy chorus together, and Lord Pembroke looked back at her. Although she could barely make out the features of his face, it wasn't a challenge to identify the sarcasm unmasked in his voice. "Friends of yours?"

> *"Wha cares for a' their creeshy duds,*
> *And a' Kilmarnock sowen suds?*
> *We'll wauk their hides and fyle their fuds,*
> *And bring the Stuarts back again."*

Peeking around the corner, she spotted the two inebriated men wandering behind the cottage. Strangers. They were attempting to reload a flintlock pistol, but both the dark and their alcoholic stupor were making it challenging. She wondered in a moment of panic where her clansmen were.

Lord Pembroke pulled her back and put his hand out flat. "Hand me your knife."

"Where's yours?" Jenna said.

He turned to whisper, "I find it challenging to sit in the parlor with a sword attached to my breeches. Now, if you please, give me your knife."

She reached under her dress and retrieved her *sgian dubh*, resignedly handing it to him. "What are you going to do?"

"Do any of the men keep a firearm in the cottage?"

"We have a musket above the door, but it's unloaded and I don't know where the powder's kept," she said, inching back toward the entrance.

"Hopefully, it won't matter." He looked around the corner at the men again, watched them struggle to reload the pistol. "Damn. Where are the guards?" He motioned behind him. "Hurry, get the gun. But be silent about it—and don't light any candles."

Jenna reached the door handle and opened it a crack to squeeze through. She felt her way to the corner of the room and pulled a stool to the doorway. On tiptoe, she unlatched the musket from its leather straps and brought the gun down, surprised at the weight of it. Silently, she slid out the door and over to where Lord Pembroke crouched, watching the men. They were singing another tuneless round of the rebellious chorus.

"Do you have a plan?" She handed him the gun.

"Well, there are only two of them, and they're well liquored. The pistol they're using isn't terribly reliable or accurate; still, I would feel more comfortable coming at them from behind." He turned to her. "If anything goes wrong—run. Go to the house, find the damn guards, wherever *they* are, and tell them what's happened. Do you understand?"

"Of course," Jenna said stiffly.

He bent down, moving closer to her and said, "And when this is all done, perhaps, at last, I shall hear the truth?"

He left with the gun poised at his shoulder, and Jenna's mind whirled with myriad wretched possibilities as to where her father and the rest of her family were when she heard the pistol fire again. It made her ears ring in pain and her whole body jump with fright.

"God bless King James the eighth!" shouted one man, clearly pickled.

"And Bolingbroke!" added the other.

"Who?"

"Bolingbroke," the first one said again.

Lord Pembroke approached the men, his body a shapeless form in the dark. "Drop your weapons," Jenna heard him order. His voice was full of authority. She would have dropped hers, had she been on the opposite side of him.

But she *was* on the opposing side, she thought anxiously, and chances were, in a few short minutes, he was going to find that out.

There was a dull-sounding thud, a soft groan, and then the noise of what sounded like a man falling to the ground. She held her breath for a moment and then heard a second body collapse onto the muddy earth. She peered around the cottage wall, and identified only one upright figure looking down over the other two.

"Bloody idiots," she heard Lord Pembroke say as he bent down for the pistol. She walked toward him, wary of the two still figures.

"What happened?" She watched him feel for a pulse.

"They never heard me coming. I just walked up to the one with the gun and hit him over the head with the butt of the musket. He went down like a stone." He pointed to the second man. "That one, I never touched. He just passed out from too much liquor, I would imagine."

"Your turn," came a husky voice from behind them, and Jenna felt a painful crack on the head.

THIRTY-ONE

"YOU SNORE."

Jenna groaned and opened her eyes to a throbbing ache at the base of her skull. "What?"

"I said, you snore." Lord Pembroke tweaked one of her fingers.

"I don't snore," she murmured confusedly.

"Well, I think you're in a poor position to dispute that if you're unconscious when it occurs." He took a deep breath. "How is your vision? Anything blurry?"

"My memory. Where are we?" She looked around and blinked in the dim light.

"By the looks of it, I would guess in an abandoned barn. But where the barn is located in relation to where we were—I'm not sure. It can't be far. It's still night."

"My head hurts—does yours?" Jenna wished she could rub the painful spot.

"Probably not nearly as much. I'm thick-headed, I've been told."

"Do you know what happened?" She tried recalling the details herself.

"I'm only guessing, but it would seem those two fellows brought friends. It pays to have backup." He turned to peer over his shoulder at Jenna. "So you're telling me neither of the men were associates of yours?"

She snorted. "God forbid." Her face took on a serious nature. "But I highly doubt you'll believe anything I have to say."

"It's not that I don't believe what you say," Lord Pembroke said, again twisting awkwardly, "it's just you've said so little to believe. I have nothing much to go on." He settled back. "Why don't you start filling in a few of the particulars for me? It's not like you can actually run away at this point, can you?" he said sardonically.

Jenna tried twisting the ropes that bound their wrists together as they sat back-to-back on the cold dirt floor.

"I find it curious that you've had these growing suspicions about my situation for some time, and have managed to squelch them successfully up until . . ." She paused and thought about what to say. She was going to answer *up until you believed I was engaged to Mr. Delafuente*, but even thinking these words sent a flush of heat through her body. Plus, it would come across as flirtatious banter, and part of her brain niggled with the admonishment that it was wrong. Lady Lucia's woebegone tale resounded in her head.

"Up until . . ."

"Are you planning to marry that fellow?"

"What?" she exclaimed. "You want to know the answer to *that*? Not *are you really a Jacobite*? Or *why is it you can calculate figures*? Or even, *how come you can't cook*? But rather *are you planning to marry that fellow?* That's the burning query?" She wrenched her shoulders around to make eye contact with him.

"You don't know how to cook?"

She turned back with a sound of incredulous amusement.

"A rule of thumb, Miss MacDuff. . . . Never ask a question you don't already know the answer to."

She turned her head to the side to see his face. It was dark, but she could make out the mud streaks that left marks on his jaw and chin, as surely as it did on hers. She watched his expression, waited to see what it would reveal. "And what is it you know?"

"As much as I need for an educated guess."

"You're lucky," Jenna said. "Until recently, most of my questions have never been answered. I simply go wherever they do. Apparently, though, I'm becoming a liability."

"How so?"

"Well, as I've gathered, my family—the clansmen—never thought I would develop an opinion of my own."

Lord Pembroke laughed. "I can't imagine it came as much of a surprise to them." His tone turned serious. "So what is your opinion about all of this, then?"

Her stomach lurched at the thought of his demanding questions. Given the circumstances, and his level of suspicion, she probably had one of two choices. Answer his question, and take her chances appealing to his sympathies, or be passed off to the local authorities, where no one would give a damn what happened to them. Jenna swallowed hard. "It's not easy to explain, I think. And honestly, all I'm doing *is* thinking about it. Everyone tells me I need to make up my own mind—find a purpose, champion a cause. It's surprising to think it could be different from all of theirs . . . if I wanted it to be."

"Is it?" he probed.

The door burst open with a thundering kick, and a snarling man in a rough shirt and dingy breeks plowed in with a gas lantern. His deep-set eyes and wide forehead displayed a temper that had been toyed with long enough.

"I canna sleep wi' the yapping going on in here," he growled. He knelt down beside them, and pulled two greasy rags from his trouser pocket. "If ye'd just kept quiet like, I wouldna have to do this, but I'm far worn out, and I've had enough of your bantering for one night."

The smell of alcohol was ripe on him, and Jenna steeled herself against the reek of his breath as he tied the oily cloth around her mouth and head. She felt Lord Pembroke's hands wrap around hers, steadying her angst.

The sour-faced man did the same to Lord Pembroke and then stood up gruffly with his lantern. He made his way to the barn door, slammed it shut behind him, and bolted it.

Jenna felt the ropes on her wrist straining as Lord Pembroke wrestled with the cloth binding his mouth. After a minute or two, he had successfully rolled the gag off his face, and it now rested like a dirty necklace around his throat.

"Can you get yours off?" he whispered.

Jenna struggled, tried to rub her chin against her shoulder to pull it downward, but it was tightly bound. She shook her head.

"Oh, the things I could say right now, if I wanted to," he murmured, chuckling and working the ropes at their wrists. His arms were long and the ropes loose enough to allow him to twist sideways somewhat. The strain on her shoulders made her muscles burn, but she realized he was trying to shift enough to get his face closer to hers to help draw the rag down.

He grabbed the bottom edge of it with his teeth and slowly pulled it over her chin. She felt his nose press against her cheek and the stubble of his chin graze her jaw as he worked the cloth loose, bit by bit. His elbow dug into her shoulder blades, pushed for leverage, but she kept quiet, as finally, he pulled the last of it away from her mouth and let it fall around her neck. He reached over one last time, covered her mouth with his, and kissed her. Whatever pains she felt from the raw rope burns and searing muscles were replaced by the feel of her racing heartbeat.

When he broke away and sat again, his back to hers, she was quiet. Finally, she whispered, "Is this your way of showing compassion to the Scots?"

Lord Pembroke chortled and said quietly, "Not all of them." And after another moment he said, "Our worlds continue to collide, Miss MacDuff. But this is the crux of it. They are two wholly separate worlds. I am compelled with a yearning to place myself in yours, but circumstances dictate that this is a choice I will not be afforded. At least not without dire consequences—those for which I would never forgive myself if they came to fruition.

"I ask that you excuse my forward behavior just now. It was selfish of me. But I am not sorry for it. I hope it will only represent a token of my affection, as much it pains me that I will never be able to repeat it."

The rush of hearing those words made Jenna both giddy with inebriating joy and grief-stricken with reality once they sunk in, but before she could respond, the sound of voices outside had them turning their heads toward the door. "It's my father," Jenna said. Relief poured through her body, and she strained to hear the conversation.

"What were ye thinking, man?" Malcolm barked angrily. "Were ye gonna hold him for ransom?" The bolt slid back and the door kicked open again. The lantern light spilled across the floor and lit Malcolm's fuming face. The grumpy guard following behind him, slightly abashed.

Jenna's father took out his dirk and knelt down, deftly slicing through the thick ropes binding Lord Pembroke and Jenna together. As they got to their feet, Lord Pembroke rubbed the raw spots around his wrists for a moment, then flexed the muscles in his hands and fingers, made a solid fist, and punched the cantankerous guard in the face. The man grunted and staggered backward, blood trickling out his nose. Lord Pembroke yanked the dirty rag from around his neck and threw the greasy cloth at him. "Try staunching the flow with this."

Malcolm looked at Lord Pembroke nervously. "I dinna ken what to say. Should we . . . do we . . . ?" Jenna could see her father trying to assess just how much Lord Pembroke knew.

He shook his head. "There's nothing to say. Clearly, a mistake was made here. No harm done." He nodded at Malcolm and briefly held Jenna's gaze. Then he walked out the barn door into the night.

THIRTY-TWO

THEY SAT AT THE TABLE, GRIMLY RUBBING BEARDS, kneading foreheads, and closing eyes in deep thought. Malcolm paced the length of the room and created a breeze as he strode. Jenna stared hard into her mug of willow bark tea, mesmerized by a reflection that would blur whenever someone jarred the table.

She had told them everything she thought they needed to know, and nothing else. What happened between her and Lord Pembroke would stay between the two of them, at least for now. Lord Pembroke knew who they were—that much she confirmed, or rather, he knew who they supported, but beyond that, it was purely supposition. What he intended to do with his theories and postulations, if anything, was the unanswered question that plagued them all.

Except for Jenna. She believed with every breath of her body that he would not allow harm to come to her—or rather, he would not himself harm her.

"He didna *actually* say what he would do now that he ken?" Gavin asked Jenna again, his fingers rubbing his temples.

She shook her head and sighed, and removed the wet, cool cloths at her wrists. "I've told you, he said he already knew—he'd put it together before tonight. The fact that Da was the one to find us probably erased any doubt he'd been harboring up until then. He never asked me what we intended to do, never questioned our purpose here. Perhaps he doesn't believe we're here to cause trouble. Maybe he thinks the garrison will be built and we'll be on our way."

Each of the men grumbled in disagreement with their own versions of *Fat chance of that*, until Malcolm cut in.

"As I see it, we've got two choices. We either pack up and leave, which would ruin months of work and countless other schemes tied to it—not to mention cause a full-blown manhunt if we're on the run, or we watch our steps and prepare for an ambush. Either way, a decision's got to be made."

Jenna discovered the men had all been at the garrison feverishly working in order to make the newly announced deadline when she and Lord Pembroke came to the cottage. They hadn't heard the gunshots because they'd been in the chambers belowground.

"Do ye think we ought not speak to the lad?" Angus ventured. "He's obviously soft on Jenna, and perhaps that's the reason he'll keep mum about what he's found out."

There was another rumble of opinions and Ian stood. "What fools the lot of ye are—and ye ken it," he growled. "If ye think he's no gonna up 'n' tell the duke this minute, then you've got less sense than a doorpost. I say we get out now, while we still have a neck."

"But surely, we'd have been questioned by now had the young man followed his suspicions from the beginning," Colin broke in. "The fact he's nay brought us to the attention of the duke says something of his intent—or lack of it, aye?"

"And who's to say he hasna told the duke of us?" Ian countered. "The lass is fit to have us believe whatever her glassy-eyed temperament dreams up at the moment. Ye canna believe the lad would hold on to something such as this."

Jenna turned to her father, desperate to placate her growing sense of alarm that the clan may decide they have no other choice than to silence Lord Pembroke. "As far as the duke's son is concerned, I think he's far too intelligent to become distressed that people living on his family's estate hold differing political perspectives. He appears to favor rational debate over violence, and as far as I've gathered from all of you"—she turned to look at the men—"that is the same path most Jacobites would prefer. Little or preferably *no* bloodshed in trying to reestablish the Stuart monarchy."

There was a cryptic silence that filled the room, and Jenna slowly took in their expressions. "Are you telling me I am wrong?" she began, feeling a cold and unforgiving dullness set in throughout her body. "Am I mistaken?"

Her father looked at her gravely. "Jenna, your interpretations are not wrong in that it is the path that most *anyone* would want in order to accomplish what they desire, but I'm afraid we've come to a point of realization that it is a not a reality we will see unfold."

Her hands and feet went numb. "Da? . . . What are you saying? What precisely is going to unfold here on the night of my birthday?"

She watched her father swallow uncomfortably.

"Are we planning to . . . to *kill* people?"

He drew in a deep breath and looked at her with an expression fiercer than she'd ever seen before. "We are planning to restore a usurped king to his rightful throne. And there may be people who would rather sacrifice their lives than see that happen. Just as we are willin' to give of ours."

Jenna cringed, recalling Daniel's words: *Each side believes they are right. And many will fight to the death to prove it.*

Malcolm made a faint nod in Jenna's direction and, turning to the others, said, "Seeing as the lad hasna done anything up to this point, and there are no guards pounding at our door, it leads me to believe Jenna may be right. Perhaps we're safe to carry on."

Safe to carry on? Safe to carry on building an arsenal of weapons that will tear apart someone's world? Does Lord Pembroke suspect this bit at all?

Malcolm tapped on the table. "But it seems there are a few loose cannons wandering about the countryside whose tongues and impatience may cost us the element of surprise we're countin' on. Apart from a few of us making rounds and spreading the attitude of forbearance, I doubt there is much else we can do."

Most everyone agreed, and a hasty plan was put together. Duncan and Gavin would visit as many village inns and watering holes as they could in two days' time to calm any aimless, hotheaded rebels, while the rest of them would keep their heads low and ears to the ground, back to work as usual. If anyone came upon information giving them rise for concern, they would all be given notice to escape and regroup.

Jenna lay awake to the sweet, drowsy sounds of Tavish's steady breathing and recalled every detail of her conversation with Lord Pembroke. She felt the skin around her wrists, where the ropes had left angry red marks, and summoned the intoxicating moment that had caused most of them.

She sighed, admonishing her indulgent thoughts, as they could come to nothing. People will act out of character if they're moved by circumstance rather than sound thought.

Funny, it was the same excuse she gave for her actions with Daniel.

Alex trekked through the woods, needing only a moment to assess his whereabouts. He knew every inch of Grizedale Forest around Esthwaite Water, and could navigate himself from most points—day or night. When he came in sight of Withinghall, he noted which windows were still brightly lit, and made the decision to seek out the occupant behind them.

He knocked softly on Julian's door and heard a disinterested reply to enter. Julian crouched at his writing desk, coat off and shirt-sleeves rolled to his elbows. He startled, and a few of the papers slipped to the floor. Gathering the scattered documents, he shoved them into the desk's deep front drawer.

"Alex, what a surprise. What are you doing here?" He leaned against the desk.

"I didn't mean to catch you unawares, Julian, but I saw your light on and . . ."

"What happened to you?" Julian said, taking in Alex's appearance. "You're filthy."

Alex had forgotten his state of disarray and looked down at his shirt and trousers. He'd shed his coat just before Miss MacDuff had given him the musket at the cottage, and hadn't bothered to collect it before coming home. His linen shirt was torn and stained with mud. He walked to the mirror by the dressing table and gazed at a face that must have been shocking for Julian to see.

The back of his shirtsleeve worked as well as a handkerchief to rub the mud and grease from his face, and while scrubbing, he watched in the mirror as Julian quietly locked the desk drawer with a key. Although his ablutions were halfhearted, he was satisfied his appearance would suffice for an informal chat.

As he'd made his way home, his thoughts had repeatedly been brought back to Julian's words of warning regarding Miss MacDuff. Alex had been keeping his distance from Julian since his frenzied attack on the girl. He'd made it clear their friendship was in jeopardy, if not irreparably damaged.

"A fall from a horse, that's all." Alex frowned in answer to Julian's worried expression. Uncomfortable, he cleared his throat and took a seat before the smoldering coals in the fireplace, aware that Julian remained at the desk behind him.

"Listen," he began brusquely, "I've had time to cool off over the whole matter at the ale house. The fact you're still here must represent your determination and faith in our friendship, so I'd like to set a few things straight."

The sigh of relief from Julian was audible enough to be heard in the dining hall, Alex thought, and he watched the young man cross to the cluster of chairs and sink into one.

"You don't know how glad I am to hear of it. I have wanted to speak with you, but understood your need for distance. You are as close as a brother to me—my dearest friend. Tell me what it is I must do to make things right."

Alex thought for a moment, his gaze on the coals in the hearth as he chewed on the scraped knuckles of one hand. "Tell me what you know of the Jacobite movement." He turned swiftly to Julian. "And don't question me about the girl—that isn't why I'm asking. The new horse handler continues to mention his concern regarding further local activity since the hangings in Hawkshead." Alex felt his throat go dry. "I'm investigating."

Julian raised an elegant eyebrow; it arched to the thick black hair falling from his forehead. "There have been riots across the country, Alex. Edinburgh, Aberdeen. Even London. Predictions of James's arrival have been rife, whether by the Episcopalian Kirk leaders, the Tories, or the dogged Jacobites themselves. It's adding up to matters getting out of hand, and groups of zealots are wreaking havoc around the country."

He pointed his finger at Alex. "Your father is doing exactly as he should. Building that garrison is his surefire way to keep us all safe, although you know I have grave concerns regarding those doing the building. By the way, when will it be finished?"

Alex looked at the glowing coals and shrugged. "Sometime soon, I figure—by summer, perhaps. But I'm asking you"—he turned back to look at Julian, his eyes blazing from beneath his brow—"I'm *warning* you—do not act on your misgivings regarding those builders. Casting wild suspicions about them will only delay the work that must be done as quickly as possible."

Julian sighed. "As I said, zealots are wreaking havoc across the country."

"What about locally, though? I know what's happening around the country—I read the *Daily Courant*, as apparently you do," he said somewhat dryly. "I simply thought since your father has returned from campaigning for the general election, he might have revealed the temperament of the towns and villages."

Julian narrowed his eyes, and Alex could see he'd hit a nerve as usual by pointing out that his father's seat in Parliament wasn't secure like the Duke of Keswick's. "Yes, he did mention local rioting, but it'll soon be of no concern."

"Because of my father's special dispensation to discipline as he pleases?" The thought made Alex's stomach writhe.

"No. It's because Parliament is passing a bill to stop rioting all together. It has become too widespread to ignore."

Alex rubbed the back of his head where he'd been hit earlier.

"Apparently," Julian continued, "the only way to get these agitating firebrands to understand we mean business is through draconian legislation. Burn the lot of them, I say. King George is here to stay." He rubbed his temples and suddenly looked weary. "I've had a draining day. Would you like a drink?"

"No," Alex answered shortly. After hearing Miss MacDuff's passionate explanation of things months ago from her family's point of view, he understood their reasoning behind the desire for change. He sympathized with this disenfranchised group of people, and it created a hair-prickling effect on him. He watched Julian carefully. "No drink, but might I have a piece of paper from your desk drawer?" Alex rose and moved toward the writing table.

Julian's eyes widened slightly. "I'm fresh out, although I think there might be some in the library, down the hall—I saw it there yesterday. Are you sure you wouldn't like a drink—a brandy perhaps?

You look like you could use it, and there's so much more for us to talk about." Julian put a hand on Alex's shoulder. "Please stay. Trust me, you need it," he pressed.

Alex backed up and shook his head, eyeing Julian's locked desk drawer. "No. I'm filthy and tired. I need to go to bed." He left the room and a clearly disappointed Julian behind him.

Trust him? Alex mused. *I trust him about as far as I can throw him.*

THIRTY-THREE

JENNA WOKE THE NEXT MORNING, STIFF-SHOULDERED and sore. She raised her arms above her head to stretch, and her eye caught sight of a piece of paper, crisply folded, attached to a thin blue ribbon and tied to the latch of her window. She reached for the note, sat up and stared at it, still thick-headed from sleep. Her name had been scribbled in black ink on the front of it, and inside, the graceful handwriting was one she didn't recognize.

> *Meet me in the stable at noon.*
> *Pembroke*

She rubbed her eyes, convinced she was mistaken. Somehow he'd made his way in here last night. Jenna glanced uneasily about the room, still half expecting to see him sitting somewhere waiting for her to wake. But it was empty. Even Tavish had left his bed.

She hastily washed and dressed before coming downstairs. The room was empty. Only Angus remained at the table, poring over a book of receipts Mrs. Wigginton had loaned him.

"Where is everyone?"

Angus looked up and smiled. "Halfway through their day, I expect. Duncan said wi' that great lump on the back of your head, it was best we let ye sleep. He and Gavin left early this morning."

Jenna sat before him and did not try to hide the anxiety she felt. "Angus? I'm worried. And afraid. I want this to be over."

He peered at her with knowing eyes. "We all do, lass."

"It's a different world here, isn't it? Different people with their own way of thinking." She closed her eyes. "I wish I could see ten years in front of me. See what I've done, know where I'll be."

Angus grunted. "Dinna wish your life away, lass. It's here and now ye need to be content with it. People spend far too much time preparing for what comes next and not enough in the present moment. I ken you'll make the right choice for yourself as each opportunity comes."

"What if I don't? Angus, do you ever wonder what could have been?"

Compassion spread across his features. But he said nothing.

"Fair enough," Jenna said thoughtfully, and rose from the table. "I'll be back shortly. I've got a quick errand to run before my studies today."

She shivered with apprehension as she stepped out into the bright sunshine and headed to the stables. March was only days away. And in less than three weeks' time they'd host the *cèilidh* for her birthday." Music, dancing, and . . . murder? She could only pray her birthday gift wasn't a fitted noose around all of their necks.

Lord Pembroke stood in between the rows of stalls, dressed in rough leather breeks, brushing the coat of a sleek red chestnut mare. He looked up as Jenna came through the stable door, and an apologetic expression filled his face. "I see you received my invitation."

"Would I be mistaken in assuming you delivered it in person?" she asked, apprehensive.

"You would not," he began. "And for this I beg your pardon, but I needed to get a message to you, and I still recall every nook and cranny of that cottage—and every window that does not lock as it should."

"And this message?" Her heart thumped loudly with suspense.

"I need you to do something—find something for me."

"What is it?"

"I don't know yet," he stated, raising a hand to run through his fair-colored hair. When he saw Jenna's look of incredulity, he added, "I'll know it when you find it."

"That's not terribly helpful," she said, eyeing him charily.

"Let me explain further," he said, offering her a seat on a tack box. "I believe someone is hiding something from me . . . something about you. I'm fairly certain I know *where* it is, but I don't have access to it."

Jenna's heart ceased beating for a moment. "Where is it?"

"In a desk drawer."

She choked on the statement. "You would risk life and limb in a house full of burly Scotsmen to deliver a note to me, yet you cannot gain access to the contents of a desk drawer in your own home?"

"It's in Julian's room," he said flatly.

There was heavy silence as she allowed the information to sink in. "No," she stated, emphatically shaking her head. "No. I cannot do it. You've seen what that maniac is capable of."

"I would make sure he'd be nowhere near you at the time. I can't do it on my own, and the only other option is"—he paused—"that I ransack the room and you divert his attention."

Jenna stared at him nonsensically.

"I didn't think you'd jump at the second choice."

"You're bloody well right I wouldn't," she said hotly. "The man nearly killed me. I would be an idiot to walk into that lion's den and not expect to be a snack."

"I implore you to reconsider. For either way, I believe it is a gamble with your life."

The next day dragged on as she contemplated different alibis for her departure after dinner. She settled on the believable excuse of having forgotten to put away some of Henry's tack after an earlier ride. Lord Pembroke told her about the ale house. That once inside, she would follow the barrel runners through an elongated tunnel stretching from under the house to the storage rooms, beneath the kitchen. The barreled ale rolled on wooden tracks along the tunnel. At the end of the runner was a keg lift, where the barrels were hauled to the kitchens. Nearby were a set of stairs where she could gain access to the house, undetected, as it was the staff's night off and dinner would be laid out as a simple buffet.

She climbed, wary of steps that might create an ear-prickling creak. The entrance to the kitchen was to her left, but quiet with no dinner service. She crept to the second staircase as Lord Pembroke had instructed. On the third floor, she retrieved Lord Pembroke's note and listened for voices. She read his further instructions and waited for the hall clock's chime to signal the hour. It was an unending hallway with doors and paintings on either side of the corridor, and a grand staircase at the end.

At the stroke of eight, her heart quickened. She made a dart past the portrait of a pallid-faced woman and reached the door. It was locked.

"Providing some early entertainment, are we?"

Jenna gasped and whirled to see the long-haired blond servant moving swiftly down the hall with her cloak slung over her shoulders.

"No worries, lass. Take heed Mrs. Wigginton doesn't see you, though. She's not keen on us making a few farthings with the lads of the house." She winked and rounded the corner.

Jenna leaned back against the door and took a deep breath. Let her think what she will. *I need to find Mr. Finch's room!* Her mind raced with the problem of the locked door. What if Mr. Finch had moved his accommodations? Or Lord Pembroke counted wrong? She grabbed the door's handle again, jiggled it, and this time the knob in her hand gave way. She opened it no more than a sliver—enough to peer in without drawing attention—she saw the glow from burning candles and oil lamps, brightening the contents of the room.

She pushed the door open farther and listened for signs of its resident. Nothing but the soft crackle and pop of the coals heating the room made any sounds. She closed the door behind her and surveyed the room. Mr. Finch must be a well-respected guest to be given such a luxurious suite.

The furniture was polished. Dark, gleaming woods outlined cushioned chairs and settees. The mantle was cast in heavy stone, decorated with masonry designs only someone like her father could truly appreciate. Oil paintings adorned each wall, richly colored and framed. Two tall windows in the room were draped with thick fabric puddling on the floor. Warmth spilled into the room from every angle.

The end of the room revealed another door, which she assumed led to the bedchamber. She spotted a writing desk in between the windows and prayed this would be the one in question, requiring her to pry no farther into the suite.

She hurried to the drawer, but as feared, it was locked. Lord Pembroke never mentioned a hiding place for the key. "Now, if I were Mr. Finch," Jenna murmured, "where would I secret my treasures?" She let her eyes wander across the room, searching for vases, boxes, or high shelves. She scanned the titles on the bookshelves. *L'Astrée* by Honoré d'Urfé and *Polexandre* by Marin le Roy, Sieur de Gomberville, both French heroic romances, sat side by side. She couldn't be sure this was Mr. Finch's private collection and canvassed farther. *A Game at Chess* by Thomas Middleton and *Fragmenta Regalia, or Observations on the late Queen Elizabeth, her Times and Favourites* by Sir Robert Naunton were both books she could easily see in Mr. Finch's hands.

She pulled the books, one by one, from their slots, and fluttered her finger across their pages. A key fell from inside and landed by her feet.

"Voilà," she said softly, and hurriedly stooped to pick it up. She carried the book to the writing desk and hastily inserted the ornate key into its lock. The drawer clicked as it came free. It was full of correspondence. The writing was neat and legible. The first letter was addressed to the procurator of Trinity House, and duplicates were made out to members of the House of Regents.

> *Dear Sirs,*
>
> *I come to offer thanks for your judicious choice in entrusting me with one of your weightiest affairs. Your doubts and hesitations have proven most prophetic, and sadly, I must impress upon you at this juncture in time that Providence has revealed to me the truth. As requested, I have kept a diligent eye upon one Alexander Paxton Clifton: Lord Pembroke. Noted of concern, is his kindled interest in local Jacobite affairs and encouraging their success.*
>
> *I have inserted in these letters, excerpts of a diary kept following the whereabouts of the individual in question, and feel the evidence sufficient enough to support your growing concern. The weight of the issue presses upon me, and sets upon my spirit, as I am sure it must yours.*
>
> *I will await further discourse as to your choice of decision in the matter.*
>
> *I remain your most obedient servant,*
>
> > *Julian William Middleton Finch*

She lowered her shaking hand and let the letters rest in her lap. *Oh God.* She felt sick. She picked up the letters again to reread them, and jolted at the sound of voices in the hallway.

She thrust the letters back into the drawer and fumbled with the key. It caught in her hair as she tried to insert it into the lock, but after a panicked moment it clicked closed and she pulled it out of the chamber. The book was still on the desk, and she only had time to insert the key between one of the pages before scanning wildly for a place to hide. The capacious drapes seemed too obvious, so with not a moment to spare, she dropped to the ground and prayed she could squeeze beneath the tall settee with its long-hanging, bordered fringe. She grabbed frantically at her cloak and skirts, pulling the last of the billowing material underneath the couch, and tried to control her frenzied breathing as two people entered the room.

She turned her head sideways, trying to see between the trimming tassels as the door swung open. Yards of swishing silk fabric sashayed across the threshold, followed by a pair of polished black boots. Mr. Finch's voice bristled with annoyance as his feet stopped in front of a lacquered liquor cabinet.

"What is it that required our leaving the salon in such haste, Lady Lucia? Couldn't you see I was enjoying a spirited game of whist with Alex? Just because he was called away does not mean I have the time to run up here for a private word at your command. He'll come back to find us gone, no doubt, and I'll have lost my partner."

Glassware clinked and was followed by the glug of spilling liquid. The carved feet of the walnut cabinet shuddered as the door was forcefully shut. "If you haven't noticed, I've been welcomed back into his good graces these last couple of days, and it would be churlish of me to spurn his revived interest."

"It is not *your* revived interest I am at all concerned about," Lady Lucia said. "I had him called away so I could speak to you alone. I want to know what it is you have been doing to ensure *my* stability in this house."

Mr. Finch's sigh was impatient. "What do you mean?"

"I mean he is not growing warmer when we are together and I am afraid he may be petitioning his parents to reverse the betrothal. You are supposed to help make sure this marriage will occur. I do not see this happening. I see you making yourself a fine place beside him and forgetting about our agreement." Jenna watched Lady Lucia's gown slither to the window.

"Shall I remind you of your ambitions? You have begged for my help, stating that if he is granted permission to leave, you will lose everything. Without a marriage to me there will be nothing to make him stay. But if this union occurs, I can ensure you have a place at his side always."

Mr. Finch's feet shifted toward her. "I need no review of the muscle you exercise. And I assure you, I shall not gamble away opportunity. But lest you feel I am deficient in my efforts to ensure this marriage takes place, I would advise you to be patient a little longer. I am doing my best. Besides, yours is not the only interest I wrestle with currently."

Lady Lucia's feet spun toward Mr. Finch. "Explain this to me."

There was a moment of silence before Mr. Finch answered. "I was never actually sent down from school." He cleared his throat. "Arrangements were made that I should observe Alex and send reports back as to his state of mind. A future Member of Parliament through peerage can be a useful tool for the school—especially if the alumnus should feel grateful for promised introductions most beneficial to one's success."

"What is this meaning?"

"Everyone needs friends in high places. It's merely a matter of back-scratching."

"And you've decided to spy on him for these people out of the goodness of your heart?" she said, her voice full of disdain.

"Like I said, milady, everyone needs friends, and I make it a matter of routine to scratch backs that are itching. It is no different from the contract we have pained each other with." He walked to the window. "The problem is, our Alex is not terribly interested in politics at present. His mind is more focused on other things. But I may have found a way around this little mess." He planted his glass and lowered his voice. "I have been preparing a most dependable way to capture Alex's loyalty and guarantee his devotion toward us."

Lady Lucia twirled from the window. "What is this thing you have?"

"This thing," he began, "is called insurance." He moved toward the desk. "I have all the protection I need right . . ." He stopped mid-sentence.

Jenna stifled a gasp, certain he had spotted the book on the writing table. She watched the shiny black boots pivot, knew he was searching for anything else out of place.

His sudden silence attracted Lady Lucia's attention as well, and she said, "What protection? What is it you have?"

He turned again to Lady Lucia. Jenna was convinced he was calculating the possibility that *she* had been the one rifling through his shelf and desk, but he said only, "You need to get out of here. Go back to the parlor, and I will meet you there shortly."

"What?" she sounded confused.

"Just do as I've said and I will follow in a few minutes. We shan't let anyone question whether we've been together."

Her skirts rustled as she gathered them up and sailed out of the room. "Fine. I will see you at dinner, but do not forget that I *must* secure my place in this house."

He closed the door behind her, and his feet raced to the desk. She heard his sigh when he found the key inside the book, heard it click into the lock, and recognized the sound of the sliding drawer. He groaned with relief and slid it shut, locked it once more. He spoke in a near growl. "I know I put this book away. Did they think I'd not notice something out of place?" He huffed. "Surely, they'd at least restore what they disturbed."

An eerie silence followed his last statement, and Jenna watched Mr. Finch get up from his chair and make a slow swivel to take in the entire room. "Unless . . . ," he whispered. "Unless you're still here."

He raced around the perimeter of the room, opening cupboards and rankling curtains.

Jenna couldn't breathe. She prayed she had successfully hidden all of her skirt and cloak.

If Mr. Finch finds me, he'll kill me. Right here. Tears began rolling down her face toward her ears as she lay staring at the underside of the settee. She had been a fool to do this.

The shiny black boots stopped at the settee. Fear grabbed her around the throat, clutched her chest. A table was shoved away, and she saw Mr. Finch's knees as his fingertips brushed the edge of the fringe.

An urgent knock made him freeze. She heard Lord Pembroke shout from the corridor and break into the room. "Julian!" he cried.

Mr. Finch quickly rose. "What is it, Alex?"

"My father has been calling for you and is losing his patience. I think we both know that if his demanding nature is not immediately satiated, well, I pity the poor fellow. I thought it the decent thing to do to hunt you down."

Mr. Finch hurried toward the door. "Yes," he said, with one quick pause and twist back toward the center of the room. "You're probably right."

The two men left and Jenna lay listening as the voices in the hall faded. Fate had been gracious to her today. But if fate lends you luck, surely it will ask for it back.

THIRTY-FOUR

JENNA RAN TO THE STABLES AND NODDED AT JEB, who was pitch-forking fresh hay. She rushed to Henry's stall, breathless and grateful for having made it out of Mr. Finch's rooms alive. Her arms circled Henry's muscled neck and she uttered a few solemn promises never to do anything so foolish again. He seemed to think her appeal for sympathy, unaccompanied by anything to eat, was inconsiderate, and gave her little compassion.

She picked up a brush and began a halfhearted rubdown, hoping to pass time without appearing suspicious. It was fifteen minutes later when Jenna heard the latch on the stable door click open and glimpsed Lord Pembroke's anxious face as he charged down the corridor.

Jeb stepped out from the narrow cupboard where the stable's tools were kept, finished with his chores. Lord Pembroke stopped short, but recovered himself and said, "Good evening, Jeb. I heard one of the foals was suffering a bit of colic, and I thought to check."

Jeb closed the cupboard door and limped toward the young man. "You heard wrong, thankfully, but there's a restless filly down that ways a bit." He motioned in Jenna's direction. "Fortunate for us you care as you do about the well-being of these animals." He raised a bushy white brow. "Couldn't ask for more attentive management."

Lord Pembroke said nothing, but simply glared at Jeb. The old horse handler cocked his head in the opposite direction and said, "Ah, that'd be my mule down around the bend. She's likely calling for her supper. Hope you didn't miss yours." He managed a meager smile and made his way toward the noiseless hallway.

Lord Pembroke rushed to where Henry's head poked out above his gate. "Miss MacDuff?"

She bounded out of the stall. "How could you do that to me?"

His features were contorted with remorse. "I am so sorry. Are you all right?"

"I thought he was going to find me . . . and *kill* me."

"Were you there?"

She nodded. "Under the settee. Had you not come when you did . . ."

"I shouldn't have asked you to do it."

She peered up at him and shook her head. "You are in terrible trouble."

"What do you mean?"

"He is plotting against you," she said.

"Wait a moment. I'm confused. Who is?"

She grabbed him by both arms. "Mr. Finch!" she hissed, looking around. "He's been keeping track of your whereabouts and has prepared letters to your school, telling them of your inclination toward . . . Jacobitism," she finished in a whisper.

Lord Pembroke stepped back and she watched his eyes wander, saw him gather his thoughts. "Damn him." He rubbed his temples.

"The letter to the procurator stated he was doing as requested—that your school had entrusted him to keep an eye on you and report to them. Have you any idea why?"

"None. He'd been sent down for trying to speak out on my behalf . . . or at least that's what I was led to believe," he said, his eyes narrowing. "I imagine the school wants to know where I stand politically—having caused a bit of an embarrassment for them. These are powerful people, and they must know who is friend and who is foe," he said almost bitterly. "I'm beginning to believe that freedom of choice is not a luxury I will *ever* be well acquainted with."

"Are the money and the title that important to you?" she asked imploringly. "Have you ever considered just leaving it all behind? You could study what you want. You're a *man*. No one would deny you that privilege."

Lord Pembroke appeared to consider her words, and she rushed on.

"If you fail to go through with your marriage to Lady Lucia, your *best friend* is willing to fabricate lies to punish you. What could possibly be keeping you here to continue on with a charade you find so deplorable?"

One of the stable doors opened abruptly, and they turned to see a mousy, whey-faced servant from the house.

"Sir, I must implore you to return."

"Whatever for?"

Looking distressed, the man replied, "Your mother has collapsed."

There was nothing Jenna could do but wait—and she hated it. She felt powerless. Again. The morning dragged on, and she paced the narrow space in the loft between her bed and Tavish's cot. What was the status of the duchess?

Grateful that news traveled like quicksilver, she was finally sent with a basket of aid to Mrs. Wigginton. Obviously the housekeeper knew every detail regarding the Cliftons, and the health and well-being of the duchess certainly fell within that domain.

Jenna knocked on one of the kitchen's back doors and viewed the bustling beyond the young scullery who opened it. "Is Mrs. Wigginton here?"

The maid turned in the direction of the voice bellowing orders at the stove.

Jenna stepped in with a basket and sidled between the running servants. The kitchen was humming, and she wondered what all the fuss was about.

"Mrs. Wigginton?"

"What is it now?" she shouted and turned from the pot she bent over. "Oh—Jenna, it's you. I'm sorry." She took a sip from one of the spoons held out to her. "Too much salt, Tom! Put some potatoes in to soak it up and add more broth." She put a quick hand on Jenna's arm and turned to her. "What is it, dear? It's a most dreadful time for a visit, ye ken. The magistrate is coming, and what with Herself being sick an all, plus the demands of the young Lady Lucia . . ." She broke off, her anger barely in check. "Oh, dear me, I'm afraid I'm just a bit taken up wi' it all today." Her eyes landed on the basket, and she cocked a brow.

"We'd heard Her Grace was ill, but not knowing from what, Duncan decided the best we could offer were his rare herbs. How is she?"

Mrs. Wigginton looked dour and took the proffered basket. "Tell Duncan we thank him kindly, but at this point it's hard to tell. No one kens what ails her, although she's sitting up a bit today and I'm about to send up some broth." With lightning speed, the housekeeper clapped a hand atop the head of a scruffy boy who had tried to sneak up on the tray of cooling tea cakes at her side. "Out of my kitchen, or I'll take your ear next time!"

"And Lord Pembroke?" Jenna ventured.

Mrs. Wigginton looked at her, confused. "What of him?"

"I just wondered how he was handling his mother's illness—if he was . . . well, all right?" Jenna wanted to pull her own tongue out. Why hadn't she simply delivered the herbs and left?

The sound of breaking glass turned their attention to one of the storage pantries. Mrs. Wigginton raced toward the chaos, leaving Jenna to thread her way out, avoiding the cooks and stewards as they scurried. She shouldn't be here—that was apparent. She would go home, where she was wanted. Where she was safe.

The room was spinning, and Jenna's heart thumped so fiercely in her chest she felt her lungs might explode with the effort of it all. Two men she'd never seen before grabbed her and hauled her back to the middle of the floor, which had been cleared of the cottage's long wooden table and benches. The fiddler's fingers moved in a blur as he began the next arduous reel—and Jenna remembered it as being an endless one. She wanted nothing more than to run as far away from this party as possible, but knew she must do as instructed and allowed herself to be redirected into the center of the dancing.

There were only a handful of women, and twice as many men—a few acquaintances her family had made in the last few months, but mostly they were the Scottish clan leaders and other Stuart supporters, who would be directing the revolt from the garrison before dawn. They whooped, hollered, and cheered one another along, thoroughly convincing in playing their part in the facade.

"We dinna want ye sitting out on your birthday, now, do we?" the shaggy-bearded one shouted above the din. He spun her like a whirling dervish and pushed her into the waiting hands of another chubby Scotsman.

"Nay! We canna have that!" the second man puffed. "A maid on her birthday's shown special favor. He's right. 'Tis ill luck to have ye sitting on your arse!" The men and women around them howled with laughter, and Jenna blushed but had no breath for a retort.

The men were unstoppable, and in between every reel, jig, or *strathspey*, they ate their fill of roast venison and red grouse, bannocks and barley pudding. If they were going to die tonight, they'd do it living life right up until their last breath. Jenna had no appetite and finally found a moment to excuse herself and escape for a few breaths into the cool, spring air.

The doors and windows had been thrown open to combat the stuffiness of the crowded dance floor, and at last outside, she was stunned to see Lord Pembroke tentatively approaching the front door.

She gasped with alarm and ran toward him. "What are you doing here?" The pace of her heartbeat now surpassed that caused by dancing the reels and jigs.

He gave her a quiet smile, took her by the arm, and led her toward the cottage door saying, "It is your birthday. I came to toast your good health."

It probably couldn't have been any worse had he waltzed in with a scarlet coat and tricorn hat. The music stopped and people stared. Jenna assumed the majority of their guests knew who he was then, but there was nothing she could do apart from play along and not rouse suspicion.

"Angus?" she nervously called to the other side of the room. "Have we any atholl brose left? I've come across a thirsty visitor."

The eyes weighed heavily upon them, especially Ian's by the fireplace. She watched Angus glance to Malcolm and then pour a drink from a round copper pot into a cup. He handed it to Tavish and nodded with his head to walk it over, when someone said, "I'll take that."

Malcolm reached for the mug and walked across the dance floor, the little crowd parting. He reached Lord Pembroke and Jenna by the door and stood for a quiet moment before them. "Milord," he said with a bow. "An honor to have ye attend. May I offer ye a drink?"

Lord Pembroke cleared his throat and stood, broad shoulders back and nearly as tall as her father. "I came to offer good wishes to your daughter on her birthday, and yes," he said, taking in the many pair of eyes, "I could use a drink." He accepted the cup from Malcolm and, raising it in the air, said, "*Slàinte mhath*, is it?"

"It is," Malcolm responded, surprised, and raised his own glass in reply. The two men drank to the bottom of their cups in one fell swoop, and Malcolm eyed Lord Pembroke appraisingly. "Another drink, then, Angus, and maybe some music to wash it down wi'?" He looked at the few men in the corner holding instruments, and they immediately started another jig. The dancers needed no more encouragement and picked up where they too had left off.

Ian crossed the room, the elixir in his hand, and poured a small amount into Jenna's and Lord Pembroke's cups. "A toast to your good health, Jenna," he said grudgingly. "Ye look more like your mother every day. I wish she were here to see it."

Jenna had no idea what to say, and as she fumbled for a reply, he continued on, addressing Lord Pembroke. "Now drink up and be gone wi' ye, lad. 'Tis getting late." He turned to Jenna. "And this party is a *family* affair."

Lord Pembroke made a brief sweep of the room and gave her a narrow look. "Welcoming bunch, aren't they?"

Jenna nodded toward the door. "I think I prefer the air outside."

He took her elbow and directed her through the gliding bodies and out the back door. They walked in silence for a minute, absorbed in the sounds of the burbling water as it began widening from brook to stream.

At last, he stopped on a slight rise and stood, eyes to the moon. A thick wedge of yellow spilled light on the hillsides and created shadows beneath the trees. The branches swayed with the wind. "Miss MacDuff—" he began, but Jenna cut him off.

"You must leave."

His eyes flashed wide with surprise.

Jenna swallowed and looked around. "Please go."

"I don't understand. What's the matter?"

Jenna scrambled for an idea, anything to get Lord Pembroke out of harm's way. She wanted to tell him what was about to happen. To make him understand. And to protect him. But she couldn't. It would ruin everything. She squeezed her eyes shut and blurted out, "I am in love with him."

"With whom?"

"With Daniel. I have always been in love with him. I *will* always be in love with him. There is no point in us—"

"You needn't say anything more," he murmured. "I understand."

"Then go," she said firmly. She looked into his eyes and saw the hurt spilling out of them. She wished she could rip her own heart out of her chest, it hurt so badly.

"Jenna?"

They spun around to see Jenna's father standing in the shadows of an old pine.

And Mr. Finch behind him.

They stepped forward, and Jenna felt her breath draw in sharply at seeing Mr. Finch's hands clasped together around the ivory handle of a pistol. Lord Pembroke stepped in front of Jenna.

Mr. Finch shook his head. "No, Alex. She goes to stand with the master mason—or rather the master of this whole machination." He gestured with the gun and Jenna dashed to her father's side. "You are such a fool, Alex, to make it all come to this. It still doesn't have to be," he said, raking a hand past his eyes as the wind threw his thick black hair into his field of vision. He tried to hold the gun steady, hands trembling despite his cool exterior.

"Julian, what are you doing?" Lord Pembroke pleaded.

"Exposing the error of your ways."

"What the bloody hell are you talking about?"

Mr. Finch took a step forward and motioned with the gun. "She's been trespassing, but of course this is the least of her crimes." He took a swipe at the hair the wind batted against his eyes and returned his hand to the weapon.

"Julian, put the gun down and we'll discuss this like gentlemen. You cannot become violent every time someone upsets you," Lord Pembroke said, putting his hands up and taking a step closer to Mr. Finch.

"I found her hair!" he shouted. "Her long, red strands lay in the page of a book where I keep the key to my writing desk." His voice rose. "No one I know has hair like her. It's unmistakable. She cannot deny it!"

Jenna's heart thudded loudly in her chest, the music from the cottage barely audible over the sound of the whipping wind. She looked up at her father, but his face was staid. He slowly pushed her behind him.

"What of it?" Lord Pembroke came back.

"She has been working her charms to her advantage, Alex—and you are too naïve to see the schemes. You *know* what her family is up to with the garrison. Yet you close your eyes to it, as you are closing your eyes to your familial duty!"

"Julian. You're delusional. This girl has done nothing wrong, and I have done nothing to harm Lady Lucia."

"And yet I continue to find you frolicking in the moonlight with a girl whose every intention is to lead you astray." His voice rose above the wind. Fat droplets of rain began to fall around them. "You have a choice, Alex. Either you marry Lady Lucia and stay here with *us*, or I will march this girl and her family straight to your father. *Tonight.* And I do believe we discussed exactly the fate of anyone who is a Stuart sympathizer, did we not?"

The rain began in earnest, and Mr. Finch drew back the hammer of the flintlock, clicking it into place and aiming it at the tall Scot.

"Wait!" Lord Pembroke shouted, spreading his hands upward. "Julian, my God. . . . I can't believe you would—"

"No more waiting, Alex. Choose!"

A whirling sound sliced past Jenna's ears. A solid thud and the deafening explosion of a gun followed. Her father simultaneously spun on his heel, leveling himself and Jenna to the ground. After a moment, Jenna raised her head and saw Mr. Finch on his back, only the shaft and tang of a *sgian dubh* revealing the fact that its blade lay sheathed in his chest. Lord Pembroke scrabbled his way to Mr. Finch's side. The man's breathing was ragged and shallow.

"I have loved you . . . always," Mr. Finch whispered, staring up into the rain.

Jenna was only a moment behind Lord Pembroke and, upon seeing the knife, gasped. "Oh my God . . . Ian."

They both turned in the direction of the knife's flight and saw the fixed, scowling expression on the dour Scotsman's face. He stood motionless, staring at them. Behind him, the rest of her clan ran toward them from the cottage's back garden. As they came close enough to see what had transpired, there was a moment before Malcolm spoke.

"Get rid of him."

Ian grabbed her, shook her to look at him. "Jenna! Run to the garrison. Hide. Hurry!"

THIRTY-FIVE

JENNA RAN BLINDLY IN THE SPATTERING RAIN, HER mind snaking from one moment to the next, a stream of consciousness fragmented with spurts of conversation and the faces of people.

You needn't say anything more. . . . I understand.

She pushed the sting of those words away with each thrust of her legs.

Get rid of him.

She skidded in the mud, sliding to a halt in front of the garrison's rain barrel. She wanted to wash away the whole night. She scrubbed ferociously. Chilly water splashed over her face.

No more waiting, Alex. Choose!

Jenna recalled the look of anger on his face, the hurt. She scrubbed to the point of rawness when the image of the buried knife flashed before her closed eyes. Water dripped from her hair and chin. She heard voices.

"Hide!" Ian had shouted. The guards surely heard the gunshot.

She threw open the door. It was dark inside, but at least it was a reprieve from the rain that soaked her clothing. She listened as the water hit the fire of the torch outside, the hiss and spit of darkness trying to overcome light. She whipped the door closed and turned to hide.

She stumbled on building supplies stored inside overnight, ran her hands along the smooth walls. It was too dark. *Where do I go?* She was beginning to panic. *Slow down. Those voices might be the clan.* She stopped to listen. *But maybe it isn't them. Where should I hide?* She crawled along the floor, her fingers searching for any piece of it that was loose, revealing where the money and artillery were stored. She pulled on the lip of a stone and found it shifted beneath her hands. Carefully, she raised the solid, removable piece, pushing it off to the side. She fumbled in the dark below and found the ladder that led to the hidden rooms beneath the garrison. She swept up her skirts in one hand and lowered herself into the nebulous cellar.

Pitched into obscurity, Jenna clutched the ladder with a death grip. She envisioned her descent into the seventh circle of Dante's *Inferno*, anticipating that any moment she'd be dipping her toe into the river of boiling blood. She was sickened by visions. The men disposing of Mr. Finch's body. How would they do it? Where would they put him? Tears streamed from her eyes, and she made no move to wipe them away.

Her father had demanded Lord Pembroke leave and be seen by as many people in the house as possible. He needed an alibi when, and if, people started to question Mr. Finch's disappearance. As much as Lord Pembroke protested the plan, he was no match for

Malcolm and five other determined Scotsman. They said they would take care of it—and they would. Jenna had been ordered to leave at once. They would come for her.

But the thought of Lord Pembroke being sent away on his own to pretend nothing happened, and to know his whole world will be ripped apart again in a few short hours plagued her to the point of breathlessness, turning her stomach to liquid. She needed to find him. To tell him. To *save* him.

The sound of voices yanked her out of the stupor she'd sunk into. With a sharp intake of breath, she realized she hadn't covered the access. The stone still lay askew. Frantic with terror, she scaled the ladder. The mud from her shoes had covered the rungs. She reached for one of them and felt it slip through her fingers, her hand scrabbling in the air. She cried out in alarm as she plunged downward, smacking her chin against a rung and biting her tongue as her head snapped back. Her foot caught a hold and, wrapping an arm through each rung, she pulled herself to the top. It was still dark and cryptically silent. *No voices. Move the stone.*

She dragged it from beneath. It grated softly against the floor. Then stopped. She pressed it farther, pushing it against whatever made it stick. *Please, please, please!*

She smelled horse dung. Her fingers went in search of the edge of the stone, the impediment blocking it. She found it . . . the toe of a boot. She gasped and heard a crisp snap. Above her, a torch was thrown into waiting hands. The snapping flames reflected into the eyes . . . of Garrick Wicken.

It felt like eternity. She'd rocked herself, crying in a tight ball, sobbing for so long she'd run dry of tears, and now only hiccupped. The spasms that wracked her, and the fear that propelled them were still present, but her mind poked through. Part of her wanted to stay curled up, to protect the terror-stricken pieces inside. But there was a niggling part of her brain that warned her, she'd better start thinking, better start acting. She rose from the dirt floor of the dungeon, muddy and drenched. She'd never even thought about the estate having one, but it shouldn't have been surprising. People did wicked things, and the duke needed a secure place to put those people. By the looks of it, its last occupants hadn't been far behind her. The place smelled dank with fear and urine, and despite a thin, high window, the interior of the room was the definition of foreboding.

She stared into the darkness. She had ruined everything. Despair crushed like a fist around her heart. Her family's losses pierced her with guilt, and a fresh wave of tears streamed from her eyes.

She ran a trembling hand along the wall and its cold square stones. It wasn't even a properly made stone wall, she observed, for some of the squares were loose and crumbling. She dislodged a smooth, flat chunk and set it on the floor. Her knees were shaking too much to stand. The stone would be cleaner than sitting on the dirt.

A scuttling sound from the corner made her jump to her feet and cry out. She was used to sleeping on the ground and the ordinary sounds of sharing space with nature, but not in the prickly darkness of a dungeon with no place to escape.

Suffering hung in the air. Death spilled through the cracks of the walls and floor, and it heightened her terror. Had it been hours of waiting? Had her father tried to find her? Did he know where she was? The dread of not knowing, the endless possibilities. Her father would come; the clan would come. They'd find a way to get her out. But she could almost hear the click . . . the shift of her faltering mind. What if they didn't? What if they couldn't? *Please be all right. Please.*

Where was Lord Pembroke right now? Was he fingering Ian for murder? Jenna slid down the wall and sat on the flat stone. She let the blackness envelop her mind. Her head nodded, the exhausting fear slipping away, until at last she slept in fitful spurts.

Whether it was hours or minutes later, she jerked awake at the whinnying of several horses outside the high window. She listened keenly, wondering if this was the start—if the Jacobite soldiers had arrived and at the crack of gunfire everything would explode in wild, lawless anarchy.

She strained to listen in the dark, and heard the ominous clipped walk of someone approaching. She recognized the guard's heavily booted feet, echoing on the flagstones. Unnerved, she pulled her skirts in around her protectively. The footfalls ended at the massive wooden door with its black iron hinges. A key slid into the catch and made a great clank to unlock the door. It swung open. A bulky, black-bearded guard held a torch in one hand and thrust it inside to locate his prisoner.

"I've been told to give you water," he began gruffly. His face, lit by the flickering torch, showed naked contempt, and sent shivers up Jenna's spine. Her teeth chattered from fear as much as from cold. It was impossible to keep them still.

He left the jug on the floor and gave her one last look of disgust before grabbing the door handle to pull it closed. "Wait!" she called, her mind reeling at a panicked speed. "Have they caught them?" she asked quickly.

The guard paused. "Who?"

"The other men—the . . . the Jacobites?" she whispered.

"Every one of 'em—the filthy sluggards." He started to pull the door shut again.

"Good," Jenna said loud enough for the guard to hear.

He opened the door a bit wider. "What'd you say?"

"I said good. They deserve to be caught."

The guard thrust the light into the cellar. "What's it to you? You're one of 'em."

Jenna shook her head. "I've never been one of them. I've been nothing but a slave to those wretched swines ever since I was a little girl—cooking and cleaning, and living in their filth. I hope . . . I hope they hang." Her teeth were fully chattering now.

The black-bearded man seemed a little intrigued. "What'd they do to you?" He opened the door and stood at the threshold.

Jenna's voice was low and faint, alluring enough to entice the stocky man to move closer. "They killed my brother," she said hoarsely. "They killed him and took me—I was just seven. . . ." Her tears began to fall.

"They'll get what's coming to 'em now, I tell you. They're being saddled up and taken to the duke's hunting lodge in Carlisle. Gonna be hanged like the animals they are." The black-bearded man nodded. "There, there, now. This'll all get sorted out."

The guard leaned down to see her face more clearly.

Jenna swung the stone she'd been sitting on into the side of the guard's head with a bone-splintering crack, and the thick-bodied man crumpled heavily over her legs, the torch rolling onto the dirt floor and sputtering out. She flipped him onto his back and crawled her way to the door, locating the key, still in the lock. After fumbling for a moment, Jenna locked the guard inside the cell.

"You've really got to watch out for those filthy Scots. Savages, the lot of them. Especially the women." She smirked.

She ran along the corridor, hoped that at this late hour there'd be no one else about, and was rewarded with nothing but the black night and stillness. When she reached the barn, she ran to Henry's stall and found him snorting and agitated that the rest of his companions had left without him. But she also found him saddled and ready. Turning to look deeper into the shadowy recesses of the barn, she saw the outline of a man walking toward her. *Limping* toward her.

Jeb grabbed Henry by the reins and pulled him out of the stall, his finger to his lips.

"God speed," he whispered.

She waited for no further explanation but grabbed only a strong bow, with its quiver of arrows, and hurried the horse out the stable. On his back, she whispered to him urgently and hoped he had the good sense to find the trail her family traveled.

THIRTY-SIX

ALEX HURRIED DOWN THE CORRIDOR TOWARD LADY Lucia's suite of rooms. He knew it was late, but he also knew exactly what needed to be done and was determined not to waste another moment waiting.

He knocked urgently on the door and only a moment passed until it swung open, revealing the anxious face of his young Italian bride.

"What is it, milord? What is the matter?" Her eyes, spilling liquid brown, expressed true fright in the dimly lit shadows of the hallway.

"Milady, may I come in? I must speak with you on an urgent matter."

The young woman looked behind her. "Mamma is in the other room, currently occupied."

"This won't take long, and I'd rather not wait. I'm sure she'll seek me out soon enough after we're finished." Alex stepped into the room and moved far across to the window. He pushed aside the drapes and spoke. "Have you ever looked through this window, milady?"

She took a few steps toward the casement and said in a quiet voice, "*Sì*."

"Do you know what it is that we see out this window?"

The young woman was quiet, but moved another step closer.

Alex went on. "We see my father's world. It is not my world, and I doubt very much that it is the one *you* want to reside in either. Would I be correct?" He turned to watch her reaction.

Lady Lucia dipped her head with the tiniest of nods. "*Sì*."

"I think it best that neither one of us forces the other to suffer a lifetime of displacement and unhappiness. You deserve better than that."

Lady Lucia simply lowered her eyes to the floor and moved away from the window.

The adjoining door opened and the countess backed in with a tray. "Lucia, *bella*, I have brought you a cup of tea."

"Mamma."

The countess looked up from her tray and jolted at the sight of Alex.

"What is the meaning of this visit?" she said, putting the tray down and smoothing her hands across the front of her gown.

"One you will not approve of, no doubt, but it has been decided nonetheless. There will be no marriage here. I cannot agree to it." Alex worked to keep his features full of resolve.

The countess's eyes flared widely. "That is not your decision to make, milord. It has been arranged by our families. An agreement that will be fulfilled because of promises made. It is your duty—and . . . and one that reflects upon your *honor*!"

"Mamma," Lucia whispered.

Alex simply shook his head.

"I still hold the letter," she said, pointing a shaky finger at Alex.

"Dear God, I hope my son will never crumble under blackmail," the Duchess of Keswick said.

They both turned to see Alex's mother, steadying herself within the door frame. She looked solemnly at the countess. "I find it highly ironic that you should remind my son of honor as you speak of extortion. No. He has *my* permission, and that is all that is necessary. We shall not be bound to a family that has ransomed their way into ours."

The countess collapsed onto a nearby settee and wept silently, her head buried in her hands.

The duchess turned a troubled face toward her son. "They've been captured," she said quietly. "The masons from the cottage. Things are very bad, Alex. Your father has already determined their fate. They will be hanged tomorrow at sundown."

One road, running north and south, passed the estate. The way to Carlisle was on this path. Henry knew it as well, and instinctively led Jenna in the direction of the rest of his clan. Whether by good fate or fortune, they were only a few miles up the road before she heard voices and the movement of horses.

Under the cloak of darkness, it was easy to remain invisible, but soon the sun would rise, and she'd have to stay well away to keep her cover. It wouldn't be as difficult as tracking an animal. She'd spent years learning how to hunt with the men. They'd taught her how to judge distance and space, as well as wind direction to keep her scent away from sensitive noses. As it was, none of the soldiers paid much mind to their surroundings. Instead, they kept a keen eye on their prisoners.

The men and horses were nothing more than shapeless masses in the dark, but gradually, in the bleary light of dawn, it became clear that all those in her clan were accounted for. Each was on his own horse and had his hands tied with rope behind his back. Four soldiers accompanied them on the trip, one of them foul of mind and temper. Jenna guessed he was in charge, because he led the procession and had the ugliest snarl. She watched and listened as he growled orders to the other three, and griped the moment any of them dared to suggest they stop to rest or water the horses. Jenna dubbed him Corporal Curmudgeon, for lack of his real rank and title.

She knew the men must be aching and tired. It pained her to watch them, mile after mile. But imagining what they must be suffering, the anxiety . . . to know they were heading to their death . . . was unbearable. She wanted to run to them, reach out to them, beg their forgiveness, and make everything all right again.

Had she not panicked and hidden in the garrison's chambers, Mr. Wicken would have only questioned her about the gunshot and not found the cache. It always ended like that in Gavin's fireside stories. It was ultimately that one thing the hero did differently, did wrong—the action that set their downfall in motion.

Why hasn't Gavin told me more stories about escape?

One of the privates made his way to the top of the parade and attempted to speak with their chief. A brief conversation ensued and after a moment of hefty snarling—lest the rear guard forget whose mission this was—the corporal turned his horse around and raised a hand to stop the line. Although Jenna couldn't hear what had been said by their fearless leader, the gist of it was they were stopping and dismounting.

Jenna spotted the reason for the stop. A stream ran alongside the road. The horses, as well as everyone else, would get to drink.

She kept Henry in the woods but let him have his fill of cold water, and then tied him to a sturdy sapling. She covered her hair with the tail end of her brown woolen cloak and crawled from one tree to the next, determined not to attract the attention of either men or horses.

She looked at her family, their faces drawn but emotionless. Then she moved to get a clear view of the corporal, with his scrunched-up angry features. His hair was greasy and drab. How can anyone have hair of no specific color? She thought of her father's wiry black hair—or rather, pewter now, as it was speckled with just as much gray as its natural coal coloring. Daniel's gleamed with shades of russet. A dark brown that made you think of rich, earthy soil, or Mrs. Wigginton's gingerbread. And Lord Pembroke's hair . . . She thought of the gold strands kept just long enough to bend at the edges, its color fair and glinting when the sun caught it.

Her own hair was simply red, and it seemed to bleed into the rest of her body with any onset of emotion. She hoped none of it was showing at the moment, for it could never blend into the background.

She pressed her eyes closed and put her hands over her face, welcoming in a patch of darkness where she touched a clear place to think. She needed a plan and guessed by the speed of their travel, they would reach the Duke of Keswick's hunting lodge by dusk.

The grumbling of her stomach made her jerk in surprise, but her hunger was nothing more than a minor distraction in her concentrated efforts to contrive a solution. She would do whatever it took to get her family back, but without a plan, she had no choice but to follow and pray one would appear.

Alex's mother put a finger to her lips and then an arm out to stop Alex from entering the duke's open study door. She pressed them both against the corridor wall, and they listened to the voices inside.

"Where are they?" Alex heard someone demand.

"What in the devil's going on?" shouted the duke. Then, after the click of a pistol notched into place, they heard the duke say, "Apparently, we have business to discuss?"

"I asked a question," the man said evenly.

"I take it you mean the Jacobites? They're dead. Hanged, I presume," the duke said, a hint of pleasure in his voice.

"Then prepare to die yourself," the man hissed at the same time the duchess moved into the open doorway.

"Wait," she said, a Queen Anne pistol raised and held in her hands, but upon seeing the gunman, lowered it.

Alex rounded through the opening behind his mother. He stopped short, caught at seeing Daniel in the study with a Spanish pistol leveled at his father. The duke was pressed against the back of his leather chair, tea staining the front of his dressing gown and the stack of papers on his broad walnut desk. "What is this?" Alex said, searching the room for an explanation.

Daniel swiveled the gun toward the doorway. "Did *you* do this to them?" he asked, aiming the pistol at Alex.

"Stop, Daniel!" the duchess said, putting up a hand. "Alex hasn't done a thing—and as far as I know, they're still alive."

Daniel lowered the gun and stood back. He drew a deep breath and closed his eyes in a moment's relief.

"How in God's name do you know this man?" Alex demanded of his mother.

The duchess's eyes were glued to Daniel. "Who found you?"

"The young apprentice. On the road an hour ago. He told me they'd been captured and he'd escaped. I was on my way back, and thankfully close."

The duke leapt up and roared, "Who the bloody hell is this man and what is he doing here?" He slammed a heavy fist onto the tea-sodden papers, splattering brown droplets.

The duchess slowly pivoted to face her husband. "The fact that this man has a gun—and a fairly accurate one, at that—states his business will come first. Be quiet and sit down while I sort things out." Her speech was crisp, but her voice remained settled as she continued.

"I can't be certain where they are at present, but I believe they're on their way to Carlisle—where the hunting cabin stands. I imagine that would be where he'd have them executed. Would I be correct in that assumption?" She looked over her shoulder.

"Yes," the duke said brusquely.

"What?" Alex said, startled. "Wait—but what about a trial?

Surely, our magistrate must officiate a trial." His face was stricken with panic.

The duke rolled his shoulders back in a shrug. "Why waste time with formalities on these people?"

The duchess put a hand out to stay her son, who was about to launch himself at his father. "Well, for one thing," she said, speaking to her husband, "it might have ensured your prisoners would actually be killed and not set free by other Jacobites who are scheming behind your back."

The duke's face pulled into a sneer. "What a ridiculous notion. We've rounded up all of them, apart from him, I'm guessing, and in a short moment, he too will be swinging from a tree."

Daniel stood fixedly but looked as if he could spring like a coil at a moment's notice.

"Well, I suppose that just leaves me, then," the duchess said.

"What?" Alex and his father said together.

"We've been preparing this rebellion for some time, and damned if I'm going to have you get in the way of it. You and your crooked politics and contemptuous attitude. You're determined to profit from your fellow man's failures—most of which you've contrived yourself.

"I feel I ought to thank you though for your healthy contributions to the Stuart cause. When James determines it's time to move, and our armies are prepared to fight, the money you've invested"—she raised an eyebrow—"albeit unknowingly, will be greatly appreciated."

The duke looked stricken. "What?"

"You're . . . a Jacobite?" Alex whispered.

"I think it important everyone be given the chance to choose their allegiance—family history or not. Pressure to conform and support simply because of one's ancestry shows poor judgment. We sent you to school, Alex, to become educated. To open your eyes to the future. To see how you are a part of it, can influence it, maybe even direct it." She shook her head. "I did not agree for you to attend Cambridge simply to be bullied into inhaling their opinions and regurgitating them as your own."

She glanced at her husband, disgust in her eyes. "Instead, I had every reason to anticipate you would come to your own conclusions as to who you were and what you stood for. . . ." She smiled now. "And I must say, it seems that you have."

"What a load of rubbish," the duke spat at her, rising and clutching his dressing gown. "You've never paid one moment's attention to anything related to government. You said talk of politics gave you a headache."

She blinked serenely and smiled. "I lied."

"You'll be hanged for this as well, you traitoring strumpet," he said, puffing.

"Oh? By whom?"

"Well, when the guards I've sent off with the first load of conspirators return, they'll have a second chance to earn their suppers, won't they?" he said through gritted teeth. "I'll make sure you get what you deserve."

"Again, I must stress the importance of paying attention to details—especially when participating in something as dangerous as a revolt against one's king. When I hired these men to build the garrison—"

"You?" Alex interrupted. "I thought that Father—"

"I'm a woman, Alex, and the mistress of this household." She flashed a look at her husband. "As I was saying, when I hired them, I knew what I was doing. Daniel could not have been more helpful, and as my liaison, I trusted him to find me the right people."

"Your liaison?" Alex choked. "Daniel is *D*? This is the man you've been writing ardent declarations of love to?"

"Not love letters. *Coded* letters. I know this comes as an awful surprise to you, Alex, but I found Daniel and he found the Freemasons—"

"The what?" Alex said.

"The Freemasons," the duchess answered patiently. "They're a fraternal group—a brotherhood. And their principles mirror mine. Soon, with their help, King James Edward Stuart will land on British soil to reclaim his rightful throne."

"Over my dead body!" the duke shouted.

"As you wish," the duchess said coolly. Raising the Queen Anne pistol with both hands, she took quick aim.

THIRTY-SEVEN

DANIEL AND ALEX LEFT, RACING THE HORSES TO THEIR limits. After each hour of hard riding, Alex stopped at one of the farms to exchange the animals for fresh ones. They had several dozen miles to cover. Their destination was not a place, but a future. The clan's fate lay in their hands.

"How come none of the guards are the ones my mother hired?" Alex shouted to Daniel as they rushed headlong up the road.

Daniel glowered at Alex. "Her Grace's soldiers were meant to arrive early this morning. They were cut off once the garrison's contraband was discovered, and these men are most likely local militia called in to aid your father with circumventing the law." He turned back to spur on his horse.

Alex ground his teeth and gripped the reins tighter. *I had nothing to do with my father's actions! Why blame me for his unseemly behavior?* Obviously, the duke had sent them to his most remote hunting cabin, to have their execution carried out in such a fashion that would call no notice.

As the afternoon passed, Alex focused on his mother's words. She had stunned him with not only her actions, but her determination. She was willing to risk everything to achieve success. His unnerving thoughts brought up sharp images of what they might find when reaching the hunting cabin. His mind imagined gruesome scenarios, but he refused to ask Daniel what he expected. At times, he'd catch the Spaniard staring at him with an expression of either anger or distrust, but mostly it was a simple appraisal.

They were a mile from the rise where the cabin lay, both breathing raggedly with the effort of hours at top speed. Daniel finally spoke to him. "They're prepared to die, you know."

Alex jolted with surprise. "What do you mean?"

Daniel kept his face aligned with his horse's, his breath coming in spurts. "I mean . . . they understood this might happen . . . that at any point they could be discovered . . . and because of the uncertainty, they never take one moment for granted . . . not like you do."

Alex growled through gritted teeth. "I hardly think you can accurately assess my life."

The Spaniard glanced at him. "Oh no?" he huffed. "You're privileged with wealth . . . a fine education. You hunger for nothing. . . . You have no *purpose*."

Alex snarled at the accusation. "All this simply from riding together for the better part of the day?" He pulled his horse even with Daniel's to glare at him. "You must consider yourself a good judge of character . . . even if the character has yet to be displayed!"

Daniel snorted and slowed his horse.

"You're dead wrong about me," Alex snapped.

"Am I? Well, pretty soon, if not already, there will be seven people wrongly dead—and what did you do to contribute to it?"

Alex tightened the grip on his reins. *Nothing. I did nothing!* But perhaps that's just what the Spaniard meant.

The sun was setting, and the day's sharp breeze was dying down. Jenna had noticed nothing of the temperature or her own exhaustion during the last several hours, but pushed herself to keep up with the corporal and the sad procession of men that followed behind him.

The men sat against a stone wall that enclosed a field of grazing sheep. Jenna lay flat in the cold soggy leaves, staring hard at the soldiers, willing herself to hate them. She needed to hate them. It was the only way she would be able to kill them. Her stomach clenched, and she curled up, retching what little there was in her stomach. She wiped her mouth with the back of her muddy hands and watched the corporal rummage through one of his saddlebags. She had a clear shot of him from her vantage point and thought it probable she could hit him.

She reached for the quiver behind her back and rose to her knees. Her breathing grew faster. She couldn't get enough air. She put her hands on the ground, felt her chest heave with effort.

I have to do this.

I must do this.

Her mind panted the words along with her breath. She rose again, this time to her feet.

It is them or us.

She notched the arrow into place and felt her thumb brush past her cheek as she slid into form. The view down the sight line was shaky. Her hands trembled wildly, so she closed her eyes and took a slow breath to steady her grasp. Her ears pricked at a rustling from behind. A strong hand suddenly closed over her mouth and simultaneously another grabbed the arrow before she could release it. The two hands pulled her roughly to the ground, and they tumbled through a mound of leaves and dirt before coming to rest at the bottom of the hill.

"What do you think you are doing?" a voice hissed in her ear. The heavy weight that kept her pressed to the ground remained motionless, the hand still firmly over her mouth. "Do not move," he whispered as she struggled for breath and freedom. Then she heard the sounds of voices above them at the crest of the edged rise they'd just fallen from.

The soldiers.

There was a moment of mumbled chatter between the men on the rise, concluding that whatever they heard or saw behind the clump of greens had been of the animal variety, and was not of immediate concern. They left, and the hand over her mouth removed itself as the owner's body rolled off her back. She looked up and pushed the hair from her eyes, stunned to see Daniel standing inches away, searching the rise where the soldiers had last appeared.

Tear-streaked and muddy, Jenna leapt to her feet and threw herself at him. "Daniel, thank God!"

He hugged her fiercely then set her down and put a finger to his lips, scanning the crest for movement. When at last he was satisfied, he grabbed her hand and the bow and pulled her farther back through the woods, away from the circle of soldiers.

Jenna heard the rush of movement behind her. She wheeled around to see Lord Pembroke, panting and out of breath. Without a thought she embraced him too.

He seized her tightly then put her at arm's length, making a cursory inventory. Lord Pembroke turned to Daniel. "Where did you find her?"

Daniel eyed Jenna. "At the top of the hill with her bow drawn. How were you planning to battle four soldiers?"

"One by one, if I had to," she said pointedly.

Lord Pembroke shook his head. "If you kill any of them, the crown has proof of a crime against you, whereas if you simply escape . . ." His face stiffened. "Well, at least they wouldn't burn you at the stake."

Her stomach dropped, twisted with fear. She dug her nails into the palms of her hands and blinked against her anguished tears. "I will do whatever I must. These men fight for something and someone they believe in. And I believe in *them*. And we will do it to our death. I won't leave them."

Daniel grabbed her arm. "You won't have to." He scrutinized Lord Pembroke. "Let's go—we've not much time."

"Wait," Lord Pembroke said and quickly turned to Jenna. "Miss MacDuff. There is so much to say—and not nearly enough time to speak it." He drew a hand down over his face as if to draw the thoughts from his brain to his lips. "We come from such different worlds, and if God grants us favor, then shortly we will both be heading back to them. But I want you to know"—he paused, searching for words—"you have altered mine."

Jenna studied his face, seeing warmth and love and gratitude.

He continued. "In many ways, I am in your debt and will find a way to repay you."

Jenna was about to say *you're welcome*, when Lord Pembroke stepped forward, took her face in his hands, and brushed his lips across hers.

"When I am able, I will search for the door to your world. Thank you, Miss MacDuff."

Jenna knew her face flushed with heat but managed to say, "When you find it, you may thank me a thousand times again."

Alex hid behind a large tree and scanned the mangy crowd that had gathered along the last of the route, intent upon seeing an early evening's entertainment. The hanging of one was enough to gain the interest of a few, but word had spread it would be as much as six, and it looked like many had put their evening chores aside to see the spectacle that had befallen them.

There were, at first, only a few minor quips from the bolder members of the audience, loud statements of disgust that these men had found their way into England in the first place.

"Bleeding Scots trying to take over with their James. The great coward isn't even here, then, is he?" one man remarked. "He's hiding 'neath Louis's skirts, he is. Now, who wants to follow his leader there?"

The head soldier didn't seem to mind the jeering, and furthermore did nothing to stop the occasional lobbing of an old winter apple at the group of men. They were lined up beneath the long, sturdy branches of two great oaks, while a rope was staked across the front of the horses, their ability to take off prematurely impeded. He watched from his saddle and smiled at the rising anticipation from the crowd as they gradually lost any remaining timidity.

Alex glanced at the clansmen on their horses, hands bound by ropes behind their backs, faces bound by oath and honor. The head soldier's face pinched with anger when he looked at them and said, "You may think your faces display courage to this crowd, but they see a mask of conceit." He smiled at the bystanders and turned back. "They're expecting me to wipe your features of their arrogant dispositions. And I must. It will show these law-abiding folk the serious nature of the new crown—the loyalty that is anticipated, that is *expected*."

Alex swung up into his saddle and looked at the clansmen, and then behind him. He had never met people with such valor. Even his mother's resolve had shaken him, awed him. The Spaniard was right. What had *he* done? Was it not time to test his self-command? This was his moment. He would do it for them . . . and for himself.

He drew in a large breath and moved forward out of the copse of trees. The crowd gasped, and the corporal's face revealed raw shock. Alex guessed it was because of what trailed behind him. It looked like he towed a dead woman flung across another horse, her flaming red hair spilling down the animal's ribs, a crimson sheet lit by the setting sun and stirring with the breeze.

Alex cleared his throat and hollered, "You there, sir, what rank are you?"

The soldier narrowed his eyes and answered. "Corporal Brummidge, milord."

Alex could almost taste the resentment that spilled out with the man's words. He knew he'd been usurped. A man who's lost his status is rarely ready to give it up so easily, and he looked like a soldier who'd been born and bred to battle.

Alex spoke again. "My father is dead. I am your new Duke of Keswick."

Two soldiers standing near the crowd saluted, but the corporal remained aloof and merely nodded.

Alex glared at the corporal and pointed. "I found this young woman trailing you. Did you know you were followed?"

The corporal arranged himself taller in his saddle, and made a quick jerk of his head to throw a condemning glance at the two soldiers.

Alex continued, his eyes burning into the corporal's. "Had I not come upon her, there's no telling what might have happened. These men might well have escaped with her aid."

The corporal's gaze wavered as he glanced at the crowd. Their glee at his humiliation was palpable.

Alex raised his voice. "I had my own man kill the woman, so you won't be short of rope for the rest, but I expect to see the remainder done properly. I won't take chances with the careless management displayed thus far." He pointed at the two soldiers. "You two, move aside. I'll have my own attendant do the ropes." And turning back to face the corporal, he continued. "Were you aware you had a deserter among your ranks?"

The corporal searched his party.

Alex snorted. "We found him beneath a tree, enjoying a late-afternoon kip. You'll find him upon your return, tied to the same tree for safekeeping."

In truth, Alex remembered, the young private had not been

found sleeping under the tree, but rather pissing by the side of it. He was tied to it though—embarrassingly, without his clothes, which now appeared on Daniel's body.

"Milord," the corporal said through rigid jaws, "I assure you I can handle the punishment of these men." He watched Daniel move swiftly from one prisoner to the next, stepping into a stirrup, securing the knot around the tree branch, and finally placing the noose over each neck.

Alex laughed. "I have no more faith in your assurance than I do in your proficiency. I might as well ask the prisoners to string themselves up."

The gathered mob howled. Ridicule on top of an execution was capital entertainment.

Alex shook his head. "No, I shall take on from here, and I will deliver seven Scots exactly as they should be, where they should be." Alex eyed the corporal fingering the smooth, rounded handle of his standard-issue pistol. He noted the bitter expression on his face as he watched Daniel finish the preparations.

"You may take your leave, Corporal Brummidge. I have no further use for you here," Alex said, narrowing in on the gun.

The corporal reeled back in his saddle, his face pulling into a sneer. "Surely you don't mean to dismiss me and my company when there might be need for our services, milord?"

"It is precisely what I mean, Corporal. There is nothing valuable you may contribute apart from directing the dispersal of this crowd. If you and your men would kindly break up the unwelcome audience—"

"Unwelcome audience?" the corporal interrupted. "This is a

lesson demonstrating the result of traitorous activities." He glanced from the crowd back to Alex. "Shouldn't they benefit from the mistakes of others? Shouldn't they watch the hanging and glean . . ."

The corporal stopped midsentence and Alex turned to catch sight of one of the ropes, previously secured around a tree branch and one of the prisoner's necks, slipping free to the ground.

Daniel dashed to the rope, but the corporal, now on high alert, shouted out to him.

"You there! Stop!" He raised his gun and pointed it at Daniel.

Alex shouted, "Now!" and an explosion of action occurred in front of the crowd.

At the same time the corporal cocked and aimed his gun, the Freemason's Daughter sprang up with a bow and arrow in her hand, expertly drawn, skillfully released.

Daniel slashed a knife through both the rope restraining the clansmen's horses and the one securing the two remaining soldiers' mounts. He leapt up behind Gavin.

The arrow hit the corporal's gun.

A shot rang out as the pistol flew out of his hand.

The crowd screamed.

Alex fired above the horse's head, striking enough terror in the animal to rear and throw the corporal from his back. The horse took flight, following Alex toward the north.

The remaining horses bolted in all directions to escape the sound of gunfire. But the nooses never tightened around the necks of those who were to be hanged. The ropes slithered from the tree branches, uncoiling from their slipknots. The clan, still atop their horses, leveled themselves to the necks of their escaping animals.

The ropes slid past the face of death and that of the corporal as they merrily dangled along in the grass, dancing with their liberty.

Jenna's mind flashed in lightning speed as her thoughts shut down and her physical senses prickled with blood-tingling friction, animal instinct taking over. She clutched the sleek neck in front of her, bending low and melting into the flow of muscles as Henry flung himself into the race with his cohorts. His instinct was as keen as hers.

They chased the crisp March wind. They felt each curve and dip of hill. The two of them headed toward the magnet of their own internal compass. She closed her eyes. Time was disproportionate, the calculation of seconds and minutes surreal as she and her horse flew across the fields in front of them. She thrilled at the notion she would live another day to make up for the terrible mistake she had made.

She heard the cries of men, and if all had gone according to plan, the voices belonged to only her clansmen, having left the three soldiers with no mounts to pursue them with. She held tightly to Henry and allowed her eyes to open just enough to see what lay in front of her. It was Hadrian's Wall and, blessedly, Henry was plowing straight for it. She closed her eyes and saw her homeland: the rough-toothed mountains of unnatural green, smooth hills blanketed with heather, the sparkling lochs with their unimaginable depths. She loosened her grip, prepared for the jump.

A familiar feeling grasped her by the shoulders when she realized, once again, that Henry had changed his mind. He hesitated and veered an unexpected semicircle away from the wall.

"Damn Newton and his theories!" she shouted as she slipped off the horse and landed with a shoulder-wrenching crunch into the grass, and then into darkness.

She opened her eyes and found herself surrounded by eight men, all shaking their heads and tsking with their familiar disappointed expressions.

"You're one lucky lass," her father growled, relief spilling from his eyes.

"Lucky?" she said. "Lucky will be to die in Scotland."

GLOSSARY OF TERMS AND FOREIGN PHRASES

Bene vale vobis. (Latin): Good luck to you.

fish chuits: similar to crab cakes

Hasta más tarde. (Spanish): Until later.

Jacobite: A supporter of James II of England or of the Stuart
    pretenders after 1688. From Latin Jacōbus, James

Mai. È brutto! (Italian): Never. It's ugly.

Mo chreach! (Gaelic): Damn! Literally, "My ruin."

No lo puedo creer. (Spanish): I don't believe it.

Non posso ringraziarla abbastanza! (Italian): I cannot thank you
    enough!

parritch: Scottish porridge

Pazya (Daniel's horse) In Hebrew it translates as "Gold of God."

receipts: recipes

slàinte mhath (Gaelic): good health

syllabub: A traditional British dessert, popular from the
    sixteenth to the nineteenth century, made from rich milk or
    cream, seasoned with sugar and wine. The frothing cream
    was poured straight into a bowl containing "Sille," a wine
    that used to be made in Sillery, in France's Champagne
    region. "Bub" was Elizabethan slang for a bubbling drink.

Tesoro mio (Italian): My love. Treasure of mine.

Tu es hermoso. (Spanish): You are beautiful.

vecchio stile (Italian): old-style

ACKNOWLEDGMENTS

A huge thank-you to Kristen Pettit, my editor. Your direction, ideas, and encouragement were treasured lodestones that kept me afloat on this journey. I continue to pinch myself with the glee of good fortune to have worked with you. Many thanks to the incredibly clever and beautiful team at HarperCollins for every ounce of effortful work you put into making this book a reality: Alexandra Rakaczki and Janet Rosenberg; Michelle Taormina, Alison Klapthor, and Emily Soto; Kim Stella and Tina Cameron; Stephanie Hoover, along with Bess Braswell and Elizabeth Ward—and definitely not to be forgotten—Elizabeth Lynch. I am indebted to you all for finding my book a home in your house where your creativity never ceases to amaze me.

To my two favorite people in the whole world: Chloe and Gabe— you guys have seen me relentlessly time-travel backward three centuries to chisel away at this tale for a dozen years, and not once in all that time did either one of you suggest I bury this book and crack on elsewhere. You have no idea how much that means to me.

As always, a massive and endless thank-you to Jennifer Unter, my agent. Your toils on my behalf and your ongoing faith in my writing make me hugely grateful to work with you.

Thanks to Alys Milner, whose affection and kindness is something so extraordinary I wish there was a way to make sure everyone in the world had a chance to spend fifteen minutes with her. To M & D, a million hugs for all the cherished dinners and drams. And lastly, to Abby Murphy. Your words, your perspective, your guidance—all a treasure beyond measure to me.